A Long Walk Home
James S. Kelly

Other Books
by
James S. Kelly

<u>MYSTERIES</u>
I Didn't Forget
Interned
Not In My Backyard

<u>WESTERNS</u>
A Man of Breeding
A Breed Apart
The Wounded Breed

<u>CIVIL WAR</u>
Magnolia

A
LONG
WALK
HOME

JAMES S. KELLY

ISBN: 978-1-963565-54-6 (Paperback)
ISBN: 978-1-963565-55-3 (Ebook)

Library of Congress Control Number:
2024926618

Printed in the United States of America

Published by:

info@thequippyquill.com
(302)-295-2278

Contents

Acknowledgments 1

Prologue...3

Chapter 1..5

Chapter 2..15

Chapter 3..35

Chapter 4..39

Chapter 5..51

Chapter 6..61

Chapter 7..65

Chapter 8..85

Chapter 9..95

Chapter 10 103

Chapter 11 117

Chapter 12 139

Chapter 13 149

Chapter 14 153

Chapter 15 171

Chapter 16 177

Chapter 17 191

Chapter 18 199

Chapter 19 209

Chapter 20 219

Chapter 21 245

Chapter 22 257

Chapter 23 271

Chapter 24 283

Chapter 25 287

Chapter 26 301

Chapter 27 309

Chapter 28 319

Chapter 29 337

Chapter 30 343

Chapter 31 355

<u>Acknowledgments</u>

<u>MY WIFE PATRICIA</u>

<u>CHILDREN</u>

James S. Kelly Jr
Mark R. Kelly
Nancy Leachman
Michelle Leachman

Prologue

The small contingent of Australian Air Force personnel at Ubon Air Base in Thailand in 1969 was there to service their two Canberra Bombers. The modified Australian version of the Canberra was suited to low-level bombing and was normally assigned to the southern district in South Vietnam. Two of the district's planes and crews had been loaned to the 22nd Fighter Squadron at Ubon for a special mission in Northwestern Vietnam. They'd already flown two missions against the designated target and estimated that it would require three more to neutralize the North Vietnamese missile site.

The Aussies were a partying lot, generous to a fault, and always ready to lift a beer to other flyers on base. The 22nd with similar views became their American Cousins. They shared whiskey, beer, and anything either could appropriate or steal such as strawberries meant for the commanding general or a case of ribs destined for the chow hall. At least once a week they'd get together and share their booty at the American's or Aussies' living quarters.

Today was no exception. Although the booze flowed smoothly at the Aussie's quarters, it was a very sad day. One of their Canberra's was shot down two days ago in the jungle within sixty miles of the base. There was an extensive rescue mission in the heavy foliage for those two days, but the wreckage couldn't be located even though the crew had radioed their position as they were going down. At midnight the party ended and the 22nd staggered back to their quarters and fell into bed. Tomorrow's mission for either country couldn't be canceled; life would go on. The Aussies notified the next of kin and asked for a replacement crew.

But things are not always predictable. One week later, the three-man Canberra Crew walked out of the jungle and the 22nd joined their Australian Brethren to celebrate the resurrection of the crew. They toasted late into the night; only tomorrow's mission could interrupt the celebration. The distinction between celebrating the living or celebrating the dead is so cloudy that sometimes no one can tell the difference between the two. The bonding between combat teams and support personnel creates such a cohesive barrier that it can't be penetrated by stress. The men who fly in combat at the direction of their respective governments know the risks involved; yet, the positive aspects of combat, such as love of country, honor, the mission, and the respect for their comrades or fallen heroes make them even more aggressive and successful.

Chapter 1

The radio signal the past two nights was weak. Those working the MARS System so servicemen could contact their families during the Korean War and now during the hostilities in Vietnam were dedicated amateurs. Larry remembered using the network during his brief tour in Guam and, in most cases, he successfully made contact with his wife, though in some cases, it took an extra day before contact was made. However, the MARS System could be held hostage by the amount of weather between Southeast Asia and home, but that didn't deter anyone from using it, nor was there any viable alternative. Last night he was fourth in line but couldn't stay awake long enough to get his call in. There was but one phone available in his building and it was located on the wall in the middle of a sixty-foot hallway twenty feet from his room. There were twenty-four rooms in the long narrow building; twelve at each end with showers, restrooms, and a lounge separating the two. Each evening, starting at nine PM, he and his fellow officers would line up against the beige-colored wall in the tile-covered hallway. Everyone tried to call home at least once a week. Majors and above were housed in separate buildings and had phones in their rooms.

Prior to the designated time, those wishing to call home each night would casually leave their rooms and line up against the wall and wait their turn. Larry would lean a chair against the wall and either read a book or pass the time talking to the other flyers in line. He flew Monday through Friday though his flight missions averaged only four hours. Takeoff was generally at seven in the morning and he'd land on or about eleven. When you add the time for briefing, preflight, and subsequent debriefing, it is a ten-hour day. The rest of the time he washed his socks, played cards, or went to a movie.

Tonight he started out second in line. The first flyer took only five minutes; he obviously didn't have much to say. Since nobody was sure when or how atmospheric interference would impact their call, he and the other flyers spoke quickly and said everything before their loved ones had a chance to respond. Such was the case tonight. "Honey, it's me. I tried to call you the past two nights but couldn't get through. Happy Birthday, Jeanie. I love you."

The party on the other side caught on fast and they, in turn, said everything all at once. "I was hoping you'd call. I miss you so very much. The kids are still in bed. We had my birthday party last night and the kids stayed up past their bedtime. I can't believe I'm almost thirty years old. The Jade Earrings and matching Bracelets are wonderful; I slept with them last night. The other gift is fabulous but I don't know what they're called."

"They're called Beggar Beads. All the guys are buying them and sending them home."

"I'll wear them today. Mom and Dad are still asleep. They said to say hello if you called. They've been great but

I know our two small children are wearing them down and after a month, they need a break. I plan to go back home next week so call me in four days; I'll be home by then. Are you flying a lot?"

"I can't talk about that but I'm counting the days when I can see you. Are you sure you can handle the trip back to Florida with two small children?"

"Well, I drove here with the two, so I think I'll be okay. It's only a day trip. Don't worry, we'll be fine. Have we been given a date for our R&R to Hawaii?"

"We're scheduled August 16th. I can't wait to see you in a bikini again."

"My old one doesn't fit. My bottom and bust are too big for the old bikini. After two children, I've finally grown a bust and a butt. I'll get rid of the excess, so you won't be embarrassed when you see me."

"I could never be embarrassed where you're concerned especially since you won't be wearing the bikini very long."

"Have you seen any of your old buds over there?"
"I saw two of our neighbors last week. They said to say hello. Honey, there's another guy waiting to call home so I'll let you go. Remember I love you and miss you very much. I'll try to call again in four days."

There was no reply; apparently the signal was lost. He knew Monday's mission was dangerous and something inside him wanted to wait a few minutes in case the signal returned but when it didn't, he handed the phone to the next guy in line and went to bed.

When he was stationed in Guam, he'd call his step-parents on a weekly basis. Theirs was an unusual relationship. Larry was one of four boys born to Thomas and Elizabeth Stephens. His mother married too young, had four children before her twenty-eighth birthday and had a breakdown. His father was immature, the depression was on and his and Elizabeth's marriage suffered. They separated and Larry and the other three siblings went into a home for boys. Larry didn't have a conversation with his biological father until he was fourteen.

Gradually, homes were found for each of the boys. Larry, the youngest, was taken by a Catholic family, Robert and Catherine Holmes. His brother Raymond was taken by his maternal grandmother; Thomas, eventually, by his mother and John by his father when he was thirteen. Larry went by the name Larry Holmes until he entered high school. Since his birth certificate never changed, the high school principal insisted that he was Larry Stephens. It wasn't unusual for some of his friends to call him Larry Holmes while others referred to him as Larry Stephens.

There was always tension between him and his foster parents who were very controlling. Larry felt his informative years were too restrictive and consequently, he was more immature than other young men at the age of twenty-two. Robert and Catherine were killed in an automobile accident while he was in Guam. He returned home for two weeks to attend the funeral and settle their limited estate. Jean never met his foster parents nor his biological parents who were still alive. Larry carried the scars of being in a home and felt that he'd been cheated out of his childhood. The few times he visited his brothers in the home were gut-wrenching.

Flying combat missions Monday through Friday the last three months out of Ubon, Thailand took up most of his week days. The weekends were down days and he slept a lot. He used the non-flying days to reflect on his role in the military and whether he could continue to justify it. He loved his country and probably would fight to the death to defend it, but why over here. He knew there was a big picture, but he just couldn't put his heart and soul into fighting against the Vietnamese. He told himself that it didn't affect his proficiency, but at times he wondered if it did. It wasn't a subject you openly discussed so he didn't know how the other members of his squadron felt.

He already knew what his next target was; it was Russian Aircraft at an airbase near Hanoi. Larry had been in that area before and he wasn't looking forward to going back. It was a target rich site protected by two SAM Battalions in the immediate vicinity. In the past, DOD refused to allow his squadron to strike the base; he wondered what got into McNamara and his aides to let them have a go at it tomorrow. It was a sore point with Larry and the other flyers in his squadron. Russians assigned there would fly missions against US targets and return to their base without interference from us. The Russians had to be laughing their ass off at all the restrictions placed on American Flyers. He hoped that Monday would be payback.

Larry slept in a little later on Saturday and walked down the hall to take a shower. Mama San and the other Thai girls were already at work, cleaning rooms and washing clothes. There was only one place in the building where they could hand wash the flyer's clothes and linens. A surprise was in store for Larry when he took a shower the first time after arriving in Thailand. He got in the communal shower, turned on the water and looked down. There were three or four young women sitting in front of him washing sheets and pillowcases. They giggled at his discomfort and he could hear one o the girls say, FNG, which meant fucking new guy. He was ready to leave when two other flyers came in and Larry said what the hell; after that it seemed natural. There were six girls assigned to his building. They'd come from the local village about seven in the morning and left around four in the afternoon. They were young and beautiful; the mixture of Asian blood and French or other Caucasians was like magic. They sported high cheekbones, small frames and beautiful faces. It wasn't unusual that one or two would stay over for one or two nights; they were there to please.

Many enlisted and even some officers took their maids home when it was time to end their tour. Larry looked but he didn't touch. He knew what was at home and he didn't want to do anything that would jeopardize that relationship.

Transportation was a premium on base. You could ride the bus to most places but those who had motorcycles felt more in control of their lives. Larry rode his motorcycle to the chow hall and then to the squadron. The few motorcycles on base were handed down when a flyer rotated home. His black and grey Honda was in good condition. He bought it from a pilot who returned to the states. When it was time to rotate home, there would be many suitors for her.

Saturday was a day off unless there was a special mission. But he had an additional duty as Squadron Supply Officer, so he went to his office at squadron headquarters and made an inventory of all the clerical equipment. Besides, he had nothing better to do other than go the Base Exchange, which he did after lunch. He bought a bottle of Johnny Walker Black and some cans of sliced grapefruit and then went back to his office to finish the inventory. There wasn't anything worth seeing at the Base Theater, so he had a couple of drinks at the Officer's Club with Phil Henry and Mike O'Connell, other pilots in his squadron. He ate dinner with them at the club and then went to his room and read a Mickey Spillane Thriller until he fell asleep. The next day would be a carbon copy of today.

He'd been flying the F4C for two years at MacDill AFB in Florida and then at Ubon Air Base in Thailand for the past three months. He was something of a celebrity among the fliers in his squadron; he was credited with a MIG 17 kill on his second mission over Vietnam. But fame was fleeting. It would last a week or until someone else shot down a plane and they'd become the celebrity of the day. Their day in the sun would be good for a couple of free drinks over the first twenty-four hours and then nothing thereafter.

Monday's mission targeted the MIG 17s and 21s at the North Vietnamese Base of Phuc Yen, about 20 miles northeast of Hanoi. This was to be a joint Marine, Navy and Air Force Operation. The micromanagers in Washington finally relented and this target was assigned a top priority.

Many targets were restricted by Secretary of Defense, McNamara for fear the Russians would enter the war; Today's target was one of those that had been off limits. These non-targets had been a thorn in the American Flyer's side, and the subject of several unapproved books. The Americans would fly over or near the Russian base and see MIGs taxing below but they couldn't attack them. They had to wait until they were fired on by the Russians before they could retaliate. That seemed idiotic to the Americans when you took into account the firepower the Russians had. If you were fired upon, you had to pray that they missed before you could retaliate. This certainly gave he and his fellow flyers a warm feeling that McNamara and his buddies at DOD were looking out for American Servicemen. Many in his squadron wondered why they were over here if they had to be a target before they could defend themselves. Why the hell would you fight a war where the other guy could decide when and where to shoot at you and all you could do is hope he missed?

Today's attack would be staggered in three waves with ten minutes of separation for each service. The Air Force would attack in the third wave. His rear for this flight was Captain Johnny Jones, a rated navigator from Little Rock Arkansas. He flew with Jones on two previous missions over Vietnam. Larry was impressed with his rear's capability.

The power of the F4C, Phantom Interceptor, was ideal for air-to-ground missions but was a little cumbersome in Air to Air Combat. He'd been flying for ten years, starting with the F-86 after graduation from Greenville Mississippi, where he finished in the top ten percent of his Pilot Training Class. The significance was that he was able to pick his first assignment, which was to the F86 Squadron at Andersen Air Force Base in Guam. A year later, he was reassigned to F-100s and subsequently to F106s before the F4C assignment materialized.

He liked Greenville; that's where he met and married Jean Washington, a pretty little southern belle. They were married two days after his graduation from flight training and had a short honeymoon before he left for Guam. Housing quarters for married junior officers was limited at Andersen and besides Jean had another year to complete her college degree. She stayed with her parents until she graduated. When he was reassigned to Luke Air Force Base in Arizona for F 100 training, she joined him.

Chapter 2

It didn't take Larry long to get ready once his alarm went off Monday Morning. After he put on his flight suit and boots, he went outside and started his motorcycle. Going from his hooch early in the morning was kind of exciting. The road to the flight line was along the western periphery of the base. No one knew who was outside the base complex waiting to take a shot at the early morning motorcycle traveler. He got the cycle up to fifty as he barreled down the main road and that's when he heard "ping, ping". He added more gas, hunched over the handlebars and made it to his squadron without getting shot. He didn't actually outrun the rifle fire; it's just that the guys firing at him were lousy shots.

"Those guys can't hit the broad side of a barn." Larry laughed as he told one of the other guys parking his cycle next to him at the squadron.

The briefing room was typical throughout the Air Force. It was a thirty by forty-foot room with a stage in front. On one side of the stage was a blackboard and on the other, a screen for a projector. The room could handle as many as sixty people at a time. Today there were only twenty in the room; Larry and his rear sat up front.

The briefing officer for the mission was Lt. Colonel Charles Bratton. "There's a squadron of MIG 17s, some MIG 21s and a few bombers flying out of Phuc Yen; Higher Headquarters wants them destroyed. The altitude for this flight is 23,000 initially; once you reach Thud Ridge, you'll drop to 5,000 feet, make the run, climb back to 25,000, and return home. The call sign for this flight is River. Takeoff is at 8:05 our time. Major Fields is team leader, Stephens, you're number two. Calder is three and Young four. We'll use the inland orbit on the way to the target to conceal ourselves as much as possible from enemy radar."

"There are antiaircraft battalions, Sa-2 SAM Sites, and MIG 17s and 21s throughout the target area. We've been having success against all three of their countermeasures as long as the rear is alert to their radar intercepting signals. Major Franklin, our ECM head, will give you some more information about the SAMs,"

"The SA-2 is a mobile weapon system and can be moved from place to place on truck beds. The system consists of electric generators, a fire control computer and about 18 missiles. They can lock on a second target while they're evaluating the first. It takes about 75 seconds to complete the sequence to fire on the first and another 40 seconds to lock on the second target. I want you to be aware that the North Vietnamese have optical guidance and will try to ambush you. Any SA-2 site in the area could start transmitting to attract your attention while another SAM site will optically track you and unleash missiles from an unexpected direction. Keep alert out there and record any attempts to lock on to you."

Larry and his rear did a pre-flight inspection of their aircraft and checked the latest weather forecast to and from the target. He was always in awe of the power of this almost sixty-foot-long aircraft with a cockpit sixteen feet off the ground. The plane carried air-to-ground missiles, an ECM POD, and 20MM guns.

They lined up in formation, made another check of their instrument panel, went to full power and waited. When the lead dropped his head, all four released their brakes and powered down the runway, taking off in formation. "Gear up." Larry informed his rear.

When they reached 23,000 feet, the lead had everyone check-in. "Let's maintain radio silence until we're ready for descent."

"Were you able to get through to your wife last night and wish her a happy birthday?" Jones asked Larry over the intercom.

"Yeah, she's with her folks in Mississippi and they had a small birthday party for her. I think she's going to head to Florida in a few days. You know, I haven't been with her more than six months at a time over nearly ten years of marriage. After my tour is up, I'm going to put in my papers. There's more to life than just flying all the time. Jeanie's twenty-nine already has two children and a husband who isn't home very much. I'm lucky if she doesn't divorce me while I'm over here."

"I know what you mean. Congratulations on your kill last mission. Who was your rear?

"Fred Jenkins. He really helped me get that MIG."

"Where did you get it?"

"We were flying cover for B52s near Hanoi when Fred spotted the MIG. I got lucky when it overshot us. After that, it was only a matter of time. The MIG is more maneuverable than this Phantom, but the power in this baby gave me an edge."

"River lead, this is three. I'm losing hydraulics, permission to abort and return to base."

"Roger three. Take it easy on the way back. Lead out."

"River two flight, descend to five thousand feet. Acknowledge." The lead said

The other two acknowledged and descended to the appropriate altitude. They could see the outline of Hanoi up ahead as they flew northwest of the city before turning southeast through Thud Ridge to the target. There was smoke on the horizon as they neared the target. "Let's stagger the formation and follow my lead." Major Fields said.

With the lead peeling off to his left and descending down to two thousand feet, the other two followed him to the target. Fields released his missiles; Stephens and Young did the same. It wasn't necessary for them to make bomb damage assessment because they carried cameras that would be analyzed when they returned. They joined up with the lead in a loose formation until they were about ten miles south of the target. Larry's rear was busy looking for SAM signals and alert to using ECM procedures to defeat any attempt to lock on.

When they were passing through fifteen thousand feet, Jones yelled. "We have a lock on."

Larry immediately took evasive action, diving below the approaching altitude of the SA-2, and then making a steep climb to defeat the missile, but the explosion in his left wing told him they were in trouble. "We're hit, I can't control the plane, eject, eject, eject." Larry ordered.

The plane was in a tight spiral and Larry had to use all his strength to pull the ejection handle; out he went. He felt a thump on his bottom when the seat pack hit him. His last position was twenty miles south of Hanoi. As he was descending; he saw Jones' chute open and he felt a sense of relief. Larry was looking down at the green foliage of the countryside and two small villages to the east. Everything seemed to be coming to greet him as his life flashed before him.

He immediately thought of Jean and his two children. How would she cope if he was captured or killed in this shithole? They didn't have enough money saved because of the cost of the numerous moves they made and the two children they had. He just knew that he'd have to survive; he saw it as his prime responsibility

He met her in the Cadet Club at Greenville Air Force Base on a Friday evening about two months after he arrived. His classmates generally went to the club on Friday nights to have a few beers and see the young women who were there to meet cadets. Many of these girls came continuously for years and were dubbed Cadet Widows. Others like Jean heard about all the young men eager to meet the opposite sex and had come for the first time. He was sitting with George Thomas when he saw this attractive brunette sitting with another girl at a table on the far wall. They made eye contact and Larry signaled, asking for a dance. She pointed to her friend.

He walked over to their table, which was three back from the entrance and introduced himself. "Would you like to dance?" He asked.

"I came with my friend Susan and I don't want to leave her alone. Do you have a friend that could come over?"

"I'll be right back."

Larry returned with George Thomas. After a brief introduction, Susan invited George to sit down. Larry took

Jean's hand and led her to the dance floor. She was five feet two inches tall, weighed about one hundred pounds, had short brown hair and full lips Both introduced themselves and after a slow dance they returned to the table where George and Susan were in deep conversation, each drinking a glass of beer. The four spent the rest of the evening just talking, laughing, dancing and being young. Larry could tell that the girl he just met was someone special.

Next Friday Jean came alone. He was waiting outside and escorted her in. No, actually she escorted him in. The club was so crowded on Friday nights that a cadet couldn't get into his own club unless a female escorted him. He and Jean seemed to hit it off immediately and he looked forward to their dates on Friday and by the sixth date he knew she was the one for him. They were on the dance floor with her hand around his neck and her cheek next to his. He could smell her cologne and her breath in his ear was making him excited. He got an erection and was embarrassed. She stepped back slightly from his embrace and smiled. "Larry, I'm really flattered and I feel the same way."

Luckily she had a car and on Saturday nights she'd pick him up outside the Cadet Club and they'd go to a movie or have a hamburger. Larry's pay of one hundred dollars a month didn't go very far after he settled his cleaning bill and other necessary expenses. She, on the other hand, was in college and had a small allowance. They'd become intimate by the third month; both told the other they were in love. One month before graduation, Larry proposed and Jean told him how much she had been anticipating it. He'd previously met her father and mother and after a few Sunday Family Dinners, they gave their blessing.

He had thirty days leave and some travel time between graduation and his reporting date to Andersen Air

Force Base in Guam. They honeymooned in New Orleans for two weeks, frequenting Bourbon and Royal streets every evening. Their favorite spot was the Court of Two Sisters. They flew home to stay with her parents until he went to Andersen and they made sure they brought back the famous Hurricane Glasses from Pat Obrien's Pub for her parents.

She'd completed her third year of college, majoring in biology, and wanted to be a doctor. There was base housing for families at Anderson and they talked of going together. But when her parents said they had something special as a wedding gift, which was to pay for Jean's senior year, they couldn't turn down the offer. The last thought he had before he hit the ground was that she wouldn't receive any of his pay if he was dead; he had to stay alive.

Trees were everywhere and he lost sight of his rear because of the dense foliage. He remembered seeing two small villages to the east within a few miles of his touchdown point. Their buildings were primarily stucco on the outside and from the little Larry knew of architecture, the villages had a distinct French influence. Both villages were surrounded by rice paddies. He hit the trees hard and his chute caught in the branches; he was left dangling with only his toes touching the ground. He pulled his chute release but nothing happened. Luckily his knife was in his right flying boot. He retrieved it, made a couple of swipes with the knife and landed on his backpack. With all his effort, he tried to retrieve the chute but it was hooked on the limbs above so he left it there. Before trying to orient himself, he cut away the straps on his fanny pack, reached inside and placed all the contents on the ground. There was a .38 pistol, a few candy bars, a map of Vietnam, two signal flares, a quick checklist of Vietnamese phrases, a homing device, some antibiotics, bandages, a survival radio with extra batteries and a compass. He put the gun in his side pocket and the rest of the items in the zippered pockets of his flight suit "What do I do now?" He asked himself out loud.

His flight leader would have reported where his plane went down and he could hear an airplane fly overhead. The leader would remain in a circular pattern over him for a few minutes and then leave. The other members of his flight were already on their way to Ubon; fuel would limit any response. The rescue choppers were notified automatically when a plane goes down but he wasn't sure they'd be able to provide any assistance this close to Hanoi. However, he knew they'd try to pick up his radio signal and they'd give it everything they had to bring him home. His flight had been given coordinates of a rescue site. By his calculation, it was twenty miles to the east of him.

North Vietnam placed bounties on downed airmen and local villagers would initially be his main antagonists; time was not on his side. Survival training instructors taught that downed flyers had a twenty-five percent chance of being rescued within two hours and that would decrease to five percent after eight hours. In essence, he had eight hours to reach the rescue site. The choppers would go to that area twice a day for a week at ten in the morning and four in the afternoon.

He thought about Jones; the last time he saw him was when his chute opened a hundred yards to his south. He decided to move south to see if he could find him before he did anything else. The trees were dense and walking was very difficult. He travelled the two hundred yards in fifteen minutes, but didn't find his rear. He decided to walk fifty yards in each of the cardinal directions from this spot and then return. It was when he walked south that he found Jones. He was lying on the ground; his neck was broken. He probably hit a part of the aircraft as he ejected. Stephens took Jones' dog tags and the items in his fanny pack and started south again; he didn't have time to bury him.

There was limited visibility through the trees so Larry used his compass to maintain an easterly heading, the direction to the rescue site. Larry was a born optimist and though he knew he didn't stand much of a chance to make it to the rescue area, he was going to try. It was Jean and his two children that gave him the incentive to push on.

Vietnam was known for its volatile weather and when it started to rain, it came down hard; he was totally drenched. He wondered what it would be like if he didn't have the thick foliage to shield him somewhat from the driving rain.

Just as fast as the rain started, it suddenly stopped and he could hear choppers nearby. That's when he saw a chopper drop two smoke grenades about a hundred yards away. The chopper crew was trying to disguise where they'd pick him up. If the enemy was in the area, they'd go to that spot, which was some distance from Larry's hiding place. Using his radio, he made contact with the chopper and gave them his position relative to the smoke grenade. Soon the chopper pilot asked Larry to fire a flare to pin point his position.

He fired the flare and immediately saw the penetrator, a heavy anchored device attached to the chopper by a strong metal line, dropping through the jungle; it worked as a seat for downed airmen. He moved toward the device, but just then two MIGs passed over the helicopter. After they passed overhead, both made a wide turn and came back; one fired a missile at the helicopter crew. Apparently the missile didn't have enough time to lock on and it went over the chopper and exploded on the hillside. The chopper was buffeted by the blast of air from the MIGS and when it finally settled down, Larry rushed toward the penetrator. He grabbed it with both hands, pulled himself into the seat and started to strap in when he was hit on the side of his head with a club by one of four or five villagers and he fell to the ground.

In his freshman year of high school, he stood five foot eight inches tall and weighted one hundred twenty five pounds. He generally was the smallest kid in his group, whether it was in sports or at a social event. He wasn't physically abused by the bigger and older boys other than they liked to hit him on the top of his head with a glancing blow with the palm of their hands and say, "how're they hanging, stud"; he was embarrassed and hated it. After school and on weekends, Larry did some errands for an elderly Asian gentleman in his neighborhood who became his confidant. After months of frustration, Larry told him he was tired of being singled out by the older boys. It seems that his new friend was of Japanese descent and had been an instructor in martial arts in his home country prior to World War II. He immigrated to the United States two years ago to be with his daughter, who married a US Army Lieutenant.

The man decided to help and over the next two years, Larry filled out his frame to one hundred seventy five pounds. He became adept at defending himself with both hands and feet; soon he was an expert in a pivoting kick. He'd be facing an opponent and could turn three hundred sixty degrees in the air, swinging out with one foot, catching his adversary in the head. Larry no longer had to put up with being teased by older or bigger boys. However, he was taught by Mr. Mihara to only use his skills defensively. After a couple of defensive confrontations, older boys gave him a wide berth.

The blow to the head knocked Larry out of the penetrator seat but he was conscious enough to roll on his side and kick out at his attackers. He slammed his foot into the groin of one villager before he rose; only one of the five had a club. Two charged him. Larry sidestepped one and pivoted on one foot catching the other with his foot alongside the head. Now there were two down and the odds were starting to even up. He hit another in the stomach and as the man bent over, Larry kneed him in the chin; the other two ran off.

The chopper was no longer in sight so he sent up another flare, but after five minutes, there was no response; the chopper had left. The crew probably assumed he'd been captured. He reviewed his options and decided to continue with his original plan to move toward the pickup point.

Soon the trees gave way to a forest of bamboo and ferns; the going was difficult. At times he had to crawl through tunnels made by animals in the bamboo; other times he had to crawl over the bamboo. One time he fell six feet to the ground slightly injuring his shoulder when he tried to crawl over the foliage.

He'd been walking and crawling for at least two hours after the chopper left. He stopped several times to check his direction and to hydrate himself from a plastic water bottle he carried in his flight suit. As he was following a random trail to the pickup point, he heard voices close by. He assumed it was the same villagers, probably with reinforcements. His main concern was that there might be armed militia with them. He didn't want to kill anyone but he wanted to escape.

As he was leaning against a tree, a shot rang out and some bark on the tree next to him broke off and hit him in the chest. He started to run, zigzagging in and out of the foliage so he wouldn't be an easy target. One hundred yards later, two more shots were fired at him. He looked over his shoulder as he was running and saw six men coming after him; one was wearing a uniform and three had guns. One of the men yelled in English, "Hands up, American."

He assessed his chances and knew he couldn't kill all six so he stopped, turned around and put up his hands. Three men rushed him while the other three trained their weapons on him. Two of those closest were with the original group that knocked him out of the penetrator. One hit him with a club and when Larry fell, the other kicked him in the ribs and then in the head. He was groggy but tried to remain conscious; he covered up in the fetal position as more blows rained down on him.

Two attackers tied his hands tightly behind him with some cord and pulled him to his feet. They took everything from his pockets and made him stand, though he was wobbly. He heard them shout, like a bunch of kids, when they found the two .38s he was carrying. They prodded him to move in the direction they pointed and he nearly fell; his ribs ached. Soon they came upon a small dirt road where a truck was parked. Four of the men picked up Larry and threw him into the back of the old truck. He hit his head on the metal floor as he landed and was dazed. He could feel the blood flowing down his cheek from the cuts on his head.

Within ten minutes they stopped at a small village. The houses were made of wood and scrap metal and had straw roofs. As he was pulled from the back of the truck, he fell, re-injuring his shoulder. Two of the villagers kicked him several more times and then dragged him into a hut in the middle of twenty or more shanties. There were at least forty villagers outside yelling and shouting at him. Inside was a soldier who sat in the middle of the enclosed area. The soldier spoke very little English. Larry was forced to kneel down on the dirt floor and was hit and spit upon as his interrogator spoke to him in Vietnamese. After he was punched in the face, he fell over on his back and passed out; the interrogation was over. The villagers dragged him to a small cage and pushed him inside; his arms remained tied behind him and his legs were bent. When he woke, he found that he couldn't stretch his legs. He immediately felt cramps but he couldn't do anything about it other than to endure the pain. In spite of his situation, he fell asleep again, but that was quickly interrupted by kids and women poking him with sticks through slots in the bamboo cage. Around midnight, the villagers settled down and he was able to gain a few hours of peace.

When he awoke the next morning, there was a different truck parked in front of the entrance to the village. Three North Vietnamese soldiers were talking to the village chief, who subsequently turned over his weapons to them, though reluctantly. The officer in charge was arguing with the village chief while others looked on. He struck the chief and stood over him where he fell. He took out his gun and shouted something that Larry didn't understand. Then one of the villagers walked up and handed the officer the maps and radios Larry had on him when he was captured. The soldier in charge issued some orders and two soldiers kicked the village chief for a couple of minutes. Hindsight was always good in situations like this, but he should have destroyed the weapons and radio prior to getting captured; he just wasn't thinking clear enough at the time.

Two of the soldiers pulled him out of the cage and he fell. They had to help him rise before they prodded him to move toward the truck, but he fell again. That brought on a series of kicks to his damaged ribs and face. He tried to stretch his legs to regain some circulation, but he needed help to rise and when he was pushed, he fell again. This brought on further attacks. His legs were numb when they dragged him to his feet and he stumbled again as they pushed him toward the truck. Two held him up while the third checked the ropes on his hands, which were still tied behind his back. They bound his legs and then the Vietnamese soldiers tossed him into the rear of the truck. One of the three got in the back with him. He assumed he was heading for a North Vietnamese prison camp and would be further interrogated. He knew there would be many beatings in the next week. While all of this was going on, the village children were taunting him while their elders stood back and watched the proceedings.

He was lying on his side facing the soldier who was sitting on a rack at the side of the truck. He moved his fingers as much as he could and found a sharp surface on the metal floor and moved slightly closer to it so he could cut his binds. The soldier saw the movement and aimed his gun at Larry's head and said something. He assumed he was being told not to move, so he lay still and the soldier leaned back, put a cigarette in his mouth and placed his rifle over his legs. Within thirty minutes, Larry's hands were free and he kicked out with both legs striking the soldiers at knee level and the guard's rifle fell to the floor. Instinctively, the soldier leaned over to reach for his gun. Larry grabbed him by the shirt and pulled him to the floor. Two judo chops rendered the soldier unconscious and Larry had a weapon. He quickly untied the ropes around his legs. The circulation in his legs was still bad so he lay on the truck bed continuously bending and straightening his legs to regain some feeling.

The soldiers in front heard the noise and yelled back to be reassured that everything was okay. When there was no response, the truck stopped and both came to the rear. One of the soldiers pulled the canvas curtain back and Larry hit him in the face with his rifle butt and the protagonist fell to the ground, unconscious. As Larry leaped from the truck to subdue the other soldier, he heard a sharp sound and felt instant pain in his left side. Instinctively he knew that he'd been shot. His momentum, however, carried him forward and he landed on top of the other Vietnamese soldier and quickly disarmed him. Two quick blows rendered him unconscious.

As Larry rolled off the man, he looked around to see if he was alone. When he was comfortable that the incident hadn't been seen, he lay on his back. It was then that he felt intense pain. He rested no more than thirty seconds before he willed himself to stand and lean against the truck. Again, he looked around but there was no one in sight nor were there any other vehicles on the road. He pulled back the canvas shield and found the remains of his fanny pack under the rack seat in the middle of the truck. Included in the contents were bandages and some antibiotics. With the heavy cord that had been around his wrists, he tied the hands of the three soldiers behind their backs and dragged them, one at a time, into the bushes on the side of the road; they would be shielded from view by the truck. He ripped up one of their shirts and placed gags in their mouths. Although this was a controlled Communist Society, no one came to investigate the sound of the gunshot; what a surprise.

Larry pulled down the top of his flight suit and looked at the blood oozing from the bullet wound on his left side. He took a clean bandage and pressed it hard around the wound, but he had to put bite on a stick to offset the intense pain. The blood wasn't flowing as fast now but it was still seeping through the bandage. He swallowed two of the antibiotics and bit into another and poured the contents over the wound, then wrapped another clean bandage as tight as he could around his waist.

He knew he was in trouble and had to get out of there. Thankfully, he hadn't killed anyone, but capture was imminent and he'd be in store for numerous beatings because he embarrassed the Vietnamese. He took the two pistols, radios and maps and put them back in the pockets of his flight suit. He thought about the rescue site, but due to his wound, he knew he couldn't make it. There had to be a place to hide until he regained his strength. He looked around and saw a sign that indicated the truck had stopped on Nghi Tam Road. He found a flashlight in the front of the truck, took out one of the maps, found the street, and estimated he was at least two miles from Hanoi but within a few hundred yards of West Lake. From what others in his squadron told him, this was the lake that John McCain parachuted into. Larry's options were few and his time to pursue any plan of action was limited.

Distancing himself from the truck was now a high priority. He made his way down a dark alley with industrial-type shacks on either side until he could see the outline of the lake. Funny, he didn't hear any dogs bark. He'd read about the Buddhist Monasteries and Pagodas in the country and saw from the map that Tran Quoc Pagoda lay on an islet in the West Lake; it was connected to Hanoi by a narrow causeway. It also was at the east end of the lake he was approaching. He wasn't a great swimmer but he had a lot of stamina. As he entered the lake, he gasped at how cold the water was and the intensity of the pain in his left side. He didn't want to be caught with radios or pistols on his person, so he threw the radios and .38s into the lake and dove in. It took him some time but he swam about three hundred yards until he was in sight of the lights of the Red Pagoda. The water was refreshing but he didn't lose sight of the fact that he had a bullet in him and had to find shelter. When he reached the grounds of the Pagoda, he hid in the underbrush on the bank, partially submerged and somewhat covered by heavy foliage. Though there were many lights throughout the compound, especially around the monuments, he saw no one.

Around three AM, he got out of the water and made his way along the periphery of the huge complex, trying hard not to attract any attention. He estimated the temple and its buildings were on about two acres. He stumbled on some vine-like ground cover and fell to his knees; a feeling of nausea engulfed him. Larry quickly consumed a candy bar he retrieved from the soldiers; the instant sugar rush helped. Although it was a warm evening, he was shivering; he had to find some dry clothing.

Other than the multistoried Red Pagoda, there was one other significantly sized building with multiple doors in the middle of the complex. He tried at least ten doors before he found one that was unlocked; it led into what appeared to be a food preparation and eating room. He carefully entered the room, waited to be sure no one was present, and then continued on. The lights outside penetrated through the windows and supplemented the illumination provided by a few lights along the walls. He carefully looked around the room. There was some cooked rice and greens in containers sitting on the counter, near a sink. An old fashioned pump was fastened to the counter next to the sink. He pumped the handle a few times and used his hands to cup the water and wash down the rice that he'd grabbed in handfuls. He was putting the top back on the rice container when he looked up and stared at a short, thin, bald headed monk standing in an open doorway. The monk was wearing glasses and was dressed in dark orange robes; sandals were on his feet. He was staring at Larry. He didn't seem threatening; he just stood there watching.

"I was hungry," was all that Larry could think to say to the man.

"You are an American flier?"

"Yes, I was shot down near here. Your English is good."

"I went to school in America. Did you kill any of my countrymen?"

"No. My mission was to damage the Russian planes at Phuc Yen Base, north of Hanoi."

"What do you want here?"

"I need a place to hide until I can be rescued."

"That's not possible. Not only are you not welcome here but you're not safe. We are Vietnamese who respect and love our country and will turn you over to the authorities, who come here often. As we speak, they are looking for you. I heard many sirens over the past three hours. It's only a matter of time before you're captured and taken away. You must know we won't conceal you from our brothers when they come."

"It's almost a death sentence if they find me. If I'm lucky, there would be hard labor and many beatings until an armistice is signed, whenever that'll be."

"That's not our problem. You made the decision to attack our country; we did not ask you to come and lay waste to our land. Staying here would put the entire monastery in jeopardy; you are not worth the lives of our monks."

"You've been to my country. We respect all people and treat everyone equally."

"If that's true, then why are you bombing my country?"

"I think our President was duped by the South Vietnamese and got caught up in the hysteria of the communist wave that could swallow up Southeast Asia. It's called the domino theory." The monk smiled.

"That's a very astute view of your country's foreign policy. How many of your countrymen think that way?"

"What do you think of our South Vietnamese brothers?"

"I haven't spent much time with them, but from what I can see, their army is well equipped and they're the best trained force in this country; however, they won't fight. I'm sure that if we leave, they'll capitulate quickly." Larry was feeling flush, so he sat down on one of the two chairs in the room.

"I'm sorry, but you must leave. We're from different cultures. Staying here places all of us in danger. I'll give you thirty minutes before I call the local authorities. That's the best I can do for you."

"That's no help at all. I might as well stay here and wait for them. It's safer than being hunted down and possibly shot."

"You cannot be found here. Please leave or I'll call some of our monks and have you escorted out of here."

Suddenly, Larry became very warm and he started to sweat. As he attempted to rise, he lost consciousness and slumped to the floor.

Chapter 3

The three soldiers who transported Larry to Hanoi were standing at attention in the office of the North Vietnamese Regional Commander, Le Tran. One soldier sported a bandage around his head where he was hit with the butt of a rifle, while another had a splint over his broken nose. Both were victims of Larry Stephens. Their Lieutenant and his superior were also standing at attention. It was a small office in North Central Hanoi, furnished with a desk and three chairs, one of which was Tran's. Everything was resting on a multicolored Burmese Carpet. On the desk was a picture of the commander's wife, a heavy set woman of fifty-five, standing with their three grown children.

Le Tran was a short, thin, baldheaded man in his early sixties. On his right cheek was a distinguishing scar, which he received from a South Vietnamese soldier brandishing a saber; he subsequently strangled the man to death. Those at attention were sweating as the man in charge rose, paced behind his desk and slapped a riding crop against his other hand. It sent a shiver down their spines when Tran said, "I could have all of you shot."

The Regional Commander was a veteran of counterinsurgency conducted by the Viet Cong in the area controlled by the South Vietnamese. He was the one who designed the tunnels that proved so effective in supporting guerrilla tactics in the south. His bold initiatives, in spite of superior South Vietnamese forces, were part of his legend. Subsequently, he served as an aide to Ho Chi Minh and won the leader's trust. Due to his exploits during this war and a recommendation by Mr. Ho, he'd been rewarded with his current assignment. As soon as he assumed command of the Hanoi District, he ruthlessly pursued his duties and purged some of his rivals; he was both revered and feared by those under his command. He had no intention of allowing an American flyer to escape from the punishment he richly deserved, unless the aviator was dead. The three incompetents in front of him put a stain on his impeccable record; he would not have such a blemish

Finally, Tran spoke and one of the soldiers openly wet his pants. "How could three of you let one unarmed man escape? He was wounded and yet, he subdued you three. How was that possible?" No one replied.

"You brought great shame to your unit, your commander and to me personally. I'm placing all of you on half rations until we catch him. Not only that, but he escaped with two guns and two radios. What do you have to say for yourselves?"

When there was no answer, he glared at them and then said to the three soldiers, "Dismissed."

The three were escorted from the room by a guard who'd been standing in the hall outside the office. Tran turned to the two remaining. "You will find this American and bring him to me within twenty-four hours. I don't have to remind you what the penalty is for failure. Get out of here and do your job."

Jean's mother asked her to stay a few more days but Jean was anxious to get back to normalcy. The children needed to be in a more stable atmosphere and not constantly being catered to by their grandparents; the children weren't dumb. They figured out that if they whined or cried their grandparents would rush to console them. She expected to leave by nine in the morning but got away at noon and therefore arrived home late. The children were tired and cranky so she put them to bed without their normal baths. Base housing was their first choice when they arrived at MacDill Air Force Base, but none was available, so they rented a three bedroom, two bath ranch style home off base in a subdivision made up mostly of military personnel. It was a mile from the main gate.

Jean rose early the morning after they returned and was having a cup of coffee when she saw an Air Force vehicle pull into their driveway. Her heart skipped a beat when she saw a chaplain get out of the passenger's side and Larry's former Squadron Commander exit the driver's side. "Oh lord, don't let it be true. I just talked to him a few days ago."

The bell rang three times but she was frozen to the kitchen chair. She leaned over and put her head on the table. Tears flowed down her cheeks and for a moment she couldn't focus until Larry Jr. came into the kitchen. "Mommy, someone is at the door."

Her whole body was unsteady as she walked to the front door and cautiously opened it; she prayed they were here for something else. Standing on the other side were the two Air Force Officers; their faces were expressionless. "Mrs. Stephens, may we come in?"

"He's dead isn't he?" Her hand went to her mouth as she spoke. She was standing in the doorway, dressed in a nightgown and robe. Larry Jr. was at her side holding her other hand, looking up at her.

"We don't know. Could we please come in?"

She led them into the living room; the three adults sat facing each other; Larry Jr. was on her lap. "Captain Stephens was alive and on the ground when last seen. He'd been shot down and we were attempting a rescue when villagers pulled him from the penetrator attached to the rescue helicopter. That's all we know. We assume that he's been captured and is now a POW." The Chaplain said.

"Thank god. When will we find out where he's a prisoner?"

"The other side doesn't give out that information. Since Captain Stephens was alive and on the ground when last seen, we assume he's been captured."

"What do me and the children do?"

"You'll continue to receive your husband's pay and benefits and complete use of the base facilities. We promise to let you know the moment we receive any confirmation of his status. Perhaps your family could come and stay with you. I understand they live in Greenville, Mississippi." Larry's former squadron commander, Colonel Newsome, said.

"That's possible." Jean replied.

"Here's a number for Mrs. Simmons who's formed a support group for wives of MIAs and POWs. To the best of my knowledge, there are two other wives whose husbands are possibly POWs living in your neighborhood. The group meets monthly at various residences; they've also reached out to wives at other bases. I'm always available for you, Mrs. Stephens, but you may be more comfortable bonding with these other women. Please call me anytime," the Chaplain said.

When the bereavement committee left, her young son asked. "Is daddy coming home?"

Trying to suppress tears, Jean replied, "Your daddy promised me he would come back. I'm going to hold him to that.

Chapter 4

Pulling himself to safety was difficult. The sea was volatile and he had to anticipate when he could use the swells to his advantage. He was exhausted as he finally pulled himself out of the water. Once on top of the wooden planks, he scanned the area for Jean. At first he couldn't find her and then out of the corner of his eye, he saw her waving at him from another pile of debris. She appeared to be yelling at him but he couldn't hear anything over the noise of the churning sea. He called her name repeatedly but she didn't respond. The last he saw of her was when a large wave flew over her and she was gone. He tried to reach her by paddling with his hands, but it was futile; the sea had claimed her.

It was dark and very quiet when he awoke. Instinctively, he looked for Jean, but slowly realized it had been a dream. He didn't know where he was and it took him a few moments to remember that he'd been shot. He hurt all over as he ran his hands over his wound and the rest of his body. There was a new bandage on the wound and he wondered how it got here. His head was warm and he felt a chill run up and down his body. Trying to move was difficult because of the pain but he continued to explore his surroundings. He traced the outline of the thin mattress he was on, first with one hand and then the other. The two inch mattress was lying on some sort of wood flooring. It was difficult to understand this because prisoners didn't lie on mattresses: it was usually concrete or dirt.

The wound restricted his movement, so he carefully explored the area around his mattress. He touched a small glass and a bowl to his left. There was no doubt that he was hungry and thirsty but he was reluctant to try any of the ingredients in the containers near his bed for fear of drugs or poison. He thought of Jean and his children again and wondered if she'd been told, and if so, did they tell her that he was alive. A pang of guilt went through his body as he realized he left her with two small children to care for and very little in the form of savings. Her parents would help but it was his responsibility and he wasn't there.

As he started to drift off again, he was blinded by a sharp light from an open door to his left; two Buddhists Monks appeared in the doorway. Instantly, he could see that he was in a six by eight foot room with no windows or vents. He remembered his confrontation with one of the two monks who was standing in the doorway looking down at him. He called himself the abbot and was next to another small man. The abbot raised his hand as Larry tried to rise. Realizing he was too weak, Larry gave in to his pain, laid back and tried to relax. The other man with the abbot entered the room, knelt down, and pulled back the gown Larry was wearing. He unwrapped the bandages around his midsection and examined the wound. He placed some form of liniment on the affected area and Larry flinched. When he finished his examination, he looked up at the abbot and spoke to him in Vietnamese. They conversed for a few seconds before the abbot spoke to Larry.

"The damage is more serious than we initially thought, but your situation is stabilized for now. The problem is that the bullet is too close to your heart for us to remove it. Our skills are rudimentary; perhaps a more gifted physician could remove the bullet, but there is no one that we could call or who would come. From everything we know, it's going to take another two weeks before we can be sure that you'll survive. In the interim we will care for you here. I want your word that you'll not try to leave this room." Larry nodded in agreement.

"How long was I unconscious?" Larry asked.

"It's been three days. The main question now is what to do with you. Our council has been talking about your situation. We've waited until you regained consciousness before we made a final decision, but now with your recovery in doubt, we'll postpone our decision for a couple of weeks. Drink water and eat the food by your bed to regain your strength. We'll come back tomorrow morning. The authorities have visited us once while you were asleep. You're safe for now, but they will come again and eventually, you'll be found. If you're here, we'll be punished."

"If there's concern about my survival, can I dictate a letter to my wife and family and would you make sure it gets to them in the event that I don't recover?"

"If you're up to it, I'll put your thoughts on paper tomorrow. I don't promise that it'll be delivered in a timely manner, but I'll make every effort if you succumb to your wound."

Even though the council of monks wanted to turn him over to the authorities as soon as his wound healed; they still sent two monks on a daily basis to care for him, bringing food and water twice daily and changing his chamber pot. Although Larry never left his room, he could hear the sounds and movement of people in the morning. He asked the abbot about that. "Visitors come every day after morning prayers and meditate in front of the many shrines in our complex. This steady stream continues until the temple is closed to visitors at four in the afternoon."

After three weeks, Larry's health had improved and he was able to go outside, accompanied by the abbot, but only after all the visitors had departed for the day. While outside his room, he was dressed in the garb of a Tran Quoc

Monk and was limited to short walks within the compound. Larry expressed his gratitude and pressed the abbot for the reason his life was saved, even though he was in enemy territory. The abbot was non-committable.

Initially his time outside the room was a tour of the Temple Complex, including its buildings and history, conducted by his host. "The Red Pagoda is a tiered tower of eleven stories with windows in each of the four sides. Each window is vaulted and contains a statue of Buddha adorned with gemstones. The building is constructed of brick and is nearly fifteen hundred years old; everything was built by skilled craftsmen. The last restoration done on any building in the Temple Complex was in the early eighteen hundreds. We receive many gifts from time to time to improve and maintain our holy place. The most recent addition was a gift from the Indian President who visited our Temple. He presented us with a fifty year old Buddha Tree from his country. This tree was placed near the Red Pagoda."

"There are three main buildings including the living quarters of the monks, which is named Vihara. Within the three buildings is a ceremonial hall, a main lecture hall, a kitchen complex, a library, a mediation room and a room for precious relics. The relics date back hundreds to thousands of years."

"Are there different forms of Buddhism?"

"The monks at this temple practice Mahayana Buddhism. Over fifty percent of the Buddhists in the world practiced this form of our ancient religion. I'll talk about the differences in Buddhism at a later time."

"Scattered throughout the complex are one and two story stone shrines. The landscaping is extensive and includes walking paths for the monks during meditation and for sight-seeing by tourists. Joining the Temple area with Hanoi is a small concrete road accessed by mopeds, autos and pedestrians. There's a large fortress like entrance with one set of wooden doors that can be accessed by autos if allowed and another door for\ foot traffic. Immediately inside the complex are the concrete and stone shrines and a room full of relics which also serves as a place to sell memorabilia to the tourists. The stone shrines serve two purposes. One is for mediating and praying and the other for tourists who want to share their food and money to help the monks. At the far end of the complex, sheltered by trees and some landscaping, is a small boat dock. I will familiarize you with other aspects of the complex in the future."

The first time Larry saw the complex was at night. It was entirely illuminated and was one of the most beautiful sites he'd ever seen. Seeing it for the first time in daylight was equally impressive.

Their conversation turned toward social things, such as where Larry grew up, where the abbot went to school in the states and what their parents did. Soon after he was born, his biological mother became ill and Larry and his three siblings went into a home or orphanage for children; Larry never met his father. Within two years he was adopted; over the next six years each of his brothers were adopted by other families. His step-father was a fireman while his step-mother taught at an elementary school. Both step-parents died in an auto accident while he was in Guam. He had minimum contact with his siblings after he left the home. In fact, he hadn't seen any of his three brothers in the past ten years.

The abbot didn't remember his mother; she died when he was very young; there were no brothers and only one sister. His father was a printer in a small company he owned in Hanoi. The two were close until he returned from college. The father was shocked to learn he wanted to be a Buddhist Monk This caused a severe strain in their relationship and lasted until his father died. The abbot said he wished he'd reached out to his father before it was too late, but he was young and wanted to assert his independence. Gradually, their conversations turned to flying and politics. "What do you like most about flying?' his host asked.

"I've thought about that many times and there is no one answer. The power of the jet aircraft is overwhelming. You push the throttle forward, lean back and you've been thrust into space. You're all alone among the stars and in awe of how small you are in the vast universe. Most of my missions had a purpose, but occasionally, I had some free time to practice different maneuvers and I'd get lost in thought up there My imagination ran wild and I felt free to sort through the problems one encounters on earth. It's as though you're communicating with God. I've caught myself many times saying his name. I wasn't praying; I was just talking. I shared with him my life and how I felt about my wife and children, without being religious about it."

"Did you always want to fly?"

"The simple answer is yes, but I'm not so sure that I want to be a military aviator anymore. It's taken over too much of my life. I've given my time to my country; it's now time to give myself something more enduring. There are more important things now than when I first went into the military. I have a wife and two small children and I don't know whether they know that I'm alive."

"What if you hadn't been shot down, would you feel the same way?"

"Yes. I'd planned to leave the military when this tour in Southeast Asia was over. I don't think it's unusual for someone my age to question whether he selected the right profession. Is this the first time you've talked with an adversary?"

"Have you ever heard of the "Deer Group"? He asked Larry

"I never have."

"In 1945, your intelligence agency, I believe they were called the OSS, sent a team into the Northern part of Vietnam to meet with Ho Chi Minh."

Larry was stunned. "You can't be serious?"

"It's true. Your people were anxious to establish a counter insurgency group in this area to combat the Japanese. This wasn't their first contact with Ho. You probably aren't aware of this, but it was your embassy that secured his release from the French in the early 1940s. That made a lasting impression on Ho. When we declared our independence from France, Ho Chi Minh used your Declaration of Independence as our standard. Interesting, isn't it that your nation and mine could have so much in common?"

"During World War II, the only method to affect contact with our group was to parachute a team into our country, hook up with some of our followers and make their way on foot to Mr. Ho, as he was called. Our organization, the Viet Minh, was the one that intercepted the American team, called the Deer Group, and brought them to our leader.

"How do you know this?" Larry asked.

"I was a young college graduate and a comrade of Mr. Ho and a Mr. Van, who you may know as General Giap."

"You were a communist." Larry blurted out.

"It wasn't as simple as that. I was part of Ho's group who fought hard against the French and then the Japanese. Our goal was an independent Vietnam."

"I thought you were a holy man?"

"I studied at Georgetown in the states, received a master's degree in philosophy and taught Buddhist Studies in a private school in Hanoi. When Ho Chi Minh put his group together, he asked me to join him."

"Who were the members of the Deer Group?"

"I don't remember all their names other than Captain Thomas and Sgt. Hoagland. You might be interested to know that Ho Chi Minh was dying when that group arrived and it was the Sergeant who saved his life by giving him Quinine and Sulfa drugs. After Ho recovered, we set up an insurgency group, made up mostly of the Viet Minh, with the Americans acting as advisors. They showed us how to use weapons more effectively and how to employ different tactics against the Japanese; subsequently we made their life unbearable. The Americans stayed until the end of the war; I believe one of the Deer Group married a Vietnamese girl. As soon as the Japanese surrendered, I along with General Giap escorted Thomas and his remaining men to Saigon and safety. You probably wouldn't be in this predicament if they had let Ho die. Our group stayed in contact with your OSS until the nineteen fifties."

"I wasn't aware of that."

"Our two countries have a lot more in common than you think. What brought Ho and our group to the attention of the OSS during World War II was that we rescued several US fliers who were shot down and captured by the Japanese. Subsequently, we were able to transport them to American lines. During one of these occasions, Ho was able to meet General Claire Chennault, a man he tremendously admired. I was with him at that meeting. For two days the two leaders met frequently. I wasn't privy to what they discussed, but our leader seemed upbeat on our way home. Politics didn't seem to be driving the agenda. Both parties wanted to defeat the Japanese and sought ways to assist each other in that objective."

Larry didn't think he was being indoctrinated, but the abbot continued to steer the conversation toward history common to the two countries including the most recent conflict. "What do you think of your involvement in this war, Larry?"

"I'm a professional soldier; I carry out the lawful orders and directives of my superiors. I'm also an American who has the right of free speech and thought. I don't know exactly why I'm here; I must accept that my superiors have an objective that must be met. I'll be honest. I don't have much respect for the South Vietnamese, who have a well-equipped and well-trained military but don't seem to have the desire to protect and defend their country. They're happy that we're here but beyond that, I'm not sure. They seem to fight well when we're present, but when we're not, they accept defeat too easily.

I'm also concerned that America is becoming involved in all kinds of wars across this planet that could get us bogged down to the point where we can't extricate ourselves, notably here and Korea. We have only so many resources and they're being expended across the globe. Our leaders seem to see every little flare up in the world as a threat to our nation. We're involved in so many treaties, that it would be impossible to come to the aid of all that we've agreed to defend. I often wonder if we could respond if only two of the countries we swore to protect, requested we intervene on their behalf simultaneously. We can't continue these policies for posterity and survive." Larry said.

"What do you think is your country's objective in this conflict?"

"I honestly don't know. If I were to guess, I would say that we want a free South Vietnamese government, one that's not threatened by their northern brothers, which I gather is contrary to your views."

On one of their walks, the tenor of the conversation changed. "If we were able to keep you safe for some time, what could you do to repay us for the risk?"

Larry was initially stunned and took a few moments to prepare an answer. "I grew up on a farm and worked as a construction laborer while I was in college. Many of your buildings are in dire need of repair. I could fix most of them. From what you've told me, this complex has been in this location for nearly fifteen centuries and the last repair to any of the building was in the early eighteen hundreds. I see that you have a garden; I could help there. But why take the risk to protect me?"

"You have been with us for over a month. It would be difficult to explain why we haven't turned you over by now. If you consider my offer to stay here, your lifestyle will be drastically altered. We rise early, have a very light breakfast, some lunch, and very little dinner. Sometimes there isn't enough food for the evening meal. Can you adapt to such an austere diet?"

"I can do what has to be done."

"If you should be allowed to stay with us, your body mass will decrease with less food. Your head will be shaved and we must do something about your skin color; tea can darken the skin. Learning Vietnamese and our customs is a necessity; you'd be restricted until it was safe for you to return to your country. Finally, you'd have to convert to Buddhism."

"I'm willing to do anything necessary to retain my freedom. Can we get a message to my countrymen that I'm alive?"

"That would incur too much risk. I'm not sure anyone outside this Pagoda can be trusted. If your secret is revealed, we could suffer the wrath of our government. Ho Chi Minh was like an uncle to me, but even he couldn't protect me or any of my monks if he were alive. I'm trying to repay a favor that Sgt. Hoagland performed many years ago that saved my friend's life. It's not my decision alone. I must speak with my council; they may overrule me. I will tell you of their decision tomorrow."

"What about the other monks? Can you trust them with my safety?"

"Yes."

Larry slept intermittently and dreamed of Jean and the life they had before he was shot down. In addition, he was feeling stressed waiting for the council's decision and what it would be. Although he wasn't a religious man, he prayed that they wouldn't send him to the Hanoi Hilton. Though there was no light in his small room, he knew it was morning because he could hear the monks chanting; he assumed it was about five AM. To pass the time he recited poetry. The "Shooting of Dan McGrew" by Robert W. Service was his favorite; it took about four minutes to recite. When he was finished with that poem, he continued with all the poetry he was required to memorize when he was in high school. He couldn't remember some of the words, so he made them up to fill out the stanzas.

An hour later the door to his room opened. He could see the abbot and two other monks blocking the doorway. They motioned him to follow them into the main lecture hall. There was a table and six chairs set up at one end of the room. One of the monks pointed to a chair and Larry sat down. He was about to hear his fate.

The abbot addressed him. "This has been a difficult decision for us. Earlier, we were visited by six soldiers who insisted upon searching the grounds and buildings for you. Luckily they didn't know about our secret room and after two hours, they went away. I'm sure they'll be back. Their commander is a very thorough man who checks things two and three times. So the question is, what do we do with you? There was a spirited discussion among the council, but the decision was unanimous. You may stay here under the following conditions. You cannot speak other than during your Vietnamese language classes. You can't have any contact with the other monks until you master our language. You will follow our way of life and learn Buddhism; we expect you to convert. I will give you chores which you will carry out without question. Should these conditions be unacceptable, you are free to leave now. No one will report you to the authorities, but once you leave here, you're on your own."

"How long do you think it will take to learn your language?"

"I would think it would take about two years of study to carry on a conversation. It will take at least three years to be accepted into the Buddhist Religion. The change in life style will not be easy. It's your decision."

"Will I be able to go into town once I can speak the language fluently?"

"When the time comes, our council will meet to determine what's best for the Temple. What is your answer?"

"My answer is yes."

Chapter 5

They cut his hair and issued him a dark orange robe and a pair of sandals. It was just like being in boot camp. For a period of time, he would be segregated from the other monks and would take direction only from the abbot. It would be lonely, but Larry was determined to survive.

The next morning, he rose at four and met with the abbot, who had a laundry list of furniture and monuments that required repair. The items were not difficult to repair, but the tools were rejected from the 17th century. There was a primitive saw, a hammer of sorts, and a chisel. Screws were non-existent and nails were a premium. He had to salvage nails from the rotten material he was replacing. It didn't matter; he was grateful for the opportunity to survive. Lumber had to be donated or reused. He started his first day of labor in the monk's living quarters. It would take at least two weeks to repair the old and decrepit furniture. "Whether you believe it or not, your decision has saved my life. I will always be grateful and I will never knowingly make you regret your decision," Larry told the abbot.

There was so much deferred maintenance that Larry wondered if he'd ever complete the tasks before new repairs surfaced on the objects he was initially fixing. He appreciated what the abbot and other monks agreed to do at their risk, but it was he, who the Vietnamese would shoot, not the monks. The number of searches by the local authorities increased, raising the issue that they must believe he was here. The monks had an ingenious method of alerting the compound if there were unwanted visitors.

They'd release about ten local birds as soon as someone spotted someone they perceived as compromising. When the first monk spotted the birds, he alerted others by whistling; soon everyone knew they had to be on alert.

He didn't move into the monk's quarters but stayed in the secret room at the rear of the building which housed the relics and treasures of the Temple. His room was secure but he wasn't sure for how long. It was only a matter of time before more soldiers would come and stumble upon his sleeping place. The last time the soldiers came, they matched each monk with a bunk or bed. Luckily, he heard the whistling and hid near the boat house in some heavy foliage.

The question was, what could he create that would solve his problem? For starters, he kept nothing but his mattress and a thin cover in his room. Each morning, he folded the mattress and blanket, tied a cord around them, and placed them on the floor in one of the corners. This made sense but he needed to do more. Over the next month, he looked at his environment and came up with three possible hiding places, but he needed some building materials. One of the sheds on the property was so run down that it was impossible to fix. With the abbot's permission, he tore down the building and stored the good lumber near his workshop.

He believed he had to create three hiding places that would blend in with the environment. The only two accesses to the Pagoda Complex were via a causeway from Hanoi or over the lake, by boat. The concrete road connecting the mainland with the Temple grounds was in constant use by pedestrians, mopeds and some autos. In the most westerly portion of the complex was a small pier. Larry hadn't seen any boats tied up there but he was sure it was used periodically.

His initial effort was to find a hiding place on a bank farthest from the causeway. The growth from bushes and trees was heavy in one area while the ground cover was thick and spreading. Larry pealed back the vine-like ground carpet and dug down into the soft dirt to create an area four feet deep, three feet wide and within seven feet of the lake. He shored up the sides, top and bottom with discarded lumber, creating a box-like structure, with access to the lake. He covered the top of the box with the vine-like sod, leaving enough space for an entrance in one end. He worked and reworked the hiding place so he could enter the box quickly by folding back the ground-like carpet attached to some old boards, crawl into the box and pull that portion of the roof over the entrance. If he had to use this hideout, he was intent to remain there until the soldiers left. In the event they found the hiding place, he'd be able to slide into the lake from the box. That portion of the enclosure next to the lake was left open. Excess dirt that he displaced was carefully dispersed into the lake. He tried entering and exiting the hiding place several times to be sure it would work and he'd be concealed. He did such a good job of camouflage that he had to concentrate hard to find the entrance.

Since he couldn't guarantee that he'd be in that area when the birds were released, he had to find or make two more hiding places. The next would be in the monastery's library which was an adjunct to the meditation room. He visualized that he could create a tall, rectangular bookcase fastened to one of the walls. It would be wide enough for him to stand up inside. It was easy to assemble and fasten the structure to a wall in the library. He found some lacquer and stained the box the same color as the walls and then made shelves around the exterior to accommodate about fifty books. Larry had worked as a finish carpenter in the past and it was within his skill set to create a door that fastened inside and seemed to be seamless from the outside. He fashioned several holes in the top of the container for ventilation.

The last hiding place would be the safest but most difficult to create. He found a spot along the lake bank near the boat dock. In this case, he dug down between two trees until he found seepage from the lake. Larry backfilled dirt so he'd be two feet above the water line at the entrance. He sloped the enclosed area to the water level proximate to the lake. The enclosure would be similar to the other he built on the opposite bank. He shored up the walls with discarded lumber and built a cover of wood, earth and foliage. The outside easily blended in with the surrounding area. He was confident that he could stay in this hiding place for a long period of time. When it was completed, he could jump into the pit quickly, pull the green cover overhead and, if necessary, slide into the lake. He knew the hiding places weren't fool-proof, but the three concealed places gave him a chance to survive until an armistice was signed.

Releasing birds was always the signal that soldiers or civilian authorities were entering the Pagoda grounds, but there was no signal for when they departed. He had no choice but to alert the abbot to his hiding places, since he had as much to lose as Larry.

The abbot emphasized physical training to maintain the body and spirit. To prepare for this austere life, Larry performed calisthenics for two hours, just after he rose, He ate a small breakfast of tea and crackers and then meditated for fifteen minutes before he started on his list of repairs. The Buddhists recommended that everyone make each day meaningful and productive. Since Larry couldn't talk to the other monks, he practiced smiling to everyone he came in contact with.

Some of his tea was used on his skin to darken the color. Within three months, his skin tone was similar to everyone else. He started to copy the mannerisms of the other monks and soon blended in during meals, meditation and prayers. The main meal of the day was served at noon; it consisted of some bread but was mainly rice and vegetables. In the afternoons, he'd study Vietnamese for two hours and be introduced to Buddhism for another two hours. After the last session, he'd return to his list of repairs and retire at eight in the evening, after another round of calisthenics.

Over the next three months he took a portion of his rations and some water and divided it among the three hiding places; he kept the rice and water in separate jars. They'd been visited by a couple of soldiers twice the past month but it was more perfunctory than a real search. Still, he didn't want to let down his guard. He was in enemy territory and one slip would be the end. He was repairing some of the benches in the main conference room when one of the monks he worked with signaled him that they had visitors. He quickly made his way to the library and entered the box he'd made. He hadn't spent much time in the box; he assumed it was large enough and would conceal him. The first thing he noticed as he entered was how small it was and that there was no way he could reach down to the floor and pick up the jars of food and water. Later he felt that his breathing was restricted; he'd probably didn't make enough holes in the top. Well, he was here and he'd have to make the best of it.

Thirty minutes had passed and there was no word that the visitors had departed. It was then that he heard the large door to the library open followed by loud voices from two individuals. He detected anger in the exchange between the two men. As they came closer to where he was hiding, he distinctly recognized one of the voices as that of the abbot. The other was unknown to him but he definitely was dictating the dialog. Larry had only a novice understanding of Vietnamese, but some of the words were unmistakable and the visitor was threatening the abbot. His identity was unknown but his importance seemed to silence the leader of this Temple. They came nearer and then seemed to distance themselves before departing. Thirty minutes later the abbot called his name and asked Larry to come out. Although reluctant to leave his place of concealment, he trusted the abbot.

"My brother-in-law, Commander Le Tran, was the one with me when we came into the library. He's positive you're here and threatened to close us down unless we give you up. Of course, we can't do that because he not only would close us down, but many of my monks would go to prison or work camps. We are caught as you Americans say, between a rock and a hard place."

"Do you want me to leave?"

"No. It's now a matter of a contest between my sister's husband and me. The other monks involved are also at risk but don't want you to leave or be found. Can you understand how they must feel?"

"Yes, and I admire them very much. Is there something I can do for them?"

"Do what you're doing. They'll know that you appreciate them."

Since Larry couldn't speak or read Vietnamese, his introduction into Buddhism was initially orchestrated by the abbot, who spent the first six months of Larry's new life teaching him the three universal truths of the religion, namely, 1.) Nothing is lost in the Universe, 2.) Everything changes, and 3.) The Law of Cause and Effect makes everyone accountable. In addition, he was taught that this form of Buddhism believes that for every event that occurs, another follows and whether the result is good or bad, it was caused by the first event. In essence, the result of an action is borne by the person who commits it. Larry learned a new phrase, "unintended consequences".

"Our form of Buddhism, namely Mahayana Buddhism, is more widespread than other sects. It's practiced in China, Tibet, Korea, Japan and Vietnam. It encompasses a wide range of beliefs and it's not as narrow in its vision as other schools of Buddhism.

Mahayana means the "Great Vehicle", and is compared to a boat that carries believers through hardships to a better life. You are going through that phase."

"Evolving around the first century; Mahayana places emphasis on meditation and believes in a multitude of heavens and hells. It makes this religion accessible to anyone, and can be embraced by all. It was exported to the United States in the nineteenth century by Chinese and Japanese immigrants. One of its main expressions is Zen which emphasizes rigorous self-control, meditation practices, and an insight into the nature of things. We need to accelerate your learning of Vietnamese and Buddhism. I believe that we'll have many more unwelcome visitors in the days to come. We must be alert."

Larry was a realist and knew that he'd be here for years because the end of the war wasn't in sight. Neither side appeared to be ready to concede that they couldn't win; hence, the conflict would continue until both sides were exhausted and would accept the gains already made. The losses in people and assets would be written off as though they didn't exist. He took to his studies with vigor and conversations with the abbot each afternoon were something that he looked forward to, especially since he couldn't have any dialog with the other occupants of this monastery. Apparently, he had an affinity for languages. He was able to memorize many of the standard phrases quickly and soon he was able to maintain a simple dialog with the abbot. Every day Larry tried to pump the abbot for news about the conflict, but his benefactor was an astute man and carefully avoided any discussion of that issue. The good news was that there was a bond developing between the two men.

By the end of his first year, his body weight had dropped from one hundred seventy five pounds to one hundred forty. He was lean and not an ounce of fat on him. He maintained his physical fitness regime in the morning and added an hour in the evening. At times, the monastic existence bothered him; he longed for human companionship. This made the daily interface with the abbot even more important.

At night, before he fell asleep, he would always think of Jean. He started to create a scenario where he remembered their life, starting with the first encounter and carried the relationship forward to the time he left for Vietnam. Then he'd repeat the storyline and add in those episodes he'd forgotten the last time he recalled the story. Escape was always in the back of his mind but he knew he wasn't ready; there were so many issues that needed to be resolved before he left the shelter of this Temple. First, there was the language he had to master and that would take years, second, his appearance and third, he needed to develop a skill to help the villagers during his escape attempt so they would assist him. In addition, he had to be able to blend in with the people in this country. Finally, he had to find a practical route to a known destination and then there was the ultimate question of how he'd survive during his trek home.

The abbot retained Larry's map of Vietnam and each week they'd look at a route he might follow to safety. The abbot had traveled extensively throughout Vietnam and his advice was invaluable. He remembered most of the villages he visited and some of the features around the villages. By the time Larry was ready to leave, he knew a great deal about the villages and what he could expect from them. He also remembered the three villages the abbot warned him against. Occasionally, they talked about the weather. May to November were the warmest months of the year, though it was also the period of the heaviest rains.

Though the Temple had only rudimentary tools, Larry was able to complete sixty percent of his repair list by the end of the first year. Lately, he'd been concentrating on the tables and wooden structure that held many of the precious relics. The abbot recognized early on that Larry had the skills of a finish carpenter and he was going to get much of his repair list completed before Larry escaped. Although Larry didn't kill anyone, he made a fool of the soldiers who were taking him to prison as well as their immediate commander, who would bear the responsibility for his escape. The abbot told him how stern the regional commander was. He couldn't comprehend why his sister took the man as her husband when she knew his true character. He didn't know for a fact that Tran beat his sister but he knew she was petrified of him.

Near the end of the first year, Larry was able to communicate a little in Vietnamese with the abbot. Dialog with the other monks was still forbidden but he soon participated with them during meditation periods. Slowly he was becoming acclimated to the ways of monastery existence. His weight dropped some more, yet he felt stronger and more alert. Psychologically, his greatest accomplishment by far was his deeper understanding of Buddhism. He looked forward to the two hour sessions each afternoon and was developing an awareness that there was more in life than he previously considered. Although he longed to be home with his family, he was developing a life-style that he was comfortable with and the best version of himself was surfacing.

Early into his second year at the temple, Larry was on his way to inspect one of his potential hiding places adjoining the West Lake. As he started down the path leading to the concealed box, he was approached by a middle aged, well dressed, Caucasian couple wanting to take his photo. He didn't understand their language, but assumed they were Russian. Pretending not to hear, he kept his gaze down and started to move away. It was the woman who forced the issue by grabbing his robe and yelling at him. He tried to pull way but the man, perhaps her husband, grabbed his arm. All eyes turned to see what was causing her concern. Luckily, the abbot, who was multi-lingual, was in the area and quickly calmed the couple by volunteering to take a photo with them. Larry stood there until the couple let go of him. From that point forward, Larry was cognizant of visitors carrying cameras. He avoided them at all costs.

Chapter 6

Jean entered the University of Mississippi's Medical School in September, five months after Larry had been reported missing. She found a four-bedroom, two-bath home for rent in Meridian, a few blocks from the medical school. Her parents moved into the fourth bedroom. Although things had been contentious with her mother since she'd married Larry, which had all changed with his capture. Phyllis Washington was like a rock and did everything she could to help with the children and allow Jean to concentrate on her studies. She still gave her opinion freely on every subject related to the family and, at times, was very contentious. When that occurred, Jean would turn to her father to provide a happy balance.

Jean's class consisted of twelve students, six men and six women. Competition was constant but so was the feeling of camaraderie. Her only social life was when she and her classmates got together on Friday evenings at a local pub to share beer and pizza. They'd talk mostly about what life would be like when they received their MDs. Each of the six male students asked her to dinner at various times during the school semester, but she explained that she was married and her husband, a POW, was sure to come home as soon as the hostilities ceased.

One of her male classmates was more aggressive than the other five and didn't take her explanation seriously. She was flattered by all the attention he was giving her, but it was annoying. He certainly was handsome enough, and she knew that she was fair game for any male, but she still held fast. One Friday evening while the others were dancing and he and Jean were alone at the table, he made his intentions clear. "Look, Jean, you and I both know that we could have an affair and no one would know the difference. Sex is a bodily function and you've had enough sex to know what I say is true. It's also a great release from all the tension were under to complete our studies. As a future physician, I'm prescribing a cure for your lack of nooky, come to bed with me and free yourself from all the stress."

"Come back in three years, Jerry, and I'll see what I can do." They both laughed but she knew that he'd persist until they went their separate ways or she gave in.

After dinner on a Sunday evening, her son asked if he and Susanne could stay up past the normal bedtime and watch Happy Days. Jean gave her permission. When their grandmother saw them curled up on the living room couch, she told them it was time to go to bed; they had school the next morning. When Jean came into the room, her daughter was crying. There was an awkward moment before Jean's mother apologized and went into the kitchen. It surfaced again when her mother suggested that she ought to date some of her classmates. "You're a young intelligent woman. You can't sit around your whole life waiting for someone who may never return. You don't even know if Larry is still alive."

"That's enough, mother. I can't begin to tell you how grateful I am that you and dad are here and how much you've helped me with the children. But my marriage to Larry is off-limits to you. He's coming home and I'll wait as long as it takes for him to get here. You've got to respect my marriage."

"You're being foolish."

"That's enough, mother."

But the holiday season has a way of bringing families together. Her father, Thomas, had always been the steadying force in their family. He had a quiet talk with his wife and most of the friction disappeared. Jean, the children, and her parents celebrated Christmas in their rented four-bedroom home in Meridian.

Medical school was absorbing most of her free time. When there was time, she spent it with her two little ones. They used to ask about their father, but now they barely mentioned his name. Reality hadn't set in yet for Jean. She still believed the love of her life was alive and would come home and life would be as it was. Thank god for Larry's check that came in monthly. It was the main reason she'd been able to pursue her medical degree. When Larry Jr. said "grace" before Christmas dinner, Jean thought of her husband and prayed that he was safe and was thinking of her as she was of him.

Larry was close to the library when the birds flew overhead; someone was on the grounds. The non-standard alarm system within the Pagoda was working and, although monks went about their business seemingly oblivious to any intrusion, they silently alerted everyone near them. He entered the library, carefully looked around and then opened the door to his hiding place and stepped inside the safe space. He heard people enter the building and he listened to the dialog between the abbot and several men, who he assumed were soldiers. He understood enough Vietnamese now to know there was someone with authority in the library; Larry remembered the voice. That man stated that he knew an American soldier was on the grounds and he wanted the abbot to turn him over immediately.

He listened as the abbot plead that he was unaware of any outsider within their midst. He assured the other man that if he found one, he would immediately notify the authorities. This must have placated the official because everyone withdrew; Larry could hear the door close. Just to be sure he waited thirty minutes before releasing the internal clasp and opening the bookshelf door. Although he modified the hideout once by making it wider and adding more ventilation, he needed to add a peep hole so he could see who was nearby and when they left.

An hour later the Abbot caught up with him in a building where he was repairing a wall. "We were fortunate today that you weren't found. The secret hiding place saved both of us, but the soldiers will continue to return. Commander Tran has taken your escape personally and looks upon it as a blemish to his record. He has made such a big issue about your capture that he either has to produce you or your body. Your escape is something he cannot accept, even though you didn't kill anyone. Just to be clear, I would not have taken you in had you killed someone."

"I know the longer I stay, the riskier it is for you and my fellow monks. I'm working on a plan but it may take one or two years before I can implement it. Is there any animosity with the other monks about the special treatment I'm receiving and the intimidation coming from the authorities?"

"You're not receiving any special privileges other than your being here. All postulates are treated the same; you are being taught our language. I've done the same for others who decided upon the Buddhist life. I've had people from India, Poland, Portugal and Germany who I instructed in our language. Not one monk has complained about your presence. To the best of my knowledge, all have accepted you as a convert. You are a convert, aren't you?"

"Thanks to you, I have found my religion."

Chapter 7

It was the eighth of December and Larry had been in Vietnam for nearly seven months. This was Bodhi Day, which is the anniversary of the day that the historical Buddha experienced enlightenment. The monks at Tran Quoc temple made cookies and to Larry's surprise, they decorated a tree with lights. It was as though he was home in America. Time had passed so fast that he hadn't realize that it was nearly Christmas. Seventeen days later, while keeping a low profile, he celebrated the holiday in his room for a half hour before pursuing his duties. He wondered what Jean and the children were doing. He assumed she moved closer to her family in Greenville, Mississippi and got a job; he wondered what it was. Most of all, he hoped that she thought he was still alive. For the first time, he realized she may think him dead and was pursuing life as though he wouldn't return. He didn't want to think about that.

In Hanoi, Commander Tran reviewed the weekly reports on the search for the American. This was the north and no one in his right mind would shield the flyer, so where was he. It was possible that he was dead although the body hadn't turned up. There were only a few places the flyer could hide for an extended period of time and only a few people who would risk Tran's vengeance by defying him; one of those was his brother-in-law, the Abbot of the Tran Quoc Temple. He learned early on to treat him carefully. He'd been a close friend of Ho Chi Minh and General Giap and that friendship went back over thirty years.

Even if the abbot was shielding the American, Tran wasn't sure what would happen if he found the flyer at the Temple. Not even he could make an accusation without definite proof. Tran hadn't gotten to his current position by being impulsive. Intuitively, he knew the flyer must be at Tran Quoc if he was alive. To succeed, Tran had to devise a plan to put enough pressure on his wife's brother to make him surrender the imperialist. How could those three idiots give him up so easily? He sent all three in addition to their supervisor to fight in the south.

Over the next two years, Tran continued to search for Larry, though he cut the number of soldiers assigned to a minimum, He now resorted to visitors on a daily basis. These were ordinary people trained to spy for him. They'd enter the Temple grounds as soon as the monks finished their morning prayers. They were required to stay for two hours and report to Tran's office if there was anything suspicious. He had coverage over the entire day and it didn't cost him anything in manpower; to date, that plan hadn't produced any results.

Jean was busy with medical school and looking forward to when she would receive her MD and earn a salary. Larry's paycheck was a life saver, but she knew those funds may not last forever. She was content to start as a General Practitioner. Earning an income to support herself and the two children was paramount for her. A tiny thought started to creep into her mind; her husband may not have survived. It was the first time she'd even considered such an idea, though her mother wasn't shy about reminding her.

It was early 1972 and several POWs had been released. Two told their de-briefers that they memorized the names of all the prisoners in the Hanoi Hilton; Larry Stephens was not on that list. The Pentagon didn't release the list initially but that wasn't a problem since the government leaked like a sieve and sooner or later the press would find out. It was Jean's mother who broke the news to her while they sitting at the kitchen table having a cup of coffee. "Mother, I know Larry's alive. He's probably in some other camp."

Her mother stirred another spoonful of sugar in her cup and then put her hand on top of Jeans. "I loved Larry like a son but you need to face reality; he's not coming home and you need to move on with your life. Your children need a father and you need a man."

"Mom, I'm going to my room and close the door. You have to stop forcing this issue on me. I'll deal with it when I have to, but not now. I don't want to even think that Larry is dead. I'll talk to you tomorrow."

Even though she went to her room, she couldn't help thinking about what her mother said. Try as hard as she could to put that thought out of her mind, she couldn't help but think it was a possibility. She really hadn't planned on that option, but now she was forced to accept that it was a possibility. But even if Larry wasn't held in the Hanoi Hilton, there were other camps that he could be in. She was going to wait. Perhaps they'd sign an armistice and everyone would come home. She said a small prayer that Larry would be in one of those camps.

Medical school was absorbing all her time. Thankfully, this was the end of her third year. She didn't know where she was going for her internship, but she knew that there was a paycheck involved. The steady income from Larry's pay had carried her and the children through these last three years. If Larry was dead, his military pay would cease and that would create a problem. She hadn't been able to save anything and she felt guilty. What if he didn't want her when he came home?

She'd been asked out frequently, but was steadfast in her belief that the love of her life would return and he would love her as he did before. Her son was eleven and looked like his father. He loved sports and went out for the elementary school's soccer and baseball teams. When she had time, Jean and her daughter Susanne would go to her son's games and cheer him on. She was active in her support of her children, being one of those mothers who would yell out to encourage her son. One of her son's classmates' father was divorced and would come to the game. He was a civil engineer who worked for the county and lived in Meridian. They talked a lot when she was able to make the game and he invited her out several times; she declined. But it was nice to talk to someone her own age and not just associated with work. He was persistent and she agreed to have coffee one day after her son's game; her daughter was at her girlfriend's house and Larry Jr. planned to spend the night with a friend.

They walked from the baseball park to a Denny's Restaurant about a block from the stadium. He seemed sensitive to her concerns and she felt comfortable in his company. When she looked at her watch, it was six o'clock and she said it was time to go. He suggested they have dinner there and she saw no harm in it. Besides, no one was home that evening, her parents had decided to see a movie. Both had left their autos near the field, so he escorted her back to her car. It was dark by now and there were no street lights where they were parked. Jean put her key in the car door and opened it. She turned to say goodnight and that's when he embraced and kissed her. Jean was taken by surprise but his kiss was so warm that she returned his kiss. He pushed his hips to hers and fondled her breasts. His tongue entered her mouth and a strong desire was taking hold of her. When he raised her skirt, guilt took over and she pushed him away. "Come on Jean, you want to as much as I do." He said.

Her keys were still in her hand as she pushed him away and opened her car door and quickly got behind the steering wheel. She locked the door, started the car and drove off as he banged on the door and asked her to stop.

She decided to end any further involvement with him and told him so when they met at the next game. He was upset and started showing up at the hospital and the grocery store where she shopped. Finally, she got up the nerve to confront him at the supermarket.

"It seems that no matter where I go, you're there. I think you're stalking me. I don't want your attention. If you persist, I'll get a court order. Try explaining that to your employer." She walked off and didn't look back.

The visible stalking stopped, but occasionally there were late calls and when she answered, the other person hung up. She hired an attorney who wrote a letter to the man stating that any more calls or stalking would be met with a court order and a notification of that action to his employer. That seemed to solve the problem because the calls stopped immediately.

When she received an offer to do her internship at Greenville Memorial Hospital, she was delighted. It meant that the children could return to a school system she was familiar with and perhaps she could rekindle some high school friendships. With her training over, it was time to look at the future and whether or not Larry would be part of their family. Her parents were delighted when she received the contract from Greenville Hospital. They missed their home and old friends. They'd rented out their three bedroom home while they were in Meridian helping

Jean. It took a couple of months before their renters found another unit and they moved back.

Larry was in his third year of study under the abbot's tutelage; he felt that his language skills had improved to a point where he was ready to be tested. He asked the abbot if he could go out with the monks early in the morning to beg for food. "It'll be dangerous for you if you make a mistake; it will also be dangerous for us. Try it tomorrow but let the other monks take the lead; all I want you to do is be there. Let them initiate everything and most of all, stay close to them and don't talk. They'll get you back safely."

It never occurred to him how many people would be out this morning in downtown Hanoi and how many soldiers were milling around. His weight was near one hundred thirty pounds and with a bald head, he look scrawny. He'd been boiling tea leaves and applying them to his skin; he could easily pass as an Asian. The only physical limitation he had was his blue eyes.

Nineteen monks, including Larry, used the causeway to walk to the western part of Hanoi. They sat down on a corner in a small square to beg. He, along with the other monks, set out tin cups or small cardboard boxes in front of them. The passing pedestrians were generous and they collected money, grain, rice and vegetables. To his surprise, one of the monks was a slight of hand artist and picked a man's pocket, Larry, with his head down, watched the monk do it twice. He marveled at the man's skill but he wondered if the abbot was aware of the monk's proclivity.

By this time, Larry started talking with the other monks, though none knew of his nationality or how he came to the Pagoda. When he had a chance, he spoke to the monk with the light fingers about what he saw and asked him how he did it. "Are you going to tell the abbot?" The monk asked.

"No. That's between you and the holy man. I just want to learn how to do it." The other monk smiled.

Over the next month, Larry became adept in the art of pickpocketing but didn't initially try out his new skill when he went out to beg. He held his allegiance to the head man above all else and wouldn't do anything to embarrass the abbot.

With his ability to speak Vietnamese and go out in public to beg, he felt a sense of security. That was broken one day when the grounds were flooded with North Vietnamese Regulars. About two dozen soldiers with bayonets came into the compound so quickly that the signal wasn't given. Larry saw many of the monks scurrying around the grounds and assumed the temple was being searched in earnest. He was near the hidden chamber in the southeastern part of the grounds, so he rushed to that hideout. This was one of two improvised hideouts with a dugout reinforced with scrap lumber and covered with a carpet of vines; it had an outlet to the lake. It wasn't but a few minutes later that he heard men running and calling out to each other.

As he lay in the hole, he was aware of voices that were near his hideout one moment and gone the next; still, he didn't move. His foot touched the containers of rice and water he'd stored inside, but he didn't reach for the jars. Soon he could hear the voices returning. He heard some of the men grunt and then there was a sound as though someone was poking at the ground, probably with bayonets. He assumed they were looking for his hiding place; now he was worried. What would happen to him if he was caught and what would happen to the abbot. He visualized pictures of Jean and whispered, "I love you. Jean".

The sounds were getting closer. Sooner or later, the bayonets would strike the wood and the soldiers might shoot into the camouflaged hideout. He had to be prepared to slip into the water and take the provisions with him. He could hear the thumping come closer. He decided to make his move. It was none too soon. As he slipped into the lake with the provisions, he could hear the wood cover split and a great deal of cheering among the soldiers, indicating they found his hideout. Larry had made large straws out of bamboo and stored two each in the makeshift hideouts accessing the lake. With those straws, he was able to stay submerged as he swam about fifty feet out into the lake, directly across from the hideout.

As the soldiers tore the hideout apart, they found his access to the lake and started firing into the water near the shore. Soon they started firing in either direction along the bank and then directed more shots further out into the lake. Larry had anticipated their action and moved much further away from the shore. The amount of gunfire brought the remainder of the NVA troops, many monks and the abbot to this side of the compound. The Captain in charge of the detail used the Temple's only phone to call for two speed boats to patrol the West Lake. They arrived within thirty minutes and for over four hours, they searched for Larry. When darkness rolled in they used searchlights to scan the waters and the banks of the Pagoda.

Commander Tran was in his office when he received a call from Captain Chu that they found a hideout on the grounds of the Pagoda. Tran immediately had his driver take him to the compound. When he arrived, the Captain in charge of the detail was still interrogating the abbot, but deferred to the Commander of the Hanoi District. Tran looked at the hole that had been dug in the ground and the old boards that were used for shoring it up. The Captain pointed out the escape hole into the lake. "I want three men on watch at this point around the clock until whoever was hiding here comes out of the water. Have the men do shifts of eight hours on and sixteen hours off. I want two boats to patrol the lake for two days. If you need more men, call my office," Tran told the Captain.

After telling the Captain to carry on, he ordered the abbot to accompany him to the Temple's office. He sat at the abbot's desk and made the holy man stand while he interrogated him. "Where is the man who was hiding in that pit?"

"As far as I know, your soldiers didn't find anyone there, or any indication that someone was hiding there." The abbot responded.

"That hole was shored up with lumber from one of your old buildings. Who did that?"

"I have no idea. Those boards are so old they probably were there before I took over the Temple. Perhaps someone used that as a shelter during the American air raids over our country."

"I know that the American is here and you're hiding him. We'll find him and it will be your neck that will be put in a vice," Tran said.

Normally the abbot would be humble in the presence of his brother-in-law and not try to antagonize him; today he lashed back. "You've been saying that for three years because of your failure to capture him. You're not the only one who has some influence in this country. I may not be able to stop your constant attempts at intimidation, but if I hear that you've sent soldiers to this Temple again without notifying me ahead of time, I'll invite some of my old friends for a visit. To satisfy your paranoia, I'll permit your soldiers to remain for another forty-eight hours. After that, I want them removed. If you've nothing else to ask me, I must get back to my duties. Give my regards to my sister and your children."

"Someone built that hiding place. The lumber came from some of your old buildings. I want to talk to the person who built that hideout. Where is he?"

"The lumber is old and rotten. It could have been there for twenty years. I don't have a clue who built it. Maybe it was used by our people to hide from the French," the abbot responded

Tran laughed. Though Tran wanted to beat the truth out of the abbot, he knew he couldn't go that far and had to swallow his pride. He'd let his brother-in-law think that he won this time. He didn't need to send more soldiers. He had enough spies visiting each day. Sooner or later they'd spot the American. As the abbot reached for the door handle, Tran said, "Your days are numbered. Soon you'll feel my wrath. I will be back tomorrow to see what our soldiers have found."

As soon as Larry heard the boats, he knew he had to get out of the water. It was strenuous but within twenty minutes he was able to reach land three hundred yards from the temple. Gradually he semi-crawled along the bank until he was near the spot he entered the water three years earlier. Luckily, there was limited population in this area. Most of the buildings were of an industrial nature and it was near the end of the work day. He stayed hidden in the tall grass along the bank and watched the boats as they scanned the area for him.

Though it was spring, the nights cooled off and besides, he'd been in the water for nearly three hours and he was cold. As soon as it was dark enough, he got out of the water and walked to the nearest metal building and tried to enter it but it was locked. He tried three other building before he was successful. It was a long narrow building made out of corrugated metal, probably where train parts were repaired. There were hoists in the middle of the ceiling and railroad tracks imbedded in the concrete floor. He took off his robe and squeezed out all the water and put it back on. He spent the next thirty minutes searching for something dry he could wear. He found a changing room at one end of the structure and there were several old and torn trousers and shirts.

"There's nothing worth stealing in here."

Larry stopped in his tracks and looked around to see where the voice was coming from. He turned toward where he thought the sound came from and waited.

"Do you have any food?" a male voice said.

"I'd be glad to share what I have if I can see whom I'm talking to." Larry responded in Vietnamese.

The silhouette of a small thin man appeared in front of one of the few windows in the building. He then approached Larry but stopped about twenty feet away. "Tell me why you're here?" He asked.

"I seek shelter from the cool night air."

"Are you sure you're not hiding from the authorities?"

"No, but I don't care to run afoul of them either. Why are you here?" Larry asked.

"Like you, I'm avoiding the authorities. How about some of that food? I haven't eaten in two days. There's a bale of cardboard in the corner where we can sit and eat. I have a small candle to provide light. We have to be careful.

There are some thugs that come in occasionally and attack people who stay here overnight."

As Larry drew closer to the man, he could see that he was Asian and walked with a limp. They sat down on the bale and he poured half of his cooked rice in a container the man provided. "If you have a cup, I can give you half of my water."

The man said his name was Nhu Tran and Larry introduced himself as Chu Diem. "Why were you wearing the robe of a Buddhist Monk?" Nhu asked.

"I'd fallen into mud and went into the lake to clean myself. Someone stole my clothes and wallet and left me with this old rag to wear."

"So you're not a Buddhist Monk?"

"No. What is this building for?"

"This is a train repair shop. It's closed on weekends. Security men who work for this company come early Monday morning and throw all of us out of here. Sometimes they use clubs. I try to leave about five in the morning if possible. The main fear of people like us is the many thugs who're looking for money, food, drugs and anything they can take and sell. Sometimes, they take our clothes. I don't think you have to worry. Those rags you have on are worthless. The best place to hide is up above. The thugs know some of us are up there, but they don't like to climb up and fight us up there. It's getting dark and time we made our way up above. I'm glad you came along; I'll need some help."

"Lead the way, I'll follow." The Asian led him to a corner at the other end of the building. There were several bales of paper piled on top of each other with a medium sized wooden box on top of the paper bales. Larry got on top of the first bale and pulled his new friend up. He repeated the action until they were on the last bale. He climbed up onto the wooden box, reached up and pulled himself up into some rafters partially covered with sheets of plywood. He lay on his stomach and reached down for his new found friend and pulled him up. When both were on top, Nhu asked Larry to pull up the wooden box so no one could follow them.

He slept only intermittently that night because he was awakened by voices below and again when a fight was in progress. Nhu said those were the thugs looking to rob anyone who was below. At daylight, Nhu said it was time to go down. "This is a good time to beg for food. People walk from their homes past this area going to town; they're normally very generous to people like us."

Larry was apprehensive at first to be away from the Pagoda for any appreciable time, but he realized the soldiers would probably be at the Temple the entire weekend waiting for him to surface. He assumed the abbot would be concerned. If he was ever going to leave the Temple, he'd have to learn some more about begging to see if he could feed himself; Nhu looked like a good teacher.

After finishing the remaining rice and water, they left the industrial area about nine AM. They found a spot alongside other beggars and put out their small cardboard boxes. There was a steady stream of pedestrians and by noontime, they each had enough food for the rest of the day. Larry kept his head down so that his blue eyes didn't give him away. He and Nhu found a place where they could relieve themselves and went back to the industrial building. Rather than stay below, they climbed up the bales and sat on the plywood about fifteen feet above the floor.

Over the weekend, Larry learned that Nhu was a former South Vietnamese soldier who'd been captured and put in a slave camp in the north. He was beaten regularly by the guards and his leg was damaged. He needed an operation but none would be provided for slaves. He successfully escaped earlier this year and had been living in the industrial area of Hanoi ever since. It was hard to get a job without proper identification, so he turned to begging and got very good at it. He asked Larry where he was from but Larry avoided the question.

"You're not Vietnamese; your use of our language is proper but not quite right. You sound more European or perhaps American. Don't worry, I won't give you away. I saw the two boats in the lake and soldiers around the banks. Was it you they were looking for? Did you escape from a camp like me?'

Larry changed the subject. Nhu laughed. "Okay, I'll let it go. Whoever you are, you seem like a nice person. I hope you can get home if that's where you want to go. For me, the north is too cold. I'm going to make my way south and see if I can find some of my family. I think I'm savvy enough to stay out of trouble and avoid the soldiers. Let's hope you can do the same. If you're still here tomorrow, we'll beg near a small temple about a mile from here. The churchgoers are very generous on Sunday. They usually donate chicken and some money to those who beg in that area."

It was painful to watch Nhu walk. His hip had been broken and hadn't healed properly; yet, he was cheerful. He had a zest for life even though he was a cripple. It took them an hour to walk the mile to the Temple that Nhu mentioned, but he was correct. Those attending services were dressed in their finest and were generous to those begging in front of their Temple. When he and Nhu had enough food in their containers, they walked to a nearby park, sat on a bench and ate some of the food given to them. Larry watched as families sat on the grass, played games and ate lunch. Soon, all kind of games, mostly with a ball, began and everyone participated. It was as though he was home in the states.

Late that afternoon, they headed back to the industrial building. Larry thoroughly enjoyed his day and the companionship of his new friend. As they entered the old building, they were challenged by three thugs who demanded what they had in their cardboard containers. Each carried a club and together they formed a semi-circle in front of Larry and Chu. Reluctantly, he and Nhu placed their containers on the floor in front of them and backed up. One of the antagonists picked up the two containers, but the thug in the center of the three wanted more. "We want your money. Turn out your pockets."

Larry and Chu complied but they didn't have any money and told the three they were penniless. But the leader of the three smiled as he and his companions waved their clubs back and forth and circled Larry and Chu. The thug to his left swung his club at Larry's head, but he ducked. As Larry shifted his weight to his left foot, he struck out with his right foot catching the man just behind his right knee and the attacker slumped to the floor, screaming in pain. The action distracted the other two thugs and Larry judo chopped the leader alongside his head and the man fell to the concrete. The last thug standing was mesmerized as he watched Larry subdue his two companions and forgot about Nhu, who picked up a nearby loose board and hit the third man on the back of the head; he fell to the floor.

"Can you find some rope or strong cord to tie these guys up before they wake up or some of their friends wander by?" Larry asked Nhu, who limped over to the nearest wall and returned with some pieces of rope.

"Their clothes look much better than ours. Why don't we take theirs and they can have ours." Nhu said.

Only one of the assailants was unconscious but they readily complied to Larry's demand that they exchange their clothes with Chu and Larry. After the exchange, they tied the three up.

"We need some old rags to put in their mouth so they can't raise the alarm when we leave tomorrow. The ropes should hold then tonight." Larry suggested.

When Nhu returned with enough rags to silence the three, Larry dragged them to one of the corners of the building and laid them on their stomachs. All three were conscious; one probably had torn ligaments in his right knee.

As before, they used the paper bales to climb up into the rafters. "Where did you learn to fight like that?" Nhu asked as they climbed up into the rafters.

"It's a long story. Let's get some sleep.

"You're right. We have to be up early tomorrow before the security people come. I'll draw them to me so that you can get away. I've been through this before. Nothing should happen to me, especially after I tell them where to find the three you tied up. I assume you're going back to where you were before the boats came. I wouldn't stay in there too long. If you do they'll surely catch you. If you are an American, they'll kill you. It's been nice knowing you. I doubt if we'll ever see each other again. Good luck and thank you for tonight." Nhu lay down and went to sleep.

He woke up Larry about five in the morning. "It's time to go."

When they reached the bottom, they shook hands. "I'll go this way and make enough noise for the guards to follow me. You go the other way. No matter what happens, don't intervene. You understand?" Larry nodded.

"Don't tell anyone about me." Larry said.

"I never saw you." Nhu smiled as he limped away.

A few minutes later, he heard some men yell out in Vietnamese to stop. He then heard men scuffling and finally heard someone say "Don't ever come back."

Larry assumed his new friend made it. He exited the building and walked toward the Temple. He was dressed a lot better than before but his clothes still smelled. He'd buried the monk's robe yesterday. If he was stopped, he didn't want anyone to find it on him. He arrived at the Pagoda as visitors were entering the temple grounds and soldiers were leaving. They didn't give him a second glance after they smelled the filthy clothes he had on.

General Tran was at the temple at seven in the morning. After a weekend report from the Captain he left in charge, he ordered his soldiers to return to their camp. He then walked into the abbot's office without knocking. The abbot looked up and then returned to the paperwork he had in front of him. "You got lucky again. Don't worry, we'll catch him and he'll confess that he'd been here all the time," Tran snarled.

"Is it possible that paranoia has set in with you? The flyer most certainly is dead and never was here. It's just a fantasy that you dreamed up to gain some attention." The abbot had never been so bold before, but he was angry.

Tran was angry as he left the temple and returned to his office. Even he was wondering if the American was alive. Perhaps he did die just after he escaped and is in the

West Lake. If so, the body should've surfaced by now unless it was caught in the trash at the bottom of the lake. Draining the lake was the only sure way to know if he was there, but that was too expensive. Then there's the possibility that the flyer was at the temple and one of the shots fired into the lake three days ago killed him. In which case, the body most certainly would surface soon.

Larry returned to the Temple and immediately went to the abbot's office, knocked and walked in. The abbot looked up from his paperwork expecting to see his brother-in-law. His face gave away his amazement that Larry was still alive. He did something he never did before. He walked over to Larry and gave him a hug. Larry told the abbot what had happened, his meeting with the South Vietnamese escapee, the conflict with the three thugs and his odyssey in begging. "I believe I'm ready to leave though Nhu indicated my Vietnamese had a western accent. Perhaps we can correct that in the next month and I can be on my way."

The next morning at breakfast, the abbot had more time to speak with Larry. "My brother-in-law said he will bring me before the people's tribunal when you're found. We must be vigilant. All the soldiers have been removed, but he's still sending civilian spies throughout the day. Please be careful."

"I think my time is limited; you've done enough. It's time for me to go." Larry responded

The most recent incident where the soldiers fired at Larry while he was submerged in the lake was an omen of what was to come, so the abbot thought. He never had children nor was he ever married. The American was as close to a son as any man could have. He feared that if Larry didn't leave soon, Tran would eventually figure it out. He remembered Tran as a fun loving boy. They played together, went to the same school and were close friends before Tran married his sister. He understood why Tran changed. He was indoctrinated and all the free spirit he exhibited through his teenage years was slowly drained from him and what was left was a hard core communist. The abbot didn't hate the man, he prayed for him.

Operation Homecoming occurred in February 1973. It was a week later when the abbot informed him about the event. Larry knew he couldn't turn himself into the North Vietnamese for fear of reprisals, not only to him but to the entire monastery. Besides, even if he surrendered, the North Vietnamese would never alert his government that he was alive. The abbot and he had several discussions over the next month about him leaving; each had to assess the risk to themselves and the other monks. Although the so-called visitor spies came to the Pagoda more often, still the district commander felt restrained and proceeded with caution which helped Larry and the abbot prepare for his departure. Leaving soon was a necessity and it had to be between May and November, when the weather was better. They finally agreed he'd leave in early May and make his way to Ubon, Thailand, some four hundred plus miles away. The route they selected would take him through valleys, mountains and the country of Laos. He marked several villages along his intended path that the abbot recommended and made sure he skirted larger towns where Vietnamese soldiers would be housed.

Larry wanted to go out with the monks a few more times when they begged for food; he wanted more practice with his Vietnamese and his new art of pick pocketing. He'd been successful on three attempts before he was nearly caught by an elderly gentleman on his fourth try. He feigned falling to mask his failed attempt. This was a good lesson; he'd been in a hurry and wouldn't make that mistake again. It was easier in a group of monks who could distract the victim while he went to work. If he did it alone he'd have to be careful because, even if the theft wasn't discovered until later, the victim would remember the monk. He decided that he would use this maneuver only during his escape if necessary.

The North had lifted the curfew the previous month and there were fewer soldiers patrolling at night. He'd made up his mind to try to escape tonight; it was the second of May. There was cloud cover and, perhaps, a chance of rain; less people would be out in the streets. All he retained while living at the Pagoda was his map and ID Card.

The Abbot called him into his office that afternoon. "Larry, I have something for you that may be useful during your trip home."

He handed Larry a passport, identification card and birth certificate. "These belonged to a Polish Monk who died of a heart attack soon after he arrived and before you came to us. He looks a lot like you and the age is about right. These might come in handy if your coloring wears off and you're stopped for questioning."

"I have my Military ID Card, but I wonder if I should destroy it. If I'm captured, the card could be a death sentence." Larry responded.

"Will your people recognize you without that identification?"

"Good point."

They had a farewell meeting in the abbot's office that evening. "I will never forget your kindness; the bond between us will last forever. I'm committed to the Buddhist religion and a life of serving others: you taught me that. Though we'll never see each other again, I will live my life as though I were here. I pray that you'll always be proud of me and never regret your decision to keep me safe."

Chapter 8

Jean met Doctor Walter Osborne when she arrived at Greenville Memorial Hospital to begin her internship. He was head of surgery at the institution and one of her instructors. He was tall, handsome, single and charismatic. All the nurses were in love with him as well as some of the younger doctors, both male and female. The rumor was that he had affairs with most of the attractive nurses and perhaps some of the female doctors.

She had daily contact with Osborne as part of her duties and occasionally had lunch with him and members of the hospital staff. He asked if she was single and when she told him that her husband was a POW, he seemed to confine his dialog with her to medical issues.

Each year, the hospital threw a New Year's Eve party for the staff and Jean decided to attend with two other interns who weren't attached; they drove separately to the party but sat together. She bought a new outfit which included black slacks, black pumps and a white over blouse which was moderately transparent. She knew that she wasn't beautiful but most men found her attractive. She was short and slender with full lips and a rear end that men admired.

Her parents and the children were very happy to help her get ready; they encouraged her to have a good time. The event started with a sit-down dinner and dancing after. By midnight many of the staff were feeling no pain. Jean had three glasses of wine and felt festive. She danced with several interns and twice with Dr. Osborne. When it was time to leave, Osborne asked if he could escort her to her car. She thought it was gentlemanly and accepted.

Several couples and singles were in the immediate area as they reached her car. Jean turned to shake hands but Osborne ignored her hand and wrapped his hands around her waist. Before she realized it, he'd lifted her off the ground and sat her on the trunk. He gave her as passionate a kiss as she ever had and she was flustered. If she wasn't off balance yet, she certainly was when he forced himself between her legs. With one hand he held her hair and he slipped his other hand under her blouse, unsnapped her bra and fondled her left breast. All Jean could think was that she was going to get fucked on top of her own car while some of her acquaintances were walking by. She raised both hands above her head and chopped down as hard as she could on Osborne's neck. She repeated the maneuver that Larry taught her twice more before Osborne relaxed his grip on her hair. "My God, what's going on? Let me down. I'm married and I don't appreciate your advances!" she exclaimed.

He lifted her off the trunk while holding her close to him as he lowered her slowly to the ground. It was a deliberate move on his part. Her blouse wound up around her ears, exposing her breasts. She straightened her clothes, said good night and started the car while Osborne waited until she drove off. She was still flushed with passion and embarrassment. She knew that she nearly wrapped her legs around the handsome man and let him take her right there in the parking lot. Her husband was in captivity and I lusted for this man. Jean had no close friends with whom she could share this experience with; her mother could never be told. Osborne had a smile on his face as she drove off. He could tell that she wanted him; he'd just have to go a little slower and she was his. There was a lot of pent up emotion in that little doctor and he was just the man to help her release it.

Jean was stressed as she drove home. She knew that she was fair game for any predatory male and had to be careful not to place herself in any compromising situations. She also knew that Osborne knew she was receptive to his advances and they'd continue. She'd have to deal with it or give in. Right now she didn't know how to cope with the situation. When she got home she was still agitated and unsure of herself; her bra was still undone. It was a good thing her mother was asleep so she didn't have to confront her. God knows she'd look for any tell-tale signs and Jean was sure she'd give off a few. She undressed in her room and lay back on the bed. She was still flush with lust and her hands explored her sensitive area. She started to massage the private spot and soon had an orgasm. "Please forgive me Larry, I'm weak and lonely. Where are you?" she whispered to no one.

It was February 1973; she and the children watched the POWs get off the first of fifty-four C-141 flights that landed in America. This was Operation Homecoming and Larry wasn't part of the first group that was released. Jean was told that those in captivity the longest would be released first. Since the US didn't know the names of the three hundred and twenty-five Air Force flyers being held, she had to wait through the entire fifty-four flights before she realized that Larry may not be coming home "Is daddy coming home?" Her daughter asked and she didn't know the answer.

"I thought he was and now I'm not sure." She answered instinctively before she realized what an impression that must have made on her two children.

"We' have to wait and see. I'm going to check with your father's commander and see what he has to say." That proved futile. The former chaplain and commander, who broke the news that he'd been shot down had been transferred and the current individuals didn't know anything about Larry. She called her US Congressman and his administrative assistant said he'd look into Larry's status. Subsequently, he called back and said Larry's status was that of an MIA; nothing had changed. There were over thirteen hundred other flyers still unaccounted for.

This was the most depressing time of her life and she feared that her professionalism would suffer so she made an appointment with a clinical psychologist. Basically, she needed someone to talk to and someone who could deal with her acute guilt surrounding her husband. She finally was able to tell someone that she waited four years for her husband to return and when he didn't, she wanted to move on. She still loved him but was willing to accept that he was probably dead and had been dead shortly after he was shot down. Saying it out loud seemed to alleviate some of the mental pain she was experiencing. God forbid that her mother would find out that she was seeing a shrink, so she made the appointments during her lunch hour. No one on the hospital staff was aware of her situation. She also discussed her social situation and the incident with Doctor Osborne with her psychologist. Although she didn't suggest moving on, the psychologist didn't rule it out either.

Shortly after the sessions with the clinical psychologist began, she accepted a dinner invitation from one of the doctors at the hospital. This event wasn't lost on Walter Osborne and soon she was receiving weekly requests from him for a date. Finally she acquiesced and agreed to meet him at a dinner house. They both arrived early and had a glass of wine at the bar before the head waiter came for them. "Your table is ready."

She was surprised how warm Osborne was and she found that he was easy to talk to. Before she knew it, two and a half hours had passed and it was time to go. She accepted a warm kiss and drove home alone. She knew she couldn't hold this man off too much longer; sooner or later she'd have to give in.

They'd been dating for two months now, but in each case, Jean would drive her car and meet Walter at a restaurant, movie or other event. Finally she knew it was time and tonight, she agreed to be picked up at home. When he came to the door, she introduced her parents and children to Walter Osborne.

They shared a bottle of Pinot Noir and each had the rack of lamb. They held hands at the table and Walter kissed each of her fingers tips. She really liked this man. As they left the restaurant, Walter suggested she see his home and have an after dinner drink before he took her home. She sat next to him on the ride to his house and placed her hand lightly on his leg.

His home was a two-story Tudor on three acres of land, guarded by a hedge circling the perimeter and accessed by a remote switch controlling a gate. The lights were on inside the gray structure as they headed up the asphalt driveway. He stopped in front and walked around and opened her door. He offered his hand and she readily accepted. He drew her into his arms and she went willingly. Before she knew what happened she was completely nude sitting on the trunk of his vehicle. Walter pushed her back and entered her; she wrapped her legs around his body and held on tightly. He caressed her breasts as he continued to thrust inside her. She cried out as she climaxed; her relief was immense. After he was spent, he relaxed and leaned against his car. Jean lay on her back on top of the trunk with her legs hanging over the side of the car; she was completely drained. Finally he picked her up and carried her inside his home, up the stairs and into the master bedroom.

The bedroom was huge with a four poster bed dominating the room. After they made love again, Walter told her that he wanted her from the first moment he saw her. "When did you want me?" He asked Jean

"I believe it was New Year's Eve in the parking lot. It was all I could do, after you kissed me, to keep from tearing your clothes off. What's with the car trunk? It this some sort of fetish," she laughed.

"I wanted to see if you were game; I could tell you were. Don't worry I won't embarrass you but I'll find some unusual places to make love to you."

"What about my clothes?"

"After breakfast and after I've satisfied you, I'll go outside and get them. Until then, you'll have to parade around in your birthday suit."

Walter wasn't kidding. She had breakfast on the rear patio with only a napkin which she placed on her lap. When they finished eating, he cleared the dishes from the table, took her hands in his and gently sat her on the table. He entered her and she cried out in ecstasy. He had both hands on her breasts as he continued to thrust inside her. "Whose woman are you?" he kept asking her.

"Yours," she gasped repeatedly.

When he was finished, he fell back in his chair, completely exhausted. She could barely stand and when she did, she climbed onto his lap. She was thoroughly drained. All the pent up emotion of four years without her husband plus the strenuous workload of medical school were finally released. He retrieved her clothes, shared a shower and watched as she dressed.

They drove up to her house and he opened the door for her. They kissed and Jean asked him to call her. Her mother opened the door and immediately knew what had happened the previous night. For once, she chose to be considerate of Jean's feeling and didn't ask any embarrassing question. The children were just happy to see their mother and then went back to watching TV.

Jean had been intimate with two men in her life; one she thoroughly loved and still did. The other she lusted for. She wondered when the flame that drew her to Osborne would burn out. Whether it would or not was immaterial; she couldn't get enough now and that was good for the time being. Their social relationship started with a once-a-week date escalating to four times a week until Jean said she'd have to spend more time with her children. They agreed on once during the week and twice on weekends.

Larry Stephens pocketed his papers in a plastic container inside a canvas knapsack and said goodbye to the abbot, thanking him for his life-saving assistance; the two men embraced. Other than the Polish man's identification papers he just received, the only other articles he carried were a map, his Air Force ID card, a razor, a tooth brush and, of course, his plastic eating bowl. If he was to escape by playing a Buddhist Monk, he had to continue to shave his head. He slipped out of the Pagoda after the other monks retired; he was on his way.

The weather tonight was in the low sixties; he decided to use the lake rather than exit via the causeway and have to go through the western part of downtown Hanoi. This way, he avoided the need to explain why he was out so late if he was stopped. He felt the lake would reduce his vulnerability to any patrolling soldiers or locals who may be out and about. He walked to the far western corner of the Pagoda, took off his clothes, put them in a plastic bag in his knapsack and entered the West Lake. He swam close to the shore until he was abreast of the southern-most portion of the city. To his left was the industrial area he visited recently and stayed for a weekend. He wondered if his South Vietnamese friend, Nhu, was still hiding out here or had traveled south. He grabbed a low hanging branch and pulled himself out of the water. After he put his robe and shoes back on, he checked the contents of his knapsack to be sure they were dry and he was on his way.

He used the area of the industrial buildings as cover so he wouldn't be as conspicuous. By morning, he was near a small village south of Hanoi. This would be a good time to find out if he was capable of begging for food. Dressed in his bright orange habit, wearing sandals and carrying a small canvas bag around his neck, he entered the village. Half of the buildings were beige in color with stucco exteriors; the remainder were made from salvaged wood and stood on stilts. He sat down on the ground surrounded by the huts used by its inhabitants and set out his small plastic container. One of the villagers served him tea and some dry bread. The village chief asked him to pray with an old woman who was near death. His command of Vietnamese was better and he knew all the prayers that the Buddhists used. The chieftain rewarded him with half a chicken and gave him a shave. To show his hospitality, the chief asked him to stay the night. For breakfast, they served him a bowl of broth filled with vegetables and noodles. The chief asked him where he was headed. All Larry would answer in Vietnamese was "South".

Over the next few days he made his way southwest and avoided any populated areas. His time with the monks prepared him for days of abstinence, so he could go several days without eating. Water was in abundance and the half chicken lasted two days. Near dawn of the third day, he moved deeper into the foliage to find a place where he could lie down for a few hours. As he settled in, he heard voices up ahead and he became alert. Crouching behind a thick tree, he saw soldiers straggling along the narrow path he'd been using. Nearly thirty soldiers were in the group, each carrying a rifle slung over their shoulder. They didn't seem to be any particular hurry. He remained where he was and waited a half hour after all the soldiers passed before continuing his journey; he'd delay his nap. The first thing that entered his mind when he saw the soldiers was that they were looking for him. After he calmed down, he realized no one knew there was an American on the loose except the abbot and perhaps the commander of the Hanoi District, who may still be looking in the Temple for him.

Within a week he'd traveled fifty miles according to his map, stopping periodically to beg and or administer to some of the elderly in the villages. Today he came across a small village and decided to beg for food and shelter. Although they shared some bread with him, he could tell that most were suffering from malnutrition and, other than a bed for the night, he was unwilling to take any of their food. The village chief told him that soldiers had confiscated nearly all their food stores. There was nothing he could do for them, so he returned the bread and left. He felt sad that he was impotent to help these struggling people. Surprisingly, the number of years he spent with the Vietnamese monks gave him an affinity for these people. It was as though he felt a form of kinship, and even more, he felt like he was part of their culture.

Since he hadn't travelled inside Vietnam before, he was relying on the abbot's experience when it came to the country's wildlife, predators, debilitating plants and poisonous insects. Because of his inexperience in the Vietnamese jungle, he gave a wide berth to snakes, such as vipers, cobras and constrictors. But it was the giant centipedes and scorpions that he was most concerned about. He knew that he'd have to sleep outdoors sometimes;

still he tried to hold that to a minimum by trying to gain acceptance at each village so there would be an invitation to spend the night. He encountered the giant centipedes early on when he stopped in a small grove of trees and sat down. The inset actually crawled over his foot and he jumped. Needless to say, from that point on, Larry checked every place before he decided to rest.

After he travelled about a hundred miles, he started to believe that he could escape and make it to Thailand and that's when he started to think about Jean and his homecoming in earnest. He fantasized what would happen when she learned he was alive. But he felt a chill go through his body when he realized she may think him dead and perhaps had remarried. Operation Homecoming was three months past. He knew she must have anticipated him coming off one of the plane and when he didn't, she may have decided to start her life over with someone else. Over the past four years, he knew that was a possibility but he had to remain positive.

There was always a time frame he had in mind. He wanted to be in Thailand by November when it started to cool off. He could probably make that schedule by bypassing the villages. Many times he had to spend extra time meditating with someone who was ill, conduct a funeral service or wedding. That took time and patience, but he needed the villages for food and shelter so it was damn if he did and damn if he didn't. If there is one thing he learned in his four year odyssey, it was patience.

Chapter 9

Ever since Jean Stephens was a child, her father took them to the Fourth of July fireworks display along the river. She invited Walter to join the family for the fireworks and a barbeque. The family arrived early and found a place where they could place blankets and chairs and set up the grill. This was the first her family spent any time with Walter. Though everyone met him when he arrived to pick up Jean, those meetings were so limited that they never seemed to have time to ask him his first name. Her mother was immediately smitten with the tall, handsome doctor; her father adopted a wait and see attitude and the children didn't seem to care one way or the other. Well, the ice was broken; everything would be easier from here forward. She'd hired an attorney and filed for divorce. It should be final in February of next year. She wasn't sure she would marry Dr. Osborne, but at least she was taking a stance and breaking with the past. For the first time, she accepted the fact that Larry didn't survive. She'd always love him but it was time to move on.

Her father and Walter handled the barbequing while her mother made sure everyone had something to drink. It was a pleasant evening along the river, there must have been five hundred families that had set up space along the concrete levee. The fireworks lasted thirty minutes and were shot from a barge about 100 feet from the Greenville Bridge. As Jean watched, she remembered that Larry went through Pilot Training here and it was the Greenville Bridge that he flew under in his T-33 jet. When she looked up, her mother was watching her closely with a frown on her face. Well, if

Jean didn't have Larry anymore, she'd at least have many memories.

Over that summer the children swam in Walter's pool and, occasionally, she and the children would stay for the weekend. Larry Jr. and Susanne seemed to accept the fact that this was the new family. Although Walter never married, he seemed to like the children and was constantly surprising them with trips to the zoo and library. He really seemed to be taking an interest in their life. He'd asked Jean to marry him at least a half dozen times and although she didn't refuse, she didn't accept him either. It was too early for her to make that decision. Osborne seemed to be satisfied with the situation. Jean was happy, her mother was happy and her skills at work improved.

As **Larry Stephens** traveled further south, the villages were more friendly and seemed to be happy sharing food and lodging with a monk on an odyssey. His communication skills were improving and, while he was in the villages, he spent time listening to the chiefs about life in the village and what was happening in the area. In this most recent village, he learned that not all the POWs may have been sent home. He hadn't thought it was possible that some of his fellow servicemen weren't released, so his interest piqued. Cautiously, he tried to solicit some information without drawing any undue attention to himself.

"Why do they want to keep them if the war is over?"

"I think they want money for them," the chief responded.

"Why not keep them in Hanoi with the others?"

"They've secreted these away on the Laos border so no one knows they exist."

"Why do they want to do that?"

"They want to give hints to the Americans that they exist; it's as though they're teasing them. Eventually, they'll ask for something outrageous and see what the other side will do. It's like a cat playing with a mouse."

"There can't be that many?"

"I was told there were six on the border working in a gold mine near the Laotian town of Sapon, just off the Ho Chi Minh Trail. Some of our villagers worked at the same mine and saw the Caucasians. There is a lot of gold there. I also heard from someone else who wandered this way, that there is a Russian camp with helicopters further east from where the Caucasians are being held."

"Do the Russian's come to your village?"

"No one sees them though we know they are here. I think there are about ten to twelve Russians and maybe six Chinese. Occasionally we see the Russian helicopters in the sky."

"Who told you about them?"

"Our soldiers tell us."

The chief invited him to stay the night. As soon as he accepted, it started to rain and the downpour lasted about an hour. The bed he slept in was adequate but other than a slice of bread, he had very little to eat. To make up for the lack of food, the chief gave him a shirt and pair of long pants belonging to one of his villagers who'd passed away. The man was about Larry's size.

In the morning, he moved on, but he didn't know what he was going to do with the information the chief gave him. It would be suicidal to go there and try to free them but maybe an assault team could, if they had the camp's location. And what about the Russians? Intuitively, he didn't want to have anything to do with any of this information. He did wonder if he could get close enough to the POW compound without getting the guards suspicious. His movement was slow through the mountains and although there were enough villages to keep him fed, he was getting anxious to reach Thailand. It was late October; he had to cover the last one hundred or so miles within a two month span; the weather was about to turn colder.

In the beginning of their new relationship, **Jean Stephens** felt pressured by Walter Osborne both professionally and personally; he definitely was an alpha male. As the months passed, she felt more confident at the hospital and more personally secure. When Walter asked her to marry him this weekend, she said yes. He was surprised at her answer and asked her again, but the answer was the same. "If my divorce is granted in February, we can make plans. I think my family accepts you and the children are comfortable around you."

"Would you be interested in moving in with me now? There's plenty of room and the children could each have their own room; I know they like the swimming pool."

"I think we'll stay where we are. They're happy in their school and I don't think it's wise to have them move just now. We can plan a wedding after the school year ends. I want them to be comfortable; it isn't good for them to make drastic changes; gradual is much better."

As the days passed, **Larry Stephens** began stretching his physical limits. One afternoon, he sat down with his back against a tree just off the trail and fell sound asleep. The further he traveled, the more confident he became in his ability and the more complacent he became in his movements. His desire to reach safety was driving him; carelessness was slowly becoming a problem. He didn't know how long he'd been asleep, but he awoke when he felt a jab in his side with a pointed object. He looked up and faced three Vietnamese soldiers who were yelling at him. "What are you doing here, monk?"

They didn't seem threatening though they carried rifles slung over their shoulders. "I fell asleep," was all he could think of to say.

"Stand up and put your bag on the ground. Where's your monastery?" one of the soldiers demanded.

He'd rehearsed a story if this question was raised. "I'm a monk from the Tran Quoc Pagoda in Hanoi. I'm on a two-year Odyssey to help my fellow man and serve Buddha. Each day I must practice generosity toward my fellow man."

"Do you have any papers?" One of the soldiers asked.

He fumbled in his knapsack and produced the identification of the dead monk furnished to him by the abbot. Larry also produced a letter that he forged with the abbot's name, stating that he was on a two-year trek as a penance for becoming too familiar with women. One of the soldiers read the letter out loud and they all laughed.

"Do you like women?" One of the soldiers asked.

"Yes, very much."

"Why did you come to Vietnam? Were you a soldier?" One of the soldiers asked.

"I was unhappy at home and came to study Buddhism. I liked the people and their culture, so I stayed."

"How long have you been in this country?"

"I think I've been here ten years."

"What happens when you go back to the Pagoda? Will they punish you some more?"

"I'll be secluded for another two months. During that time, they'll reduce my rations and give me extra chores. After that, I'll be allowed back into the order." Larry was winging it but they seemed to buy his explanation.

He shared some of their bread and grain and they asked for his blessing. They wished him good luck and left him standing on the trail. He'd overcome his most serious threat so far, so he continued on with his journey, but he learned a good lesson. From now on, he'd have to be more careful in everything he did.

The rains came early and the north-flowing stream he wanted to cross swelled beyond its banks and wasn't fordable. He had to alter his course somewhat to find a place where it was safe to cross. When he couldn't find a safe spot, he decided to stay close to this location and wait until the stream receded enough. Finding a place that was dry so he could sleep was almost impossible. The best he could do was cut some limbs and create a makeshift shelter that leaked a lot. He still had some bread and cooked rice in reserve as he stayed holed up for another three days; he had no other choice.

Intuitively, staying in one place too long was not a good idea. He decided that he would cross the river today even if he had to swim downstream part of the way. Just as he was taking down his shelter, he saw three young men come into the clearing at the river crossing; they saw him at the same time. One was taller than the other two; each had a beard and unkempt clothing. They looked like they were scavengers. Since they didn't appear to be soldiers nor were they armed, Larry relaxed and decided to see what they wanted. He continued pulling the branches down from his shelter while keeping an eye on the three.

"Do you have any food we can have?" one of the young men, asked.

"I have two days of rice. I can let you have half." Larry responded.

As the three approached, Larry took off his knapsack from around his shoulder and placed the container with rice on the ground. "Leave me half."

The shortest of the three picked up the plastic container of rice and put it in his knapsack, while one of the other men asked Larry what else he had in his bag.

Larry replied that he only had some personal papers and a few vegetables."

"Lay them on the ground, so we can see for ourselves." One of them ordered.

"No. You've taken all my rice, so I think you should be on your way." Larry had a sturdy stick in his hand as he turned to face the three who were within six feet of him.

They rushed him at once. He stuck one of the three in the solar plexus with the stick and the man fell down, yelling out in pain. Larry grabbed a second by the shirt, and pulled him forward. As they fell backward together, Larry stuck his foot in the man stomach, pushed out hard while holding onto his shirt and the man went flying headfirst into a tree behind him. Larry rose quickly to defend himself against the third man, but he ran off with Larry's knapsack.

Chasing him in the heavy foliage was futile. After thirty yards, he lost the man. Realizing that his possessions were stolen, he immediately returned to his campsite to question the other two, but they had disappeared. He could always replace the food, but the forged letter from the abbot, his Air Force ID card and the late Polish Monk's identification he was carrying, weren't replaceable. It would also be damaging for the abbot if those documents fell into the wrong hands.

The river was still moving swiftly, but Larry had no choice. He had to get to the other side. If those three gave the documents to the authorities, they would come to this spot. But they'd have the same problem in crossing the river that he had even if it was only about fifty feet across at this point. Larry felt if he didn't fight the current and tried to flow with it, he could probably make his way to the other side, grab some of the branches and pull himself out.

He put his shirt on over his robe, put on a pair of pants and tied them to his ankles. He put his sandals inside his pants and dove in. He was under water immediately but soon surfaced. He tried to keep his head above water, using his hands to stay with the current, while making small moves toward the other side. About three hundred yards into his swim, he grabbed a branch on the far bank and broke his momentum. He held on tight and slowly pulled himself ashore. All he could think was he made it. He took off his clothes, wrung them out and put on his sandals. Soon he was dressed but wet. He travelled about five hundred yards north until he found some shelter in the heavy foliage; soon it stopped raining. A half hour later he smelled fire and decided to go in that direction. He travelled another half mile and came upon villagers who were sitting around a small fire. He asked if he could have food and shelter for the night. They welcomed him to their fire and gave him some rice. An hour later his clothes and sandals were dry and that night he lay on the ground near the blaze.

Chapter 10

It was idiotic, but there seemed to be a magnet drawing him to the area where the POWs reportedly were being held. Instead of traveling as close to a straight line from Hanoi to Ubon, his ultimate destination, he was continuously heading closer to a westerly direction. He should've crossed over into Laos by now but for some reason, he was heading toward Sapon Mine, which was about 100 miles directly east of Da Nang, Vietnam. He didn't exactly raise the issue when he stopped at villages along his route to beg for food, but eventually the conversation always seemed to go there. With so many sightings of Caucasians being held at the gold mine, he was now sure it was true. As he came closer to the mine area, he kept telling himself that it was too risky to try to pinpoint their location. The villagers were more than happy to host a travelling monk; most times he received food and a bed in return for evening meditation or perhaps a marriage or funeral ceremony.

It was getting colder at night. At one of the previous villages he was given a pair of socks and a warm shirt; today, he received a pair of pants at this village. The shirt and pants he previously received were torn by shrubs and trees while travelling off the main trails. After he changed and discarded the rags, they washed and repaired his torn robe. In return he conducted a Buddhist service with some meditation and a lot of spirited chanting. The more he practiced the Buddhist Religion, the more comfortable he was with it. It was as though Larry saw this as his calling. The thought crossed his mind that if Jean had moved on with her life, he would consider becoming more involved with the Buddhists, maybe even becoming a priest.

He was continuously warned by local village chiefs of the number of marauding bands, consisting of four or five ex-soldiers, who were threatening the countryside. Larry had taken their advice and was now travelling parallel to the main trails and staying in villages at night. The local villagers were happy to allow a visiting monk stay in their village overnight. It was always a sheltered place though not necessarily a bed. It wasn't that he was afraid of sleeping in the countryside, it was the warm manner he was received by the villagers that gave him a feeling of belonging. He actually looked forward to the visits, though it would be hard to explain.

"They haven't killed anyone in this area, but many travelers and businessmen have been robbed and beaten. One village was burned to the ground when they refused to give the thugs money. The authorities have told us they would help, but I don't think so. The gangs must be paying off the local commandant. That's how it works here." The chief at the next village seemed sober as he told Larry about the gangs. Inwardly, Larry knew that scenario played out in the so-called civilized world as well.

He knew that, sooner or later, he'd run into one of these gangs; he hoped that he'd be in a village when they made their move. He stopped at this village of about twenty shanties about an hour ago. The ground was higher and none of the huts were on stilts as he was accustomed to. He could see five or six people milling around and two scrawny dogs. As was his custom, he placed a small plastic cup down in front of him as he sat on the ground. He was given rice by the village chief and, in return, was leading a group in meditation when five thugs wearing old South Vietnamese uniforms rushed into the village. Each had a beard and smelled as though they'd never been in the vicinity of soap. Their weapons were slung over their shoulders; they assumed there was no threat and that the villagers would comply to avoid being shot.

Initially, they asked for food and when the village chief said they didn't have enough for their people, the leader slapped him several times and forced the chief on his knees. The leader of the thugs hit the chief in the back of the head and the chief fell unconscious on his face. They ordered everyone out of their shacks. Larry knew it was going to get ugly when two of the soldiers pulled two teenage girls forward and started to undress them in front of everyone. The two soldiers pulled the girls toward one of the shacks and forced them inside. Larry could hear the girls cry after several loud slaps. No one in the village moved. They were huddled together for fear they would be singled out by the thugs and killed.

Larry had moved closer to the three ex-soldiers who remained outside and were calling to the two in the shack to hurry up; they wanted their turn. When they squatted down in front of the fire, he made his move. He judo-chopped the one nearest him in the neck and the soldier fell into the soldier to his right side. Larry pulled the rifle from the third man and swung it around and hit him the face with the barrel. The soldier screamed and fell to the ground. In the same motion, he jammed the butt of the rifle into the stomach of the middle man who was prone on the ground; he threw up on the third man. The first man was getting up by now and was reaching for his rifle but he had no chance. Larry hit him on the side of the head with the rifle and the man fell back down.

Three men in the village rushed forward to subdue the soldiers while Larry went into the shack. Both soldiers were on top of the two nude girls who were crying. He hit both in the back of the head with the rifle butt and then dragged them one at a time near the three who were prone in front of the fire. They'd been tied up by the villagers. The chief, who was bleeding from his nose and head, was being attended to by his family. One of the elders seemed to take charge; he ordered some of the villagers to tie up the other two soldiers. Larry handed over the rifle to the elder and knelt by himself away from the fire. He'd betrayed his Buddhist teachings by submitting to violence; he started to meditate. He knelt for nearly an hour and was oblivious to the many gifts the villagers placed at his feet. He was their hero.

The elder knelt beside him and offered Larry some solace; he seemed to understand Larry's concerns. "You should not punish yourself. You saved two of our children. There is no telling what they would've done if you hadn't acted. All of us will pray to Buddha to protect you throughout your odyssey; no one will hear of the violence you showed today."

Before he left the next morning, Larry checked on the chief and received his thanks. "You need not worry about what will happen to the thugs when you leave. I know you can't take all the gifts, but take as many as you can. We'll always be grateful to you and we'll pray for you every day."

As he was leaving the village, the two young girls and their families hugged him. He started to cry. He left the village with a heavy heart.

The moment of decision had come for Larry. The location of the POW camp was twenty miles to the west. He could either go there or pass it by. All his life he'd been a responsible individual; could he ignore all his training? As he lay awake on the ground in this most recent village, he thought of Jean and his children and what they meant to him. But before he fell asleep, he knew he was going to go to the mine.

He saw the suspected POW site from the top of a nearby ridge. He knew it was some sort of prison complex because of the barbed wire and the number of patrolling guards. From his vantage point, he could see what looked like a mine entrance at the rear of the compound. He couldn't make out whether there were any prisoners, but there had to be some. From what he could see at this distance, they'd cleared about fifty feet around the square shaped facility. Approaching the site to get a better look would be tricky, but he had to find out.

Before he even assessed the risks, he changed into his orange robe, walked up to the gate, pounded on the wooden barrier and begged for food. The guard told him they didn't have any food to give to a filthy looking monk. As he started to walk away, he was told to halt by someone else; an officer had come up on the other side of the gate.

"State your business," a Lieutenant said.

"I'm a poor monk in need of some food and shelter."

"Who said you could get shelter here?" the officer asked.

Larry knew at that moment that he'd made a serious error. Now was not the time to enter the enclave and now was not the time to be anything but self-effacing. He hunched over somewhat and shivered. "I saw the gate and I was hungry. I don't mean to cause any trouble, just some bread and I'll leave."

"Get out of here." As the Lieutenant yelled at him, he threw him a piece of bread and then laughed. Larry scurried to pick up the bread and shuffled off. When he was far enough away, he darted into the foliage. No matter how many times he was told there was a Russian complex close to the POW compound, not one of the village chiefs was able to tell him where it was located; he was not going to look for it. His view of life at this time was, he'd done everything he could for his country, now it was time to do something for his family; he was going home.

Major Nhu Nguyen commanded a rifle company at the Da Nang Army Base on the eastern coast of Vietnam. The 310th Battalion, to which he was assigned, had control over the central part of Vietnam, which included the POWs held at Sapon. His responsibility encompassed nearly 3,300 men under his command. He was what was known as a high flyer in the NVA, primarily because he was the nephew of Commander Tran of the Hanoi District. The three thugs who had a confrontation with Larry were intercepted by Sergeant Le Quon, leader of one of Major Nguyen's squads two days after they stole the knapsack. They surrendered the bag which included some papers and an ID card that Larry had been carrying. Sergeant Quon released the three and didn't pay any attention to the documents until ten days later when he returned to his headquarters and presented the papers to his commander. Major Nguyen immediately saw the significance of the documents

"Where did you find these documents?" His commander asked.

"We took them from three young men."

"Who and where did they get them?"

"They told us they took them from a Buddhist Monk who was camping by the Rho River."

"Did you try to find the monk?"

"No. It wasn't within my orders to deviate to that location."

"I want you to take some men and go there tomorrow. See if you can find the monk and bring him back here. I'll take these documents and notify my superiors."

As Major Nguyen looked at the ID card of Captain Larry Stephens, he wondered if the monk came across a flyer's body and took the man's ID. But, what was the significance of the Polish Monk's identification and then there was the letter from the Abbot at the Tran Quoc Pagoda? He knew that his uncle would know. He didn't have a teletype in his office, but there was one in the commander's office across the base.

It was late and he had a date with a hottie so he decided to wait until tomorrow morning to send the documents. After a brief exchange with his superiors the next day, he tele-typed the documents to Hanoi. General Tran was on an inspection tour in the southern part of the country when the documents arrived. When he returned he reviewed the documents and then wondered out loud if he had the information in his hand that would rid him of his nemesis, the Abbot of Tran Quoc Pagoda.

The first issue was whether Captain Stephens was a POW. He looked at the list; Captain Stephens was not among them. He then looked at the Missing in Action List, sent by the Americans. Captain Stephens was on that list; he'd been shot down 20 miles southeast of Hanoi. His nephew was correct; the monk may have come across the body of Stephens but what about the other documents?

The letter signed by the abbot alone was damaging. Could Stephens, as he suspected, been protected in the Pagoda the entire time he was in Vietnam and did the abbot give him this letter to use during his escape. Tran hoped that was the case. He then looked at the two pieces of identification for a Josef Poleski. Who was he?

Since the end of hostilities, the monks had no use for signaling with birds. Today they were surprised by a visit from the Regional Commander of the Hanoi District. General Tran walked into the abbot's office who was talking to two of his monks standing before him.

"This is an official visit; I wish to speak to you in private." The abbot asked the two monks to excuse them; he'd talk to them after his visitor left.

Tran tossed Larry's ID on the desk in front of the abbot. "This is the flyer you hid in this Pagoda for three years, don't deny it."

The abbot said nothing. He stared back at his brother-in-law and waited for his next outburst. Tran placed the letter Larry was carrying in front of the holy man. "This, in your own handwriting, is a letter he used during his escape."

Again the abbot said nothing. "Have you anything to say in your defense or is your silence confirmation of your treachery." Tran shouted.

The abbot took two letters he was working on and handed them to Tran along with the forged letter Larry was carrying. "Compare the writing. Anyone, who doesn't have an agenda, can see that's not my handwriting. I deny your accusations. Now if you're finished, please leave my office."

"Who is Josef Poleski? Tran asked

"I have no idea."

"You deny that the American Flyer, Lawrence Stephens, was here in the Pagoda?"

"Your accusation is without merit and not worthy of my response. Please leave."

"The man was wounded when he came here. Which of your monks took care of him and doctored his wounds?"

"We have no doctor here or anyone with medical training. You know that. You only see what you want. Our conversation is finished."

"It's finished when I say so." Tran stormed out of the abbot's office and left the Pagoda. He wondered out loud if he could approach the Central Committee with his suspicions. Not at this time was his answer to himself.

The first thing that crossed the abbot's mind was that Larry was dead or captured. He dismissed both quickly, because Tran would've taken pictures and brought them with him. No, he came across the documents the American was carrying by another method; they were probably stolen from the flyer.

Since his brother's son, now a Major in the army, sent him the package, Tran decided to find out how eager his nephew was to please his uncle.. He ordered him to Hanoi for a meeting. It took two days for Nguyen to make the trip by boat.

"How much more do you know about the documents you sent me."

"Other than that the documents were taken from a Buddhist Monk by three thugs at the Rho River, I don't know any more about the incident. I dispatched one of my men to lead a squad to find the monk. He hasn't reported back yet." Nguyen said.

"I want that monk found and brought here. Do you understand?"

"Yes sir."

"Do you trust the man you sent to lead a team and chase him down?"

"My Sergeant can get the job done."

"I assume the monk is headed to Thailand. From the information I've received from America, I suspect the monk is an American Captain, named Lawrence Stephens, He was shot down near Hanoi over four years ago; Stephens flew out of Ubon. You may have to chase him into Laos and perhaps Thailand. If you or your Sergeant need help in those countries, let me know and I'll make the calls. If your people can't catch up to him, they can lay in wait at the bridges across the Mekong. I want that monk."

"I'll not fail you." Nguyen left his uncle with a smile on his face. Getting that monk would be worth a promotion, maybe even more.

When he returned to his outpost, Sergeant Quon reported that he didn't find the monk his commander sought. In fact he didn't find the three men he previously intercepted. "I want you to select nine men you can trust, and bring the monk back. We believe he's headed to southern Thailand, perhaps Ubon. You have to work fast. Once he gets to the Mekong, it will be difficult. Of the nine, I want you to dispatch two men to each of the bridges over the river; we can't afford to lose him. Check with the village chiefs along the way. They know what's going on in their area and perhaps the monk stopped at one or more of the villages for food. If it's the same man my uncle is looking for, be careful. He subdued three soldiers who captured him even though he was wounded.

Quon picked his men and supplies, including food for seven days, and reached the Rho River some one hundred miles from Da Nang in three days. They found the makeshift shelter Larry left behind, but nothing else. The team decided to cross the river, though the current was still swift. They found a spot within a hundred yards of their present location and crossed over. It was at the second village where the chief remembered the monk. He suggested a route that Larry might have taken and the team of four was on their way. Quon had selected the six to be deployed at the three rope bridges: they went via a different route.

Larry Stephens slipped into Laos in September on a cold and rainy day. He found a village close to the border on the Laotian side whose inhabitants spoke mostly Vietnamese. He'd been told by the abbot that approximately fifty to sixty percent of Laotians spoke that language. One of the villagers had a sick wife and Larry meditated with her for two days before she died. The husband was so grateful that he gave his own jacket to the holy man. Larry initially refused, but the village chief told him it would be an insult to refuse the gift. Even though he spent long hours meditating with the sick wife, he had a bed and was fed by the chief. When it was time to go, he told the chief he was on his way to Thailand; it was the first time he divulged his intentions to any villager. He asked about routes. There was a villager who travelled extensively and he looked at Larry's map and suggested two routes. One was much longer but somewhat safer. The other was over a mountain range and could be perilous when the weather was bad.

Even though it was the dry season, he took the safer route through a deep valley. When he stopped at the next village and begged for food, he asked questions about mountainous routes to Thailand. He was surprised to learn about a trail in the mountains that was traveled widely and would save him considerable time and, according to the village chief, it was safe. He was anxious to complete his journey, he was anxious to see his wife and children and he was anxious to put as much distance between himself and any pursuers. The villagers gave him four days of rice and showed him how to access the trail and off he went

The foliage along the trail was extensive at the lower part, but as he climbed higher, it gave way to patches of shrubs and low ground cover. He encountered very few people along the route, other than families coming back from Thailand. He had no problem finding a place off the trail each night, though he refrained from lighting a fire. He was in his third day and had started down the other side of the mountain when he met a Laotian family of four who were moving quickly. When they saw him, they signaled him not to go any further. He asked them in Vietnamese, "Why".

One of the children spoke some Vietnamese. "There are gangs preying on travelers ahead. Don't go any further. Turn back." The family hurried down the trail that Larry had used.

He thought about it for a few minutes and assessed his options. He didn't want to take a chance, so he followed the family back down the hill. He shared his rice with them; they shared some vegetables with him. They found a spot to sleep at night, with Larry, the father, and a son alternating four-hour watches throughout the night. Going up and back down the mountain cost him five days. He stopped in the village that recommended the trip across the mountains; he wanted to tell them about what the Laotian family said. He was shocked when the villagers didn't offer him food and lodging. They'd been so friendly when he stopped there before.

Seeing no reason to stay, Larry got up to leave and asked the chief if he'd done anything to offend him or the villagers. The chief said the army was looking for him; four

North Vietnamese soldiers said he wasn't a monk, but a thief. "Go. Don't come back or I'll set the dogs on you." The chief said.

"Did you tell the army which way I went?"

"No. Be on your way."

He thought long and hard why there were soldiers after him. The only two things that came to mind were the POW encampment he tried to visit. Then there was the documents the three thugs took from him. Did they find their way into the NVA's hands" Intuitively, he knew the latter was the case. Somehow, those documents ended up in the army's hands and probably Commander Tran's; he wasn't dumb. He'd probably go to the Pagoda and confront the abbot. Larry prayed his friend would be okay. If for no other reason, Larry had to escape.

He wondered how much authority the NVA had in Laos. He certainly didn't want to find out. The only advantage that he had was that he was following them. From this point on he'd have to live off the land, perhaps pickpocket for some money and avoid the villages. Anyone ahead of him would stop at each village along the route and ask if they'd seen him. Once they realized he hadn't been at any of villages ahead, they'd know he was behind them and they'd set a trap.

Just to be sure, Larry stopped at the next village at the end of a lush green valley and asked for shelter and food. He was denied both and told to move on. He frequently saw travelers on the trail and asked them if they knew a route going west over the mountains. Most did not or wouldn't converse with him and rushed off. One traveler was walking leisurely and stopped to talk to him. Larry took out his map and the traveler showed him a trail others used, though he did not. Larry thanked the stranger and when he reached the start of the path, he went up a mountain trail.

With very little food, Larry pressed on, stopping only when he was too tired to continue. With great effort, he made it about three-quarters of the way to the top in four days of hard climbing; he felt the pressure of being pursued. He still had some vegetables and water left. He found a clear spot in some small trees about twenty yards off the trail and laid down. He was so exhausted that he forgot some of his rules and fell asleep immediately. He dreamed what his homecoming with Jean and the children would be like. They'd gone to the beach somewhere in Texas on a Sunday Afternoon; the entire family was swimming in the water. They were splashing each other with water and having a festive time and that's when he awoke suddenly; he was drenched with water. Four soldiers were standing over him; one had thrown water in his face. "Stand up Captain Stephens." One of the four said and then kicked Larry in the ribs when he didn't move immediately.

Chapter 11

He assessed his chances and knew they were limited but, he couldn't go back to Hanoi. He kicked out with one leg and caught a soldier on his right in the groin. While the soldiers were initially stunned at his fierce retaliation, he rose and lashed out at the nearest man, hitting him in the head and then twisting his arm. He kicked the third in the groin and started to run. That's when he felt the bullet hit him in his left shoulder and he fell forward. Two soldiers were on top of him quickly, pinning him to the ground and then methodically tying his legs and then his arms in front of him. In spite of the pain, he didn't call out or fight back; he just lay on the ground.

His captors let him lay there until dawn. One of the soldiers had a broken arm and was being treated by his Sergeant. Another was holding his groin; two of the four seemed to be okay. Larry knew the four would have a hard time getting him back; they didn't know what he was capable of. None of the soldiers made any attempt to treat his gunshot wound; he'd remember that. Larry was going to make them carry him; they weren't going to like it. Even though his shoulder was damaged, he assessed his chances of escaping at fifty/fifty.

Sergeant Quon wanted badly to notify Major Nguyen of his success. The major had promised a helicopter pickup when he captured the monk. The only problem was he couldn't make radio contact. He either had to move to higher ground or go back down to the valley to get reception. In either case, he wasn't confident that he and his only functional man could handle the American, even if he was wounded. According to Major Nguyen, the monk was shot by one of the three soldiers who captured him and yet he subdued all three. Quon had to make a choice.

He ordered Larry to get up and when he didn't, he kicked him in his wounded shoulder, but the prisoner didn't cry out or move. He kicked him three more times and Larry passed out from the pain. They were going to have to carry the man down the trail. He sent his man with the broken arm ahead to act as point and the one with the sore groin to bring up the rear while he and the remaining soldier tried to carry Larry, who still hadn't regained consciousness. They'd gone twenty yards when the man holding Larry's feet fell and Quon had to let go and Larry rolled a few feet downhill. "Sergeant, this won't work. The trail is too rough. Perhaps if we built a stretcher we'll have better success." They spent the remainder of the morning building a stretcher. Quon decided to hold the stretcher in front while two men would carry the back end.

It was apparent they didn't think he spoke or understood their language because they spoke freely. He initially was surprised when they called him by his name, but he learned that they'd been sent by Major Nguyen at the direction of his antagonist, Commander Tran. They travelled this way for two hours and were ready to take a break when Larry, who'd been awake for some time, lashed out with his feet and caught the soldier with the sore groin in the jaw. He let go of the stretcher and the other man holding the other handle fell over him and both lay on top of Larry.

Quon let go of the front of the stretcher and yelled, "What happened?"

"The prisoner kicked Chu in the jaw; he dropped the stretcher and I fell over him and the prisoner."

When Quon kicked Larry in the head, he nearly passed out. Let's take a twenty-minute break and see what the damage is. We'll place the prisoner on his stomach and tie his legs to the stretcher. How bad is Tien?

"I think his jaw is broken. I can wrap a bandage around his head to hold it in place, but he's not going to be much help. It's you and me now."

"I'd shoot this son-of-a bitch right here if they didn't want him so bad in Hanoi. We have to do the best we can. As long as the American is alive, I think they'll be happy," Quon told his subordinates.

They stopped for the night and, out of necessity, they had to feed and hydrate Larry or he'd die before they returned. They got him up and made him walk a little before they finally looked at his wound. Quon cleaned and bandaged it, while Larry smiled at him. The sergeant was so irate that he backhanded the flyer across the face and Larry fell. "If you give us any more trouble, we'll kill you right here and say we didn't find you."

Larry rolled over, looked at Quon and laughed. "If you don't get me back to Hanoi, Tran is going to cut your balls off and make you eat them while you're still alive. You're never going to make it. Quon looked at Larry with utter hatred. He prayed that Commander Tran would let him kill the American once they were done with him. It didn't matter how long it would take, he'd be ready. Quon could understand why it took so long to track down Stephens. He looked like a monk; he acted like a monk and his language was nearly flawless. Quon was in a tough spot here without communication. One of his men had a broken arm and another had a broken jaw. He and Corporal Ly had to carry the American.

Just then Private Hoang ran back up the trail. "There are about ten Hmong coming up the trail."

"Put a gag in the American's mouth and move him out of the way. I don't want to tangle with them today. If we're quiet, they'll pass and we can be on our way."

The Hmong seemed to be taking their time as though they were looking for something or someone. Quon wondered if they were looking for his squad. He hated them as much as the Americans. They worked with the CIA during the war and were not friendly toward his government. Their day would come, but not today.

It took thirty minutes before they could move. Quon ordered Private Ly to tie Larry to the stretcher. But, as Ly reached for Larry's arm, he lashed out with both hands that were now tied in front and caught Ly in the neck; the Corporal fell to the ground. Larry kicked him in the neck and solar plexus and was about to deliver a life ending blow when Quon hit him from behind. Larry fell and hit his head on the ground; he was unconscious.

Ly was conscious but throwing up on the ground. When he tried to talk, he couldn't; Quon helped him to his feet, gave him some water and leaned him against a tree. He gathered the others around Ly. "This American is not going to defeat the soldiers of the NVA. How would we explain to our superiors that one man, who's wounded and tied up, got the best of us? I don't want to tell my superiors that; do you?" The other three shook their heads, "No."

"Hoang, you have one good arm. You'll hold onto one side of the stretcher up front. Chu, you'll handle the other side. I'll carry the back until Ly feels able to spell me. We will not give up. We will persevere. Are you with me?" All three nodded yes.

Larry was placed face down and his arms and legs were tied to the stretcher. He was still unconscious. Quon tried the radio again, but there was too much atmospheric interference and he gave up after fifteen minutes. They stopped again at dusk, found a place to camp off the trail and didn't light a fire for fear of attracting the Hmong.

They fed Larry sparingly, gave him water and then tied him to a tree. Larry didn't sleep. He knew they were vulnerable but so was he. There wouldn't be many more chances to escape once they got to the valley floor.

"I've got to take a shit."

"Do it in your pants. I don't care."

"Come on, I won't try to escape but I need to go." Larry kept it up for nearly ten minutes before Quon relented.

He untied Larry and told him to get to his feet. He trained his revolver on him and led him through some trees to a bare spot fifty yards from camp. "My hands are tied behind me. I can't unzip my pants, unless you want to do it and then pull them back up and zip them after I'm done." Quon stared at him and then told him to turn around. He unfastened the ropes around his wrists, backed up and Larry squatted down and did his business. Quon was cautious and kept his distance.

When it was time to retie the ropes around Larry's hands, Quon stayed back and said, "We'll tie them when we get back to camp. I want you in front of me at all times on the way back. Don't think I won't kill you."

It was nearly dark now. Quon could still see him while staying five feet back of Larry as they returned. When they were near the camp, Larry grabbed a low-lying branch and pulled it forward and when it wouldn't bend anymore, he released it. The limb snapped back fast and caught Quon on the side of his head and he dropped the gun. Larry turned to his right and threw his shoulder into the Sergeant and the two went down. Larry made quick work with two judo chops to the neck and Quon was unconscious. Larry was free now, and had a gun.

He tied Quon to a tree and stuffed a rag in his mouth and then cautiously made his way back into their camp. The other three were sound asleep. He carefully took each of their weapons which were resting near each man. The three were confused as he woke them and forced the three to tie each other up. He took all the ammunition from their weapons and belts; he planned to drop it along his escape route. After taking most of their rice and water, some liniment and bandages, Larry started up the mountain. Even though it was dark, he had to create some distance between himself and the four soldiers. They would come after him when they were able to free themselves from their bonds.

Larry didn't have time to treat the bullet wound in his left shoulder. His entire left side hurt and his movements were restricted. He didn't know if it was the bullet wound causing the pain or the many kicks he'd suffered to that area. Stopping only to rest for five minutes every hour, he was able to walk the trail until the following evening. He estimated that he'd created a half day of separation from his pursuers but he still had a long way to go before he was free. He slept about three hours in the early evening and then continued on. With a full moon to help illuminate his way, he moved forward and was able to follow the trail to the summit and start down the other side. But fatigue was starting to set in and even though the bleeding had stopped, the wound hurt like hell. He was aware that he might be susceptible to infection but there was no time to dwell on that. He either had to move on and create distance from his pursuers or he'd spend the rest of his life in some version of the Hanoi Hilton.

Quon was groggy for some time after he woke up. He knew he screwed up by letting the American get the best of him. All he could think about was what his commander would do when he found out they captured Stephens and he escaped from four armed soldiers. He wondered where his men were and whether they were looking for him.

The other three had finally gotten loose and after stumbling around trying to figure out what to do, Corporal Ly directed them to fan out to find Quon. It was Ly who found his sergeant and untied him. Back at their camp, Quon took inventory. They had little food or water and although they had guns, they were without ammunition; Quon was embarrassed in front of his men. He couldn't give up and he couldn't return without the prisoner. There was no choice but to continue on. They'd get food, medical attention and some ammunition at the next village or at some Laotian Army Outpost. If he came back without Stephens, Major Nguyen would kill him; if not, Commander Tran would. There was always defection, but that would leave his wife and two children at the mercy of the regime. No, he had to get Stephens.

Larry realized he had a head start but he knew that he would still be pursued; he couldn't afford to be taken. The weapon he took from Sergeant Quon balanced the odds somewhat but he was still outnumbered. He didn't run on the trail but he moved as fast as he could while the pain in his shoulder became more acute. Although completely fatigued, he willed himself forward and made it half way down the other side of the mountain before resting for thirty minutes. He wondered where the next village was and whether he could get some help there. At dawn, he ate some rice and flushed it down with water. Fifteen minutes later he was up and ready to go, though he noticed that his movements weren't as steady as before.

Quon and his men rested that night; they'd continue the chase at dawn. Without ammunition and with very little food, Quon had to make some decisions. He decided to send Hoang and Chu back; they were too injured to help with the job and would slow down the chase. Before Quon left Da Nang, he made two copies of the orders Major Nguyen had given him; he gave one of the copies to Chu. Without ammunition, no food and injured, Chu and Hoang were at a disadvantage but both were young and healthy and could stop at the villages in Vietnam for assistance. Stephens, on the other hand, was wounded in the shoulder; that would slow him down. Quon was confident they'd run him down within one or two days.

At dusk the following evening, the trail was barely visible but Larry chose to continue. He needed to stretch the distance between the NVA soldiers and himself. He'd gone without sleep for over a day and was planning to walk through another night, but he was running on adrenalin. Although he was continuously stumbling, he willed himself on; he had to get home. It was after midnight when he stumbled and fell in a green patch alongside the path; he was thoroughly exhausted. He lay there for ten minutes before he literally crawled to a more secluded spot forty yards off the trail and hid in some dense brush and sat down. After a few sips of water from Quon's canteen, he passed out.

Larry dreamed he was captured by Tran's men and taken to Hanoi by helicopter where he was interrogated for ten days. He initially struggled with his captors but finally gave in and told them about the abbot. When he woke, he was in a moderate-sized village of about twenty huts laid out in two semi-circles, one behind the other in a large clearing. Subsequently, he would learn that the village was located near the crest of the hill. There was a lot of activity but no soldiers. It appeared to be lunchtime; communal dining seemed to be the norm. There were numerous tables around pits in the ground and several fifty-gallon drums that had been cut in half and were being used to cook meat. At least twenty adults and fifteen children were eating at long tales in front of the two semi circles of homes. He started to rise but his shoulder hurt. That's when he realized there was a young woman kneeling over him, bandaging his shoulder. She was slim, dressed in a colorful brocade vest with pantaloons. Larry was awake but didn't seem to be coherent. It was as though he'd been on drugs. He looked around at all the people going about their business as though he wasn't there.

The woman spoke to him in a language he didn't understand; he responded in English. Soon an elderly man walked over and asked him in broken English if he was Vietnamese or American. Without thinking, Larry responded that he was an American. The man signaled to another of the villagers who was eating with a group and he came over.

"We are the Hmong People. Luckily we found you when we did, you were in bad shape. We fought alongside the Americans in the war with Vietnam. "I'm Truang Le, the chief of this village. You are in safe hands, though your shoulder is damaged and the bullet is still in there. We can take it out but I think you'd be better served in one of your own hospitals. Tell me what you're doing here wearing a Buddhist monk's robe."

Larry told him most of the story and the fact that he was being chased by four NVA Regulars. "I must get to Thailand."

"We can't take you there but we can protect you until you are ready to travel. My guess is that you need a

week or two to recuperate; until then, you'll be our guest."
The chief said.

"I feel as though I've been drugged."

"Our folk medicine woman gave you some opium
to ease your pain."

"Tell her I'm grateful, but I don't want any more
opium. I'll handle the pain. What about the four soldiers
who are pursuing me?"

"There are only two now and they went down the
trail toward Thailand this afternoon. The other two are
injured and appear to be heading back to Vietnam. Who
knows where the two who are chasing you will be in a week.
I'm sure we can help you find the best route to your
destination; if you're lucky, you may never see your pursuers
again. Once you reach the Mekong, there should be boats
that will take you the rest of the way. So lay back, relax and
enjoy our village."

Over the next four days, he slept most of the time,
though he knew the medicine woman was tending to his
wound. He ate little but consumed a lot of warm broth and
some rice. When he woke and tried to walk, he stumbled
and fell a few times before he willed himself to stay upright.
He tried some calisthenics and then walked around the
village until he had to lie down. Soon he was about eighty
percent normal and getting the urge to move on.

He learned that the Hmong were primarily an
agricultural society and practiced slash and burn type
farming here in the highlands of Laos. He, the chief and
another of the Hmong, who spoke passable English, had
many conversations over the next week. Though it was
tedious because of the language problems, Larry learned
about the involvement of the CIA with the Hmong People

going back to the nineteen fifties. The other gentleman, whom the chief introduced as Pao, fought for the CIA in Laos and Vietnam, where he was wounded.

"Pao came to this village with his family two years ago because he was wounded and tired of fighting. His group had functioned as guerrillas and blocked the Ho Chi Minh Trail, slowing down the supplies coming from the north to the south. Pao and his compatriots rescued many downed flyers and safely brought them to this village. It was our villagers who saw that they made it to Thailand. .Thousands of our people were killed in the war and the animosity between our people and the Vietnamese is real, even to this day."

"We're not happy with your government either. By stopping the North Vietnamese from extending the Ho Chi Minh Trail into Laos, we saved thousands of Americans. They promised aid but have sent nothing for years. We did what the CIA asked and what do we have to show for it. We live like this and are hated by the Laotians and the Vietnamese. Perhaps you can tell your leaders to send us help. What you see here is all that is left of a village of one thousand people."

"This is the first I've heard of your people. Where did you come from?"

"We are descendants of the Miao people who lived in Mongolia some four thousand years ago. Gradually we migrated to the Yangtze River Basin in China almost two thousand years ago. Our people were persecuted there and, in the eighteen hundreds, migrated to Laos, Vietnam and Thailand. Our village has been here nearly one hundred years; almost one half million Hmong live in Laos. In the early nineteen sixties, the North Vietnamese invaded Laos and we were recruited by the CIA to fight against the invaders. This was called the Secret War. Prior to that, the

French recruited us to fight the North and South Vietnamese Armies. We're not a warlike people. But we needed so many things to survive in an unfriendly country that we hired out as mercenaries."

"I can understand now why you believe you're owed aid from the United States."

They found Larry's robe in his knapsack and asked him about it. "I'd been posing as a Buddhist Monk during my escape from Vietnam."

"Have you converted to Buddhism?" The chief asked.

"Not officially, but for all practical purposes, Buddhism is my new religion. I have been conducting funeral and wedding ceremonies at the various villages on my way here. There's a sense of peace about the religion that I find very attractive and fulfilling."

"Our Shaman performs our ceremonies. Would you like to assist him and learn our ways?"

"If it's acceptable, I would love to participate."

"We are going to perform a Child Naming and Buddhist Wedding Ceremony at the end of the week. My nephew has been waiting for the Shaman to come from one of our other villages and marry him and his intended. They are anxious." The chief smiled at Larry.

"This is a very special event for us who are Green Hmong. Three days after a birth of one of our children, he or she is given their first name, while the father is given a second name. The Shaman offers his blessing while bestowing words of wisdom to the child. The village sacrifices a pig or cow prior to the ceremony. We try to conduct the naming ceremony in conjunction with a wedding ceremony if possible. Soon we will celebrate a wedding and a naming."

On the day of the blessed events, the dining tables were decorated with flowers and different embroidered scarves. About one hundred twenty-five villagers were dressed in their finest and most colorful apparel. Larry was told that the birth name of the child was Nao, while his father was to be given the second name of Vang. The women of the village wore colorful costumes consisting of embroidered jackets in contrasting designs which were so well done that they could be sold in any of elite shops in America. During the ceremony, they drank some native drink and later there was fruit and rice at the wedding dinner.

Before he left, the village chief presented him with an embroidered jacket and matching pants. Larry retained his orange robe and sandals, but dressed in the embroidered outfit. The chief trotted out three young women, including the medicine woman who treated him. "If you would stay with us, I will give you one of these women in marriage. What do you think?" The chief asked and the three women, who were about eighteen years old, giggled.

"I thank you for this generous offer. Any one of the three would be more than I could ask for. However, I'm married and want to return home to my wife."

With the weather changing, the warm clothing provided by the villagers would be appreciated the remainder of his trip. Larry left at noon the next day on the trail he previously used. At least half of the village was there to see him off. One of the villagers guided him the first half mile and, when he was sure Larry wouldn't get lost, he left.

His thoughts during his week with the Hmong never moved very far from Jean. He wondered what she was doing and how she'd receive him when he got home. He had so much to make up to her and the children; he'd been gone too long. It was a foregone conclusion that he wouldn't stay in the service longer than the time it took him to process out. His time in the military was over.

He was so close to escaping from the North Vietnamese that he could almost taste it. He knew that Sergeant Quon would never give up, but Larry was determined to make it home. He swore that he would never be in any conflict ever again. He didn't know how Jean would feel about his conversion but he hoped she wouldn't be embarrassed. This new religion came to him out of necessity but it was as though it was something he was meant to do.

When he reached the valley floor, he stopped at the first village on his way and begged for food; no one mentioned whether anyone was looking for him. At least two in the village spoke some Vietnamese. They were most gracious and replenished his supply of rice and water. He asked them about the route the Hmong suggested and they said it was the best way to travel to the Mekong. It would probably take him four days.

Larry felt that if he could reach the Mekong River, he'd be able to obtain transportation aboard one of the many river vessels that used the river for trade and transportation. His two main problems were money and identification. He wouldn't be able to use any official point of entry into Thailand. He'd probably have to swim part of the way and complete his journey by foot. Then there were the two Vietnamese Soldiers who were looking for him.

Quon and Ly stayed on the trail up to the summit and then down to the valley floor. They knew Stephens had started this way and they saw no reason why he would deviate. When they reached the bottom, they checked with the first two villages in the area for the American. Either the villagers were lying or no one had seen him. They asked for food and when it wasn't forthcoming, they took it by force. It was obvious the flyer had chosen another route down the mountain so they asked the villagers where the other routes would be. They settled on one of those routes and made their way to the villages on the valley floor closet to those paths.

But the villagers hadn't seen the American either. Quon and Ly wondered what happened to him. One answer was that Larry's wound was more serious than they thought and he didn't survive his escape. Another option was that there was another route that Larry used. They were convinced that if he came down the mountain, it would be by one of the two trails the villagers recommended. They decided to find the nearest Laotian Garrison and get some ammunition for their weapons and then come back. If the American hadn't surfaced by then, they'd look at other alternatives. They couldn't accept the possibility that Stephens was dead.

Although his shoulder was sore, the two weeks in the Hmong Village improved his spirits; most of his strength had returned. He felt positive and was sure he was going to reach Ubon. He'd retained his Buddhist robe but was wearing the brocade clothing the Hmong had given him plus a wide brimmed hat that the boatmen wore. With his thin frame, his dark complexion and his bright clothing, he could easily pass as one of the Hmong. He struck out along the valley floor, traveling southwest most of the time. The Hmong figured it would take him four days to reach the Mekong; he made it in five. The river was wide and too swift for him to swim across. He wanted to walk as far as he could and then either hop a ride with one of the river craft or cross one of three rope bridges the Hmong told him about. The number of dams and rapids precluded a river craft from traveling too far on the Mekong; therefore, that couldn't be his only form of transportation.

Quon was knowledgeable about the three rope bridges. Six of his soldiers he selected were dispatched, two each to the three bridges. Quon stopped at the first rope bridge and found the two soldiers from his squad. The American hadn't tried to cross at this point. His men had been sent with seven days rations. Even though they ate sparingly, they'd run out of food three days earlier. The locals were reluctant to feed his soldiers without being paid. There were many markets along the river, so Quon went to two of them and demanded food for his soldiers. One of the vendors acquiesced but the other resisted. Quon stuck his rifle in one vendor's ribs, took what he wanted and returned to the bridge. Rather than wait to see if they were ahead of the American, Quon and Ly continued to the next two rope bridges, leaving the two soldiers behind. The situation with his men at the next two bridges was the same and as before; he quickly solved their problem.

He knew that he and Ly were the only ones who knew the American by sight. Since they couldn't watch all three bridges at the same time, they'd only watch the last two. Ly would go back to the middle bridge while Quon would stay at the third. Quon didn't feel as though he had a choice. Coming back without the American would be a death sentence.

Larry knew he'd be safe once he made it to Thailand, so his plan was to cross the river using the second of the three rope bridges. He'd seen one of these before in South America. The bridge was anchored on both sides with parallel load bearing cables or thick rope. The deck or flooring was made of wooden slats and the bridge swayed when you walked on it or if there was a slight wind. Due to the weight of the flooring and the length the cables or ropes must span, there was a downward arc on the bridge initially. The middle section leveled off and the last portion had an upward arc as one approached the other side. Generally, there was netting on either side of the walkway for safety, while the traveler held onto the load bearing cables as he walked.

During this odyssey, Larry had plenty of time to reflect on his last three years at the Pagoda. He learned to speak Vietnamese fluently and he learned to be part of the Buddhist religion. But more than that, he was a propagator of the religion. He found that his ability to bond with those who were sick or hungry was surprising to him. He liked being a monk. He liked conducting meditations, as well as wedding and funeral ceremonies. He wondered what part Buddhism would play in his future and was this to be his calling in life?

When he reached the Mekong, he estimated that he was one hundred twenty-five miles from Ubon with maybe two days of rations left. There was no guarantee that he wouldn't see Quon and Ly again; therefore, he needed to get to Ubon as fast as he could. To accomplish this, he wanted a ride on one of the river craft. He couldn't speak Laotian but perhaps some of the river people spoke Vietnamese. There were several boats with their cargo sitting on the dock along the river. He approached a group of men and asked if anyone spoke Vietnamese. When no one responded, he tried English.

"What you want?" one of the men asked.

"I need to reach Southern Thailand. I'd be glad to work for the trip."

"Only go part way. You load those in that boat." The man pointed to ten small crates lying on the bank next to a long, narrow dugout. The boat appeared to be carved from a large tree with planking added to provide a flat surface over the boat to carry supplies and one to two boatmen. The boat was powered by a small motorboat engine with a steering oar to guide it in the river.

In spite of his damaged shoulder, he loaded the ten crates and hopped on board when the boatman signaled. They were on their way. He never steered one of these boats but when the man handed him the tiller, he took hold. After pushing the oar in the wrong direction a couple of times, he got the hang of it. It was a short trip of thirty miles down the river but he was finally on the Thai side; he was closing the gap between himself and Ubon. The boatman asked him if he was hungry. When he nodded, the man fed him some raw fish and rice. Larry unloaded the cargo and asked the boatman where he might pick up another ride.

"About five mile down river, ask for Hoa, he speaks Vietnamese. He has yellow boat."

An hour later he found Hoa, who told him to load twenty crates onto his boat and take the tiller. Hoa's boat was similar to the other he'd steered. As soon as he fastened down the crates, Hoa told him to push off, start the engine and get underway. This time he was aware which way to move the shaft and off they went. After ten miles he saw the second rope bridge ahead. He put on his jacket and wide brimmed hat and hunched down.

Hoa looked at him and asked. 'What are you doing, fool?"

"There're three men on the bridge with guns. They're after me, so watch out."

"What did you get me into?"

"This has nothing to do with you; they're after me and want to take me back to Hanoi."

"You think that's going to make any difference to them. Give me the tiller and get behind those crates. I'll get us out of here."

Just then, two shots were fired from the bridge; both shots hit the craft. Hoa turned toward the bank and Larry got behind the crates. After two more shots hit the water, the firing stopped. People crossing on the rope bridge stopped and watched the action. Soon, three other men came running up to the bridge entrance on the Laotian side and the three Vietnamese soldiers started to run away. Larry assumed that Laotian Policemen came in the nick of time. Surely the Vietnamese Soldiers would either follow the boat or go to the third bridge. Well, they found him but catching him wasn't going to be that easy. He was armed with Quon's revolver and getting closer to safety; his resolve became more intense.

Hoa steered the boat to a small dock on the Thailand side. He gave Larry some cooked fish and told him to jump off; Hoa would unload the boat. "Good Luck," he said as Larry hopped off the boat and went up the bank. He estimated that the last rope bridge was thirty miles away. He had plenty of time to formulate a plan; he'd be ready and, besides, he was on the Thailand side.

Once he reached the area around the third rope bridge, he'd be about sixty miles from Ubon. He assumed that the North Vietnamese would rush to the third bridge, crossover, and try to set up a trap for him as he was making his was to the Air Base. The road on the Thailand side was wide and crowded. There were other roads parallel to the one by the river yet he decided to stay on this one until he was near the last bridge. Larry was tired; he found a secluded spot about two hundred yards from the road he was using.

He knew it was a calculated risk but he needed all his strength when he reached the third bridge. He lay down and went to sleep. Tomorrow he'd be fresh and would be able to take on the North Vietnamese.

Quon and Ly and the other six soldiers discarded their uniform shirts and mingled with the crowd of people at the Thailand side of the rope bridge. They waited but the American didn't show. One thing that went through Quon's mind was that Stephens had already passed the third bridge but Ly assured him that he was at the second bridge and couldn't have beaten him to the third. There was another option. Stephens could have taken another road to Ubon. Ly asked him what he wanted to do.

"We'll wait another day and if he doesn't show, we'll go to Ubon and see if we can apprehend him before he enters the base."

Early the next morning, Larry checked his revolver. He was ready for the showdown. As he approached the third bridge he was conscious of the number of people coming across and, to him, it seemed like a family reunion of sorts. As the group crossed the bridge and reached the Thailand side, they were greeted enthusiastically by about twenty people milling near the entrance. Those people were carrying banners and balloons. Ly and two of the soldiers were at the bridge entrance on the Thailand side and Quon and four others were on the bridge. As Larry neared the bridge entrance, Ly saw him, separated himself from the crowd, and raced at Larry with his two soldiers ten paces behind him. Just as Ly neared him, he leaped. Larry ducked and when he felt Ly touch his back, he lifted up quickly and the Vietnamese soldier went over the guard rail and tumbled to the river bank twenty feet below and then roll into the water. Larry saw him go under. The other two soldiers following Ly stopped and looked at the location where Ly went over the rail. It gave Larry enough time to attack. He rushed at them and hit both with chops to the back of their necks and down they went.

Quon lifted his rifle and, using the cable to steady his aim, fired at Larry. The bridge was swaying as he shot and he hit a family member who had run to greet a relative. It was as though a curtain had been pulled down over the scene and the plot changed one hundred eighty degrees. One moment there was laughter, the next, dead silence. As what happened started to sink into the crowd, knives were drawn and Quon was quickly overwhelmed as were the four soldiers by his side. The two that Larry had subdued, ran off, with many in the wedding party chasing them. Larry could hear the screams of the soldiers as knives slashed at them. He walked quickly around the crowd until he was out of sight.

Chapter 12

Larry Stephens walked up to the security post at the main gate at Ubon Air Base on December 10th, 1973 and told the two guards who he was and asked that the 22nd squadron commander be notified he was here. Larry was dressed in a brocade shirt and pants; he still wore sandals. His hair was starting to grow back but it was covered with a peasant hat. The American soldier manning the gate told him to sit down on the concrete curb and wait there. Fifteen minutes later, Lieutenant Harris arrived in a jeep, driven by another MP.

"Who are you", Harris asked while standing in front of Larry.

"I'm Captain Lawrence J. Stephens, United States Air Force. I was an F4C pilot in the 22nd Flight Squadron stationed here at Ubon. I was shot down twenty miles southwest of Hanoi on June 5, 1969."

"You don't look like one of ours. Show me some identification."

"It was stolen from me."

"You look like a freeloader to me. You get out of here or I'll call the Thais and have you arrested. Don't show up here again." Harris was close enough to push Larry away.

Larry was stunned. "You can't be serious. All you have to do is check my fingerprints against your own records and you'll see that I'm telling the truth."

Harris turned to the guard at the gate. "Call the Thais and tell them to come pick up this guy who's trying to infiltrate the base." When Harris turned back, Larry was gone.

Larry moved away from the main gate and stood in the shadows of the trees nearby. It never dawned on him that he'd be turned away after he'd come so far. The layout of the base couldn't have changed too much in the four years he was gone. The runway and airplanes must still be in the same area; most of the other buildings were too large and expensive to move. He assumed personnel and base headquarters were located in the same large buildings in the middle of the base, as before.

It took him several hours to find the place were some of the Thais had shot at him and the other pilots as they rode their motorcycles to the flight line. He went under the barbed wire and made his way to where he thought base headquarters was located. He found the back door but it was locked. It was still warm in the daytime this time of year. Intuitively, Larry knew there'd be a window partially open somewhere on the first floor. He found it and was able to squeeze his small frame through the opening; he was in. The personnel division was on the first floor but the door was locked. He took out a credit card from Lt. Harris' billfold and opened the door. The young Lieutenant was going to be mad when he realized Larry had picked his pocket.

All the filing cabinets were locked with a steel bar through all the handles of each drawer. He checked under the blotter on the nearby desks and found the combinations to all the personnel safes. He looked for T through Z files, opened the drawer and found nothing with his name on it. He searched for a drawer marked suspense. It was in one of the other filing cabinets, which he opened with one of the other combinations. There was his file. He opened his folder and saw his picture and a fingerprint card inside. He put the NVA revolver in the drawer, locked up everything and exited through the window he used to enter the building. "I'll bet finding that NVA revolver will give them pause," he said out loud.

He had about two hours before dawn to find his old squadron's headquarters. He retraced his steps to where he entered the base and then paralleled the road to the flight line. Finding the 22nd Flight Squadron was easy; there was at four by four foot sign on the lawn, identifying the building. He used the credit card again to open the rear door, shut it carefully and walked to where he thought the commander's office was located. That door wasn't locked, so he entered the room, sat down at the commander's desk, pulled out a drawer and put his feet on top of the drawer. He eased back in the chair and waited; sleep was out of the question.

Promptly at seven AM, a Lieutenant Colonel walked into the room, turned on the light, put his hat on a rack and turned to find a civilian with dirty clothes and a wide brimmed peasant hat sitting in his chair; he stared at the man. "Don't be alarmed Colonel. Let me explain my presence before you call the Military Police," Larry said as he rose.

Larry signaled the Colonel to use the desk and took off the peasant hat. "I'm Captain Larry Stephens. I flew F4Cs out of Ubon in 1969. In June of that year I was shot down twenty miles southeast of Hanoi and I've eluded capture for four years. I don't have any identification but I went to personnel last night and borrowed my file. My picture and a copy of my fingerprints are inside."

Larry handed the file to the officer. "It would be easy to check my fingerprints against this file or, if you're cautious, you could wire Washington and have them produce the copy they have on file. I assure you, I'm not going anywhere and I'm not a threat to your presence. I've come home."

"I know you won't be happy that I broke into personnel, but Lieutenant Harris of the Military Police wouldn't believe my story last night at the main gate and threatened to have me arrested. This was the only way I knew of to prove to you who I am. I'd like you to notify my wife and children that I'm alive. I don't know where they live in the states but her father's name is Thomas Washington; he and his wife lived in Greenville Mississippi."

"Okay Stephens, or whoever you are, I'm Lt. Colonel Martin, the squadron commander of the 22nd. I'm going to check out your story, so sit down while I make a few calls."

Larry listened as Martin made the calls he would've made had he been in the Squadron Commander's position. Within twenty minutes, Lt. Harris, a Major from Personnel and two air policemen arrived. When Harris saw Larry, he turned to the colonel. "This little bastard stole my wallet. I'll take him to the lockup and hold him until the Thais get here."

"Just hold it. He's not going anywhere just yet. This situation needs to be sorted out. He may be a little bastard to you Harris, but we're going to check out his story. If it doesn't match with what we have, you can give him to the Thais. Everyone have a seat while Major Phillips looks at the personnel record I have here and makes sure it hasn't been compromised."

Larry handed the wallet to Harris, who checked to see if everything was still there including thirty dollars. "Thanks for lending me that. I didn't take anything." Larry smiled.

"Everything seems to be here, though the picture in this file doesn't look anything like our friend here. Of course, he could've switched fingerprint cards and his picture, since he stole the file out of personnel. I need to take his prints and send them to DC to see if there's a match to be sure he's authentic." Phillips answered after about a ten minute check of the folder.

Martin turned to Larry and asked him a series of question relating to the F4C, such as its capability, thrust ratio, range and armament. Larry took his time and discussed each issue in detail. "Even though you don't look like one of our aviators, you certainly know the F4C"

"To evade in enemy territory, I darkened my skin by using tea leaves and lost over forty pounds so I'd blend in with the populace."

Martin then asked Larry a series of question about Luke and McDill Air Force Bases where Larry had been stationed. He then asked question relating to the mission Larry was on when he was shot down. He used the mission report signed by the lead for that mission which was in his file. When Martin finished asking questions, he turned to the others. "There's a strong possibility that Stephens may be who he says he is."

"Here's what we're going to do. Harris, you escort this man to personnel with Major Phillips so he can take his fingerprints and check them against those in this file. If they check out, call me. Assuming that he checks out, take him to the chow hall and feed him while Phillips wires Washington and has the pentagon check his prints against the official file. In the interim, I'll call Air Force Aid and authorize five hundred dollars for you, Stephens. After he's fed, take him by Air Force Aid so he can collect the money and then to clothing sales for a uniform that fits and then to the exchange for some personal items such as a tooth brush and comb. It may take a day or two to get confirmation from Washington. However, if his prints don't check, turn him over to the Thais."

"Just so Lt. Harris can feel comfortable, Stephens will be housed in the jail until this is all sorted out. Stephens may come and go as he pleases, so long as it's on base and he's escorted by an MP at all times. If Major Phillips finds his prints match his file, he will be treated with the respect of his rank."

As they were leaving his office, Colonel Martin signaled Corporal Jones, an MP who came with Harris. "One thing you should know. Stephens is an accomplished Martial Art's expert. He competed in one of those Thai tournaments and won; he's lethal. Let Harris know about this and be alert until we check out his story."

It took about thirty minutes before Phillips matched Larry's fingerprints to the ones they had on file for him. Larry breathed a sigh of relief, figuring that it was only a matter of time before confirmation came back from Washington and he could go home. "Take me to the chow hall, I could eat a horse."

Jones and Waiters sat with him while he ate. "Tell me, Captain, were you in the Hanoi Hilton and if not there, where were you?" Jones asked.

"I was hiding out the entire time. I assume I'll be debriefed shortly, so I'll withhold any information until that time."

"The color of your skin has changed and so has your body mass. How do you explain that?"

"In order to blend in, I used tea leaves on my skin to darken it. Cutting my hair was easy. The weight took some time. I was on an austere diet for four years. It was natural that I lost forty pounds."

"The colonel said you won a martial arts tournament. Is that true?"

"Well, I won the one hundred seventy-five pound division."

"What made you enter the tournament? I understand some of the contestants were killed in the ring. Weren't you scared?"

I had free time and certain skills. I guess it was my ego that got the best of me. I wanted to find out how good I was."

Sleeping on a real bed was uncomfortable for someone who led an austere life and slept on a thin pad or on the ground for the past four years. He tossed and turned all night and apparently spoke in his sleep because the jailer came back to see if he was alright. The two MPs took him to breakfast. It was the first time since he took off that fateful morning four years ago that he had eggs; he ate six. When they came back, Harris was waiting for him. "I'll take over here boys; go get a cup of coffee. I want to talk to Stephens alone. Jones looked at Waiters and smiled; they'd seen this action before. Rather than leave the building, they went to the monitoring room to see what Harris had in mind. They turned on the audio and video devices.

Both men were facing each other inside the cell, when Harris said. "I didn't appreciate you taking my wallet. I was embarrassed in front of my men. I can't have them thinking that someone got the best of me. I'm going to teach you a lesson."

"Look, I'm sorry. It seemed like something I needed to do at the time, nothing personal. I apologize. Let's shake hands and forget the whole thing."

Larry reached out to shake hands but Harris slapped his hand away and swung his right hand at Larry's head. Harris was over two hundred pounds and at least six feet tall. Larry moved out of range easily and put out his hands as though to say, let's talk this over. Harris crouched as he came forward. He jabbed with his left and swung with his right. Larry grabbed his right arm and pulled him forward while he moved to the side. Harris' momentum propelled him forward and he hit the bars and went down. Blood was streaming from his nose and he was swearing. He changed his tactic and dove for Larry's legs but Stephens danced out of the way. When Harris rose, Larry kicked out with his left leg and caught Harris alongside the head and the MP fell to the floor. He was slow in rising but wanted to continue. Larry hit him in the solar plexus and Harris threw up on the cell floor. Just then, Jones and Waiters walked in. "He's our boss, but he's not well liked. We'll clean up here and this won't go any further. I think the Lieutenant will take a few days off, or at least until you leave; if not, all his men will see what happened here. For a little man, you sure are potent. Why don't you wait in the monitoring room while we have this cell cleaned up?"

Chu and Hoang made it back to Da Nang and reported to Major Nguyen after they had their injuries attended to. "Do you know if the monk was the American?" Nguyen asked.

"Sergeant Quon said he was and spoke to him as though he was the American. All I know is that he spoke Vietnamese and was lethal. He broke my arm and Private Hoang's nose, and this was after Quon shot him in the shoulder. He also disarmed Quon and escaped with a weapon. We wanted to kill him but Quon said you wanted to interrogate the monk and we had to bring him back alive," Private Chu told Nguyen.

"How could he manage to escape the four of you?"

"He took every opportunity to lash out when we weren't looking. His feet were as lethal as his hands. I've seen men like him; they're trained to kill."

"Where are Quon and Ly now?"

"We don't know. Since we were injured and had no ammunition for our weapons, Quon sent us back here."

"Do you know anything about the other six soldiers we sent to the rope bridges?"

"No sir."

Major Nguyen took his time writing a report to his uncle, General Tran; he sent it through channels and waited for a response. It came within a few days; he was to report to Tran's office in Hanoi. He wasn't looking forward to the meeting with his uncle. "I'm very disappointed in you, nephew. You sent ten men and they couldn't subdue a wounded American!"

"Quon is a good man and persistent; he'll bring him back or die trying. I'll keep you informed, general."

"That's how much you know. Quon and Ly and four other soldiers are dead."

"The American killed all six?"

"No, most of them were killed by Thai civilians. Apparently Quon fired at Stephens and hit a member of a wedding party and they killed him and four of the guards we sent to watch the bridges. Ly was killed by Stephens We have an international situation on our hands now. The Thais want to know why we sent soldiers to invade their territory. I'm going to let you explain to the central committee how you screwed this mission up. You're dismissed."

Tran wasn't giving up. He'd check with his delegation in the states to determine where Stephens was and how they could deal with him. No one was going to embarrass Tran and get away with it. After he took care of Stephens, the abbot would have an accident and a score would be settled.

Captain Larry Stephens had been waiting two days since his encounter with Lieutenant Harris when one of the MPs came into his cell. "The Colonel wants to see you in his office at eleven. He should have word on your status by then. Waiters and I hope it works out for you Captain; you did us a small favor," Jones smiled.

Lt. Colonel Martin was waiting for him at eleven. "Captain Stephens, we've confirmed your identity. I apologize if I was somewhat overbearing, but I wanted to be sure. I contacted the pentagon last night. We're flying you out late this afternoon to Washington on commercial air. Two senior officers are waiting to debrief you. A telegram has been sent to your wife notifying her that you're alive and coming home. She lives in Greenville, Mississippi; here's the address and phone number. Due to the time differential, we're not sure if she's received the notification yet. Someone will go to her home to be sure she knows."

"I'd like an advance of one thousand dollars so I can buy some clothes at the exchange and perhaps some gifts for my wife and children."

"My secretary has your orders detailing who and where you are to report to; I'll tell her to put an advance of one thousand in the orders. Go back to personnel; they'll issue you an ID Card. Jones will escort you during your out processing; over to finance, personnel, the exchange and then, to the plane. Welcome home, Captain." Martin got to his feet and saluted Larry. It was December 15th, 1973; he'd be home for Christmas.

Chapter 13

Just after Thanksgiving, which she and Walter shared with her children and parents, Jean and Walter decided to visit Las Vegas to gamble and have some alone time. They planned to fly in early one day and fly back out late the next. Both checked their schedules and found that the 15th and 16th of December would work for them. They'd been dating for nearly ten months and planned to marry after her divorce was final, which was sometime in February of the following year.

Their non-stop flight from Greenville landed in Vegas at one in the afternoon. Jean couldn't help but put two dollars' worth of quarters in the slot machines at the airport. As they walked to the baggage claim area, she spied a flowered dress in the window of one of the many boutique shops in the airport.

"Come on Walter, I've got to try on that dress. I have some nice clothes, but nothing for dinner and a show tonight."

Walter looked at his watch, but reluctantly followed her into the store. The pink and blue dress with a round neckline fit her perfectly. The saleswoman started to wrap it up and Walter moved to the checkout station, but Jean told him she needed a dress for the hospital Christmas party. She spied a simple black dress and immediately fell in love with it; she purchased some imitation pearls to go with it. She was laughing and almost dancing while holding onto Walter's arm as they took a taxi to the hotel.

It was three o'clock by the time they checked into the Desert Inn Hotel. Walter was unusually quiet on the ride to the strip. After they checked in, they went to their room and ordered a bottle of champagne. When it arrived, Walter opened the bottle, grabbed two glasses and dragged a small table out to the balcony. They were up four floors. "What's the matter, Walter? You've been so quiet since we landed."

"It's really nothing. I just hate shopping. Here's to you, the future Mrs. Osborne." They clicked glasses and sat down.

"I checked with the concierges and took the liberty of reserving two tickets at the Flamingo's ten o'clock show. I also knew you liked prime rib so I made reservations at the Copper Kettle for eight. The question is, what are we going to do between now and then?"

Jean stood up, unzipped her dress, which fell down around her ankles, and kicked off her shoes. She was wearing only her panties. "Does this give you any ideas?"

Her gesture seemed to break the spell Walter was under and he sprang into action. He put the champagne and glasses on the small table and moved it inside. He grabbed two blankets from the closet and placed them on the balcony floor. He picked Jean up and laid her on the blankets, took off his clothes, and lay on top of her. "I'll have to take my dress off more often if that's the reaction I'm going to get." Jean laughed.

Occasionally, when she was making love to Walter, her thoughts would wander to the other man she was intimate with. She accepted the fact that he was dead but she worried that he'd suffered and a tear would come to her eyes. Although she loved Walter, he could never be her first love. The remainder of their stay was filled with food, champagne and love making. It truly was a weekend for lovers. They held hands during the entire flight home.

"I've got an operation at ten tomorrow and I'm exhausted. Do you mind if I go to my home alone tonight?" Jean asked.

"No. It's not a problem. I'll drop you off and see you tomorrow at work." Jean squeezed his hand.

They exited baggage claim and found his car. She sat next to him on the way home with her hand resting on his thigh. He drove into her driveway and got her bag out of the trunk. "Do you want me to see you inside?"

"I'm fine, Walter." They embraced and he gave her as passionate a kiss as she ever had. "I love you, Jean."

Chapter 14

His **overnight** bag was full of gifts for his family. In addition, Larry purchased a Class A service uniform and an overcoat and put them on; he knew it'd be cold in DC. He was surprised that there wasn't a military flight heading to the States but that thought was quickly erased from his mind when the stewardess moved him from economy to first class. The food and service were great but he abstained from the free liquor that was offered. He wondered if he'd revert to his pre-Vietnam days when he enjoyed a couple of high balls or if would he practice the Buddhist Religion and abstain from alcohol. The biggest issue he had on this flight was the comfortable seat; he couldn't get accustomed to such luxury. His itinerary was to fly from Ubon to Seattle and then Dallas, before connecting to the flight to Washington, DC. He was again upgraded to first class on the Seattle to Dallas leg.

As he walked off the plane in Dallas, he glanced at the departure board and saw that he had a six-hour layover before his flight to DC. His eyes instinctively swung further down the board. There was a flight to Greenville, Mississippi in one hour. It didn't take him long to make up his mind. He found the United Air Line counter and asked to have his itinerary changed to a round trip ticket to Greenville with a connecting flight through Dallas to DC, which left at three-thirty tomorrow afternoon. The charge was an additional seventy-five dollars.

His anxiety level was high. He was close to Jean and the children and he couldn't wait. Whatever was waiting for him in Washington could be dealt with later. The flight was a little over an hour long before he was on the ground, catching a taxi to the address Colonel Martin had given him. The taxi driver, looking for a generous tip, pointed out all the landmarks from the airport to the Greenville center. It was about seven in the evening when they pulled up in front of a two-story white clapboard house; the name Stephens was on the mailbox at the curb. Larry was somewhat stunned at the price the meter read; he'd been gone a long time.

There were no lights on in the house and no one answered the bell. He went around the side and opened the gate to the backyard. The slider to the kitchen was unlocked and he went in. He called out the names of his wife and children and when there was no answer, he went to the front door. Mail was lying on the floor along with a telegram. He opened it and saw the notification that the Pentagon had sent Jean, telling her he was alive. The amount of mail indicated she'd been gone for about two days. He didn't care, he was finally home.

All three bedrooms were upstairs. Susanne's was decorated in pink. Larry Junior's in blue and his and Jean's was painted white. He went downstairs, opened the refrigerator and took out a Coke. He sat in the dark in the living room, drinking the soft drink, and thinking of all the things they would do together now that he was home. He knew his Air Force Career was over. And though he had no idea what he'd do in the future, he felt comfortable in his decision. He'd resign when he got to the Pentagon tomorrow. He found her parent's number in the phone book and called, but there was no answer. Perhaps they were all together. He turned on the TV but couldn't get interested in local news, so he turned it off and sat in the dark, waiting.

It was eleven o'clock when he heard a car pull into the driveway. It stopped but its lights were still on. He looked out the front window and could see it was a sedan. A woman opened the passenger door, embraced and kissed a man who handed her an overnight bag and then walked toward the front door. She opened the front door, set down her bag and started picking up the mail that had accumulated inside. She didn't hear Larry come up behind her, but she stiffened when he put his arm around her waist and his other hand over her mouth. "Please don't cry out, Jean. It's Larry; I'm alive and I'm home for good."

Jean starting to struggle by backing up, bending over, striking out with her heels and twisting her body in an attempt to free herself. Larry put his head next to hers and pushed her against the wall so she couldn't strike out at him. "Jean, its Larry. I'll let you go but please don't scream. Don't be shocked at my appearance; I'm really your husband."

He released his grip and backed up. As soon as he released her, she turned and swung at him and then tried to kick him. He continued to back up as she screamed. "You son-of-a-bitch, get the hell out of here before I call the cops"

"Jean, its Larry, your husband. Please calm down."

She flipped on the light switch and he could see the terror in her eyes as she tried to equate what he said with what she could see. "My husband is dead. You don't look anything like my husband; now get the hell out of here." She started to move toward the phone.

"I've lost forty pounds, shaved my head and darkened my skin. I had to in order to survive these past four plus years.

"Liar, I would've been notified if you were alive."

The telegram is on the telephone table. He picked it up and handed it to her. "You haven't been home. It was put in the mail slot when they couldn't reach you. There's also a note from a chaplain who came here to give you the news." He handed her the note.

As she read the telegram and the Chaplain's note, she started to sob hysterically. Larry tried to put his arm around her but she shrugged it off, pushed him away and sat down in one of the living room chairs. "Just because Larry's alive, it doesn't mean it's you."

He took out his ID card and handed it to her. "This was issued at Ubon, Thailand yesterday. The picture is me and the name is Larry Stephens. They wouldn't have issued it if they didn't confirm that I'm who I say I am."

She continued to look at the ID card and up at him. "Oh my God, what am I going to do? I waited so long, but you didn't come back. When they released all those men last February, I lost faith. Please forgive me Larry, I lost faith. My mother and children have to be told."

"I believe they know. There're several messages on the phone from your mother. She was notified by the chaplain. Where are the children? I want to see them so badly."

"They're with my mother; they've been with her for two days while I was away. I know you don't want to hear this but I filed for divorce two months ago. It should be final in February. I've also been seeing someone; we just got back from a two day trip together." Jean started to cry again

"Was that the man who kissed you outside?"

"Yes. I'm weak Larry. I was unfaithful to you with this man. You put up with all the hardship and returned home to a wife who wasn't true to you. I'm so ashamed."

He reached out and touched her hand and she pulled away. "Jean, I don't care about the infidelity unless it's a permanent thing. I still love you but the real question is, do you still love me enough to continue with our marriage?"

"I honestly don't know. I never thought a day would come when I didn't jump into your arms and beg you to hold me if you came back. I need some time to sort all this out. I've been seeing Walter for nearly a year."

"Do you love him?"

"I told him I did."

They sat for thirty minutes looking at each other in the dim light, without speaking. "I think I need a drink; what do you say?" Jean asked.

"I haven't had any liquor for so long I don't know what's available these days."

"I'll fix us a couple of Scotch and waters."

"There are some other things you need to know. While you were gone, I completed medical school and my internship here in Greenville. Since September, I've been a resident physician at the hospital here; I'm Doctor Stephens to them. I didn't save much of your salary while you were gone. I felt guilty living off your pay while you were a POW, so I've started placing some in a savings account. It would pass to the children if you didn't come back. Were you beaten while you were in captivity?"

"A little, and I was shot twice. Once, soon after I was captured, and recently, while I was trying to evade capture."

You had the bullets taken out, didn't you?"

"No."

"Let me see them."

He took off his uniform shirt and Jean could see how thin he was but muscular at the same time. He pointed to the two marks and she carefully probed his shoulder and could see the discoloration and swelling. "The bullet is still in there."

"Yes. The one near my heart is there, as well."

She felt around the scar and her fingers found where the bullet was. "Those need to be x-rayed and, if possible, taken out immediately. I want to set up an appointment so we can have those taken care of by tomorrow."

"I've got to go to Washington tomorrow for a debriefing. If it's okay with you, I'll come back as soon as possible and have them removed."

"How did you get shot?"

"The one near my heart happened within a few days of my capture. I was shot while trying to escape. A monk did his best to heal the wound; in fact he saved my life. The second happened less than forty days ago while I was evading capture in Laos. Unlike the first, I didn't receive much medical attention for the shoulder wound. A village medic gave me some opium to handle the pain and did a nice job of bandaging the wound."

"You mean your captors shot you and didn't try to heal the wound."

"They were mad at me. I broke one soldier's nose and another's arm. I guess they thought I'd be easier to control if I was wounded."

"I'll bet they got a surprise. Are you still on opium?"

No, after the first dose, I declined any more." Jean smiled.

"I don't know how much I want to tell you about where I was and what happened to me after I was shot down. The less you know would be better for you and the children. There're a lot of people who are praying that I don't divulge where I was during the past four and one half years; their lives would definitely be in jeopardy. I don't even know how much I can tell the people in Washington."

"You didn't desert, did you?'

"No Jean, I did not desert. I lived with some people while I was gone."

"With a woman?"

"No, I've been celibate the entire time."

"Do you have a place to stay tonight?"

"I was hoping that I could stay here. If that's a problem, I'll call a cab and go to a hotel."

"No. Though I don't know how to deal with our situation, you certainly can stay here. I just don't want to be forced into facing reality at this time. I need time to think. This happened so fast."

"Did you keep any of my uniforms and civilian clothes?"

"I kept everything. I always thought you were coming back; at least until this past year. They're in the hall closet." Jean pointed to the door under the stairs.

"How did you escape and travel all that distance?"

"Well that's another story. I'm kind of tired. I've been up over twenty-four hours. I wonder if we can continue this discussion in the morning. I fly out tomorrow afternoon at three-thirty; we should have plenty of time in the morning. I hope I can see the children before I leave?"

Larry walked over and opened the closet door and saw his Class A service uniform. He took the coat out of the plastic bag and off the hanger and went into the bathroom and tried it on. It was several sizes too large. He did the same thing with his civilian jacket. It was equally big but looked better. "It's a good thing I bought some new clothes in Thailand. The old clothes won't fit for another year."

"I have your underwear and socks boxed up. We'll get them out tomorrow. I believe that you're my husband but I don't recognize you at all."

"I gather you don't want to sleep in the same bed, but could I at least have a hug and a kiss before we retire tonight? I really missed you; I've waited so long to come home."

She walked over to him and put her arms around him and kissed him. "All I could think about for months was that kiss. I pray that there would be more in the future. Where do you want me to sleep?" Larry asked.

Jean led the way up the stairs and switched on the light to their son's room. "There's a connecting bathroom with new toothbrushes and combs under the sink. The bed is small, but I think you'll find it comfortable."

Sleeping in a strange place was nothing new to Larry, but sleeping in a room next to his wife, whom he'd rushed home to be with, was uncomfortable. He couldn't sleep. He wondered what he could do to resolve the situation. He watched as the hours passed on the clock on the nightstand next to him. It was three in the morning when Jean came into his room and crawled into bed with him. "I don't want to make love, but could you please hold me like you used to?"

She was barely five foot two inches tall and weighed one hundred five pounds. He put out his arms and she lay on top of him with her face in the crook of his neck. He didn't sleep that night. For the entire time he was away, he thought about this moment. He wasn't sure there'd be another so he wanted to savor it as long as he could. They rose at seven, and while he was taking a shower and shaving, she made him breakfast. "I'll take you to the plane this afternoon. We should get there at least an hour before takeoff. If you need some money we can stop at the bank on the way."

"Thank you. I remember the omelets you made when we were first married. It's funny what things you think about when you're in captivity."

"You said you weren't a POW."

"That's true, but for all practical purposes, I was confined for the first year while North Vietnamese soldiers were searching for me. Subsequently, I had more freedom to walk around the grounds, but the searches continued. I built three hiding places on the grounds where I was staying. Two worked very well, but one was discovered while I was occupying it. I barely escaped into a lake. That close call told me I needed to leave and make my way home. About eight months ago, I began making my way home."

"Why didn't you try to leave earlier?"

"I hadn't mastered the language nor did I have a plan to evade. I think the North Vietnamese relaxed a little after the Armistice was signed. If I tried to leave earlier, I would have been recaptured and perhaps never released. I caused them to lose face, so to speak. The commander of the Hanoi District has made it his mission to capture me. He may try even after I'm separated from the service."

"Do you speak Vietnamese?"

"Fluently."

"You look so strange. I know you don't want to discuss some things, but there's an air of serenity about you, one that I'd not seen before. You seem to have taken the situation with my lover as calm as you could be. How do you explain that?"

"He hesitated for a few minutes, trying to decide whether to tell her. "I feel that I'm on trial with you and don't want to tell you everything for fear it will scare you and the children off. While I was gone, I converted to Buddhism. In fact, I've functioned as a monk for several years, conducting wedding ceremonies and funerals. Many of the villages I entered on the way home had need of spiritual services. I tried to provide those."

"Will you continue practicing that religion?"

"I believe I will. It should have no impact on you or the children."

"You're so thin, your hair is gone and the pallor of your skin looks as though you're ill. Pardon me, Larry, but the doctor in me is looking at you. I would never recognize you had you not told me who you were. As I look at you now, I would think you're of oriental descent."

"I used tea leaves to change the color of my skin so I could pass as a Vietnamese."

"How did you survive on your walk home?"

"I begged for food and, basically, traded Buddhists ceremonies for food, shelter and in some cases, clothing."

Jean started to cry and he put his arm around her and held her to him. The old feeling that had been put aside for almost four years was surfacing, but she soon recovered and stood up. "What happened to the other flier?"

"He was killed during bailout. Wasn't his kin notified?"

"Not that I'm aware of."

"I must tell the authorities how he died."

"So you weren't captured?"

"I was captured by villagers and handed over to the North Vietnamese soldiers but I escaped and hid out."

"Is that when you were shot?"

"Yes."

"Did you kill anyone?"

"No, I was able to evade most encounters during my seven month trek to safety; however, I did injure four or five soldiers." Jean smiled; she remembered how lethal Larry could be.

A car pulled into the driveway and a man got out and walked up to the front door and knocked. "Oh shit, it's Walter. I rescheduled an operation I had at ten this morning. He must have come over to see if I was alright" Jean said.

"Let him in." Larry directed.

Jean looked at Larry as though to disagree, but she walked to the front door and opened it for Doctor Walter Osborne who embraced Jean and quickly stopped. He looked at Larry and turned to Jean. "Who the hell is this?"

"This is my husband, Larry Stephens."

"You must be kidding. He's dead. You said he was."

"He escaped from Vietnam and came home to his family. Have a seat."

"Does he know about us?"

"Yes."

Larry stood, stepped away from the table and put out his hand. "I'm Larry Stephens. Have a seat. We might as well get to know each other. It may take time to sort through this situation." Walter ignored the hand.

"It should sort out next month. Jean has filed for divorce, so the sooner you're on your way, the quicker the situation will be resolved," Osborne said.

"Walter, you're in my house and you won't speak to my husband that way. It's possible that I may go through with the divorce, but it's not your decision; it's mine and I'd appreciate it if you'd remember that from this moment on."

"I love Jean very much and she's agreed to marry me," Walter said.

"I didn't know that but Jean was left to fend for herself when I was shot down. I've always trusted her judgment. A person can get lonely waiting for a spouse who's been gone as long as I was. I'm not one to judge the choices she made." Larry responded.

Walter let his temper get the best of him and swung at Larry who stepped back, took Walter's arm and pulled it toward him so that Walter rushed forward, stumbled and fell on his stomach. Larry turned quickly to the fallen man. "Please don't get up just yet. I want you to promise that there'll be no further violence on your part."

Walter ignored the threat and started to rise. Larry kicked his hands out from under him and Walter fell on his stomach and hit his chin. He started to rise once more but thought the better of it. "I'm okay. I got angry. I apologize and won't try anything else."

Jean smiled. You really are my husband. I saw that maneuver on one of our dates when that thug tried to take your wallet. "Walter, my husband is an expert in hand-to-hand defense, as you just found out."

Walter smiled. "Thanks for telling me too late. You led me to believe that your husband was a robust man. This guy looks anemic."

"Larry was wounded twice, once four years ago and again, about a month ago. He still has two bullets in him. He had medical attention for the first but not for the second. I want him operated on immediately; he wants to wait until he comes back from Washington."

"Do you think it's wise to put off the operation?" Jean asked Walter.

"Do you want me to take a look?" Walter asked.

"It's okay. When I come back is time enough." Larry said.

"Time is running out. Please call your mother and have the children come over. I must see them before I fly to the capitol."

Jean went to make the call. "Why are you flying to Washington?" Walter asked.

"I have to report for my debriefing at the Pentagon. They want to know where I've been for almost four years."

"Are you coming back here after your debriefing?"

"Jean seems ambivalent about our relationship, so I'm going to let her decide what she wants and I'll accept her decision."

"Where were you a POW?" Walter asked.

"I'd rather not discuss the issue now, if you don't mind," Larry said.

Thirty minutes later he was reunited with his children and in-laws. The children were apprehensive and didn't want to make eye contact. Larry didn't look like the father they remembered. "Perhaps we could go for a short walk. I think your mother wants to talk to Walter."

They walked down to the corner where there was a coffee and donut shop. "Let's go in here and get something to eat and drink, if you wish."

Larry Junior was the first to speak. "Can you tell us what happened?"

"I was shot down over North Vietnam and, just as I was about to be rescued, I was grabbed by some villagers, beaten and put in a cage. They turned me over to North Vietnamese soldiers the next morning and I was transported by truck toward Hanoi. While I was in the back of the truck, guarded by one of the soldiers, I freed my hands and subdued the guard. The two soldiers in the front heard a noise and came back to investigate. When they opened the canvas flap at the rear of the truck, I knocked both out and escaped. I hid out with some Vietnamese for three years and learned to speak their language. For the past seven months I've been walking home. I must fly to Washington this afternoon, report to my commander and tell him where I've been since I was shot down."

"Are you hurt? You seem so thin and your hair is gone." Susanne said.

"My hair will grow back and I'll gain weight now that I'm home and can have some good home cooking."

"Dad, do you know about Walter?" Larry Junior asked.

"I just found out. I also know about the divorce. I don't know how you feel about all of this but your mother was placed in a very awkward position after I was shot down. She had to work and raise two children; she was lonely. Many people, including her mother, told her I was dead. Don't be hard on her. It will all sort out eventually. I just want you to know that I thought about you two all the time and I love you very much. I plan to resign my commission and come back to Greenville so I can be near you two. Your mother has a right to determine if she wants to be my wife again or go a different direction."

Walter Osborne asked Jean if they could have a moment alone. They stepped into the backyard, closed the kitchen door behind them, and sat in the swing Walter helped her buy. Jean started to cry and Walter put his arm around her shoulders. There was a small breeze in the air.

This situation is a mess. How are we going to resolve it?" Walter asked.

"I don't know. Everything seemed so simple yesterday." Jean replied.

"Do you still love me?" he asked.

"Yes. In spite of the ass you made out of yourself, I really do. But I'll always love Larry, too. Do you understand?"

"Not really."

"Well just reverse the roles for a minute. If you had to make this decision, what would you do.?"

Walter wrapped his arms around her and kissed her passionately; Jean returned his passion. "I trust you, Jean that, you'll make the right decision. What do you want me to do?" Walter asked.

"Have patience with me. He's leaving for Washington today, so I'll have a few days to think this thing through. When he comes back, I'll make my decision. I owe it to him to help him through this ordeal."

When Walter left, Jean's mother joined her in the kitchen. Jean was sitting in the nook and her mother sat down across from her. "You're not going to dump Walter for the husband you haven't seen in four years. You'll be making a big mistake. Walter seems like such a caring individual. Think this out," her mother said.

"Thank you for your opinion but I didn't ask for it. My relationships with Larry and Walter is my business."

Larry and the two children walked back to the house and joined Jean and her mother in the kitchen; Susanne was holding his hand. Walter had left, but his in-laws were still around. "What did those people do to you, Larry?" his mother-in-law asked.

"Nothing, other than giving me a chance to live and come back home."

"You didn't desert or anything like that, did you, Larry?"

"No, but since both you and Jean asked me that question, I think I'll be asked that many more times. I was kept by people who I can't identify for fear that they will be persecuted, imprisoned or even killed."

"What do you think about Jean's affair with Walter?"

"Mother!"

Before the mother could respond, Larry answered. "That's between Jean and me, and I won't judge her. I've always valued her judgment. She was placed in an awkward situation, not of her own choosing. I want her back, but it's her decision. I love you and your husband as though you are my parents, but this is the last time we'll discuss this issue. I don't want you pressing Jean for a decision; let her make it on her own. Now if you'll excuse me, I have to get ready to leave."

He changed into his Class A service uniform. The children hadn't seen him dressed in his military uniform. Larry Junior wanted to know about his medals; both kids wanted a picture with him. He, Jean and the two children drove to the bank; she went inside with him.

"Do you have a safety deposit box at this bank?" he asked.

"Yes, do you need to get into it?"

Larry had written a detailed account of his capture and escape, naming names and places. He wanted that kept in a safe place if anything happened to him. "For all our married life I trusted you. I still trust you. I want you to put this envelope in the box and not tell anyone about it. If something should happen to me, you may look at it."

"You're scaring me, Larry. Are you in trouble?"

"I won't know until I go to the Pentagon. Can you do this for me?"

Jean took the envelope, went downstairs and came back in ten minutes. Here's a thousand dollars. If you want more, just ask. I owe you a lot."

At the airport, Susanne cried when she kissed him and made him promise to come back. His son hugged him and Jean shook his hand. He left them after he checked in. As he was about to hand his boarding pass to the stewardess, he heard people running behind him. He turned as all three came up and hugged him again. Jean kissed him passionately and hung on to him and Susanne cried. "Please come back home, daddy."

"Yes, please come home," Jean said as she squeezed his arm.

Chapter 15

Since his conversion to Buddhism, Larry's didn't react to annoying things as he did in the past. His time at the Pagoda gave him a new perspective on life and the Vietnamese people. But how would he react in a world that was fast paced and achievement oriented? He knew he could never return to Vietnam, but he felt a bond with the people in the villages. What started out as a means of escape became something he didn't want to exclude from his life. The situation with Jean was something he thought about while he was in hiding. She may not want to relinquish the role of 'Head of Household' that she'd filled for the past four years and share it with him, or anyone. What if she wanted to move on with her life, which was entirely possible; what would he do? Certainly, the way he felt about his religion would have a bearing on that. The abbot had told him about the Buddhists in America. He didn't know if he wanted to be a monk but he did want to be involved in the religion and at a Temple, if possible.

This debriefing was something that needed to be completed; he didn't fear it, it seemed to be part of the process of coming home. At the same time, he knew there could be problems. It was going to be hard to explain where he was for over four years, especially since he wouldn't tell them who hid him. To an outsider, his intent to shield his benefactor could be viewed as self-serving and, therefore, not credible. It was a matter of trust. If he felt that his source could be protected, he'd share his information readily. The question would be, how could he determine who to trust?

His conscience was bothering him about the forged letter on the Temple's letterhead that he used to make his way out of Vietnam. If his pursuers in Vietnam knew his name, they'd had access to his ID card and the letter identifying the Pagoda of Tran Quoc. He was sure the authorities had visited the Temple and questioned the abbot. Larry had seen the abbot's signature, so when he forged the letter he made sure that he didn't try to replicate the man's handwriting. If anything happened to the abbot because of the letter, Larry would never forgive himself. He wanted to try to communicate with the abbot to let him know that he made it home but that would be folly and be tantamount to putting a noose around the holy man's neck.

His plane landed at seven in the evening, DC time; it was snowing and two inches had accumulated on the ground. Prior to going to a hotel, he stopped at the USO room in the airport, showed his ID card and asked to see a telephone directory. He made a list of law firms in the greater Washington area and then took a cab to his hotel in downtown Washington. After checking in, he went to the restaurant on the tenth floor and ordered dinner. It had stopped snowing and he could see the lights of the city from his table. He was proud to be an American and happy to be home, but he couldn't help but think about tomorrow. He was supposed to report today but the day after tomorrow was closer to reality and that's if he found an attorney who would represent him.

The bed was comfortable but he couldn't sleep; he didn't know why. He was safe; no one knew where he was, or did they. Larry wondered how long it would take before his paranoia vanished and he wouldn't see an enemy around every corner. He called the attorneys on his list at nine the next morning. On the sixth call, he found one he hoped would be suitable. He arranged for a meeting with Amos Frank that afternoon at his office on Jefferson Street.

Normally, the issue of reporting when ordered would be significant, but he didn't think it would matter in the main scheme of things. He picked up a newspaper and a soft drink from one of the street vendors and then took a cab to meet the attorney. The firm's office was located on the sixth floor of a twelve story building on the corner of Jefferson and Center Street. The woman sitting in the modest reception area took his name, called Frank's secretary, and asked Larry to be seated. "Mr. Frank will be with you shortly," she said.

Soon he was escorted down the hall by Mr. Frank's secretary; she asked if he wanted something to drink, he declined. Amos Frank was a man of about sixty years of age, slight of build, moderately short with hawkish features and gray hair; he wore a bright bow tie. Frank rose from his desk and greeted Larry. "Sit down young man and tell me what trouble you're in and I'll see if I can help you."

"Is it true that everything I say stays with you alone?"

"Unless there's a crime committed, everything you say is confidential and I can't repeat it. Tell me why you're here."

Two hours later, Larry sat back and waited for Frank to ask questions. During his entire narrative, Frank didn't ask any questions; he just took notes. "What are your plans for the future, Captain?"

"I want to separate from the service as soon as possible and see if I can salvage my marriage. Beyond that, I haven't thought about what the future may have in store for me."

"How vulnerable is the Abbot of the Tran Quoc Pagoda?"

"It's imperative that he not be identified. His brother-in-law is General Tran, the commander of the Hanoi District. Tran wants to bring him down in the worst way."

"Could he still be an avenue to the power structure in the north?"

"He might prove to be valuable if we could take some of the heat off him."

"When do you intend to take care of the two bullets you're carrying around in your body?"

"My wife is a surgeon. I believe she's making plans to operate on me at her hospital as soon as I return."

"I think it's best the military know about the bullets up front and under what circumstances you were shot. It will reduce some of the concern about you deserting." Frank said.

"That's a good point. My wife and mother-in-law asked if I deserted. If they think that way, imagine what the debriefer will think."

"Are you sure you can find the POW Camp near the Laotian Border?" Frank asked.

"Yes."

"What about the Russian installation?"

"I don't think so. One of the chiefs seemed to think it was about ten miles away from the POW Compound, but I didn't see or hear the helicopters the chiefs saw. None of the villagers that I talked to had been there."

"Let's hold that information back. I want to see who's going to give you a bad time and who seems to believe your story. Other than the abbot's name, the Russian base and your stay at the Pagoda, you should be forthright and answer all questions candidly.

"I'll call the JAG Office and let them know we're available at one tomorrow afternoon. I know what your orders say, but we can handle the three-day delay. I'll need some time to prepare for our meeting. Don't worry; I'll keep you out of trouble. If you're uncertain about any question, take your time before responding. I'll get you through this. Be at the west entrance of the Pentagon tomorrow at twelve forty-five. Go to your hotel and get a good night's sleep and above all, don't worry."

He'd made hotel reservations for only one night, so he called Andrews Air Force Base from Frank's office and asked about the room availability for a field grade officer; he was in luck. He took a cab to the Visiting Officer's Quarters at Andrews and went to the officer's club for dinner. Next morning, he called a cab and went to visit the Supreme Court. He was in awe of the small chamber where constitutional law was debated and made. After visiting the Jefferson and Washington Monuments, he took a cab to the Pentagon. Mr. Frank was sitting on one of the benches near the west door.

Since she'd been gone for a week, Dr. Jean Stephens decided to go into the hospital to see what her schedule would be for the next week. She was talking to one of the nurses on the second floor when Walter Osborne came down the hall. "Doctor Stephens, could I have a minute of your time in my office?" The nurse smiled. It wasn't a secret that Jean and Walter were going to be married.

Jean followed him down the hall to his office and closed the door behind her. "I haven't much time, I have three operations today."

Osborne frowned but didn't push the issue; he decided to whisper. "I want to talk about us. I felt our relationship was great and then your husband showed up. I'm concerned that he's going to foul everything up. You mean everything to me."

Walter put his arm around her waist; Jean kissed him on the lips. "I know you want to know my decision but I haven't had time to think. Please Walter, give me time." She hugged him and left his office.

Chapter 16

Larry Stephens wasn't sure what awaited him at the Pentagon. Over his four years of evasion, he never gave this aspect of his journey a second thought. He focused on escaping and anything else was immaterial, but he was still on active duty and subject to military justice, whatever that was. There were six men and a woman waiting for them in a second-floor conference room at the Pentagon. Each had a nameplate on the table in front of where they sat. Colonel French and Captain Foster were Air Force Officers. Two men, Mr. Ridley and Mr. Jones were from the State Department and two others, a Mr. Higgins and a Mr. Minh were from the CIA. The woman, Claire Goodwin, was the stenographer. The room was austere with just chairs and the table in the room. An Air Policeman was stationed outside the door, which was closed.

Colonel French chaired the meeting and asked Larry to stand and be sworn in. Mr. Frank grabbed Larry's arm. "No one is going to be sworn in until you tell my client what the purpose of this meeting is and what the agenda is," Amos Frank said.

"This is a debriefing of Captain Stephens who's been MIA for nearly four years. This panel wants him to take an oath to tell the truth," French responded.

Frank produced Larry's orders. "I don't see anything in these orders he received that indicates he's on trial for anything. Have you issued new orders that Captain Stephens hasn't been given?"

"No."

"I can see what your intent is Colonel, but I won't let my client be sworn in for a debriefing that may be an interrogation, as a prelude to a trial. You have your Senior Jag attorney present. The only thing I can deduce is that you intend to put Captain Stephens on trial for something."

"This is standard procedure in situations such as this."

"Not true Colonel. If you wanted to debrief the Captain, it would have been done at Ubon when he reported in. No sir, this is some form of interrogation to see if you want to prefer charges. I think we need to conduct a debriefing, but he's not required to be under oath. Just so you gentlemen and ladies know my background, I've been a practicing attorney in DC, Virginia, Maryland, and Pennsylvania for around thirty years. Prior to that time, I was a Lieutenant in the Army, assigned to the JAG office for two years, with the primary responsibility of debriefing POWs and MIAs from the Second World War. I'm quite familiar with these procedures."

Colonel French turned to Captain Foster, the JAG Representative. "Perhaps we should have a brief recess. Captain Stephens and Mr. Frank, will you please step out of the room for a few minutes? We'll call you when we reconvene."

While they were outside, Frank wanted to be sure that Larry was comfortable. "Mr. Frank, I've faced worse than this continually for four years. Anything they could do to me pales in comparison to what the NVA has tried. I'm not the least bit worried. I think they came into this debriefing with an agenda and you made them rethink their game plan. I'm confident with you."

Ten minutes later they were called back into the room. "We'll do the debriefing without a swearing-in unless we feel that the information Captain Stephens tells us is incorrect." Colonel French said.

"One more thing before we begin. I see that we have a lady who's functioning as a court reporter. What do you intend to do with the transcript?" Frank asked.

"We intend to review it to see if there are any other issues that need to be addressed by Captain Stephens, then we'll file it away."

"I want to be able to review the original transcript before any additions or deletions are made to that document," Frank responded.

"Agreed," Colonel French responded.

"Make that agreement part of the official record."

Colonel French made the statement to the recorder and directed Captain Foster to begin the questioning. "In your own words, will you tell this panel as much as you can remember from the time you took off on June 5th 1969 to the time you showed up at Ubon in December 1973?"

Larry did his best to cover his capture, his evasion, his wounds and his journey out of the country. When asked about his return route, Frank produced a map showing the route Larry took to escape.

"How did you pick these particular villages?"

"When I was planning my escape route, I had an advisor who'd traveled the area and knew the villages. He felt that these villages would be the least likely to turn me over to the authorities."

"Who was this advisor?"

"I'm afraid I cannot divulge his name for fear that he would receive reprisals from the North Vietnamese."

"Was he a senior official in the north?"

"I'm sorry but I can't answer that question."

"I find it hard to believe that you could evade the enemy for seven months while you journeyed through their country. No one before you was able to accomplish the feat," Ridley from State spoke up.

"I was given food and water at some of these villages which are off the beaten path. But I didn't evade the enemy the entire time. I was captured, shot and tied up before I managed to escape."

"Where were you captured?"

Frank produced the map and Larry pointed to the approximate location where he was shot, captured and then escaped, both times he was shot. "So you had a bullet in you the second time and made your escape from four soldiers. You had to be very lucky."

"Yes, I was lucky. I was found by a group of Hmong, taken to their village and cared for by one of their medical people. I stayed with them for two weeks and then continued my journey home."

"Where is their village located?"

Larry used the same map and indicated approximately where the village was located. "Can't you tell us exactly where they're located?"

"That's the best I can do, but why not ask the CIA people at this table. The Hmong were assets of the CIA during the secret war in Laos. The chief of that village indicated that his people are still waiting for the aid promised by the CIA."

Ridley turned to the CIA men at the table but they declined to add any more information than Larry had.

Ridley wasn't sold. "What did you do for the people in the villages you visited who gave you food, water and shelter?"

Larry hesitated. "I fixed some things that were broken, such as a roof."

"Not one of our airmen who tried to evade the enemy was successful. You had to have help and I don't believe any of the villages you pointed to could give you that help. You say the four soldiers that were pursuing you were North Vietnamese. Why did they pick you out?" Ridley asked.

"I'm not positive how they knew who I was. I'd saved my ID card but it was stolen from me by three thugs. The authorities may have intercepted it and put two and two together."

"That's a long shot at best. Did you come across other NVA?" Ridley asked.

"Yes, several times, but I evaded them."

"You traveled nearly four hundred fifty miles with soldiers following you, through three countries and were never captured."

"Sir, you must have missed that part of my statement. I was shot and captured by four Vietnamese Soldiers on my way home. After four days I escaped."

"You initially escaped from three soldiers after you were shot down and ten NVA in Laos. Who are you, superman?"

"Sir, six of the NVA were guarding the rope bridges from Laos to Thailand. Although they fired at me, their fate was decided by members of a wedding party after one of them was shot."

"Okay, okay but four soldiers, by your own words, had you tied to a stretcher and yet you immobilized two of them. I find that hard to swallow."

"While I was being subdued by the four, I broke the arm of one of their soldiers. Subsequently they tied me to the stretcher. My legs were tied together but not to the stretcher. As soon as I got the chance, I struck out with both legs and broke the jaw of another soldier."

"It sounds more like a Hollywood script rather than real life," Ridley was going to have the last word.

Just then Mr. Minh spoke to Larry in Vietnamese. The others in the room were startled and turned to look at the CIA man. He asked Larry for the village chief's name in the first village he stopped at on his way home. Larry was caught by surprise and looked at Amos Frank, who nodded that Larry could tell them. He responded to the CIA man in fluent Vietnamese.

"You speak Vietnamese?" Colonel French asked. Larry nodded yes.

"You were able to follow this route because you're fluent in their language but that doesn't answer Colonel French's question. What did you do for the villagers that made them want to feed you?' Minh persisted. Larry shrugged.

Minh asked the question two more times and, in each case, Larry refused to answer. The CIA representative changed his tactic. "What are the three universal truths of Buddhism?"

Larry responded quickly in Vietnamese, "Nothing is lost in the Universe, Everything Changes and there's a Law of Cause and Effect."

Minh smiled. "I know where you were for three years, I know how you interfaced with the villagers and I know what you did for them."

"Mr. Minh, please tell the rest of us what is being said." French asked.

"Like Mr. Ridley, I came into this meeting doubting Captain Stephen's account of his survival. As I listened to him tell the story, I decided to take a different tact and put myself in his place. I asked myself how I could evade the enemy in a very hostile country. To accomplish an escape from North Vietnam, three things are necessary. I have to speak the language. I have to do something that would incentivize the villagers to cooperate with me and give me food. And third, I would have to disguise my appearance."

"Mr. Stephens is fluent in Vietnamese. Obviously, he was taught the language while he was evading the enemy. To travel through three countries on foot in seven months, one would have to be fluent in one of the local languages. Second, a Caucasian couldn't accomplish this feat even if he spoke the language. Captain Stephens had to disguise himself somehow. You can see by the pallor of his skin that he looks more Asian than Caucasian. There are many natural things that can darken one's skin. My guess is that he posed as a soldier, a physician or a holy man. A soldier would incite fear and the villages would only cooperate to a point and then complain to higher authorities. A solitary soldier would probably be seen as a deserter and the villagers would turn him over to the first soldiers they encountered. A physician would definitely be an aid to the villages, but then again, Stephens would have to get his medical training somewhere in Vietnam while trying to evade the enemy; it's possible, but unlikely."

"Look at a picture of Captain Stephens before he was shot down. He passed copies of Larry's picture around the room. I reviewed his file before this meeting. He had a full head of hair and a one hundred eighty pound physique when he bailed out. The Captain Stephens here today has his head shaved. With a loss of forty pounds, he fits the profile of the ordinary Vietnamese. My guess is that Captain Stephens has been shielded by a religions group for the three years in question, most probably Buddhist. It's possible they're the ones who taught him Vietnamese and hid him out for three years. Captain Stephens doesn't want to divulge their names for fear this information will leak out and there'll be recriminations against his benefactor. If it were me, I wouldn't tell either."

"As far as Mr. Ridley's comment about Stephens being superman, I refer those in the room to Captain Stephens personnel file. He is an expert in hand to hand combat and won the open one hundred seventy-five pound title in Martial Arts in a tournament in Thailand. I know what these tournaments are like. You have to be one tough hombre to enter and you have to be more than tough to win. That's how he kept getting away from the enemy. I believe Mr. Frank's presence here today is because Captain Stephens has information that would be valuable to our government." Minh said.

Before any of the other members of the debriefing team could ask a question, Amos Frank spoke. "Minh is correct. Captain Stephens has some extremely valuable information he'd like to share with you if there are no charges pending against him."

"We're not bargaining here. He hasn't answered for his whereabouts well enough to satisfy me," Colonel French was adamant.

"Then I don't think we have anything more to say to this group. Perhaps someone more senior could make a decision and Captain Stephens could tell you where some more POWs are being held."

It was a though a bombshell had exploded in the room. "You have a responsibility to tell us," French shouted.

"We fully intend to do just that. Are you satisfied that Captain Stephens did not desert, that he evaded the enemy and reported back as soon as he could?"

"My superior won't accept this form of a trade," Colonel French said.

"Why don't we talk to him? Perhaps Captain Stephens can be of some help in rescuing more Americans."

"That's blackmail," Colonel French was furious.

"Sir, I resent the accusation. I'm here to represent Captain Stephens. We've answered every question posed, other than who shielded my client in Vietnam. We feel that if that identity is released, the advisor most certainly would be killed," Frank responded to Colonel French."

"Anything Captain Stephens says in this room would be treated as confidential material."

"Sir, are you living in a dream world? Everything, and I mean everything, leaks in this community. If you have no further questions, my client is finished here. You have my number; we can meet with your superior anytime," Frank said

"Stephens is not going anywhere. He's under arrest," French countered.

"What are the ground for his arrest?"

"He's a deserter and he's going to stand trial."

Amos Frank turned to the Air Force attorney and asked him if he could substantiate an arrest at this time.

"Let me talk to Colonel French and see if we can compromise."

Ten minutes later, French adjourned the debriefing and said that Stephens was free to go pending a meeting with French's superior.

Minh spoke to Larry after the meeting broke up. "I'm convinced that you did everything you could to escape. I know you got lucky initially by learning the Vietnamese language from your benefactor. But it was your perseverance that got you home; don't forget that. I understand that you're planning on resigning your commission. My company would like to talk to you about a position."

That evening, he and Amos Frank had dinner downtown. Frank was quite confident that they'd be able to work with someone other than Colonel French. I don't know what his background is, but my sources tell me that he's on his way out. He'd been passed over twice for star slots by officers junior to him. You have too much to tell them; they don't want French to play hard ball. As soon as I find out anything, I'll let you know.

It was the following afternoon when Larry received a message to call Amos Frank. "I've had a phone call from General David Sweeney, Chairman of the Joint Chiefs of Staff. A meeting is set up tomorrow morning at ten between him, his staff, you and me. It'll probably be in the same room as the last one; we'll be told when we check in. I'll meet you at the same place at nine forty-five and we'll walk in together."

There were four people sitting at the same conference table when he and Frank arrived. Their nameplates identified them as General Sweeney, Chief of Staff of the Air Force, Colonel Ratliff, his chief of staff, Captain Morley his aide and Mr. Minh from the CIA. Larry and Minh exchanged smiles. The meeting was cordial but the conversation wasn't very candid. Larry covered in greater detail, his visit to the POW Compound. Although he didn't see any of the men, nor could he confirm their nationality, Larry was assured by several village chiefs that there were American flyers being held in captivity.

"What's your gut reaction?"

"They were there."

"Do you think you could find this camp again?" the general asked.

"I do."

"I also understand that you think your benefactor could act as a conduit between us and the North Vietnamese."

"Yes, but I'm not going to tell you how I know that to be true. Once I do that, you're smart enough to figure out who it is. He's not in the military is all I'll say."

"What if we want to open up that avenue?"

"I'll meet with whoever is heading the delegation and see if I can get his assurance that he'll protect my source; only then will I divulge his name and who his friends are."

"Would you like to be part of that delegation?"

"I believe that the soldiers pursuing me in Vietnam and Laos were personally directed by General Tran, the Regional Commander of the Hanoi District. Until he's neutralized, neither I nor my benefactor are safe. I also feel that Tran's tentacles may extend to the United States."

"I have a report from the Commander of the 22nd Squadron at Ubon. There was one thing that stood out in this report as unusual. He said you were a martial arts expert and won a tournament in Thailand in your weigh division. I've been to Thailand and I know how much skill it takes to participate in those games. Our state department friends question how you could keep escaping. You must be really good. I wish you luck in the future and I'm sorry to hear that your marriage is in difficulty. Bring her flowers; she may come around. I will give you an answer in forty-eight hours as to how the Air Force views your status," General Sweeney saluted Larry and he was excused.

Colonel French wasn't finished yet. He requested a meeting with his superior and explained why he so was concerned about Stephens. His supervisor was a personal friend of General Sweeney. He called Sweeney's office and asked if he'd be receptive in listening to Colonel French. The general had completed his investigation and was going to make a ruling tomorrow. He welcomed French to his office. "I know you think Stephens collaborated with the North Vietnamese. Do you have any proof?'

"None of our men who tried to evade the enemy were successful. In some cases, two or three tried together and still were unsuccessful. The other issue is that Stephens won't divulge where he was and who helped him. Then there was the invincibility issue. He was captured twice and as many as ten of the NVA were pursuing him and he was still able to escape. I don't believe it. I've read his file and know about his martial arts training. I firmly believe he's a North Vietnamese plant. They released him on the condition that he become a mole in this country."

"A mole in what? He's not remaining in the service, has no educational background and no prospects with a job in our government. Although the CIA is interested in him, they won't touch him if he can't pass their stringent security clearance.

The boys you reference didn't speak Vietnamese, didn't have a plan of escape and had no way of providing help to the villages in return for food and shelter. I, for one, believe him and do you know why? He could have held back the location of the POWs and sold his story to a magazine for big bucks. You aren't the only one who's going to question him from this day forward, but I believe him and I'm willing to welcome him home."

Two days later, Larry was out of the Air Force, had been cleared of any potential charges of desertion and had revealed the location of the POW camp. The Air Force insisted on a physical which was completed at Andrews Air Force Base. Larry signed a waiver stating that he wanted his wife to operate on the areas where the bullets were located. The following day, he was interviewed by Minh and several other CIA officers. They offered him a position, conditioned on him passing a rigorous security clearance. He wasn't naive. He knew why they were asking him to join them and what they were going to ask him to do; he was committed to help.

His tentative new employer told him to take thirty days to make up his mind. If the recovery time from the two operations exceeded the thirty days, they'd wait a little longer for his answer. Prior to departing the next morning for Greenville, Minh had a private conversation with Larry. "Have you converted to Buddhism?"

"Who wants to know?"

"I do. I think you were holed up in a monastery and learned Vietnamese and Buddhism. I think that's how you made it back. You prayed and meditated with the villagers who thought you were a Buddhist Monk.".

Larry smiled, "I think I'll leave it at that."

Chapter 17

Amos Frank was the key. Larry was called for a debriefing by six men who had a preconceived idea that the only reason he was back from Vietnam was that the enemy helped him and now wanted to use him as an asset. In spite of his new religion, Larry was angry as hell. He'd given too much to his country to be treated this way. Flying airplanes was all he could think about when he was young, but that was in the past. It was time to make a new life. His future plans were undecided, but whatever he pursued would include his Buddhist religion, with or without Jean.

They sat in Frank's small office, decorated with pictures of old time Basketball Stars, both collegiate and professional, with a small Christmas tree standing in the corner. It took Larry by surprise; then he remembered the tree at the Temple in Hanoi and he nearly shed a tear. He just kept staring at the tree until Frank broke his concentration. "I don't think Colonel French is convinced of your innocence. He could be a dangerous enemy in the future. If it wasn't for Mr. Minh and General Sweeney, we'd be knee deep in court martial paperwork. It's a pleasure to know a real hero. I'm amazed at your accomplishments. Don't let them talk you into going back; that's not your job anymore."

Larry responded. "I feel guilty that I had help and others didn't. Since my wife is going through with the divorce, I need something concrete to work on to take my mind off losing my family. I may have already made a commitment."

"That's all well and good, but you've paid your debt to the military. You've shown them where they can find our men and you may have opened up a diplomatic avenue that they didn't know existed. They have more resources to complete the task besides you. Go home and talk to your wife again; she may have second thoughts."

He paid Amos Frank the thousand dollars Jean had given him and thanked him for his support. He'd collected payment for two months of accrued leave, plus his last month's pay, before the paymaster closed that afternoon; he felt richer than he'd ever been. Even though it was close to Christmas, he still put his name on the standby list. When his seat was confirmed, he called Jean and told her of his plans to stop by this evening and pick up his things. She said she'd be home. His airplane landed at five PM in Greenville. Before he took a cab to Jean's home, he bought a dozen long stemmed roses.

His future plans with the CIA were tentative. Other than the mission he knew they'd ask him to accomplish, he had no plans beyond the next few months. Satellite photos of the POW area he visited had been enlarged. The analysts determined that it looked like some form of stockade. They could make out twelve guards and six prisoners, though they weren't sure that Americans were being held there. However, they weren't able to locate the Russian base nearby. Minh told him the president had been briefed and he'd directed the CIA and State Department to come up with a plan to extract the POWs.

Jean knew that she needed someone to talk to about her situation. In the past, she'd talked to her priest, Father John Mahoney, about her husband and her relationship with Walter Osborne. Although he didn't specifically indicate what action she should take, he was a good listener and the questions he did ask allowed her to sort through her options. Jean called him the afternoon that Larry left for Washington and set up an appointment at four that afternoon at the parish.

One of the parish priests directed her to Mahoney's office. He rose to greet her and clasped her hands in his. "It's always good to see you, Doctor Stephens. Please sit down."

His office was sparse with an ornate desk and two chairs for visitors. There were pictures of all the former parish priests on the wall behind his desk and a statue of the Virgin Mary taking up most of one corner. "How may I help you, Jean?"

She told him about her husband's return, his conversion to Buddhism, his appearance, the divorce she filed and her love for Walter Osborne. "I know you can't tell me what to do, but you've always been a comfort in the past; I just needed to talk to someone."

"What does Larry have to say?"

"He accepts my infidelity and wants to continue with our marriage, but he's leaving the decision to me."

"Do you love both men?" The priest asked.

"I love Walter and the man I married. I just don't know if I love the new Larry Stephens."

"I could give you the church's position on marriage, but that doesn't take into account how you feel. I think both men trust your judgment and so do I."

On her way home Jean made two calls. The first was to Walter Osborne, inviting him to dinner at her home at seven. The second was to her parents. She asked her father, who answered the phone, if they could watch her children tonight. Her father immediately said yes and drove to Jean's house to pick up the children.

Walter Osborne was apprehensive but as the clock struck seven o'clock, he walked up to Jean's front door and pressed the bell. He was reluctant to take her into his arms but that point was mute because she threw her arms around his neck and kissed him passionately. He handed her a bottle of Pinot Noir. She asked him to open the bottle and pour two glasses. Walter handed her a glass and she took a small sip and smiled. "Dinner will be ready in five minutes. You picked the correct wine because we're having Lasagna."

Jean sat at one end of the table with Walter at the other end. He offered a toast to their love and refilled both glasses. Each had second helpings of the main dish and finished the bottle of wine. He kept the conversation light and avoided any mention of the pending divorce. Jean was her most vivacious self and made him feel that he was the only person she loved. As she finished off the wine in her glass, she got up, walked to Walter and sat on his lap. She put both arms around his neck and kissed him firmly on the mouth. "I want you to spend the night and make love to me. I love you very much."

Walter picked Jean up in his arms and climbed the stairs to her bedroom. They took their time undressing each other and then made love with a fervor neither had experienced before. In the morning, she made breakfast before he left and told him she loved him. He put his arms around her and held her tight and she told him what her decision was.

Larry's taxi pulled into Jean's driveway; he paid the fare and walked to the front door. As he reached the stoop, the door opened and Jean walked out onto the landing. She had on the flowered dress she bought in McCarron Terminal in Las Vegas. "Come on in Larry, I've been waiting for you."

He presented the flowers; she smiled and held them to her bosom. "I won't stay long, Jean. I'll pack up my things and move to a hotel. I don't want to pressure you in any way."

"I've done a lot of thinking while you were in Washington. If you agree, I want you to stay here through the holidays and see if we can put our married life back together. I've told my attorney to suspend the divorce proceeding for four to six months to see if we can work out our problems. That should be enough time to see if we're meant to be together.

"What about Walter?"

"I love Walter and I probably always will, but you're my husband and my first love. I want a chance to see if we can have the love we knew before you went away. I want to make an effort for six months, if you're willing. I promise to be faithful to you while we're together.

Jean walked over to Larry, put her arms around his neck and pushed her hips against his. There was no doubt in his mind what she was saying. He picked her up, kicked the front door closed and carried her up the stairs into her bedroom. He took his time undressing her as he fondled every part of her body. When he entered her, she gasped as before and he told her that he loved her more than ever. He also thanked her for giving him a chance. She sobbed openly.

After they made love again, they went downstairs and Larry sat at the kitchen table while Jean heated up some leftover macaroni and cheese. "Have you given any thought to what you plan to do in the future?" she asked.

"Well, for one thing, I'm a civilian now. I resigned yesterday and collected money for two months of accrued leave in addition to last month's pay. We need to talk about our finances. The CIA was at my debriefing and offered me a position. I didn't know what would happen when I came here tonight, so I tentatively accepted it. I wish I had consulted with you first, but I wasn't sure you wanted to go on with me. There are several things you need to know. I was cleared of any potential charges of desertion. They all agreed, well, at least all but Colonel French, that I evaded the enemy and came home by myself as soon as I could.

For your information, for three years I was housed in a monastery in North Vietnam. The abbot was kind to me and saved my life after I was shot in the ribs while trying to escape from my captors. I learned to speak Vietnamese fluently. I also converted to Buddhism. I was able to escape because I altered my appearance and wore the clothes of a Buddhist Monk. During my escape, when I entered a village, I'd sit down among the people and beg for food. In almost every case they fed me what they could. Sometimes I conducted services and meditated with them. That's how I was able to walk over four hundred miles to freedom. I feel very strongly about my new faith and plan to practice most of its teachings."

"My God, Larry, I never imagined anything like this. I saw the bald head and the slight build, but I thought that was from malnutrition." The tears were running down her face.

"I'm thin because I trained my body to survive on only one meal a day. The pallor of my skin will change and I'll put on more weight with some of your cooking. I believe

I'll look as you remember me in about three or four months."

"Before I forget it, I've scheduled an appointment with one of my doctor friends to look at your wounds after we take x-rays. My guess is that it'll be a simple procedure to remove the bullets. You should be laid up no more than a week." Jean said.

Jean seemed so happy and he didn't want to spoil their reunion, but he had to tell her. "There's something else that I haven't told you."

"You got married while you were there."

"No, nothing like that. I've been celibate the entire time. You are the only one I ever want to make love to. I love you so much. I have to tell you about this other issue, but it might make you unhappy and you may go forward with the divorce."

"Tell me and let me decide."

"While I was on my way back, I learned some information from one of village chiefs which was corroborated by two other village chiefs. There may be other POWs that haven't been released. I went to a stockade near the Laotian border and tried to confirm that they were there. It definitely was some sort of prison, but I couldn't make out who the inmates were."

"Oh my God, they want you to go back and help release them. You can't do this. We've suffered enough. I can't bear to lose you again and I don't want the children to lose their father a second time. Please don't do this, please."

He got out of the chair and wrapped his arms around her. She clung to him and wouldn't let go. "I'm not hungry now. I want to go to bed and have you hold me and promise me that you won't leave again," Jean said.

She was hysterical as they made their way upstairs and into bed. She crawled on top of him and put her arms around him and wouldn't let go. She sobbed again and then asked him to promise not to go back.

"I promise that I won't do anything without your approval. Don't tell anyone what I said about the POWs. It could jeopardize their lives." He didn't know if she heard him. They slept that way until morning. He tried to go to the bathroom around six, but she held onto him and wouldn't let go.

She got up first and went to their bathroom. When she came back, he was sitting on the side of the bed and she sat on his lap. "I prayed that you would come back to me. When you weren't identified with any group, I lost faith and took up with Walter. Please don't leave us."

When his in-laws brought their children home the next day, Larry met them at the door and told them he was here to stay. He could see the apprehension on their faces as he told the two young ones that he and their mother were going to make their marriage work.

"Is mommy going to get a divorce?" his son asked.

Jean walked into the parlor as Larry Jr. asked his father that question. "No, she is not. We are a family and were going to stay a family."

Everyone hugged and Susanne asked, "Will daddy be with us for Christmas?"

"He'll be here for every Christmas," Jean said as the adults toasted each other with a glass of wine.

The tree was beautiful. They were so busy with each other that he hadn't seen the tree until the children arrived. He instantly remembered the tree the monks used in the Pagoda.

Chapter 18

The bodies of Quon, Ly and the other four soldiers laid along the bank of the river for over three hours before the authorities arrived and took them to the nearest town. When they checked for identification, they were shocked to learn that all six were North Vietnamese soldiers. The first question the local magistrate asked was, what were they doing on the Thailand side of the Mekong River?

When the North's ambassador was notified in Vientiane, he wired Hanoi with the names and identification numbers and asked for direction. Two days later Major Nguyen flew in by helicopter and claimed the bodies. The first question he asked the ambassador was who killed them.

"There is limited information. From what the Laotian authorities learned, the mutilated soldier had fired on a wedding party and they, in turn, attacked him. It's assumed that the other four came to his aid and were killed by the wedding party. The sixth was found in the river, thirty feet below the bridge. He either jumped or was thrown from the bridge, and broke his neck in the fall. The two soldiers guarding the first rope bridge decided to return to Da Nang.

General Tran sent a helicopter to pick up Major Nguyen after he returned with the bodies, and transported him to Hanoi. To show his anger, he kept Nguyen waiting in his reception room for two days. When he finally allowed the Major into his office, he berated him for a full five minutes. "I trusted you to carry out my orders. Six men were killed and two others badly injured while trying to capture one man, who I might add, was wounded. You're a disgrace to your unit; you're a disgrace to me. I'm ashamed to be related to you. What do you have to say for yourself?"

Nguyen was shaking but he had some backbone. "Those were some of my best men. They gave it all they had. Quon and Ly are going to be missed by our battalion. They were good soldiers. I take full responsibility for the mission's failure and I'm prepared to accept your decision."

"We'll get him yet. I want you to go with me to the Temple of Tran Quoc. Almost a year ago, we found a tunnel on the grounds leading to the lake. We didn't catch anyone, but we uncovered his hiding place."

They drove to the Buddhist Temple, had the diver wait with the vehicle, and walked inside the temple grounds. Tran knew where to look and the two walked directly to the site. The hole had been covered over, but when Tran stepped on the remaining old boards, they creaked. "This is what we're dealing with. I believe Stephens was here and had a few hiding places throughout the complex. We nearly caught him. His escape is an embarrassment to me, to you, and to our country. He's probably back in America, but we have some resources there and we'll bring him back. Next time I won't be as gracious to you; remember that."

Two days after Christmas, **Larry Stephens** went in for x-rays on his shoulder and heart. Although there was a slight infection in Larry's left shoulder, Doctor Bill Ponder, with Dr. Jean Stephens assisting, took out the bullet the next day. Two days later he was released from the hospital and sent home. Neither Bill Ponder nor Walter Osborne would recommend an operation on the bullet near Larry's heart. It was too close to remove; they thought he could live with it without any lasting effects. They suggested to Larry and Jean that it be looked at on a yearly basis. The children and grandparents were allowed to visit Larry during visiting hours. The kids were fascinated that their mother operated on their father and that their father was coming home for good.

Gradually, the Stephens' clan settled into a daily pattern. She'd go to the hospital and he'd take the children to school in the morning. Subsequently, he found a Buddhist Temple in Jackson, about sixty miles away, and met with the abbot who was of Indian Dissent and practiced the Vajrayana form of Buddhism, which is newer than the Mahayana form that Larry practiced. There were many similarities, and yet, some differences how the two sects looked at enlightenment. But, for all practical purposes, their teachings were similar and Larry was welcomed into the temple. Finding a place to worship and meditate gave him a feeling of fulfillment. Subsequently, he was asked to be the abbot's assistant and perform some of the ceremonies. Larry was thrilled. The first wedding ceremony he performed was attended by his entire family. Jean's mother was a little embarrassed but Jean and her father were so proud that anything the mother said was ignored by everyone.

In addition to visiting the Temple each week, he joined a gym in town and spent two hours in the morning and two hours in the afternoon working out before he picked up the children from school. He also found a martial arts teacher and continued to hone his skills. Jean saw Walter daily at the hospital and occasionally they had lunch, but he gave her the space she demanded.

Although she wouldn't commit to Larry's religion, Jean saw to it that he had an hour in the evening for meditation. Sooner or later, the issue of Buddhism would surface with either the children or his wife. They were enjoying Saturday morning breakfast with the two children when Larry Junior asked if the entire family was going to become Buddhists. Larry and Jean knew that his mother-in-law was behind the question, so he had to be careful in his response. "I'm perfectly happy that you, Susanne and your mother continue to practice Christianity and attend Mass. Most Sundays, I'll be there to support you."

Young Larry wasn't finished. "But Catholics believe in God and Buddhists don't. Sister Ann said that if you don't believe in God, you can't be saved."

"Throughout the world, there are many religions; many do not believe in the concept of heaven and hell. Does that mean they won't be saved? Not all of Christianity, which the Catholic religion is part of, believe in the same things as Catholics. The answer is that you must be tolerant of other religions and the people who believe in their own faith. I'll talk to Sister Ann. Maybe she was trying to say one thing and it came out wrong. I was raised as a Catholic as was your mother. It's a fine religion but I chose another religion. Maybe I was forced into it to save my life but the more I practiced it, the better I felt. If you feel good about your religion, then you should continue to practice its teachings. I'm not going to tell you mine is better than yours. Are you uncomfortable coming to my temple once a month?"

"No, I thought it was neat. I just don't understand the loud chanting."

"It's like a song or prayer, similar to many things in your religion, like psalms."

"What about meditation? Mom says you meditate for an hour each evening. Is that true?"

"For me, meditation helps reduce stress, clears my mind and allows me to calmly look at negative things that have happened to me each day. I know you feel stress when you take a test or talk in front of people. Meditation would help reduce that kind of stress. I'd be glad to show you a way to meditate that would prove helpful."

"If my son is not interested, I am," Jean smiled and Larry squeezed her hand. It was Jean who spoke to Sister Ann, not Larry. The next day, Sister Ann made it a point to clarify who would go heaven.

Jean's mother and father came over for New Year's dinner and Larry couldn't ask for a better life. He hadn't told his new employer that he wouldn't be reporting for training, though there were several administrative calls from the agency that he didn't return. He did however, check into the GI Bill and the possibility of completing his degree. With Jean's salary and the GI Bill, there was enough income to allow him to attend college. He didn't know what profession he'd pursue, but it had to be outdoors.

The four year separation had a positive effect on their marriage. Similar to the first two years of marriage, they would explore different aspects of their relationship. Everything seemed new and exciting as before. It was as though they were dating again. About two weeks after he was released from the hospital, they were driving down the highway after an afternoon of shopping and Jean asked, "Do you remember some of the crazy things we used to do?"

"Such as?"

"Well do you remember the time I took off all my clothes in the car and you found a turnoff and we did it with cars driving by? We didn't care whether they saw us or not."

He looked at his wife with a puzzled expression as she slouched down in her seat, took off all her clothes and smiled at him. He took the next exit off the freeway, got out of the car in a light rain and went around to the passenger's side. It seemed more difficult this time than the last, but he finally was beside Jean with his clothes off; she'd already lowered her seat to a reclining position.

"I love you Larry, but could you take your socks and shoes off?"

"Not a chance."

Afterward, Larry dressed, stepped out onto the wet grass, ran around the car and got back in the driver's side while Jean put her clothes back on. As soon as they were dressed, a police car pulled up alongside. An officer rolled down his window and asked if they needed assistance. "No thanks, officer, we just stopped to change drivers."

"Do you think he believed us?" Jean asked.

"Probably not."

Procrastination had never been part of Larry's character, but he wasn't looking forward to the call he had to make. He called Minh the day after New Year's and told him that he wasn't accepting employment with the CIA. "We need you Larry. We couldn't do an extraction without your being part of the team."

"I nearly lost my wife; she filed for divorce and was going to marry someone else. I don't want to put any undue pressure on her and my children at this time. I was gone four years; they couldn't handle my disappearance again."

"What can I say to make you change your mind? Think of the expertise you have for a mission like this. You'd just be repeating what you've already accomplished."

"I appreciate the support you gave me when I needed it, but I can't go."

"You didn't tell her about the POWs, did you?"

"Jean is no dummy; she figured that out immediately; it was obvious to her what you wanted me to do. She promised she wouldn't tell anyone about what I saw in Vietnam."

"I hope you're right. It could foul up our plans if that information is leaked."

He was called four more times that week; each time by someone further up the food chain. The Director of the CIA called on Friday, but Larry wouldn't commit. Each time the phone rang while Jean was home; it created more tension between the two.

"Are you reconsidering going back to help rescue the POWs?"

"Not as long as you're opposed to the idea. I'm not going to jeopardize our relationship."

The Saturday after New Year's the family was sitting around the kitchen table having breakfast when the phone rang. Larry answered the phone and listened for about two minutes and then hung up. The color had disappeared from his face and he was solemn. Jean was in a good mood and started to kid him, "Larry you look like your stock broker called and said you lost all your money." She playfully patted his rear.

When he didn't answer immediately, she persisted. "What's going on, Larry?"

"That was the first lady on the phone. She's parked on the ramp at Greenville Air Force Base in Air Force One. She wants us to come out to the base and talk to her."

"Oh my God. I don't know whether I can handle this pressure. They're after you all the time. Do we have to go?"

"It's either that or she's going to come here with her entourage of Secret Service agents. I don't think we have a choice."

"We can always run away."

"Be serious, Jean."

"What about the children?s Mom and Dad are in town shopping."

"She suggested that we bring the children. If nothing else, they get to see Air Force One."

"I'll go, but it won't do her any good. I've made up my mind. When I tell her no, will the president come next?"

Larry smiled. "It's possible.

"I haven't had my hair done and my nails need work. It'll take me at least an hour to get ready. I'll shower first while you clean up the children. Tell them to put on their Sunday clothes."

Jean was like every other woman; it took her longer to get ready than she planned. She had to try on six outfits before she was satisfied that she found one that was good enough to visit with the first lady. When she was ready to go, she said "let's hurry everyone, were going to be late."

They were met at the gate by three Secret Service agents and after a thorough screening, they were escorted to the president's plane. They were searched before boarding and again before they were ushered into a small room where Pat Nixon, the first lady, sat in a soft chair. She rose as they entered and asked them to be seated. "Thank you for coming on such short notice. I must be in California for a dinner and fund raiser, so I don't have much time. Can I offer you something to drink?

Larry and Jean declined.

"I wonder if we could spare the children from our conversation and have Agent Richards give them a tour of the airplane?" Both children smiled and were led out of the room by Agent Catherine Richards.

The first lady looked directly at Jean. "I've heard the story of your husband's remarkable escape from Vietnam and the problems you've both encountered since he's returned. I don't know what my position would be if I were faced with your situation. Still, I must make a plea that your husband reconsider his position and take the assignment so more of our men can be released. I know you both have suffered enough for three or four families, but what do we tell those wives and children who still have hope that their loved ones can come home?"

Tears welled up in Jean's eyes and Larry handed her his handkerchief. "Why should I give up the man I love for an almost suicidal mission? I'm not a dummy. Larry's the one who knows the land and it's Larry who can infiltrate the country and talk to the people. You may even want Larry to pose as a Buddhist Monk again, and enter the prison camp at his peril; not yours, his."

"The only thing I can counter with is, what about the wives and children of those men in captivity. If it was your husband who was in a POW compound, wouldn't you want someone with your husband's expertise to make the attempt? I can't give you any guarantee because I'm not qualified in the art of insurgency. I just want to do everything I can do to help them."

The silence between the three was overwhelming. Finally, the first lady spoke, "I've taken up too much of your time. The decision is yours. There'll be no further calls pleading with you. Additionally, there will be no leak to the press to pressure you to go on the mission. I see that Agent Richards is back with your children. Thank you again. I'd like to stay longer and chat with you, but I must be on my way."

She stood up, shook hands, and Agent Richards escorted them to their vehicle and bid them a good day.

"Mom, what was that all about?" Larry Jr. asked.

"The president's wife came to ask your mother and father for a favor." Larry said.

"Are you going to do her a favor?" Susanne asked.

"We don't know." Jean replied.

"Do they want you to go to war again, dad?" Susanne asked.

"Not quite, but pretty close."

Everyone was quiet the remainder of the day. It was as though a black cloud had descended over their home and was threatening them with a major storm. Larry retreated to his room and meditated; Jean sat at the kitchen table and had a glass of wine; the children went outside to play. Larry knew the first lady was correct, but so was Jean. He didn't realize until last night how much she loved him. Yes, she'd been unfaithful, but in her defense, she'd been told he was dead and just wanted to provide a stable home for herself and her family. He could never fault her for that.

Chapter 19

The neighbors had come calling several times while Jean was either at the hospital or off with Walter. They'd seen him come and go and occasionally stay over on weekends. The neighbors assumed he was her boyfriend. When Larry arrived, most thought he was a visiting relative, but when they heard one of the children call him dad, they wondered where he'd been. One rumor was that he'd been in jail for some time. Most assumed that the couple had been separated and decided to reconcile.

Jean was happy to have her husband home. He was someone who loved her and could protect her. She'd had several incidents with one of men in the neighborhood, who thought it was his right to come over whenever he felt like it and just walk into her kitchen. On two occasions, he caressed her bottom and suggested that he could comfort her. When she started seeing Walter, the unwanted overtures ceased. Now that Larry was home, the neighbor was taking liberties again. Perhaps he saw an emaciated husband who couldn't defend his turf. After a couple of recent incidents where the intent of the man was made very clear, Jean told Larry.

Johnny Lagard had lived in the neighborhood for the past ten years with his wife, Linda, and their three children. He fashioned himself a lady's man and had two or three conquests in the neighborhood. He was employed by Blue Star Realty in town and generally had Thursdays free. His wife was a secretary/bookkeeper at the All Brand Tire Company located in Greenville. Jean had told Larry that

Johnny would normally come by on Thursday afternoons, just as she was getting home. He'd come twice since Larry returned, but while he was in Jackson at the Buddhist Temple.

The Lagard house was on the opposite side of the street, but two houses down from them. Johnny was able to sit in his living room and keep track of the Stephens when either or both left. This Thursday, Larry left the house about two PM and drove toward downtown. As was normal on Thursdays, Jean had come home early and was doing the washing. Johnny saw his opportunity and slicked back his hair and casually walked over to the Stephens' house. He checked to see if anyone was looking before he pushed open the gate to the back yard and walked in; he closed the gate behind him. He could hear the radio in the kitchen and he smiled as he neared the back door.

Just as he started to open the kitchen door, he heard a male's voice say, "Can I help you?"

He stopped, turned around and saw Larry standing about ten feet away. "I had some time off this afternoon, so I thought I'd be neighborly and come over and see if your wife needed any chores done,"

Larry smiled. "That's very good of you, but I wonder why you didn't come to the front door and ring the bell, rather than sneaking in the back gate and looking into the kitchen," Larry said as he drew nearer.

"I don't like the tone of your question mister, whoever you are?"

"Well I'm Larry Stephens and I'm Mrs. Stephens' husband. I have a right to be here but you, you look like a sneak or a Peeping Tom," Larry smiled at the man who was about forty pounds heavier and four inches taller.

"Listen Stephens, I'm leaving and if you get smart with me, I'll knock you on your ass."

Larry stepped closer. Oh, I don't think so. You're all mouth. My guess is that you'd wet your pants if you ever got in a fight with someone."

Lagard turned crimson and swung his right fist at Larry, who stepped closer to him, ducked and then drove his right hand into Johnny's midsection. Lagard threw up and fell on his face. When he stopped retching, he swore at Larry and said he was going to sue.

At that moment, Jean came out of the kitchen holding a motion picture camera. "Well Johnny, the court will certainly get to see who started the fight. No I don't think you want anyone to see the movie of my husband kicking your butt. I forgot to tell you that Larry's an expert in hand-to-hand combat." She laughed and went back into the kitchen.

By this time, Lagard had started to rise and Larry helped him up, but pushed him into one of the lawn chairs. Larry grabbed another chair and sat across from Lagard and grabbed his right hand firmly in his. "I want you to understand something. I'm a peaceful man but if I wanted to, I could break ever bone in your body. I'm probably the most lethal person you'll ever meet. Don't ever come over here again, don't talk to my wife, and don't do anything that will annoy me." With that last statement, Larry squeezed harder on Johnny's hand and the man screamed. Johnny Lagard retched one more time before he left the backyard.

There was a block party in their neighborhood two weeks after New Year's. It's been an annual event for ten years; the Stephens were invited. They didn't know anyone on the block but decided to go anyway. Larry Jr. was old enough to be able to call them if there was an incident, especially since they'd be directly across the street.

There were twelve couples who accepted the invitation; each brought something to the party which was held indoors. Food was laid out on the dining room table while refreshments were available at a makeshift bar set up in the living room. Johnny Lagard and his wife, Linda, said they had a previous engagement. Larry hadn't seen the man since that day in his backyard.

Jean made a chocolate pie; she and Larry went to the party around nine. Everyone was friendly; some became a little tipsy and as the evening wore on; two passed out in their chairs. Jean drank wine and Larry had 7UP. It wasn't as though he felt abstinence was his goal in life, he just didn't feel like any liquor, especially that night.

He was asked repeatedly who he was and what he did for a living. The questions weren't probing; it was just something people asked to break the ice and enter into a conversation. He told them he was Jean's husband and the father of Larry Jr. and Susanne. He'd been working in a foreign country for a few years and was now home for an extended period of time. He wouldn't tell anyone what country or what company he worked for; no one pressed the issue.

The party broke up just before midnight after the host and hostess toasted their friends and neighbors. He and Jean toasted each other and kissed each other passionately. One of the neighbors said, "Hey, you two, you're married. You seem like you're on your first date."

Jean blushed and Larry laughed. She looked directly at him. He held her tightly as they walked back home.

Over the past few Sundays, Larry would get up early, go to the store, and pick up some donuts and the New York Times. The kids liked to have a snack before going to church. Afterward, the family would go to lunch before coming home. Jean was a practicing Catholic as were the two children. Larry had been a Catholic and, although now a devout Buddhist, he'd go to church with his family.

Jean and Larry liked to read the Sunday paper in bed for an hour before getting ready for church. Today's headlines chastised the Vietnamese for not releasing all the POWs. There had been sightings by foreign journalists and enough pressure was being put on the White House to take some action. The editorials in the back of the paper further outlined reasons why the US had to take action. The article said that the country and the military families were owed some action to bring our boys home; the administration was really feeling the heat.

Larry wondered why Jean was so quiet, and then he read the paper, he knew what was going on in her mind. They dressed and went to church. After mass, Jean asked Larry to watch the children; she wanted to talk to Father Mahoney, the parish priest.

"Good to see you and the family today. Is Larry adjusting?"

"He seems to be, but that's not what I want to talk to you about."

"Is it the divorce?"

"No Father, there'll be no divorce. Larry is going to be my husband until one of us dies. I don't want to go to confession, but what I'm about to tell you cannot be divulged. If we have to go into the confessional to keep this confidential, I will."

"That won't be necessary. Unless it's about some crime, I'll not betray your confidence."

She told him about her husband's escape, what he had to do to survive, what he uncovered on his way out of Vietnam, and what he was being asked to do.

"There's so much pressure on us from as high as the president; I need some advice."

"What do you want to do, Jean?"

"I'm sorry for my language, but I want to be a self-serving bitch and keep Larry home with me. I don't want to lose him twice. I don't think I could take the uncertainty again. Everyone knows I've been unfaithful to him, but that was because I was weak. I'm still weak; I need him."

"Then why come to me? You seem to know what you want."

"We visited with the first lady at Greenville last month and this morning, there's a newspaper account about other POWs not being released and what the MIA families are going through; I doubt my own judgment."

"Is your husband essential to a mission inside Vietnam?"

"I'm not a military person, but Larry had the skills to walk 400 miles in enemy territory posing as a Buddhist Monk. Yes, father, he has the skills they need. But Larry is fearless. I'm afraid he may go into that camp all by himself to initiate the extraction. The risk to him is much greater than the others that would be with him. The North Vietnamese know he was in their country and escaped. It would be a death sentence to send him back. I don't want my husband to go back there, but I'm feeling guilty. I know what I would do if there was a man like Larry who could go back into that country and save my husband. I would scream to the world that I'd want him to try."

"I can't tell you what to do. You have all the information and know what you're going to do. Whatever you do, I'll always be here. I won't divulge our conversation to anyone. You are a strong woman; not a weak one. May God give you the guidance you're looking for."

Jean knelt at the altar in front of the candles that people light when they want to ask God for a favor. She dried her tears and lit two candles, looked up to the ceiling and asked God to keep him safe; she walked out of church into a beautiful sunny day. Okay kids, where do want to go for lunch?" Jean asked.

"The pancake house," both children said simultaneously.

Back home, Jean told the two young ones to do their homework for tomorrow while Larry went to their bedroom to meditate for an hour. When he was finished, Jean asked if they could go for a walk.

There was a park a couple of blocks from their house. They held hands as they walked there and found a bench to sit on. "I used to come here and watch families spend their Sundays together and I wondered if we could ever be able to do that. I was okay for the first two years of your absence, then I really began to wonder if you'd ever come back. I prayed to God and told Him that if I could have another thirty days with you, I wouldn't ask Him for anything ever again. I've broken my promise to God. This afternoon while you were meditating, I asked Him to keep you safe and return you to me after this next mission. I've been selfish and I know it; there are families that need your help. You'll never know how much I love you at this moment and how proud I am to be your wife. I will be your wife forever, no matter what happens next."

There was silence between them for a few moments before Larry spoke. "This had to be a hard decision for you. I promised I'd come home the first time and I promise that I'll return again. We were meant to be together. I'll not let you down. Thank you for taking me back, especially since I know you love Walter." He held her tightly and she kissed him several times, then they walked back to their house.

"We have to tell the children. When do you think you'll leave for training?"

"I'll call Minh when I get home and work out the details if they still want me. I think the shoulder wound needs further healing, but that can be done during training. I'll tell the children some of it, but not all. I think your parents need to be told as well. They're going to want to help, as before."

Susanne cried and Larry Jr. went to his room and didn't say anything. Her mother was very vocal and accused Larry of deserting her daughter again. "Mother, I'm the one who made the decision, not Larry."

"He doesn't have to go; he could refuse," Jean's mother responded.

Her father took a different tact and told Jean how proud he was of her. "I know this was a very difficult decision for you, but you showed me what you're made of. The many POW wives in this country will also be grateful that there is someone like you who thinks so much of their country. My main question for Larry is, how can you put yourself in a treacherous situation with that bullet near your heart? That's something that could really jeopardize the mission."

"It could, but I've had it for over four years, it's not slowed me down."

"When do you leave?" her father asked

"Minh wants me in Washington on Thursday for two months of intense training. I won't be able to come home, but Jean could visit if she wanted."

"Try keeping me away."

Both of her parents said they wouldn't divulge his mission and they would help Jean any way they could. Larry took the children out of school for a day. They went to the pancake house for breakfast, then to Greenville Air Force Base to look at the airplanes and finally they walked along the canal in the center of town. To his son's question, Larry told them he would be away for about three months but he'd be back. He asked them not to tell anyone about his plans. "If someone asks, tell them I'm in Washington, trying to get a job."

"Are you doing a favor for the first lady?" Larry Jr. asked.

"Yes. Is that okay with you two?"

"We liked her."

The last night he was home, the children stayed at her parent's home. Jean cooked his favorite dinner of chicken piccata and they finished a bottle of wine by candlelight before they retired. They made love and Jean laid on top of him all night and held him tightly. She rose early and had breakfast waiting. "I told them I'd be late this morning because I was taking my husband to the airport to go job hunting in Washington."

They stopped at Jean's bank on the way to the airport. Larry gave her most of the cash he still had and asked her to deposit it in her account. "My monthly pay is being wired into your checking account and the CIA has purchased a five hundred thousand dollar life insurance policy, with you and the children as beneficiaries."

"You're starting to scare me, Larry."

"It's what they do for all recruits. There's nothing ominous about it. I'm not worried."

"I'm not going to release you from your promise that you're coming back to me. I'll wait for you forever."

Chapter 20

His training started the day after he arrived and, although he'd been working out on a daily basis, he hadn't expected this much training. Some of his training had to be delayed for a month until his shoulder healed. Jean said he'd have full movement in about two months. At the end of two months, he was in magnificent condition and had gained back some of his weight. He was at one hundred fifty-five pounds and he was quick. He honed his martial art skills and took classes in all types of communications, weapons, explosives and first aid. The only physical problem was an infrequent pain near the bullet in his chest. The physician attending the training said Larry would have occasional pains there but he'd be okay to go on the mission.

He met the other members of the four man team at the end of the second week and was pleased to learn that Minh would be the senior member, though Larry would be directing the team once they reached Vietnam. The other two members were Jack Curtiss and Jim Long, both former Navy Seals who'd been working for the CIA. Each member had specific skills the others could rely on. They would carry minimal food, be prepared to survive on one meal a day and for all practical purposes, live off the land. To supplement their dietary needs, they'd rely on Larry's ability to obtain food from the villages. Larry had the map he used when he'd escaped from Vietnam and, although they wouldn't take the same route, he spent a day briefing the other members what to expect once they were inside Laos. He covered the terrain, insects, plants, animals and some of the sanitary issues they'd encounter.

He liked Jim Long immediately and knew this was a team member he could rely on. Curtiss was a little different and hard to penetrate. The former Seal saw martial arts as a competition and body slammed Larry on their first training exercise. Larry was slow to rise and the instructor monitoring the training rushed over but Larry assured him that he could continue. Curtiss moved in fast but Larry sidestepped and tripped him, but he regained his balance and continued the attack. Within thirty seconds, Larry had him in a hold he couldn't break and the instructor called time. Curtiss glared at Larry and wouldn't shake his hand.

Curtiss didn't take the loss well. Larry assumed that this was just part of his competitive personality and he'd be a good team member. Yet, Larry didn't let down his guard during any training where Curtiss was involved. During the martial arts training, Curtiss attacked Larry unnecessarily on two occasions. Larry was alert for the maneuvers but it certainly gave him pause. Although Larry was proficient in firing all the weapons they were taking, he concentrated on throwing a knife. It would be difficult to conceal a gun in the monk's garb he'd be wearing.

Jean came to DC his last weekend before the mission; they stayed at the Four Seasons in town. They didn't get in much sight-seeing because most of their time was spent in bed, relying on room service for food to keep them going. "I don't know if I could take another weekend with you. I'll have to go back into training to get my strength back; I'm exhausted," Larry said.

"I just wanted to show you what it'll be like when you get back home again," Jean replied.

"I may have to send a younger man in my place."

"Don't you dare? You can handle it and you know it."

"Let's be serious for a moment. How comfortable are you with your team? Do you think you can rely on them when it gets tough? You're a finisher. Are they?" Jean asked.

"We've trained together. If they're as good as their training, the answer is yes. I have some reservations about Jack Curtiss. His only drawback is that he wants to beat me all the time and, therefore, I'm not sure he'll follow my lead, but he trained well, didn't complain and was as good as anyone of us."

"What about Minh? Is he in charge?"

"No, I'm team chief once we're in country. If he goes along with me, so will the other two. Curtiss worked for him in the past."

"Let's be realistic, Larry, you are the team. You're the only reason they're going. Without you, they wouldn't even consider it. You're a patriot and I think that's clouding your judgment. Get rid of Curtiss and don't go until you're satisfied with his replacement. You're smart enough to know that."

"I'm worried that the window may close and they'll move the POWs around so we con't find them. I've got to go now."

"Will you confide in Minh about your reservations of Curtiss?"

"I already have."

"I feel strongly about your situation. All I ask is for you to have one more meeting with your group before you go. I'd put Curtiss on the spot and see if you can count on him."

He knew she was correct. "I'll do it."

Minh told Larry that the president was briefed and had signed off on the operation. The team was to be moved to Ubon, Thailand three days from now and would use the first two days after they arrived getting acclimated to the time change. Larry asked for a meeting with the team before they departed. Minh said they could have that meeting once they were in Ubon. "I'm sorry Minh, but I'm not going on this mission unless we have a team meeting and the issue with Curtiss is resolved to my satisfaction."

"You can't do this. We have a schedule to make."

"Let me know when the meeting is set up. I'm not going anyplace until we meet."

Minh met with his superior and told him about the latest developments. "Is he serious?" his boss asked.

"I'm afraid he is."

"Why did he wait until the last minute to bring this up?"

"He didn't. Stephens shared his concerns with me about a month ago. I felt that it could be resolved by me talking to Curtiss."

"You should've informed me. Set up the meeting; I want to be there. Do it today."

Curtiss must have been tipped off about the meeting because he glared at Larry when he walked in. John Ross, the supervisor in charge of the mission, started it off immediately. Mr. Stephens has raised the issue whether Jack Curtiss is suitable for this mission." You could hear a pin drop after he made that statement.

Ross continued, "At the end of this meeting, we'll either have a delay, a cancellation, or three or four of you will fly to Ubon tomorrow. Mr. Stephens, you have the floor. Please be direct."

Five men sat around an oval table, Minh was to Larry's left and Long to his right. Ross and Curtiss were directly across from him. "The success of this mission depends upon teamwork. Although Minh is the senior man, I'm in charge once we leave Thailand and I'm concerned that Jack Curtiss will not follow my direction."

"You son-of-a-bitch." Curtiss stood up but Ross grabbed his arm. "Sit down, you'll have your turn."

Larry continued. "I and my family have been pressured from the highest levels in this country to not only join this mission; but to lead it as well. Yet, I had no input on who would accompany me. Only one of you speaks passable Vietnamese. The other two do not, which puts an added burden on me and Minh. Throughout our training, Curtiss has not been a good teammate. He's challenged everything and especially me. I don't believe I can go into a hostile situation with someone who won't follow my direction. I spoke to Minh about a month ago, but the tension between Curtiss and myself hasn't changed. I ask that the mission be delayed to give us sufficient time to find a replacement for either myself or Curtiss."

Curtiss started to speak but Ross interrupted him. "Minh, what do you think?"

"Curtiss has been on two difficult missions with me and has performed in an extraordinary manner. He always has a chip on his shoulder and is a little temperamental, but he's a solid performer and one you can count on. As far as replacements are concerned, Larry cannot be replaced."

"What about you, Long?"

"I served with Curtiss for a year in the Seals. He's a royal pain in the ass but he's solid in the clutch. I'd go with him."

"Okay, it's your turn, Curtiss."

"This is a bunch of bullshit raised by the prima donna in this group who's probably a deserter. He's scared to death to go back. Who put him in charge, anyway? Long and I are Seals; we can get this job done without Stephens. Let Minh be in charge and we can leave on time."

"Now I know the problem. This mission is delayed as of now until we can find a replacement for Curtiss." No one responded and Ross got up to leave.

"You can't do this; I need to be on this mission." Ross stopped and turned around. Curtiss had his hands over his face as he slumped in the chair,

"Why do you have to be on this mission?" Ross asked

"My sister's husband is a MIA. He might be one of those that are still being held. I owe it to my sister to see if he's there and bring him home. This would be her last chance"

"Why the animosity toward Stephens?"

"He's kind of a one-man show and probably will leave all of us out of the decision making. I need to be involved."

"Jack, I'd like you to leave the room. I want to talk to Minh, Long, and Stephens. I'll let you know what my decision will be."

When Curtiss left, Ross turned to Larry, "What's your take on this?"

"I'm concerned that the window of opportunity is now. If we delay, the POWs may be moved before we get there. I don't know whether three men can accomplish the task, but I do know that a four-man team where one is working against the one in charge is a disaster and I don't want to be part of it."

"Minh, can three do the job?

"I don't know, but I think we need to give it a shot. I agree with Larry that the window of opportunity is now."

"What about you, Jim?"

"Larry is the perfect leader and I'd be willing to go with only three. I like Jack, but he can't go. He's too involved and I'm concerned about the friction he brings."

The team had two days before their departure and Ross still hadn't made a decision. He talked to his superiors to see how they felt. Larry and Jean decided to make the most of whatever time they had left. They rented a car and drove to Chesapeake Bay, had deviled crabs at Jason's on the Boardwalk and took a moonlight cruise around the bay. They went to bed around two in the morning. The next morning they drove back to DC, had a lunch of shrimp and lobster along the way and dinner at their hotel.

"Thanks for the second honeymoon. I had a great week here and, although I'm scared, I know you'll pull this off. The kids think you're a hero. I think you're superman. Let's get to bed early tonight and let me show you my appreciation."

That night Ross called and said the mission was a go and he was adding another man; Jack Curtiss was out.

Departure was at noon the following day, but Ross wanted everyone to meet for breakfast at nine the next morning. Larry and Jean agreed that she wouldn't see him off, so they said their goodbyes at the hotel; she'd take an afternoon flight back to Greenville. He took a cab to Andrews AFB and met with his team.

The others were at the officer's club when Larry arrived. He walked in and took his seat and was introduced to Jud Kelly. "Larry, the others know Jud, who's probably the finest seal member we've ever had. I personally asked him to go with you. On the flight over, you can learn his capability and brief him on the mission. He'll have your back."

There wasn't much said as they boarded a C-2 cargo plane. Their first stop was in Hawaii for refueling. Larry requested that Kelly sit with him on the way over so they could get acquainted. Kelly was a wiry, one hundred sixty pound, gray-haired individual on a five foot ten inch frame with a distinct scar on his nose. He said little but when he spoke, he commanded attention. Larry assumed the man was about fifty years old. "I've been in your position several times when a new man joined the group. I know you don't know much about me, but I've heard a great deal about you. I admire you and what you're doing. When I was asked to replace Curtiss, I agreed immediately when I heard you were leading the team."

Kelly continued. " I was in the Navy for twenty years before joining the Special Operations group of the CIA, which is seventy percent former Seals. I've been a Seal for ten of my twenty years and honed my skills in Vietnam, training the South Vietnamese, principally in Hit and Run Tactics; it was very successful against the Viet Cong. Like you, I speak fluent Vietnamese and I was on five missions in the North near Hanoi, so I know a good bit about surviving. My main skills, other than the language, are weapons and guerrilla tactics. I've worked with Long and Minh before. I also worked with Curtiss. That man is okay; the only problem is, it may take a year to find that out and you don't have that kind of time. I was briefed on your escape from Vietnam and I know what your capabilities are."

They landed at Ubon in the middle of the night. A CIA support team on the ground handled their gear and drove them to the VIP quarters on the base; they'd be here for two days.

Their entire last day in Thailand was used for briefings, especially the one on intelligence for the area they were visiting. Since they were traveling light, the instructors familiarized them with the plants that could be eaten and the small game available in Laos and Western Vietnam. Bamboo shoots were plentiful as were squirrels and fish. Long was a survivalist, Larry had lived off the land previously, Kelly had been in country for seven years and Minh spent his childhood in Vietnam.

Representing the CIA, Minh was the last speaker and went over the rules of engagement. "We will not overtly engage any of the military or civilians. If there's a threat to life, we can use our weapons. Larry is team chief once we're airborne from Ubon. He will make the final decision as to the feasibility of rescuing the POWs or whether to abort. If we become separated for any reason, your duty is to return to Ubon; we don't want anyone taken prisoner."

Their plan was optimistic to say the least. They would be dropped off in North Central Thailand along the Mekong River. A small inflatable boat had been provided for the crossing, which would be done at night. Once inside Laos, they'd rely on stealth to reach the POW area. Their plan was to neutralize the guards at the stockade and then radio for the rescue choppers. Though there were two choppers for the mission; one would be held in reserve. They still didn't know how many men were being held in country but either helicopter could carry as many as fifteen men. They calculated that it would take no more than three weeks to travel by foot to the remote POW site.

Larry shaved his head and donned a Buddhist robe similar to the one he wore on his escape home. The CIA produced a passport for a German monk and a letter from an abbot of another Temple in North Vietnam, authorizing his odyssey. He would use the same cover story, as before, if and when he was stopped by soldiers. Larry was the only one of the four who wasn't armed, other than with a small knife.

Since Laos was a communist state, they planned to avoid any contact with the populace, other than the villages. Larry's job was three fold, namely, procuring food, assisting the villagers any way he could and gathering information about what was happening in and around the villages, such as soldiers or other threats. The other three would make themselves inconspicuous while he was in the village.

They were dropped off about halfway between the northernmost rope bridge and the city of Vientiane on the Thailand side of the river and paddled across the Mekong about two in the morning. They deflated their boat and hid it among the brush on the Laos side of the River. They didn't intend to come back to it unless there was an emergency; Jim Long carried a canister to inflate the raft; he hid it near the boat. The POW compound was due east of the trail they took when entering Laos. They hadn't traveled five miles before they spotted a camp fire in a clearing ahead; it was near dawn. The team hid in the underbrush waiting to see who was in the camp. At first light, they saw a squad of twelve soldiers camped there; two were on guard.

They waited to see which direction the soldiers would move at daylight. When it appeared that the squad was breaking camp and heading directly toward them, they beat a hasty retreat back to the river and hid in the foliage along the bank until the soldiers took a trail north.

"I believe we can wait another ten minutes and use the same trail. I don't think we exposed ourselves, so our plan is still viable. We probably lost a half day; that can't be helped. There'll be some unknowns that will be encountered; we'll just have to handle them as best we can when they arise. If anything, we need to be more alert. Let's load up and move out," Larry said.

This time Larry took the point with Long on his left flank, Kelly was on his right with Minh bringing up the rear.

Since they got a late start, they only travelled fifteen miles before they found a place to set up a cold camp. The four took turns keeping watch that night and they left at dawn the next morning. The second day was without incident and they were able to travel twenty miles before stopping. Near the end of the third day, they came across a village similar to those Larry had previously entered. Minh and the other two men found a place to rest while Larry went into the village, set his paper bag down in the center of the village and meditated. Soon some of the villagers put three handfuls of rice and some greens in his bag. No one conversed with him, so after being there for over an hour, he picked up his bag and went on his way. He met up with the other three and shared his food.

Although the terrain today was more difficult to travel than the last two days, they estimated that they walked at least ten miles. Their food supplies were low, but they were in good physical condition. At the next village, Larry was able to obtain some pork and a scoop full of rice. As he walked back to join his comrades, he found some indigenous fruit and filled his knapsack. The delay of the first day was forgotten and every member of the team was upbeat.

At night, they tried to camp at least fifty yards off the trail they were using. Tonight was no different. It was Larry who took the first watch, and heard a group coming up the trail. He quietly woke each member and alerted them to the situation; they took up positions behind some trees. Their rules of engagement dictated they not engage in a fire fight with any troops; yet, they could defend themselves if attacked. Larry knew that once they engaged any soldiers, they'd alert the entire region and have to abort the mission. He crawled closer to the trail and counted twelve soldiers heading east. He wondered if they were members of the same squad they'd encountered on their first day.

Before they started the next morning, Minh asked Kelly, in front of the other two, if it was possible that the soldiers who came through last night had a set region to patrol. "It's possible. The group numbered the same as the one we encountered our first day. If they're on a routine patrol, it should be easy to track them and therefore stay far enough away so they won't know we're in the area," Kelly responded.

"Won't the soldiers find out from the villagers that you're in the area?' Long asked Larry.

"The villagers will know about me but I've been discrete and haven't done or said anything that would make them suspicious enough to contact soldiers in the area. That's my experience from several months ago. It's common for the villages to accept strangers such as traveling monks. Besides, they're our main source of information and food. If I don't visit them, we don't know what's going on in our immediate area and we may not have enough food to complete the mission."

After a week, the team settled into a cohesive group and by the next week, they successfully caught some fish, dug up some bamboo shoots and began enjoying each other's company. Larry had been in six villages and the closer they came to Vietnam, more villagers spoke Vietnamese and therefore he was able to learn about patrols in the area. Today, the chief of the village spoke of the prison which contained some prisoners. He was evasive about its location; Larry didn't want to press the issue for fear the chief would become suspicious. He did allude to a location which was exactly where Larry had been the last time he was here.

During this latest adventure, he performed two funerals and one wedding in the villages he visited. He and his team looked forward to these ceremonies although the other three didn't attend. After each of the ceremonies, there was a feast and food was plentiful; Larry loaded up his knapsack before he left.

They reached the vicinity of the prison camp in North Vietnam at the end of three weeks. They split up into three units to approach the compound. Long and Kelly would come in from the west. Larry would come from the south and approach the entrance gate while Minh would circle around the camp and come in from the east. It was Larry's intent to enter the compound and try to determine how to extract the men kept there. They waited for Minh to get in place before the other team members made their move.

As he approached the entrance gate, there didn't appear to be any movement around the barbed wire exterior or inside; the front gate was unlocked. Larry went up to the gate and called out in Vietnamese. "Hello inside there. I'm a traveling Buddhist Monk. I seek shelter and food for the night?"

There was no response. He pushed the gate open and went inside. No one came to meet him. He walked around the interior of the compound and inside the few buildings that remained. By this time Minh and the other two arrived and entered the compound. "It's deserted," Minh said.

"Let's take a look around and see if we can determine if any Americans were here and, if so, how long have they been gone," Minh suggested.

After an hour they re-grouped in the building that appeared to be housing for the senior officer. "I found names on some of the posts in one building which I believe was used to house the prisoners. There were no last names, just first names, perhaps of wives or children. Six straw beds were in one room. They were here, alright," Kelly said.

The mine hadn't been worked in some time. The equipment was outdated and the shoring had come down in places. There may have been a cave-in and they stopped until it was cleaned up," Long reported.

"I'm not positive, but I believe that there were people here until thirty days ago. I think Larry is correct. This compound held six POWs and I believe all or most were Americans. I don't know whether they were Air Force or Army, but by looking at the names, they spoke English," Minh said.

He turned to Larry, "Your thoughts?"

"I'm disappointed. The question I have is, where did they go and why? It's possible they may be rotating between several camps and this was just one of them."

"Does this mean we're turning back?" Long asked Minh.

"Larry?"

"I'm not willing to give up without checking with some other villages to know what they heard or saw."

"Our food supply is low. We didn't plan on walking back out. Helicopters were to be our ride back. I don't think we can risk the choppers without the POWs. I think we may have to hoof it on limited food," Long said.

"What if you three go back and I stay another two weeks to see what I can find out?"

"There is no way that's going to happen. I know you're in charge in country, but we stay together," Minh responded.

"But I can make it here. The villages are willing to provide me enough food to survive. If they don't have food, then I can forage off the land. I've done it before and I can do it again. You three can make it back with the food we have left. You know the route and should be able to avoid any civilians or soldiers. It makes sense."

"I'm sorry Larry, I can't let you do that. All of us will go back together. That's an order," Minh said.

"The Op calls for me to be in command while we're in country. You three are going back and I'm going to stay another two weeks and see if I can find where they took the POWs. I've come this far; I don't want to go back without an answer."

"What if you find them?' You'll have no way of communicating with us or the helicopters, and no way of bringing back six or more men whose condition could be such that it would jeopardize everybody. If the three of us have to hogtie you, you're coming back with us." Minh was angry.

"Look, all of us know how to survive off the land. Long is the only one who has a problem in that he doesn't speak the language, but if he's with one of us, he's protected." Kelly said

"I agree." Long responded.

"Is there a way we could compromise on this? I suggest all of us go with Larry for a week and then if we don't have anything concrete, we get the hell out of here," Long said.

"Would you be willing to look for one week and then go back to Ubon?" Minh asked.

"It would be dangerous because I'd have to press the villages for information. If it's the only way it can be done, I'll agree to at least one week."

"Not at least one week; only one week or you're coming now. What's it going to be?" Minh was steadfast.

"I'll agree to a week, but if something concrete surfaces, we'll revisit the time limit, Larry responded.

"Where do you suggest we start?" Long asked.

"I want to go back to the last village. That chief knows more than he's telling me. I suggest we work it the way we did before, with you three out of sight." Larry answered.

It took them an hour and a half to travel back to the last village Larry visited before they went to the stockade. With the other three hidden in the forest, he made his way to the village, sat down in the middle of the shacks and placed his paper bag in front of him. Soon the chief walked over, placed some bread in the bowl and asked him what he was doing back here.

"I saw four men who seemed to be laying a trap for solitary travelers. I thought I'd come back this way; it was safe when I was here last."

"My wife has taken ill since you were here, perhaps you could meditate with her and soothe her pain?" The chief asked.

The woman was lying stretched out a makeshift cot in a small hut; there was an old trunk on one side of the bed and a wooden crate on the other side. Her breathing was heavy and sporadic. Larry placed his hand on her forehead; it was hot; he suspected a fever. He asked the chief if they had any antibiotics or alcohol. When he was told there were none in the village, he asked for a wet cloth which he used to wipe her face and neck. Larry stood over the woman, chanted for nearly fifteen minutes and then, with some of the other villagers, proceeded to meditate. When he was finished, he sought out the chief.

"Your wife is ill and needs some medical attention. Why not take her to the prison compound? They should have a doctor or some person who could give your wife some medicine."

"They're no longer there. They moved to another location two weeks ago."

"If its close, we could have some of your people transport her to their new location."

"It's too far. It's almost twenty miles due east of here. It would take too long. She wouldn't be able to handle the trip."

"What if I go and ask them for some medicine and then return with it? Your wife is ill and should have medicine as soon as possible."

The chief looked at Larry for some time, then told him where the camp was and that there were fifteen soldiers guarding six prisoners. All of the prisoners were white.

"What if you were to give me something in writing so they'd know it was for your wife?"

The chief wrote the request on one side of an old paper bag and handed it to Larry. Just then, multiple shots rang out, followed by several bursts of fire. It was as though there was a running battle. The shooting kept up for a full five minutes and then ceased. Villagers scurried to their huts. The chief asked Larry to join him in his hut where his wife lay ill. Thirty minutes later, the chief, under Larry's urging, sent two of his people to see if they could find out what the shooting was all about. In the interim, the chief directed everyone to remain in their huts. It was an hour later when the two villagers returned.

"Four of our soldiers are dead and there's some blood leading toward the Laotian Border. Three of our soldiers survived; two will probably come this way. They said foreigners were hiding in the trees and, when ordered to come out, they started firing at our soldiers. Our radio was damaged so we couldn't call for reinforcements. One soldier is following the foreigners."

"Are the two who are coming here wounded?" Larry asked.

"Yes. They'll have to go for medical attention to the camp where they're holding the foreign white men."

Rescue of the POWs seemed out of the question; perhaps his own squad had been eliminated. The best he could hope for was to visit the camp to the east and verify that there are POWs still inside Vietnam; it would be risky. If any of his group survived, Minh's responsibility would be to save the squad and get to Thailand as best they could. Larry knew he was on his own. Well, he did it before; why couldn't he do it again? The risk was the North Vietnamese soldiers. He couldn't rely on their restraint. They would be on full alert at the POW camp because foreigners had been seen in the area.

Before he was able to leave, two soldiers came into the village and sat down; one was wounded in the shoulder. The chief found some clean cloths but deferred to Larry to treat the wound and bandage his shoulder. While he was attending to the soldier, he asked one of them what happened. His story was similar to what the two villagers told him and the chief.

"Two were white, one was Vietnamese, maybe Laotian; the two white men were large. They were dressed in camouflaged clothes and had automatic weapons. They killed four of our men but they lost their radio in the battle. It lay on the ground were they hid; it had a bullet hole in it. I think one of the large white men is wounded; there was blood on the ground."

"Which way did they go?" The chief asked

"Toward the Laotian border."

"You should go with the soldiers to their camp. You can help the wounded man and get some medicine for my wife and bring it back," the chief told Larry.

It didn't seem like he had much choice, especially since one of the soldiers said they would do that. Larry wasn't nervous; he had an innate confidence in his ability to handle the mission, but he knew it was risky. He looked back over the initial trek home and drew upon his inner strength; he would succeed.

They made their way to the compound in two days. They could've been there earlier, but the wounded soldier needed to stop and rest more frequently. Larry changed his bandage twice but the blood was still flowing. Larry wanted to show up around noon, when the soldiers were eating, but it was later in the afternoon when they finally arrived. As they approached the gate, four guards came out to meet them and told them to halt. Larry let the soldiers he was with do the talking.

The two soldiers told the guards what happened when they encountered some foreigners. "Who is this?" One of the guards asked, pointing at Larry.

"I'm a wandering Buddhist Monk. I wonder if I can have shelter and some food."

"You can't be here. Go away. The guard nearest him yelled loud enough for an officer to come up to the gate. "What's going on here?" he asked.

Larry responded, "I'm a Buddhist Monk. I'm in need of some food; I have a note from the Quoc Trac village for some medical supplies for the chief's wife. It was I who bandaged this wounded soldier and helped carry him here.""

"Let me see the note." The officer held out his hand."

"What's wrong with the woman?"

"She has a high fever and is coughing. It's probably a form of flu."

"All we have is aspirin."

"If that's all you have, I'll take it back to the chief."

The officer turned to the wounded soldier. "Did he help you?"

"He bandaged my arm and assisted me to get here. I don't think I would've made it if he hadn't been along."

The young officer motioned the two soldiers to follow him but told Larry to wait.

"I'll be right back with some aspirin. You can't come in here. This is a restricted area."

As the young officer was returning to the gate, he was intercepted by a more senior officer. They conversed for a few seconds and then both approached the gate. "Captain Vang wants to talk to you, monk." The younger man said.

'Can you perform a funeral service?" Vang asked Larry.

"Yes, I've led a few of those."

"What's in your bag?"

"Some crumbs, a pair of socks, a razor, a hat and some identification."

"Dump the contents on the ground." As soon as the senior man said that, the four guards became alert and trained their weapons on Larry, who dumped the contents in front of them. One of the guards opened the gate and pointed his rifle at Larry's chest. The senior officer followed the soldier outside the gate and examined the contents of the bag.

"What are these?" He said pointing to some documents?"

"Those are my passport and a letter from the abbot directing my three year odyssey."

"You are German?"

"I was born in Germany."

"Your Vietnamese is excellent. How long have you been here?"

"Twenty years."

"Why does this letter say you must atone for your transgressions?"

"I was weak. I touched a female disciple inappropriately and was caught. My punishment is to wander the countryside for three years before I can return to my monastery." The senior officer couldn't contain a smile.

"What monastery was that?

"Tran Quoc, near Hanoi."

"Why do you need a razor?"

"To shave my head."

"I want you to perform a funeral service. The guards will hold your bag until you leave; come with me."

On the other side of the main building, a corpse, covered by a sheet, was laid out on a table. "This is my brother. He died two days ago. I want you to perform a funeral service and then cremate him."

"I'd be glad to perform a funeral service for your brother. There are some things I'd like completed by tomorrow morning. First thing I need is a wooden altar. Can you have one made?"

"Yes."

On the altar I want a picture of your brother, some flowers and fruit. I plan to stay and meditate with the body all night. Do you have some incense to burn around the body?"

"We can have all that for you. I understand you've asked for some food?"

"If you have enough to spare, I would appreciate it."

The Captain barked out some orders and Larry was given a bowl of rice with some cooked vegetables, chicken and a slice of bread. It was getting near sunset when they finished making the altar. The soldiers decorated it as Larry wished and stacked wood and brush near the table. He squatted down near the corpse and started to chant. The captain stood nearby for thirty minutes, then went into the main building.

Larry would alternate chanting and meditating throughout the night. A sentry stayed close but it didn't prevent Larry from looking around to see what else was in the compound. He didn't see any prisoners the entire time he was inside the compound, but he did recognize that food was being delivered to a small building about one hundred yards from where he squatted. There were only three buildings inside the compound. He assumed the main building housed the compound's headquarters, kitchen and eating area. There was a smaller building which probably housed most of the soldiers and the small one they were taking food to.

At dawn, he rose and under the careful eye of the sentry, did basic calisthenics and then sat down waiting for Captain Vang, the camp commander, to arrive. Vang directed there would be a service at nine in the morning, followed by a cremation. At the directed time, ten soldiers and two officers stood around the dead body and Larry started chanting. Some of the soldiers joined in. Then they meditated for thirty minutes before Larry gave a sermon. He spoke about life and death and he finished it with a saying from Buddha:

> Life is a journey
> Death is a return to earth
> The universe is like a nice inn
> The passing years are like dust
> Regard this Phantom World
> As a star at dawn, a bubble in a stream
> A flash of lightning in a summer cloud
> A flickering lamp, a phantom and a dream

After the brush was ignited, the ten soldiers, with the man's brother trailing behind, picked up the table with the corpse on it and placed it over the brush. Larry supervised the entire service and, when it was over, he asked if he could have some more food and he'd be on his journey.

He wasn't nervous during the entire twenty four hours he was here. It was as though this was his life's work. It must have seemed the same to the Camp Commander because he came up to Larry and thanked him. "I haven't seen a service this beautiful even in the main Pagodas of Hanoi. This is a military installation and I reported your arrival and what you did for us. My parent command is seventy miles to the northeast. The two men you helped must report there; I want you to escort them there. This shouldn't be an imposition for you since your odyssey hasn't been completed. I hear the food is very good there."

Larry knew that the next few hours could change his life forever. He couldn't afford to go further in country and he couldn't object to the request by the captain. "I would be happy to comply. How do I reach this outpost?"

"I'll have one of my soldiers drive you and the two soldiers who came with you. If I never see you again, I'm Captain Vang and I want to thank you for my brother's beautiful funeral service."

He handed Larry his bag with his papers inside. The two men shook hands. He knew the POWs were here but at no time did he see them.

Chapter 21

Their plan called for his group to take three weeks to reach the POW encampment, neutralize the guards, rescue the POWs, call in helicopters to perform the extraction and then everyone would go back to Ubon on the choppers. Larry called Jean the night before they departed and told her to expect a call within three and a half weeks, if everything went according to plan. She was a nervous wreck for the entire time and on the twenty-fifth day after performing a morning appendectomy, she called Langley to talk to Larry's boss.

"Jean, I don't have any word yet. None of them have reported in and we don't know where they are."

"What do you mean you don't know where they are? They have radios. Call them to see what the problem is."

"It's not that simple. We don't know what they've encountered and we can't risk trying to contact them for fear they may be compromised."

"What are you going to do?"

"We have a meeting this afternoon to see what our options are. I can't tell you more than that. As soon as we hear from them, I'll let you know. I'm sorry Jean, but that's the best I can do for you right now."

She made a call to the Base Commander in Ubon, Thailand, but he didn't have a clue as to what was going on.

"Mrs. Stephens, if this is a CIA operation, I'd be the last person to know. You have to go through their channels to find out anything. I'm sorry. All I can do is say a prayer for your husband and his group."

She wanted to call someone else, like her congressman, but she knew that wouldn't be wise. This was a top-secret mission and any leak would put her husband in jeopardy. She didn't like it but she had to wait and hope for the best. Though Larry was paramount in her life, her days were filled with her duties at the hospital and her children at home. She rose at six in the morning, reached the hospital at seven to begin her rounds and then would assist in one or two operations before she'd end her day at the hospital. She'd have lunch with Walter each week as part of a staff get-together. Though he asked if they could have dinner, she declined.

Her dad would come in the morning, fix breakfast for the children and take them to school. He'd pick them up in the afternoon and wait until Jean got home. Today started the same as every other day, except there was a major accident on the highway south of Greenville and, instead of assisting at the scene, she was called upon to repair the femoral artery of a male victim of the crash. Normally, the Vascular Surgeon would perform this intricate procedure but Doctor Williams was up to his armpits in trying to save a female victim of the crash. He felt Jean was qualified since she'd assisted on two other vascular surgeries, one of which was on the femoral artery

Jean wasn't the least bit flustered and checked the intravenous line in the man's arm. Then she monitored his heart rate, blood pressure, breathing and oxygen flow by the anesthesiologist. After she made an incision in the leg and stopped the flow of blood, she attached the graft and then performed an arteriogram on the affected area to ensure that blood was flowing steadily and sufficiently. Doctor Williams came by as she was finishing the graft of the affected area and assisted her in finishing up. "Great job, Jean. That was first class; you're going to make a fine surgeon."

After the vascular surgery, she assisted Walter Osborne on two other operations. They finished after seven in the evening and after he cleaned up, he suggested they get something to eat. She accepted. The Embassy Restaurant near the hospital specialized in French Cuisine; Walter made a reservation for eight. Jean called home and told her father that she'd be home around ten. They arrived separately just after the peak rush hour and had no trouble being seated at a good table. Jean ordered a Scotch and water; Walter a dry martini. They hadn't spent any time together, other than at work, since Larry came home. Jean had previously told Walter that she planned to spend the remainder of her life with Larry. He told her he was still in love with her and would wait a reasonable amount of time to see if she'd change her mind. Walter didn't know anything about Larry's second incursion into Vietnam. He, like everyone else, thought he was in Washington seeking employment.

The Embassy emphasized an intimate setting and good food. Some of the old feelings for Walter had surfaced after two drinks and Jean knew danger could be lurking close by. She ordered Coq-au-Vin and he ordered Steak au Poivre; they shared a lobster salad and a bottle of Pouilly Fussé; she insisted they split the bill. They'd both parked in the restaurant parking area and he walked her to her vehicle. When she turned to say goodbye, he took her into his arms and kissed her; she returned the kissed with equal fervor before she broke away. "It's true that I still love you and I always will, but I gave my word to Larry that I wouldn't be unfaithful as long as we were together and I'm going to hold you to that promise."

There were two ZI trucks parked inside the compound in front of headquarters. **Larry Stephens** watched as a soldier walked over to one of them and got into the driver seat. After several attempts to start the vehicle, it finally caught. The driver turned the truck around and signaled Larry to get in. The other two soldiers, one of which was wounded, walked over. After they put the wounded man on a cot in the rear of the truck, Larry and the other soldier got in the front with Larry in the middle. After a couple of coughs and sputters, the engine settled down and they were signaled through the gate by the guard. He didn't know exactly where they were taking him, but he knew the dirt road leading from the stockade was about five miles in length before it intersected the main gravel road leading east and west.

The two soldiers loosened their ties and the passenger put his feet up on the grill and lit a cigarette. The talk soon turned to the many girls at the gin mill just outside the gate of the installation where they were headed. Luo's name came up many times; apparently there was a friendly rivalry between the two soldiers on either side of him. They asked Larry if he liked girls. He smiled.

Their rifles were behind the head rests in the cabin of the truck; it didn't appear that they were carrying side arms. As soon as they stopped at the intersection of the access road and the gravel road heading east and west, Larry elbowed the man on his right twice in the head and the soldier slumped forward. The driver didn't react at first, and by the time he did, Larry placed two judo chops on his neck and he slumped forward. Although both men were somewhat subdued, they were still conscious. Larry opened the driver's door and pushed the driver to the ground; he followed right after him and hit him one more time in the head. He reached back into the cabin and pulled the other soldier to him and placed him alongside his fallen comrade.

He tied them up with their shoe laces and belts. Just then, he heard the soldier in the back ask what was going on, so Larry went to the rear of the truck, pulled back the flap in the rear, reached in, grabbed the man's hand and pulled him out of the truck. He tied him up and put him and the driver in the rear with a cloth in their mouths. He tied the other soldier to the passenger's seat in case someone saw a monk driving a vehicle and alerted the authorities. He placed the soldier's hat on his head and leaned him back in the seat. Anyone seeing him would think he was taking a nap. He turned west and was on his way.

After Larry left with the three soldiers, Captain Vang called headquarters to speak to Major Nguyen and make his daily report. Just as he finished, he remembered the monk and told his superior he had a surprise for him. He told him about the German monk and the odyssey he was on. "Where is the monk now?" Nguyen asked.

"He's on his way to you with three soldiers," Vang responded.

"He may not be a monk; there's a strong possibility that he's an American flyer who was shot down near Hanoi over four years ago. He's probably with that group of foreigners our men had a fire fight with a couple of days ago. They want to free the POWs. "Did the monk have a letter from the abbot of Tran Quoc Pagoda?"

"No, it was signed by an abbot of a different temple."

Take a squad and go after him; I want him alive. Put the rest of your men on high alert until I get there. I'm leaving here immediately and I'm coming your way with reinforcements for the compound. If you move quickly, you should be able to capture him. Either way, we'll have him in a vice. He's very dangerous and has been directly responsible for the death of six of our soldiers. Don't take any chances."

Before Nguyen left to intercept Larry, he called his uncle and told him about the monk. "I want reinforcements sent to that compound immediately. They can't take the POWs from us. We'll lose our bargaining chips. Don't fail me," General Tran said. Nguyen didn't have the nerve to tell his uncle that he'd already thought of that.

The main question for Larry was what to do with the three soldiers and the truck. He made a quick decision and drove to the compound they'd initially come to see. The gate was still open. The three soldiers were conscious by now; the one in the front asked him what he was doing.

He ignored the question and put the soldier in the main building, found some rope, and tied him to a chair. He did the same with the other two soldiers who were tied up in the rear. With all three secured to chairs, he field stripped their weapons, took their ammunition and put a hole in the truck's gas tank; he watched the gas siphon out. Larry found a radio in the glove compartment along with a map of the area. He took the map and destroyed the radio. He spent the next ten minutes looking around the compound and found a couple of cans of vegetables that had been left behind. He didn't worry about the three soldiers. He was sure they'd eventually free themselves, but they'd have to walk back to their installation.

Larry knew it was risky, but he made his way back to the last village he'd been in. The chief was waiting for medicine for his wife. Although he wanted something stronger, he was happy to receive the aspirin. The two men chatted and Larry was given a bowl of rice and some dried bread. He asked if he could have more bread for his journey. "We're short of bread, but I can give you some more rice."

"The last time I was here there was some shooting close by. What was that all about?"

"There were some foreigners in the woods. They killed four of our soldiers. The soldiers wounded at least one of them, but I don't know what happened next. They may have gotten away and escaped to Laos. Will you be coming back this way?"

Larry wasn't sure why he asked that question, so he decided to hedge his bet. "I'm heading south toward Saigon."

Larry suspected that if any of the three CIA men were wounded, chances were they'd head back the same way they came Minh had a good sense of direction and a level head. Larry was sure Minh could find the trail they'd used coming through Laos. So there would be no question in the Village Chief's mind, Larry left the village the next morning travelling south and then made his way back northwest until he found the trail his squad had taken.

At the next village of ten huts where he begged for food, the chief spoke of foreigners in the area. They had been spotted last week about five miles from here. He didn't want to ask the chief directly about the foreigners, so he wondered out loud what they could be doing here and let the chief tell him. "They're heading to Thailand, most likely. We sent a runner to an army post to alert them about the foreigners. Our military doesn't work fast, but I know there are a couple of six man patrols in the area looking for them. If you are heading west, be careful. Those men are thugs."

Just when he was about to leave, six North Vietnamese Soldiers came into the village and asked the chief if he'd seen the foreigners recently. The chief told them he hadn't seen the foreigners.

When the soldiers saw Larry, they asked him who he was and what he was doing here. The chief told them that Larry was a wandering Buddhist Monk."

"Show us your papers. Where is your Temple?" one soldier asked Larry.

He produced the letter he forged with an abbot's signature from the monastery near Hanoi. The soldier read the letter and seemed satisfied, but he asked the obvious question of why he had to wander for three years."

"I placed my hands inappropriately on a nun at the monastery. For that I'm being punished."

The soldiers broke out laughing and said something to the effect, "you're a good man." They left the village as fast as they entered. He could tell they were headed north.

Sensing that Minh and the group were one to four days ahead of him, he left the village and told the chief he'd be careful. A half day later he found where Minh and the other two had previously camped He checked the area and found some bloody rags behind one of the trees; they'd been lucky to avoid capture this far. His goal now was to reach them as soon as he could and help them escape. Even though they failed to extract the POWs; finding where they were might save their lives in the long run.

Two days later, believing he was in Laos; he decided to rest. He found a place about twenty-five yards off the trail in a small thicket, leaned against a tree and shut his eyes. He sensed he was being watched and opened his eyes; three men looking down at him and he stood up. Their clothes were shabby and ill fitting. One spoke to him in a foreign tongue; he assumed it was Laotian. Even though he'd learned a few phrases, they spoke too fast for him to comprehend. He assumed what they were after so he took off his bag, placed it in front of him and backed up. The leader of the three grabbed the bag, dumped the contents on the ground and sorted through the items while the other two brandished knives at Larry. The leader looked up at Larry and put out his hand.

"I have no money, I'm a poor monk," Larry said in Vietnamese as he placed his hands out with his palms up.

This didn't seem to appease the men. One came toward Larry and raised his fist to strike him, Larry closed his hand over the man's fist and struck out with his other hand, driving his knuckles into the man's Adam's apple; the attacker collapsed to the ground grabbing his throat. The other two were stunned and that was long enough for Larry to jump over the fallen man, kick one of the thugs in the groin and judo chop the other in the neck. While they were down, he hit all three until they were unconscious. He dragged one at a time into the brush but not close to each other and tied them up. Their possessions were limited but he confiscated their rice, bread and knives. None of the three had a firearm. It occurred to him that he'd been careless and allowed the thugs to get too close. Sleep was out of question now; he had to create some distance before they freed themselves and alerted the authorities that he was in the area.

The spots he picked to rest during the next few days were more strategic. He set up alert signals around him so he wouldn't be caught off guard and he slept with one eye open. Three days later, he sensed he was close to his group; he found one of the camps they'd used recently. He knew they had to be short of food and probably might even be ill. On his two missions into Vietnam, Larry learned how to track humans and how to come upon anyone without being heard. He saw them huddled together in a group of tall trees. Minh was keeping watch while Long and Kelly rested. He could see that one of the former seals lay on the ground; there was blood on his pants and shirt. Larry crouched behind a tree and called out.

"Minh, it's me, Larry Stephens. Don't shoot, I'm coming in."

"You may be Larry and you may not be. Come in slowly with your hands on your head or I'll blow it off," Minh said.

Larry took his time and did as he was commanded. Minh's face was drawn and Kelly and Long were lying down. "Am I ever glad to see you, Larry? We thought you were dead. Well, we made it this far, but were out of food and water. Long and Kelly are wounded."

"You keep watch while I tend to Kelly's wounds," Larry told Minh.

"We're glad to see you," Kelly said as Larry checked his bandages.

Kelly had been shot in the shoulder and leg. The initial determination was that the wounds weren't life threatening, but they hadn't been treated properly and there was a good chance of infection. Kelly had bled some and his face was drawn and his were eyes bloodshot.

They were near a stream and Larry found a rag in Long's knapsack. He washed it in the stream and then cleaned Kelly's wounds. The man winced and cried out a little when Larry cleaned the area and removed all the dried blood around the wounds. He'd found some bandages at the Vietnamese POW outpost and used them to re-wrap Kelly's wounds. Long's wound was more superficial. His leg had been grazed by a bullet and was easier to tend to. Long was tired because of the energy he expended while walking with the damaged leg. He thanked Larry and told him how glad he was to see him. Although they couldn't light a fire, Larry took some of the rice from his bag, put it in a bowl and added water. The water reduced the clumps in the cooked rice and he fed Kelly. He gave Minh and Long some of his bread.

"I haven't been able to sleep for two days. Do you think we can rest a little before we continue?" Minh asked Larry.

"I'm sorry, but we need to cover more ground before I'm comfortable with taking a rest. I subdued some bandits yesterday and another three soldiers two days before that. If any of them gets loose, they'll be looking for a Buddhist Monk. Let's get through today before we stop. I'll take the watch tonight while you sleep. Long seems okay but Kelly is weak and will need assistance to walk."

Larry helped Kelly up and put the man's arm around his neck. The four made their way west. Near sunset, they found a secluded place off the trail near another stream. Larry said they could rest here overnight. He took the rest of his rice, added water to the bowl and, when it soaked up enough water, he fed all three. He took Minh's firearm and told them to get some sleep. He'd be awake all night.

Chapter 22

Captain Vang rounded up supplies, food and ammunition for himself and five soldiers. He got in the remaining ZI truck and started down the access road from the compound. When they reached the intersection, they turned left. The ZI was in poor condition, barely reaching thirty-five miles an hour, but they weren't more than thirty minutes behind the monk when they left. An hour into the chase, Vang yelled at the driver. "We should've caught them by now. Go faster; we've got to apprehend that monk."

"The truck is moving as fast as I can make it go. These are Russian rejects that we have." The driver was courteous, but Vang got the message,

The captain tried several times to reach the soldiers he'd sent with Larry by radio, but no one was answering. He estimated they were half way to his battalion's headquarters when they saw another truck approaching from the opposite direction. The two trucks pulled up alongside each other. Major Nguyen yelled at Vang from the other truck. "If you don't have them, then they didn't come this way. He must have overpowered the soldiers and gone another way. Follow me back to your compound. I want to be sure we have enough men to repel any attack; we'll have to move the POWs soon."

Major Nguyen's group reached the compound five minutes ahead of Vang. He unloaded his ten soldiers and had them construct a barricade about twenty feet back from the main gate and then man it with five of the soldiers, they'd be relieved by the other five in eight hours and by five of Vang's men the remaining eight hours. They'd be under a high state of readiness for two days. The following day, two NVA helicopter gunships flew in and extracted the six POWs and Major Nguyen. They delivered them to his headquarters in Da Nang. He'd keep them there for three days before moving them to another secret location, which was being made ready for them. Nguyen called Commander Tran when the extraction was complete. "Well, at least you didn't lose the POWs. What's the status of the American Monk?"

"I'm sending Capt. Vang and nine soldiers to capture him and bring him back. I've impressed upon Vang your concerns. He understands that he must bring the American back."

"What about the foreigners who were involved in the fire fight?"

"I'll have Vang keep an eye out for them. The American may try to join up with them. If possible we'll capture or kill all of them."

"We can't have foreign mercenaries running around in our country. They must be eliminated to set an example."

The major had taken over Vang's office until the arrival of the helicopters. Once the POWs were moved and the threat eliminated, his plan was to have Vang go after Larry and any of the foreigners that were left. He called the captain into the office and laid out a plan.

"Here's a map marking the monk's most probable route of travel. From what one of the surviving soldiers that chased him last year told us, the monk used this trail over the mountains inside Laos. They were about here when the monk disappeared. It's possible that he had help from one of the villages or ethnic groups," Nguyen said, pointing to the map.

"We also know he visited these two villages and was supplied with food. Chances are that he'll go to one or both of these on his way out of the country. This could very well be an American CIA operation including the monk. I don't believe they'll enter Thailand near Ubon as before. They'll probably cross the Mekong and get helicopter support in the northern part of Thailand, probably as close to a straight line from where he was last spotted." Nguyen plotted a ruler over the suspected course.

"General Tran wants that monk captured, not killed; I don't want to disappoint him. Take nine men and supplies. If you have to kill some of the foreigners, do it, but save the monk for the general. Are there any questions?"

"What about the Laotian Government?"

"I've made contact with their military in Vientiane and have received their cooperation. We've told them that you'll be in the area chasing some CIA thugs. They'll help if they can. I want you out of here by sunup. Check in with me on a daily basis. Don't fail me."

Larry's conditioning and his faith were what was carrying him this far. He'd been trained at the Temple to go extended periods of time without food or sleep; he'd become the ultimate warrior. He wanted to be home with Jean, yet he was comfortable in this setting and glad he came upon the three. Their eyes gave them away. Minh's effort to this point had been herculean but he needed sleep. Larry allowed them to sleep through the night and when he woke them at dawn, they seemed to be in good enough shape to make it through the next day. That's all that Larry wanted. If they could take it a day at a time, he knew they'd make it.

Minh took his time getting up but he said he was ready to move on. "I was too exhausted to ask if you found the POWs."

"I didn't see them but I was in the camp where they were being held, I'll bet my life that they were there at that time, but they may have been moved after I left. We'll talk about it when we travel a little further."

"You think we're going to make it?" Minh asked.

"You bet."

The next day, Larry begged at two villages and although most of the people in the village didn't speak Vietnamese, he was still able to get extra food. The other three hid out about a mile from the village and when Larry returned, they split the food. It wasn't much but it was enough to get them moving and to look forward to the next day. He also wanted to be candid with them about their chances of reaching safety.

"I didn't say anything about what I did while we were separated, but I think you have a right to know about that and what we may need to do."

No one said anything so Larry continued. When we separated, I went to the village, as planned. While I was there, the village chief asked me to look at his wife, who was ill. After I examined her, I told the chief that she had the flu and needed some antibiotics. He told me there was none in the village, but he was sure they had some at a camp where they were holding some foreigners. I was now pretty sure where the POWs were. I asked him for something in writing and I'd go to that camp and get the antibiotics and then return. About that time, you had a fire fight with some NVA. I was about to leave and try to find you when two of the NVA soldiers who were in that fire fight came to the village; one was wounded. The village chief suggested that I take a look at his wounds and see if I could help him. The bullet had passed through the soldier's side. All I did was put on a fresh bandage. The chief then suggested that I help the wounded soldier back to his camp twenty miles away. He felt the commandant of that camp would be receptive to giving medicine to someone who helped their wounded."

"When we reached the compound, they asked me to perform a funeral ceremony and were so pleased with the ritual that they insisted I go to their headquarters, seventy miles away, and meditate with their soldiers. To make sure I was going, they sent the two soldiers I'd escorted to their camp, along with a driver. I subdued all three when we were about five miles away, then took them to the deserted compound we visited. I left them tied up, without ammunition or a vehicle. When I didn't show up with the three soldiers, my guess is that they would send out a search party for the monk on an odyssey. There's a history here. Significantly, that's the same cover story I used to escape from Vietnam last year. That time, they sent ten men after me. I was captured by four of them and held for two days. To my surprise, they called me by name. Apparently they had my ID card which had been taken from me by bandits during my escape. The four soldiers were part of a group of ten sent from somewhere in Vietnam but directed by the Commander of the Hanoi District. He's the one who's searched for me for over four years. .Of the ten that were sent to bring me back, I disabled two and escaped two others prior to reaching the Thai border. The others who were tracking me were killed by Thai civilians at the border."

"It isn't going to take much to put two and two together and realize that I'm the same monk who escaped them a year ago. My point is that I'm toxic. They will probably send many more troops to apprehend me; you may be more at risk with me than you'd be separated from me. I know we had this discussion before, but all three of you may want to reconsider."

"It still doesn't matter. We came together and we're going back together. I see the risk being greater without you," Minh said

"When I escaped before, I had some help in the latter part of my journey. I traveled some distance after I was wounded and eventually passed out on the trail. I was found by a group of Hmong villagers and taken to their camp. My wound was treated and I was fed until I regained my strength. The reason I'm telling you all of this is that my instincts tell me we're going to need the Hmong to get through this. I think I can find their village again. Since we're close to the trail I took through Hmong country, I suggest that we deviate a little and see if we can find that village, get Kelly healthy, and then be on our way. I don't like the odds of the NVA versus us."

Over the next two days, Kelly was improving and Minh had returned to his old optimistic self. They stopped twice each day near some villages so that Larry could procure food, then they'd move on. All four were feeling optimistic; Long and Kelly were able to handle some of the night sentry duties so Larry could sleep. They weren't sure if anyone was pursuing them and, if they were, they couldn't tell how far behind they might be. Larry guessed it depended on how bad they wanted him; he'd get his answer soon.

They were nearing the crest of the hill, close to where he was wounded months earlier when shots rang out; they appeared to be coming from down the trail. The four dove for cover and took up defensive positions behind some rocks along the trail. They had a good view of the trail below.

Long was the tactician in the group. "Let's spread out more so they can't outflank us. We can hold this position for a short time, but we're going to have to find better cover or they'll overrun us at night."

"Larry, do you think you can find the Hmong Village?" Minh asked.

"I'm pretty sure, but we don't want to deplete our forces. It could take three hours before I'd get back and that's if I find them right away and if they'll come."

"I vote you go." Minh said. Long and Kelly agreed."

"I'll be back as soon as possible."

Larry stayed on the left side as he crawled up the trail. Once he found thicker vegetation, he rose and hurried in the direction he thought the Hmong Village was located."

He was moving as fast as he could when he heard gunshots coming from the location where he left his group. After several wrong turns, he came upon a clearing in the heavy vegetation. There was the Hmong Village straight ahead of him. Several villagers came out to meet him. He remembered some of their language and asked for the chief and a glass of water. The chief remembered him but it wasn't the chief who spoke English or Vietnamese. There were two other villagers who he conversed with the last time he was here; neither was in the village. He remembered their names and was able to communicate with the chief that he needed to talk to both. Chu was on a hunting expedition while the other, Akamu, who previously worked with the CIA, was at another village.

He didn't know how he did it, but he was able to communicate to the chief that it was important that he talk to Chu. One hour later the man came into the village and threw his arms around Larry. Speaking slowly, Larry told him the problem and what he needed. After a long discourse with the chief, Chu told Larry they would send ten men and Akamu, who'd just returned.

It was four hours before he and the Hmong returned to the site of the attack. No one was there. Akamu sent out four men to see if they could pick up a trail. Only four of the Hmong had weapons, namely AK 47s, probably confiscated from the North Vietnamese. Three others carried spears, two had bows and arrows while one carried an axe. Larry wondered if they had any chance against the NVA with automatic weapons.

Within thirty minutes, three of the scouts returned. Minh, Kelly and Long were alive but had been captured by the NVA. They were tied up and being held at the bottom of the trail. All three had been wounded.

Akamu sent the three with weapons to join the one who was left to watch the Vietnamese and told them to get behind the NVA while four others circled the North Vietnamese to come up behind them. Larry, Akamu and the other two carefully took the trail toward where the Vietnamese were camped. When they were within one hundred yards of the aggressors, Akamu signaled his men via a bird call and Larry heard gun fire. More shots rang out as though fire was being returned by the Vietnamese captors.

He, Akamu and two other men crept closer until they could see where the NVA was camped. Two Vietnamese soldiers lay on the ground; they weren't moving. Just then he heard another soldier cry out and stumble forward; there was a spear in his chest. He still didn't see Minh or the other two. The odds were getting better.

Captain Vang was in an indefensible situation. He couldn't retreat and he couldn't go forward. And someone from the south threw a spear that killed another of his men. Well, he had the three hostages and decided to use them. "If you don't leave, I'm going to kill the three hostages I have, one by one. Now get out of here." He said in Vietnamese.

Akamu asked Larry what he said and Larry told him. "I'll respond," Larry replied.

"You're welcome to leave, but the three prisoners will be released to us. The longer you resist, the more men you'll lose; eventually we'll prevail."

"You can't defeat us before we kill them all," he responded.

Larry knew the remaining soldiers could hear the interchange between him and Vang. "There's an ant hill near our friend's village. We outnumber you and will take all that survive and put them near the ant hill. It's your choice but we want the prisoners released now. I give you my word that you will be allowed to retreat." Larry wasn't sure he could make that promise. Akamu and his friends were very angry and remembered the many atrocities by the North Vietnamese during the Vietnamese War.

Captain Vang was no dummy. His men were loyal, but given the chance to live or be captured and put to the ant hill, wasn't much of a choice. They looked at him for a decision. He decided to make one last threat. "We're going to take these prisoners with us and go back down the trail; if we see anyone, we'll kill all three."

"We have you surrounded and you know it. This is your last chance to get out of here alive. Leave the prisoners there and we'll not attack. Cause them any harm and we'll kill all of you," Larry responded. Akamu's men started firing on Vang and his group; soon the white flag went up.

"Leave the weapons of your dead and start walking down the hill," Larry ordered.

As Vang and his remaining men started retreating, the Hmong moved in and secured the prisoners. All three had been shot. Long was in especially poor condition and Larry wasn't sure he'd survive. The villagers quickly made wooden stretchers and carried the three to their village. Before they started back to the village, Akamu voiced his concern to Larry. "They have their weapons and their orders. Chances are that they'll go a short distance and come back looking for us. They may not want to go back without you and the prisoners. We either have to kill them or follow them back to the Vietnamese border.

He and Larry discussed the situation for a few minutes. "Okay, can your people keep out of sight and follow them to their border. If they should turn around, kill them." He and Akamu shook hands.

Minh told Larry that as soon as he went for help, the NVA charged and he and the other two were wounded and had to surrender. Minh was shot in the left shoulder and had been kicked repeatedly in the ribs; he was sure two were broken. He wanted to shoot the remaining seven NVA. Long's wounds were in his right hand and right shoulder. He, too, had been beaten badly; his reactions were slow. Kelly was shot in the right leg; previously he'd been shot in the left leg. Neither of his wounds were life threatening. The three men needed medical attention and at least two weeks rest before they'd be ready to complete their journey. It was Larry and one of the villagers who cleaned and dressed the wounds, but it was Larry who took the bullets out of Kelly's leg and Minh's shoulder. He'd never treated a bullet wound before, but the training he'd received from the monk who saved his life at the pagoda and his wife's explanation of his operation, gave him a feeling of how to treat bullet wounds.

It was Long who was a problem. With multiple wounds on his right side and possibly broken ribs, he needed constant care. Larry took the bullet out of his shoulder and bandaged his ribs and tried to reset his hand that had been broken by a bullet. Two of the women, who acted as the medical team from the village, spelled Larry so he could get some rest. Seven days passed before Long appeared to be gaining strength and could sit up; it was then that Larry slept for nearly two days straight.

They lost their radio in the fire fight and had no way to contact the CIA, so a helicopter rescue was eliminated; they'd have to walk out. The NVA survivors had been tracked to the border but Larry wasn't sure they'd heard the last of them. Someone wanted him badly and chances were they'd come back and hide at the bottom of the trail toward Thailand, waiting to pounce on him and the others.

Larry was correct. He hadn't heard the last of Captain Vang. As soon as the Vietnamese were across the border, Vang reassembled his men and told them they were going to go after the American and his friends. He decided not to report his status to his commander until the job was completed. They'd made it very clear they wanted the monk and he'd better not come back without him. He assessed the condition of his men, the amount of ammunition he had left and how much food remained. They were short of food but they could take it from the villages on the way. He'd sent four men to bring back as much food as possible from the villages in the area; they brought back half of his needs but he was ready.

Jean Stephens was distraught; she hadn't heard from anyone; after four more calls, the CIA wasn't responding. She prayed that Larry was still alive, but she was having doubts. There was no one to talk to, other than her parents, and she didn't want to discuss the situation with her mother. The only thing her fellow workers, including Walter Osborne, knew was that Larry was in Washington looking for a job. They could see the change in Jean's demeanor and her immediate supervisor, Dr. Brown, asked her what was wrong.

"There's nothing wrong. I just had a couple of tough cases and haven't been sleeping well. It'll pass. Whether Brown accepted the explanation didn't matter, but he must have talked to Osborne. The next day Osborne stopped Jean in the hall on her rounds and asked if everything was okay at home and when would Larry return. "Larry's having a hard time finding the correct opportunity. We'll be fine. He has two interviews tomorrow and both seem promising." Jean hoped that would keep the staff off her back for at least a week.

The neighbors also seemed to be interested in Larry's whereabouts, though Johnny Legard was not one of them; he was keeping his distance. She gave them the same explanation she gave Osborne.

The children asked repeatedly about their father and when was he'd be coming home. Jean tried to give a reasonable explanation but the kids weren't dumb. They sensed there was a big problem; Larry Jr. was moody and got in a couple of fights at school. The principal called and Jean had to meet with him and a counselor. She assured them that as soon as her husband returned from the nation's capital, everything would be fine.

Akamu was nobody's fool. He sent three of the villagers to follow the Vietnamese to the border. But what Larry didn't know is that Akamu told them to stay a week after they reached the border to be sure the NVA weren't coming back. The three watched Vang assemble his men just over the border and then sent four out for food. When they returned a few days later, Vang made his move to return to Laos. Two of Akamu's men followed the Vietnamese Soldiers while the other raced to alert the village and the Americans.

Akamu and the elders of the village met with Larry and the other three to discuss the situation. "We cannot allow them to reach this village and alert other NVA groups of our location. These men must be intercepted as soon as possible. They will not be allowed to surrender. This will end here; we gave them ample warning of our intentions. If there are any objections, state them now," Akamu said.

No one objected. It was decided that Larry would join the villagers in their attack; Minh, Kelly and Long were recuperating and would wait in the village. Long made several suggestions on strategy, but in essence, they were going to surround the soldiers and open fire; no one would be allowed to surrender. Their weapons and ammunition would be confiscated. Larry took Kelly's automatic weapon and would be with Akamu during the attack. Mink asked him if he had any reservations in carrying out Akamu's direction. "None in the least, we gave them ample opportunity to live."

Vang was alert to an ambush and had his seven soldiers properly deployed. He had a scout, a rear guard and two soldiers each on the flanks. His was a solid defensive posture. However, the ground cover along the trail was thick and the trees dense. No sooner had they reached the top of the trail, just past where they captured the Americans, when the Hmong and Larry opened fire and wounded all of the NVA, The Hmong did the mop up and killed all those still alive. The firefight was over quickly and the victors returned to the village, sporting the captured guns and ammunition. It was nearly time for the Americans to go home

Chapter 23

It was the second time he'd left the Hmong village. There was a warm feeling between him, Akamu, and the other villagers. In fact, the chief asked him to stay; they had a nice wife for him. Larry smiled and thanked him and said if he was interested, he'd come back. Thinking that the NVA threat had been neutralized, Minh left two of their automatic weapons and most of the ammunition with the chief. He promised that he'd tell his superiors about the promise of aid from the CIA. Kelly was the only one who was ambulatory, so the villagers built a cart that he could sit in and be pulled or pushed on the trails.

They had twenty miles to travel to the Mekong River. As was the custom, Larry would visit villages along the way and beg for food. In some cases he was successful; in others, he was turned away because the villagers had only enough food for their own. They completed the journey in three days without any mishaps. Once they recovered and inflated their raft, they rowed across the Mekong. He and Minh alternated rowing until they reached the Thai side, then made their way to the first sizeable town in Thailand; Kelly was pushed in the cart by Larry. Minh called Ubon and requested a helicopter to pick them up. Three hours later they touched down at Ubon.

Using a secure line, Larry called home, even though there was nearly a half day's difference in time. When the phone on her nightstand rang, Jean instinctively knew it was news that Larry was dead, captured or it was him calling home. When she heard the voice say hello, she could hardly speak. All she could say was, "Please come home, we need you."

"I'll be home as soon as the other members of my team get out of the hospital and they debrief us."

"Are you wounded?"

"No. I'm fine. The others were captured and we rescued them."

"Who's we?"

"Jean, some of this is classified. I'd rather tell you when I get home. I'm fine."

"Do you need anything such as money or clothes?"

"No. I have the thousand I left with. I'll be okay. I'll call you when we're ready to leave for the states."

Three of the team were in need of medical attention. Larry was exhausted, had lost ten pounds and was hospitalized as well; he was released after two days. Minh and Long remained in the hospital three more days; Kelly stayed five. Once they all were all released from the hospital, the team would be debriefed and sent home.

The CIA sent two senior men to conduct the debriefing. They arrived aboard an agency jet within forty-eight hours of the team's return to Ubon. In the interim, Larry and the other three spent most of their time sleeping, being treated for wounds, recuperating and eating some good food. Kelly was receiving the most care; he became fond of one of the nurses and stayed in the hospital an extra day. Kelly told Minh that he was in love. Although Larry removed the bullet from Kelly's right shoulder, he didn't have the skill to take out the one in his left shoulder. Luckily, there was a skilled surgeon at Ubon; he operated on Kelly and removed the remaining bullet. Minh's and Long's flesh wounds were examined and the pair were released from the hospital and advised to seek medical attention as soon as they returned to the states. Time would take care of their broken ribs. Other than being slightly dehydrated, Larry was in good shape.

They'd been issued lockers in the base gymnasium before they left on their adventure. This is where they stored their valuables and clothes. Larry picked up his clothes, and personal items and checked his money. He had nearly a thousand dollars in cash. He went to the BX and bought gifts for his wife and children.

Minh knew the two debriefers and went first, then Long and Kelly. They took two hours each to debrief. Larry was scheduled the next morning. He didn't know any of the debriefers nor did they volunteer any information. Larry's fear was that this wasn't a debriefing but more of a criminal interrogation, and what had happened to him when he first came home could happen again.

However, nothing is always as it seems. Around 3 PM on the seventh day back, he received a call to report to the Base Commander as soon as possible. He wasn't sure why he was singled out so, with some trepidation, he walked over and entered the building. The first person he saw was Amos Frank and standing behind him was his wife, Jean; he was speechless.

"All you had to do was say the word 'debrief' and I was on the phone to Mr. Frank. He rearranged his schedule and agreed to accompany me and be your counsel at the debriefing. I hope you don't mind?"

"Mind, hell no, I'm delighted. Hello Mr. Frank. If you don't mind, I want to say hello to my wonderful wife first." She was in his arms and it seems that they kissed each other a hundred times.

The base commander's secretary arranged for quarters at guest housing. "Mr. Frank is in one room, you and I are in another. I don't know about Mr. Frank, but I'm dead tired. Why don't the three of us check in and get an hour or two of sleep. We can discuss the debriefing at dinner tonight at the Officer's Club. If that's okay with both of you, let's go," Jean said. Larry and Amos Frank just smiled; Larry carried Jean's overnight bag out the door.

It was a race to see who could get their clothes off first; Larry lost. They made love, but mainly he held his wife and told her how much he loved her and that they'd never be apart again. After a short nap, they enjoyed a quick shower, then walked over to the O Club. They met Amos Frank in the lounge. After dinner, they went back to the lounge where Larry told Jean and Amos what happened on his incursion into Laos and Vietnam. Frank had a few questions but Larry covered everything he could think of. "I think I have it down. Don't worry, we'll find out what's on their mind very quickly and respond accordingly."

"Do you think they're going to prefer charges against you?" Jean asked.

"Normally, I'd respond that I didn't do anything wrong, but these days, I'm suspicious, especially since the other three went first and they're holding me off until tomorrow. I think something's up."

"Larry, I think it's fruitless to speculate. You know what happened; the debriefers don't and neither do your other mates. Let's get a good night's sleep and meet them head on tomorrow. They're probably not aware that I'm here. When they find out, it will give them pause," Frank responded.

They met for breakfast at the O Club and kept everything loose. "I guess I can't sit in on the debriefing?" Jean asked.

"Probably not, why don't you go back to our room. I'll call you when we're done."

"Not a chance. I'm going to hire a guide and go into town for some shopping. This opportunity may never come along again; I intend to make the most of it. First thing I'm going to buy is a large suitcase. I'm not worried about the debriefing. I know you can handle yourself, but with Mr. Frank at your side, you're invincible."

There were three men in the room as Larry and Frank entered. Two were CIA civilians and the other was Captain Gerald Duncan, of the Staff Judge Advocates Office in Ubon. The CIA nameplates reflected a Mr. Anderson and a Mr. Strong. At first, the three didn't know how to handle the presence of Larry's attorney. "I'm sorry, sir, you can't be present during this debriefing due to the classification of the mission," Captain Duncan said.

"Mr. Stephens isn't in the military and it's his decision whether to attend this meeting, not yours. There'll be no swearing in of my client. He'll be glad, with counsel's concurrence, to answer any pertinent questions you may have."

The taller of the two debriefers, Mr. Strong, started the meeting. "Mr. Stephens, in spite of your counsel's statement, you'll be sworn in by Captain Duncan and your attorney will leave the room. He's not cleared for any of this information."

"No he won't, nor will I leave." Frank responded.

"What do you mean, no? He's required to give us a statement under oath," Strong said.

"Who says so? You?" Frank fired back.

"His contract with the agency says so."

"Frank turned to Larry. After a brief conference, Frank responded. "My client advises me that he's resigning from the agency, effective immediately. We'll bid you good day gentlemen. We'll let ourselves out." Larry and Frank got up to leave.

"Your testimony is essential to this mission. We need to know what you found out."

"You already found out everything you need to know from the three who preceded my client."

"Perhaps there's something they left out since Mr. Stephens was separated from the others for some time; it's essential that he provide that information," Strong responded.

Larry couldn't control himself. In spite of Amos Frank's counsel that he refrain from making any comment, he responded. "I don't know either of you and I don't like your attitude. You're not going to force me to take any oath. I volunteered for this at the request of the President of the United States, as well as the Director of the CIA. I'll be glad to answer any of your questions relative to the mission, but that's after I see the written testimony of the other three and I confirm with them individually what they said. If not, I'm going to get on a flight and go home this afternoon." Larry stood up to leave.

Strong was red in the face. "I can have you arrested and thrown in jail right now if your attitude doesn't change immediately."

"I could break both your necks right now, before anyone could reach the door and you wouldn't see the light of day ever again. Don't threaten me. The best have tried and failed."

The other man hadn't spoken a word until now. "Mr. Stephens, we appreciate everything you did in support of this mission and especially saving the lives of your three colleagues. We need your information so we can decide what to do next. How would you like to handle the debriefing?"

Frank grabbed Larry by the arm. "I know you're angry but let me handle it from here out. Okay?" Larry sat down and nodded to Frank.

"Gentlemen, this is the second time that a debriefing group like yourselves has tried to strong-arm my client. We're not going to stand for it. We recognize you have to know all the facts, but so do we. Who did you interface with prior to coming here?"

"We met with Colonel French for an hour on the morning of our departure."

"I don't know what your orders are, but it seems to me that you're trying to establish blame for the mission's failure so you can use that information as leverage for what, I don't know. I want to read the written statements of the other three so I can ascertain your motive. If the questions to them were straightforward, we'll cooperate, other than taking an oath. There can be no transcription and no video or tape recorder present. I also want the other three members present while my client is being debriefed. Those are our terms. It's your call." They waited for a response.

"We'll accept those terms. Here are their statements. You are free to talk to each of them before we continue with you. This other gentleman works for me and

I work for the Deputy Director of Operations. Can we set a time of two o'clock this afternoon to get back together?"

Individually, each of the other members of his group met with Larry and Frank to discuss their testimony. Their answers were straightforward to the questions posed, but there seemed to be an inordinate number of questions relative to where they thought Larry was after they were fired on by the Vietnamese soldiers. To the question of whether he could have caught up with them sooner, all three said they thought he caught up with them in the appropriate amount of time. Minh and Long suspected that the debriefing's priority was to suggest Larry was a collaborator; that's why they went first; that's why he was held to last and required to be under oath while they weren't.

At two PM, the four team members and Amos Frank met with the two debriefing officers minus the staff judge advocate. Larry gave a statement to include exactly where he went, why he went and what he saw. He produced the map he was carrying and showed everyone his route from the time the team was separated. He told them why he went to the military outpost and what happened while he was there. He sketched the layout of the deserted camp on a piece of paper, as well as the other camp where he conducted a funeral service. He pointed to where the two watch towers were and where he suspected the POWs were being kept.

"When it was strongly suggested that I go to another outpost seventy miles further into the interior of the country, I thought my cover was blown and I took action. I restrained the three soldiers accompanying me and took them to the first outpost we targeted. Shortly after I left the deserted outpost, I was accosted by three thugs and had to subdue them and hide them so I'd have time to escape.

"I felt my three comrades would try to return to Ubon via the way we came, if they were still alive. The main priority of our mission was to find where the POWs were being held and then rescue them. I believe I fulfilled the first part of the task. Since I couldn't perform the rescue operation, my goal was to find my group. I did everything possible to save my team. It was also me who found the Hmong village and convinced them to come to our aid. I was with the Hmong when we freed Minh, Long and Kelly from the NVA. .I'm not trying to pat myself on the back, but it's entirely possible that none of my three comrades could've returned to Ubon without my help."

Minh spoke up. "I agree with Larry. This whole debriefing was designed to cast doubt on him. I resent the hell out of that. This man volunteered for this mission and to go back a second time into hostile territory. He deserves our thanks, not what you guys tried to do here. What we should be doing is planning a mission to go to that other outpost ASAP and save our men."

"We've asked the agency to develop such a plan. It'll take the president's approval before we can launch one. Do all of you want to be part of the team?" Anderson, who finally identified himself as the Assistant Deputy Director of Operations at the CIA, asked.

Minh was the first to voice his intent to go back immediately. Long, although nursing a hand wound was almost as quick to reply. Kelly said he needed some time back in the states and begged off.

"I've escaped twice from that country. I don't intend to ever go back. It's time I give my life to my family. I'm resigning from the agency effective this day. If you won't provide return transportation for me, my wife and my attorney to the states, I'll pay their way back," Larry responded.

"We'd hoped that you would lead the next mission. I know you're angry and don't feel that you've been treated fairly, but I and the director want you with our team," Anderson implored Larry.

"When I came back last year, my superiors thought I deserted. They couldn't fathom the possibility that I could walk out of that country. Your intent when you came here was the same. I don't need to work with people like you. I'm out as of now. Whatever paperwork you need me to sign, I'll look it over, but even then I may not agree to sign it. When I think of the pressure put on my family, from as high as the first lady, I'm shocked at my treatment. I'm also sorry I ever met any of you, with the exception of Minh, Long and Kelly."

Two days later, Long and Kelly were cleared to fly to Washington. Anderson and Strong agreed to fly Larry, his wife and attorney, back to the states. "Mr. Stephens, once you're home you may have second thoughts and I, for one, would welcome you back into our small group," Anderson said as they all boarded the CIA Airplane.

"Mr. Anderson, I really don't trust any of you. I also don't believe that there'll ever be a mission to liberate our men. I think you have enough satellites up and running to see movement from the targeted compound to the one where they are now. I think our mission had another purpose other than what you told the President. I'll just leave you with that and one other thing to think about. I recorded a narrative about my mission, who was there, who debriefed me and what was said. I sent it someplace you'll never find. If I should die or any of my family is harassed for any reason, the tape will be released to at least three major newspapers. I don't want to see any of you or your people ever again. I'm going home to live in peace."

He and Jean deplaned in Dallas, said goodbye to Minh, Long, Kelly and Amos Frank, who were headed to Washington. "I hope you consider me your friend. I admire you very much. There should be more Larry Stephens in the world."

Frank hugged Larry and Jean and asked them to stay in touch. He and Jean made their connection to Greenville, picked up her vehicle in the airport parking lot and drove home.

Chapter 24

Jean's vacation extended through the next day. They called her parents from the airport; they wanted to pick up the children on their way home. Since the children were already in bed, they agreed to let them stay the night and pick them up the next morning; the four went for breakfast at the Lunch Wagon, mainly because the restaurant served pancakes all day. The children were quiet and hanging on every word Larry said. "Are you going to stay home now?" Larry Jr. asked.

Before he could answer, Jean spoke up. "He'll be with us forever."

When they dropped the kids off at school, they took a drive down to the bayou, got out of the car and walked along the concrete bank. "The divorce papers came while you were way and I had them shredded at work. I had dinner with Walter last week and told him I was going to stay with you. Unless you're going to dump me, we're stuck with each other for the rest of our lives."

She smiled at him and when she saw his long face she asked. "What's the matter? Aren't you happy that we're not getting divorced?"

"I'm happy to be with you no matter how long. But I must tell you some things."

"She laughed again. "You got somebody pregnant?"

"Jean, I want you to listen carefully to what I have to say." He definitely had her attention.

He was sitting directly next to his wife on one of the benches overlooking the river. He leaned toward her so they wouldn't be overheard even though there was nobody within a hundred yards of them. "Do you remember how much pressure there was for me to go back there?" She nodded.

"From everything I could see at the compound where the POWs were being held, they'd been moved at least two to three weeks before we left Ubon and I think the CIA and Pentagon knew that. I also think they knew where they'd been moved to."

"How would they know that, Larry?"

"They have satellites in the sky taking pictures of the entire earth. They can magnify the pictures to a point where they can make out a woman's breast."

"What are you telling me?"

"I think the goal of the mission was something other than rescuing prisoners. I think they've known about them for some time and where they were located. Perhaps I'm being paranoid, but I think the objective of the mission was to eliminate me and, if necessary, the other three members of the team. They don't want anyone to know about the prisoners."

"I may be naive, but it's difficult for me to believe that our government sent you into harm's way just to eliminate you. But if you're right, should we consider moving to a more secure location? I believe I can always get a job and I can support us until you find something worthwhile."

"I think my life is in some kind of limbo, though I think you and the children are safe. I made a tape recording of everything and everyone that's been involved in this mission, including the lead up to the mission. I sent the tape to someone who they'll never find. If I or any of my family should meet with an accident, the tape will be sent to the media. Jean, I seem to be a magnate for trouble. You don't deserve any of this. I would suggest you go through with the divorce and find someone else. I could have crosshairs on me for the rest of my life."

"I don't care how much time we have together, I want all of it. Is there someone we can contact that could help us?"

"Well, you can see how far up this has gone. The First Lady made a special trip to pressure us. One of my debriefing officers was the Assistant Deputy Director of the CIA."

"Do they know you think this way?"

Larry smiled. "You know me fairly well. I told them what I thought and that I had the recording. I've also resigned from the CIA."

"What do you plan to do?

"If we can swing it with the GI Bill, I'd like to get my degree in botany. I enjoy the outdoors and would look for a position in a wildlife preserve or a national forest."

"We have some savings and my salary is adequate until I complete my residency. After that, my salary can more than handle all of us."

"You wouldn't mind being the bread winner for a couple of years?"

"As long as I can have you, I couldn't ask for more. Let's go home, I'd like to have some cuddle time, if you're not too tired?"

"No way. I've been saving up for a long time."

Chapter 25

Major Nguyen knew he was in trouble. If Commander Tran wasn't his mother's brother, he'd be in an outpost along the Chinese border. He was escorted to Hanoi by a Colonel and two Sergeants to meet with his uncle. Seven bodies, including Captain Vang's, had been recovered, though they were partially mutilated. After an extensive two-day search, they gave up on the other one. The seven were buried with honors at Da Nang.

He was ushered into Tran's austere office and stood at attention for over five minutes while his uncle looked at correspondence sitting on his desk. Finally, Tran looked up and frowned. He then tilted back in his chair and put his feet up on his desk. "You've made a mess of this situation. I told you how important it was to me, you didn't take enough precautions to make sure you would succeed."

Nguyen knew better than to argue with his uncle. He was here to accept his fate and hope he could recover from whatever punishment his mother's brother dictated. "I have no excuse, sir."

"This isn't over yet. The American is probably at home now. I want you to find out where he is and keep him under surveillance until it's time to act. Here's a contact in the United States who can help get that information. Report back to me in three months with a plan to bring the American back."

Born in 1942, Nguyen was the second son of the owner of the Oriental Fish Company in Hanoi. Although his family wasn't part of the powerful elite, he grew up comfortable and was twelve years old when his countrymen defeated the French at the Battle of Dien Bien Phu. The subsequent division of Vietnam into two countries didn't occur until 1956 and didn't have an immediate effect on his life.

As soon as he graduated from high school, he was sent to the United States to study biology at Northeastern University in Boston. It was there that he met two other Vietnamese students who would have a significant impact on his future. Their names were An Phong and Dai Chien. Both were enrolled at Boston University in Political Science. Over the next four years, they subtly indoctrinated Nguyen in Marxist Philosophy. By the time he returned home, he was also committed to the unification of his country. His uncle, by this time, had made a name for himself by employing counter-insurgency in the South and was more than willing to accept Nguyen as his protégé. Subsequently, Tran was able to secure a commission for his young nephew.

His early career was forgettable. It was during the TET Offensive that he distinguished himself and was promoted to Captain. Subsequently, he commanded a battalion during the Easter Offensive of 1972 and was promoted to Major. Although the North didn't gain a major victory, his battalion captured some territory held by the South Vietnamese, giving the North a better bargaining position at the Paris Peace Talks. .He was considered by his superior to have potential and possibly be general material. He married a woman from a middle-class family and fathered two sons whom he seldom saw. He wasn't considered to be much of a family man by his wife. Theirs seemed to be a marriage of convenience.

After enrolling at Mississippi State University, with a schedule to complete his degree in two years, **Larry Stephens** was able to fit all his courses into three mornings a week. With free time on his hands, he wanted to contribute to the family income. He scanned the want ads for a month before deciding that the handyman training he received at the Pagoda in Vietnam, more than qualified him for that type of work. He could repair most things found in a home, plus he had a good understanding of plumbing and electrical work.

He made up a flyer and circulated it throughout his neighborhood; Jean put one on the bulletin board at her hospital. Within days he received some calls; most he turned down primarily because they conflicted with his college schedule. His first client was Walter Osborne. He didn't know it was Osborne's home when he knocked at the front door; the doctor had no idea that ASAP Handyman Company was owned by Larry. After an awkward moment, Walter showed him the kitchen door that had come off its hinges and Larry fixed it within thirty minutes. "Even though I'd hoped you go away forever and leave Jean to me, you did a fine job on the door. I'll let my friends know of your capability." Osborne paid him in cash.

Over the next year, he was able to work about sixteen to twenty hours a week and felt good that he was helping his family.

Minh visited him a few times to see how he was doing. He knew Larry would never come back to the agency, but he hoped they could call upon him for some advice on CIA incursions into Vietnam since the end of the war. Larry didn't ask one question about their plans to rescue the POWs, but he did learn that Curtiss took a medical disability retirement and was living in New York City. Long had recovered and was still working for the agency. Kelly's injuries lingered and, although he was still on the CIA payroll, he was on injured reserve.

In his senior year of college, Larry's grade point average was near the top of his class and he was able to obtain a small scholarship. Jean extended another year at her hospital with a significant increase in salary and an opportunity to spend that year perfecting her skills as a surgeon. She was able to work under the tutelage of Hunter Brand, considered by many as one of the finest surgeons in the south, with a specialty in neurology.

Prior to going back to Vietnam, Larry spent one day each week at the Buddhist Temple in Jackson, Mississippi. He was welcomed by the abbot and gradually he integrated into their community where he was especially adept at funeral and marriage ceremonies. Because of his college schedule and his handyman company, he could only participate in the temple activities on a once-a-month basis. He and Jean agreed that the family would attend Catholic services on the first, second and fourth Sundays of the month and go to Jackson for Buddhist services on the third Sunday. Jean wanted the children to have an insight into the way their father worshiped.

Today, Larry conducted a Buddhist Wedding Ceremony dressed in a blue business suit. The bride wore a brocade dress similar to a long sarong; the groom was similarly dressed but had a waistcoat over the long dress with a sash around his waist; he also wore a cap made of brocade. The wedding was limited to closest friends and relatives. The groom's family brought eight trays of food containing tea, meat, fruit, wine and candles. They also brought some jewelry for the bride to wear during the ceremony.

At the start of the ceremony, the bride and groom simultaneously lit candles as a symbol of the togetherness of both families. Before that, the shrine of Buddha was decorated with flowers. Near the end of the ritual, Larry, the bride, groom and their families stood in front of the Buddha Shrine and recited traditional hymns, followed by the vows of both bride and groom. Then Larry placed a sacred red paste on the foreheads of both bride and groom. The ceremony was concluded when Larry led all the guests in reciting versus from various holy books, after which he gave his blessing to the newly married couple.

Jean and the children were fascinated with the way the ensemble listened attentively to her spouse and their father. However, they were unaware that one of those gathered in the Temple was there to take pictures of the American Buddhist. He was of Asian descent and sat two rows behind the Stephen's family. Le Nhu had spent the last three days in Greenville tracking all members of the family. Today, he followed them to Jackson to observe the American up close without creating too much attention.

Similar to going to lunch each Sunday after services in Greenville, the family went to lunch afterward in Jackson. Though there was plenty of food and drink at the temple, and he was paid handsomely by the groom's parents, they begged their leave to maintain their ritual of pancakes and waffles after church. The family owned restaurant, similar to Denny's, was two blocks away; they'd eaten here previously.

Larry noticed the Asian sitting behind Jean and the children during the ceremony and assumed he was one of the distant relatives. He thought it was most interesting that the Asian was at the same restaurant and sitting three tables away, especially since it was part of the ritual for family members to dine with the newly married couple. As they left, the Asian was still at his table and didn't appear to follow them to their car. However, Larry was suspicious and made a mental note of the Asian's face. Le Nhu had accomplished his assignment and saw no need to follow his target; tonight he'd write his report, then drive to Dallas tomorrow and leave on the next flight to the nation's capital. The report was addressed to the head of the Vietnamese Delegation. The Asian assumed it would be sent immediately to Hanoi.

Since the Buddhist Wedding, Larry's radar was alert for any Asians in the Greenville area and especially the man who followed them to the restaurant. The man was either an anomaly or he was able to maintain his secrecy while tracking Larry; he didn't surface again. Eventually, Larry dismissed it as a coincidence.

Near the end of his second year of college, Larry and Jean sent out resumes to see if they could locate in the same area and perhaps make that a permanent home. Jean's applications went to the hospitals in the western part of the United States while Larry applied to the US Forestry Service. He was told that there were openings in four locations that matched the locations where Jean applied. Subsequently, they received letters requesting interviews at two of the four locations for Larry and all four for Jean. They decided to fly to the two destinations that wanted to interview both he and Jean. If the interviews were positive, they'd spend two or three days looking over the towns and especially the schools while the grandparents watched the children. They were surprised at how well they were received at each destination. Larry Jr. turned thirteen and would start high school in the fall while Susanne was eleven.

When Larry received a contract to be a ranger at The Medicine Bow-Routt National Forest near Steamboat Springs, Colorado, Jean accepted a position as County Surgeon for a fifty-bed Memorial Hospital in that city. Steamboat Springs, with a population of over 5,000, was best known as a world-class ski area with an excellent school system. The small-town atmosphere was the main reason for their decision. They left Greenville behind in mid-June and drove to Galveston, Texas, and stayed at the Jack Tar hotel overlooking the gulf. Most days they either swam in the hotel pool or walked across the street to Stewart's Beach. The idea was to let the children have ten days enjoying the warm southern beach area before they tackled the cold North Country.

They'd rise early each morning, have a quick breakfast and either go to Stewart's Beach or hang out at the pool. They spent so much time at the Coney Island Hot Dog Stand that Larry asked the owner if he could be an investor. Fish and chips was the mainstay at night while they watched a movie or played Canasta. The time passed quickly; soon it was time to leave. Any shyness the children had toward Larry was gone by the end of the trip. Their marriage was back on track and all the trials of previous years were set aside.

On the way to their new home in Colorado, they stopped at various state parks and historical monuments. Since his return, Larry had a special feeling for America and wanted to share his love of country with the children, hoping that they would learn to accept his vision. They arrived in early August, near the end of the two-month summer season in Steamboat Springs. Two weeks later they made an offer, using his VA Loan, on a home on Dartmouth Lane, just north of the city airport and in clear view of the North-South freeway dividing the state. Thirty days later they moved into a three-bedroom, two-bath, ranch-style home with a full basement. The former owner's hobby was model trains, which took up about one-fourth of the basement; Larry purchased the train set for the children. They met the neighbors and there were at least five children who were near Susanne's and Larry Jr's age, living on Dartmouth Lane.

Colorado had a reputation for superior schools and Jean enrolled the two children in the system. Bus service to and from their schools was but one house away at the intersection of the frontage road and Dartmouth Lane. Larry Jr. would take the bus, but Susanne would be driven to school by Jean.

Their first big surprise was the early coming of winter accompanied by the fierce cold and blowing snow. They'd previously lived in Florida and Mississippi; it would take them an entire winter to adjust to the dramatic change in their living conditions. Both he and Jean purchased four-wheel drive vehicles; Larry installed a snow plow on his. Their garage was the width of a one-car garage but the length of two. Larry would back his jeep in last so that he could be first out. If the county snow plow hadn't plowed their street before he left for work, or Jean had an emergency at the hospital, Larry would plow a lane one-half mile to the state highway; Jean would follow in her vehicle.. With a short summer and a long winter, they gradually adapted to winter sports and especially skiing at the many resorts nearby.

After their first Christmas in town, they decided to drive to Keystone Ski Resort and rent a two-bedroom condo. He and Jean had skied a few times early in their marriage, but neither had the skill of their two children, who seemed to be on the black runs the first time they put on skis. The four would be on the lift around eight-thirty in the morning, stop for lunch and ski until four; then they'd gather around the fireplace in their condo enjoying hamburgers, hot dogs and warm cider. They were becoming a very close knit family and enjoyed doing things together. They left the ski resort around noon on New Year's Day and drove home. They turned off the freeway and exited onto the frontage road at about five that evening. As they turned onto Dartmouth Lane, they noticed a black station wagon parked at the curb in front of their home.

"It seems as though we have visitors," Jean said.

Larry hit the remote control and the garage door opened; he turned into the driveway and drove into the garage. Larry had been cautious and protective of his family since he'd come home. He sensed he had a target on his back in Vietnam; that feeling carried over once he was back in the States. He'd discussed his feelings with Jean on several occasions and they agreed on a plan if and when they felt vulnerable.

"Let's not take any chances. You and the children go inside and I'll see who's sitting in that car. Larry, help your mother with the luggage. We can leave the skis until tomorrow. Jean, you know what to do if there's trouble."

As Jean and the two children made their way inside, Larry walked down the snow-covered driveway toward his visitors; there were three of them. All had exited their vehicle and were dressed appropriately for the weather, with large parkas, gloves, and heavy boots. He was within ten feet before he recognized Minh but not the other two. "What can I do for you gentlemen?" Larry asked.

"There's been a new development and we came to talk to you about it." Minh said.

"You're going to have to be more specific than that or this conversation is over."

"I wonder if we couldn't discuss this inside. It's cold outside and our heater isn't too good," Minh said.

"Not unless you tell me what brought you here."

"Look, shit head, we've been cooling our heels for three hours waiting for you. If you don't get rid of your attitude, I'm going to kick your ass right in front of your house," one of the other men with Minh said, and to emphasize his point, he tapped Larry in the chest with his gloved hand.

Larry grabbed the man's hand in both of his, pushed down on the hand while pulling him forward. At the same instant, he kneed the man in the groin. The startled man fell forward onto his knees in the snow and screamed. The other man with Minh started to move toward Larry but Minh held him back.

"You broke my wrist," the man on the ground shouted.

"You haven't lost any of your skills, it seems. I told him before we got here that you were no one to fool with. He's young and has to learn. We still need to talk," Minh said.

"Put all your weapons in your car and give me the keys. There'll be no weapons in my house." The other man with Minh objected but was overruled by him. The man on the ground had gotten up and was holding his wrist. "I need to go to the hospital."

"My wife is a doctor; I'll have her look at it. If it's broken, she'll know right away."

After their firearms were locked in the station wagon and the keys turned over to Larry, the three followed him into the garage and then into the kitchen. Larry could see the concern on Jean's and his children's faces. They must have witnessed the confrontation out front.

"Honey, this man's hand needs attention. Do you mind looking at it?" Larry asked.

Jean sent the children to their rooms. All five sat down at the table in the small dining area off the kitchen. Jean examined Frank Colter's hand. Minh introduced his other companion as Gerald Frank. "What we have to discuss shouldn't involve your wife." Minh said.

"She stays and you have thirty minutes to tell us what this is all about. I don't work for you and I don't have to entertain you. So let's get to it."

"Jack Curtiss left the agency on a disability soon after all of us came back. Last year, he approached the agency with a draft of a book which told the story of our attempt to rescue the POWs. He was turned down because much of it was too sensitive and he had no first-hand knowledge of our incursion," Minh said.

"Someone leaked the information. Who was it?" Larry asked.

"We don't know who leaked it," Minh responded.

"That's baloney. You have a good idea who it was and I'll bet it wasn't any of the four of us."

"We can't be positive, but I think you're correct."

"What about Colonel French."

"He's retired, but he's at the top of my list."

"I'll bet you never went back for those men after what you put my husband and our family through?" Jean said.

"It wasn't my decision. I wanted to go," Minh responded.

"So what's the problem?" Jean asked.

"Curtiss went ahead and published it through one of those underground publishing companies. He also revised the book and included what he knew of Larry's original escape from Vietnam, posing as a Buddhist Monk."

"I gather you can't find Curtiss?" Larry asked.

"He's off the radar."

"What do you want me to do?" Larry asked.

"My superiors seem to think you helped Curtiss with the book and that you know where he is."

"You and I know that's nonsense but there are still a few in Washington, including Colonel French, who think I betrayed our country in spite of everything I did. They're never going to change their minds. I can't help you. I didn't help Curtiss, I don't know where he is and, if I did, I'd break both his legs for what he's doing to my family."

"This isn't going away."

"Here are your keys. Don't come back, I won't be as nice the next time."

Minh smiled.

Colter's hand was sprained, not broken. Larry and Jean were tense for at least thirty minutes after they saw the three drive off. Susanne had gone to bed but young Larry was worried and joined them at the table. "Dad, when did you learn to do what you did to that man?"

"When I was your age."

"I'm sorry, but I overheard one man say you escaped from Vietnam by posing as a Buddhist Monk. Is that true, dad?"

"It's true and, if you love your father, you can never repeat what you heard. There could be people that would harm your father if they knew," Jean said.

"I know we went to that church in Jackson but I didn't know we were Buddhists."

"No son, only me."

Things went back to normal after News Year's; the children went to school, Larry to work and Jean to the hospital. This morning, Jean finished her rounds by ten and was having a cup of coffee in the doctor's lounge. The hospital administrator came over to her and complemented her on her level of professionalism as a surgeon. He then sat down with her at a table to enjoy their morning coffee. "You have an admirer at Greenville Memorial. I talk to Walter Osborne on a weekly basis. He's always asking about you and asking how you're progressing. I gather he was one of your sponsors."

"Not really. He and I dated when I thought my husband was dead. He didn't take it well when Larry came home. I'd rather he not be kept informed about me and my family."

"Oh my, I'm sorry. From the way he talked, I was under the impression that he was a friend of the family; he asked about your husband and how he was acclimating after the move. I'll keep our conversation strictly professional from here on. I'm sorry Jean. It seems that I wasn't sensitive to your position."

Chapter 26

Walter Osborne hadn't lost contact of Jean Stephens. He knew that she was given a permanent position at the hospital in Steamboat Springs. The chief administrator at that hospital and he were friends so he used that to keep track of her. He still loved her and was angry that she'd pass up a great life with him for that short, balding, ex-flier. Though he hadn't spoken to her in two years, he longed for the intimacy that they'd shared for almost a year before Stephens came home. She was the love of his life and it wasn't easy giving up.

He heard about the novel, 'Escape from Vietnam', authored by Jack Curtiss, and bought a copy, but he didn't have time to read it. He decided on a fishing trip in Baja California and took the book along for something to read. He was nearly through the novel when it dawned on him who the author was referring to as the Buddhist Monk; it was Jean's husband, Larry Stephens. The author seemed to imply that the escapee may have colluded with the North Vietnamese to enhance his escape.

He checked into the San Diego Library prior to his return flight home. He wanted to see if there was much attention given to the character in the novel by members of the press. The CIA had blasted the novel as nothing but fiction and the White House was equally adamant that there was nothing to the POW story. There were a few reviews that wondered if it was possible for someone to pose as a Buddhist Monk and escape. Another review thought the plot was preposterous.

However, one particular reviewer of the book, who worked for a national magazine, stated that in spite of the government's denial, there was a strong possibility that much of the book was accurate and that the American who assumed the role of a monk, exists. Walter wrote down the reviewer's name, his magazine, and caught a flight back home

The next morning, Walter called the magazine and asked for the reviewer, but he wasn't there. He left his number and gave a brief summary of what he wanted to discuss. When he hadn't received a response within a week, he called again and this time he indicated that he knew the identity of the Buddhist Monk in the novel, 'Escape from Vietnam'.

Obviously, he didn't tempt the journalist, because after three weeks he still didn't have a response. Walter didn't want to let it lie, so he called again and talked to someone at the magazine and asked for the reviewer. He was put on hold for five minutes before a reporter came on the line. "This is Howard Schultz, how may I help you?"

Walter went through his spiel again and this time he must have hit a nerve. "How do you know so much about the monk?" Schultz asked.

"The individual I'm talking about was presumed dead because he wasn't on any of the POW rolls. After Operation Homecoming, his wife decided that he really was dead and we started dating; we planned to marry the following year. We're both doctors. It was as much a surprise to her as it was to me that he showed up one night. I saw him the next morning. The man was very thin and had shaved his head; he was, however, in good physical shape as I found out in a confrontation with him."

"So you have a vested interest?"

"Absolutely. There's a couple of strange incidents that you may want to investigate. I know he was debriefed In Washington within a few days of his return."

"How do you know this?"

"He told me that's what he was going to do; he was gone for a few days in the DC area and then came home. For the next month, he had constant visitors who I assume were CIA; then he was gone for six more weeks. His wife said he was in DC looking for work. Prior to his leaving for the six weeks, the First Lady flew into Greenville Air Force Base and met with a family. I assume it was the Stephens family."

"How do you know this?"

"I have a patient, an aircraft maintenance man, who told me about the First Lady's flight and the couple with two children who visited her airplane at Greenville Air Force Base."

"Do you know that to be true?"

"Not really, but it would be easy for you to find out if Air Force One landed at Greenville and, through deduction, you could probably ascertain that it was the First Lady who came here."

"Why do you think that happened?"

"I think the government was trying to pressure him to go back and see if he could find other POWs. The author of the book indicated that the Buddhist Monk did go back to search for POWs."

"What do you want out of this, other than the wife?"

"I'm trying to be a good citizen. Stephens could have betrayed his country. If so, I think he should be unmasked and pay the consequences."

"Where is this individual living at present?"

"The family is in Steamboat Springs, Colorado. Stephens works for the federal government as a forest ranger and his wife is a physician at Memorial Hospital."

"I'll see what I can find out and then get back to you. Thanks for the heads up."

His girlfriend was teaching a class in journalism tonight at City College, so Howard ordered a pizza and decided to spend the evening looking up Larry Stephens. Neither Schultz nor Mary Eaton, his love interest, saw marriage in their immediate future, even though they'd been living together for five years. They wanted a relationship but no commitment. She'd been at the magazine for a year longer than he, but worked in a different division, so there wasn't any conflict in their career paths unless they both were up for the big job.

Over one thousand fliers were considered MIA during the Vietnamese Conflict. Most of them were probably dead, though the rumor persisted that some had made their way to North Korea, China and Russia. Since the Russians had given aid to the North Vietnamese, the odds were that many were hidden in Russia's vast interior and would never be seen again.

Stephens was on the MIA list from the time he was shot down in June 1969 until 1973, when he showed up at Ubon Air Base in Thailand; he was never officially listed as a POW. The prisoners who came home before Operation Homecoming had memorized a list of those who were in their camps. Stephens wasn't on any of those lists, so where was he for nearly four years? During that time, he learned to speak Vietnamese fluently and become a Buddhist.

Howard had a source at the Pentagon who Schultz knew would still be working early into the evening. He called the contact who he used in the past to verify his facts; Lt. Col. Charley O'Neal was still at his desk.

"Charley, its Howard Schultz, How are you?"

"Still trying to get promoted, what can I do for you?"

Howard decided to play it straight and not give his acquaintance some bogus story. "I'm following up on a review the magazine did on the novel, 'Escape from Vietnam.'"

"That's a touchy subject here. I don't know what I can tell you."

"Tell me what you can about a Captain Larry Stephens who was shot down in June 1969, about twenty miles southeast of Hanoi. He showed up at Ubon in November 1973 but was never on any POW list or in a camp that we know of. My question is, where was he for all those years? Can you call me back tonight?"

"I'll see what I can do, but I can't draw any attention to myself."

"Fair enough."

While he was waiting for a return call, he looked into the log of Air Force One's flight schedule. He found that it did land at Greenville Air Force Base the Saturday after Christmas. The President was in Washington, so someone else used Air Force One. It took him only five more minutes to verify it was the First Lady.

An hour later, Charley O'Neal returned Schultz' call. "The general attitude at Air Force Command is that it's possible that Stephens hid out in a Buddhist Temple during his time after he was shot down, but since he won't tell which Pagoda he was in, some feel that he collaborated with the North Vietnamese."

"Wasn't he cleared of any wrong doing?"

"He had an attorney at his debriefing and some feel the Air Force was coerced into clearing him to get the information about where some more POWs were being kept."

"How could the Air Force be coerced if Stephens was still on active duty?" Shultz said.

"Your guess is as good as mine."

"Were there some POWs left behind?"

"I can't comment on that."

"Was his information corroborated?"

"I don't know."

"Did Stephens find a POW compound when he was escaping?"

"I can't comment on that."

"But they sent him back to Vietnam to help extract POWs?'

"I can't comment on that subject."

"Anything else you can't comment on?"

"Whatever you do, don't reference any conversation with me or this source is dried up forever."

"I got your message."

Commander Tran wasn't living in a vacuum. He'd written a report detailing his investigation of the downed flyer, including the men who were lost in trying to capture the American. Since it was presumed that the flyer was safely in America, the report was sent to the Vietnamese UN Delegation. One of their departments at the UN Delegation reviewed all literature published in the United States pertinent to Vietnam. The novel, 'Escape from Vietnam', caught Binh Hao's attention and he purchased the book. To him, it seemed utter fantasy that anyone could hide out in his country during wartime and walk out without being captured. However, the memo from their UN Representative was to send anything dealing with that subject to Commander Tran in Hanoi. In addition, Binh forwarded a report from one of their agents detailing a Buddhist wedding ceremony conducted by Lawrence Stephens in Jackson Mississippi. He also included several recent photos of Stephens with the dispatch.

After reading the novel and the report form Jackson, Mississippi, Tran sent them to Major Nguyen and asked him to come to Hanoi. Nguyen thought the novel to be credible, especially since he sent two teams to intercept the American flyer and they failed. He compared the name listed for the American in the novel and the agent's report with a copy of the captured ID card; they were the same. There was no doubt in Nguyen's mind that it was the same man. Just to be sure, he sent for the two men who were injured by the American. Both were positive that the man who injured them while they were in Laos was the same as the one conducting a Buddhist ceremony in America.

He expected Tran to be appreciative of his efforts, but that wasn't to be. His uncle treated him with indifference. "Our agent in American also found out where the American lives. I want you to send two of our agents and bring him back here."

"Do you have some agents in mind?"

Tran handed him a piece of paper with two names on it. The major took that as his cue to leave, he saluted, did an about face and walked out of the office. He always had a chill in his bones when he was here. He hoped his visits in the future would be fewer in number.

Nguyen met the Abbot of Tran Quoc many times when he was a teenager. There were three siblings in the abbot's family, he and two sisters. One married Commander Tran while the other married his father. The three siblings seldom got together because of the hatred Commander Tran had for the abbot. He asked his mother and father many times why his uncle disliked the abbot so much. It seems that the abbot was close to Ho Chi Minh, General Giap and their current leader, Le Duan. They were part of the resistance against the French and established a long-time friendship. The only thing his father could deduce was that Tran was jealous of the abbot.

Chapter 27

Howard Schultz ran the story past his editor and then up to the editor-in-chief. Finally, the magazine's lawyers gave the green light and the article appeared on pages 40 to 42. The article was entitled, "Is this man a Hero or a Collaborator."

Most of the source material for the article came from the book written by Jack Curtiss, "Escape from Vietnam'. Curtiss crafted a narrative that an Air Force flyer bailed out over Vietnam and was hidden in a Buddhist Monastery for nearly three years. It was there that he learned Vietnamese and became a Buddhist convert. When he escaped or left Vietnam, he travelled by foot from near Hanoi to Ubon, Thailand posing as a monk; he made the trek in a little over six months. What angered Jean and Larry was that the magazine article stated where the flyer lived, where he worked, who he worked for, and that Jean was a surgeon at the hospital in Steamboat Springs, Colorado. Schultz didn't name Stephens outright, but he identified both husband and wife just the same.

"No one called me and, to the best of my knowledge, no one came here and verified where we live or work."

"I think I know how they found out. Walter Osborne has been keeping tabs on us. He's been talking to the hospital administrator and asking questions about us. I wouldn't put it past him to be the source for the story that you were the Buddhist Monk that Schultz described.

"This is going to affect you and the children. You may be better off without me in the picture. Since mine is a federal job, pressure may be put on my superior to fire me. I can handle that. What I'm concerned about is: what if the North Vietnamese take it into their head to retaliate. That could be a major problem for us. I don't think they'd visit the hospital, but if they did, call me immediately."

Minh called that evening and said how sorry he was. They still hadn't found Curtiss. They tried to stop the story from being published but were unsuccessful. "Some of us are sorry. We're going to keep a lookout for who may come into the country and try to harm you. You may not believe it, but the Deputy got involved and called Newsweek."

The next day at work, Jean felt very uncomfortable. As she tried to make eye contact with some of the staff, they immediately looked away, seemed embarrassed and wouldn't make eye contact. She knew she should let it go but she made the call anyway.

"This is Doctor Walter Osborne, how may I help you?"

"You set this up, didn't you?"

"Who is this?"

"You know who it is. If I had any feeling for you in the past, it was a mistake. You are a vindictive asshole who never did anything for others, only yourself. Stop calling my hospital administrator to pump him for information. That source has dried up. You are persona non grata from this point forward. If I ever have the chance to repay you for what you've done, I will." Jean hung up without allowing a response.

Osborne was devastated. He gambled that she would come to her senses and leave her husband. His call to Schultz only exacerbated the situation with Jean; she was lost to him forever.

Jean told Larry what she'd done and he smiled. "It won't matter but it probably made you feel much better. My superior called me into his office and showed me an inquiry from the Department of the Interior. He asked me several questions relating to the magazine article. I told him I was completely exonerated by the Air Force and given a position in the CIA. I told him that it was true that I became a Buddhist and escaped Vietnam posing as a Buddhist Monk, but I still didn't see the similarity between the character in the book and what I did. He wanted to know if there were POWs still in Vietnam. I told him that was classified, but it wouldn't surprise me if there were. I asked him if they were going to ask for my resignation. He said he didn't know, but would keep me informed and then he shook my hand and said, "You're a hero to me, Larry."

"I don't know if we can ride this out. I got some funny looks today. We can always move. My professional skills are always in demand and you had a great business as a handyman in Mississippi." She couldn't control a smile.

"To be serious for a moment, our finances are in good shape and I believe the house will sell quickly; we could recover most of our investment. It's the children who I worry about. They like it here, but children are children, and they're going to receive some heat from the kids at school and the neighborhood." Jean said.

"Anytime you think it's getting too tough for you and the children, I'll move on."

"I lost you once and will not lose you again. Please don't raise that issue again. I get sick to my stomach when I think of life without you. I'll tell the children what to expect and see what they have to say. I want our family to be together, always."

After three weeks, the fallout from the article was limited. Everyone in the family went about their business and, although there were some comments to the children, they handled it with grace. The school principal had gotten to know the Stephens family and he made sure there were no incidents involving the children. Soon, everything was back to normal, although Larry and Jean weren't being invited to anyone's home for dinner even though it was obvious that other people on their block were socializing.

Minh called and alerted Larry that there was some unusual traffic to the Vietnamese UN Delegation, referencing the Buddhist Monk in the book. Additionally, Minh noticed that this particular delegation had been supplemented with two new members; their names were Kim Dong and Ngo Linh. The CIA believed them to be a hit squad. "I'm flying out to see you today. I'll stay downtown with an associate; we have our own transportation. It's possible that we're overreacting, but I don't want to be unprepared. I assume that someone could get lost indefinitely in that preserve you're working in."

"It's possible."

The district office for the Medicine Bow-Routt National Forest was in Steamboat Springs on Weiss Drive about a mile from his home. The one-story building sat on an acre parcel surrounded by indigenous plants and flowers. The six room, wood framed building was painted red with white trim around the windows; it included a large greeting room and office for the head ranger, receptionist and six rangers, two to an office. The entire preserve was divided into districts. Larry's main job was to keep track of the campers, hikers and visitors to his district. All visitors were required to sign in at the district office and give their itinerary to the receptionist. Larry would arrive at seven AM, park his car, work at his desk in the office until nine AM and then review the registry book to see who would be in his district that day.

He'd try to reach the entrance to his area before any visitors appeared and then offer any assistance they might need. In addition, he was responsible for several camp sites and supply shacks strategically placed, where he kept emergency equipment such as flares, radios, blankets and some basic medical supplies. He made a habit of checking these locations on a daily basis to be sure there were no break-ins.

This morning the reception area was manned by Ranger Grace Heller. "I've directed about fifteen novice hikers to use the Lodge Loop; it's a good beginner's trail for them. You may want to head that way before you make your rounds," she told Larry.

As was his habit, Larry always looked around the office to see who might be visiting. He noticed two oriental men dressed in business suits looking at the maps on the wall. He exited the station, walked to his assigned vehicle and started it up; it was cold. He sat in the front seat for nearly ten minutes with the heater on, but neither man exited to follow him. After he checked out the vehicle's equipment, he drove to the entrance of Lodge Loop. His backpack was on the rear seat and, after strapping it on, he walked the trail. Within thirty minutes he saw most of the main group who were using this trail, stopped along a path. They seemed to be resting. Larry asked them if they needed help, but all declined and he continued on. He completed the loop in two hours and returned to his car. He took off his backpack and returned it to the rear seat.

Today he wanted to check two of his supply shacks, located on a dirt road off highway 40, to see if they needed to be resupplied. He didn't drive fast on the dirt roads in the preserve, primarily because he wasn't sure how many potholes, caused by the spring run off, he'd find. As he made a turn to avoid one of the holes, he saw a flicker of something red in his rear view mirror. Civilian vehicles were prohibited from using these roads; they were strictly for ranger and emergency vehicle use. As he neared another bend he distinctly saw a red sedan following him. He was only about a mile from one of the shacks he planned to check. He sped up and when he arrived at the building, he immediately got out of his car, grabbed his backpack and made his way behind the wooden structure.

Kim Dong had been a sleeper agent for the North Vietnamese while serving in Saigon at MACV Army Headquarters. He infiltrated into the South's Army and reached the rank of Major during the war. His main role was to transmit any South Vietnamese offensive plans to the north. Ngo Linh was a journalist attached to the main newspaper in Saigon. He interviewed American and South Vietnamese generals on their conduct of the war. By trade, he was an assassin; he personally eliminated seven fellow journalists in Vietnam.

The two men were fluent in English and had been in the United States many times since the end of hostilities in Vietnam. Initially, they went to Greenville and learned that the family had moved. Their work was made easier by the magazine article and they took the next flight to Denver and drove to Steamboat Springs yesterday. They'd been a team for the past six months and had worked successfully on two assignments.

Larry looked around the corner of the cabin and saw the red vehicle stop near his Jeep and two Asian men exited the vehicle; they were the ones he'd seen in the office this morning. They carried automatic pistols in front of them.

The terrain at the rear of the shack was steep and the tree coverage very thick. There were multiple man-made trails as well as natural ones frequented by deer, wolves and a few bears. Larry didn't have a weapon and there wasn't one in the cabin, so he made his way down the slope away from the structure. He created enough noise for his two pursuers to know where he was. Although the two had pistols, Larry's advantage was that he knew the terrain. He stopped periodically to be sure they were still following him and when he was sure they were committed to capturing him, he moved further down the slope.

Taking on both men at the same time was foolish. He had to get them to separate. He took a good sized rock and threw it as far as he could to his right and waited to see what their reaction would be. Both went in that direction. Once they took a few steps in that direction, Larry threw another rock to his left and the two men stopped. He could tell they were confused and didn't know which direction to pursue. He heard them discussing it in Vietnamese before they split up. One went toward the noise to the right and the other went to his left toward Larry. When he was sure that the one following him was keeping up, he moved another twenty yards down the trail and climbed up a cottonwood tree. He could hear the Asian move and then stop; he was confused but very cautious. Larry was completely concealed in the thick branches of the indigenous tree. He waited patiently while the intruder came closer and stopped directly below him. Larry dropped on the man and as they hit the ground, Larry hit him twice in the head with a small club he was carrying.

Quickly tying up the Vietnamese and dragging him behind some boulders, he picked up the man's gun, put it in his belt and waited for the second man to approach. He heard him call out in Vietnamese, asking his compatriot, "Where are you?"

"I think he went this way," Larry responded softly in Vietnamese.

As the second man drew nearer, Larry waited behind a large tree that was nearly three feet wide and when the man leaned against the tree, Larry brought his club down hard on the man's hand and his gun fell to the ground. Instinctively, the Asian lashed out at Larry and parried his blows with his arms. For two minutes neither was able to gain an advantage until Larry pivoted and caught the other man on the side of the head with his foot and the pursuer fell on his side. It was only a matter of time until he was subdued and tied up like the other; Larry pocketed the other gun.

First one, and then the other, was dragged back to the shack and placed by the steps leading into the enclosure. He searched their pockets and found a piece of paper with his name, address and several unknown phone numbers. He checked their IDs and from the information in their wallets, he assumed they were North Vietnamese agents. Larry paged Minh and gave him the phone number inside the wooden structure. Soon it rang and Larry told Minh what happened and how to find him. "My associate and I will be there in an hour," Minh responded.

Larry looked in the vehicle the two drove and found a map, a piece of paper with several more phone numbers and two airline bags. He opened the bags and peeled back the lining inside each bag. He found a small notebook written in Vietnamese. Larry took his time and read the four pages, which in essence, were the orders these two were working under. They were to bring him back to Hanoi, alive if possible.

When he was finished, he sat down for a few minutes next to the two who were tied up. The order to bring him back came from the highest level and directed that the head of the Vietnamese Delegation to the United Nations make every effort to see that this mission was accomplished successfully. The two were fully awake by now and asked for water.

They were surprised when Larry responded in Vietnamese. "I'll be glad to give you both water, but first I want to know why you followed me." There was no answer to his question.

"Since you're never going to see your homeland again, you may as well tell me who gave you the order to come after me?" Again, there was no response.

"I could shoot both of you with your guns and no one would ever know what happened to you. I want to know who sent you."

Larry waited for a response; there was none forthcoming.

"The CIA is coming to get you. You are as good as dead. I'm the only one that can intercede for you. Tell me who sent you." He could tell the three-letter agency made an impact but they still wouldn't respond, so he didn't give them water.

Minh and Felix Santiago, his associate, arrived ninety minutes later and the two agents and Larry discussed the situation. "That magazine article has stirred up a hornet's nest and I'm in the middle. They may try to harm my family. Get word to the President that I did what he asked and this is how I'm being repaid. I want some action out of my government."

"You're lucky to have escape these two. When they came through Dulles Airport, we took their pictures. They're assassins."

"I know. The question is, what happens next? Are they going to keep sending assassins or will it be kidnappers next time?"

"I can have a personal talk with the head of the delegation." Minh said.

"What are you going to do with these two?" Larry asked Minh.

"Don't worry about it. I'll take care of them. They won't bother you or anyone ever again. I'll leave another associate in the city for a week to be sure no one else is on the way. After I dispose of these two, I'm going back to Washington to see if we can put an end to this and you can go on with your life. I don't know whether we'll see the President, but he sure as hell will know what happened. Felix and I'll take their car so you can forget them."

"I'm counting on you and the agency to see to it that my family is protected. They had nothing to do with my escape and return to Vietnam."

He told Jean what happened and she exploded. "What do we have written on our foreheads, 'Fuck us'?"

"It's me, not you or the children that is the lightning rod for all this. I can't sit and wait anymore for something to happen. I'm going to figure out a more proactive role. I can't let them decide what is going to happen to us. Let me think. I won't do anything without talking it over with you. Okay?"

"Will Minh help?"

"He has so far, but I don't know what he can do to stop them from coming after me."

"Don't forget that all of us love you and we'll stand behind anything you do."

Chapter 28

Over the next sixty days, life returned to normal for the Stephens family, though they took the threat seriously. Winter was here and, of course, there was always snow in Colorado. Larry usually left home early to get to work on time. Today he plowed to the frontage road so Jean could get to the hospital; she had an appendectomy to perform but wanted to drive her daughter to school first. "Come on Susanne, mommy has to get to the hospital, so hurry up."

Jean took Susanne to school each morning. Her school was closer than her brothers and, although they could see her playground and buildings from their house, it took only five minutes by car. Jean felt that her daughter was too young to walk by herself or with other children; besides it was snowing. She drove out of their driveway, turned right and stopped at the frontage road. As she turned left onto the frontage road, she instinctively accelerated. At the same time she looked at Susanne to be sure she had her seat belt on; that's when they were hit broadside by a large white panel truck coming down the street, parallel to Dartmouth Lane. The impact was significant and their Jeep Cherokee overturned into the ditch on the right side of the road. Susanne's head hit the passenger's window. Jean was thrust forward and hit her head on the steering wheel and then fell toward Susanne. The driver of the truck backed up as though he was going to ram her Jeep again, but as he started to put the vehicle in drive, he noticed another vehicle coming down the frontage road with its lights flashing. He bypassed the damaged jeep and drove toward the airport.

Deputy Sheriff John Bigelow was on his way to a two-car accident on the freeway when he saw the collision. Initially, he thought it was another mishap caused by the snow, but something about how the truck backed up and seemed poised for another strike caught his attention. He hit the flashing lights and was immediately on the radio directing others to apprehend the driver and send another car to the freeway accident. His main job now was to see what happened to the passengers in the vehicle lying on its side in the drainage ditch. Bigelow put out some flares, called for an ambulance and checked on the occupants of the Jeep.

He climbed up on top of the driver's side of the overturned vehicle and tried to pull the door toward him but it was damaged and wouldn't budge. With his revolver he broke the window and looked inside. There was an adult woman hung up in her seat belt and harness leaning toward a young girl, who had her head on the passenger's door, blood was running down the young girl's head. Both occupants seemed to be unconscious and there was blood on the woman's forehead as well. "Lady, can you hear me?' Bigelow yelled.

He continued calling out to the two, but there was no answer. The ambulance arrived and he jumped down and let the paramedics get to work freeing the two. They were able to pry the driver's door open, cut the seat belts and harnesses and carefully lift the two unconscious females from the vehicle.

Bigelow got on the radio and checked on the pursuit of the truck. "We found a white panel truck in the airport parking lot; it was empty but the engine was warm. It had damage to the right front fender, the bumper is bent and there's red paint marks on the bumper," Deputy Strong reported.

"Call for backup and find the driver. I could be wrong but he looked Asian to me. See if there are any flights that are about to leave. I'll follow the ambulance to the hospital and see what the victims have to say when they come around."

The paramedics strapped the two victims, probably a mother and daughter, into the gurney-type stretchers and put them in the ambulance. They found a purse in the back of the car and Bigelow went through it and found the mother's ID. "Hey guys, the woman is Doctor Stephens from Memorial Hospital. I'll follow you there."

Bigelow called into the station and asked to have someone go to Stephen's residence on Dartmouth Lane and see if anyone was home. Mother and daughter were taken to the emergency room and Doctor Rhodes immediately examined Susanne, while Doctor Overhold treated Jean.

Two hours later, Jean regained consciousness and Bigelow received permission from the attending physician to talk to her. "Doctor Stephens, I'm Deputy Bigelow. I was close by when you were struck by the panel truck. What can you remember about the incident?"

Jean seemed confused and continued to rub her left shoulder. "Please, how is my daughter?"

"The attending physician is still examining her."

"I must be with her; she needs her mother. Help me up."

Just at that moment, Doctor Overhold came into Jean's room. "You're not ready to get up yet, Jean, but I understand you want to be with your daughter. We'll move you into her room soon. Give me a couple of minutes to get someone to help. When Jean was moved to the other bed in her daughter's room, she asked the doctor for an update on Susanne.

"She's still unconscious. I believe she has a concussion and I don't know about a skull fracture. You've got to stay in the room while we take her down for X-rays. Doctor Rhodes is with her, Jean. The Deputy has some questions for you; he's waiting in the hall."

When they took Susanne for x-rays, Bigelow came back into the room. "I need some information from you, Doctor Stephens. I'll try to be quick, but we do want to catch whoever did this. Tell me what you remember."

"Actually, very little, I turned my head to check that my daughter had on her seat belt and when I turned back to the road we were hit. After that I don't remember much until I woke up in the hospital. Has anyone called my husband?"

"No, give me his name and telephone number."

"He's employed by the US Forestry Service and works out of the Steamboat Springs Office." If you have a piece of paper, I'll give you his pager number and office number."

Deputy Bigelow called the Forestry Service Office at Aspen and the receptionist was able to find Larry. When he came on the phone he was out of breath. "Give me a second, I had a long run. This is Larry Stephens."

Bigelow told him what happened, where they found the vehicle and the condition of his wife and daughter. "Were you able to catch the hit-and-run driver?" Larry asked.

"No, we're still looking."

"Do you think it's possible that there were two vehicles? Whoever did this may have used the second vehicle to get away after dumping the crash vehicle at the airport?"

Bigelow acknowledged. "It's entirely possible that whoever did this is on his way to Denver."

"Thanks for the call, I'm on my way. Give me the hospital number and the number of my wife's and daughter's room."

As soon as Larry hung up, he called the CIA on Minh's private line. "This is Larry. A hit-and-run driver crashed into Jean's vehicle early this morning. Whoever did this dumped their vehicle in the Steamboat Springs Airport Parking Lot and could be on their way to Denver. No one saw the driver and we don't know his or her nationality, though I suspect it's our friends from Vietnam. The deputy who saw the accident said he thought the driver was Asian. You have time to get on top of this. I'm on my way to the hospital. Here's the hospital number and Jean's room number."

His mind was working at the speed of sound. This wasn't going to end unless he was dead or he could negotiate his way out of this. He hadn't lost his confidence, but any reaction on his part would come after his wife and daughter were safe, but he was going to do something. He wondered if anyone told Larry Junior what happened. He stopped at a gasoline station and called the high school. He explained what happened to the school's principal. "I'm about an hour out and would like you to call a cab and send my son to the hospital to be with his mother. Can I count on you?"

"Mr. Stephens, I'll take him myself and wait until you arrive at the hospital."

Doctor Rhodes was waiting for Larry as he came into Jean and Susanne's room. "Mr. Stephens, your daughter has a concussion and is still unconscious, but she may wake up any minute. I took a CAT Scan and her skull is intact. There's some blood around the brain but I don't believe it's anything to be worried about, though there's some swelling. I intend to treat her with cortisone shots to bring down any swelling. I went over my diagnosis with your wife and she concurs." Jean nodded.

Larry went over to his daughter and kissed her on the forehead and squeezed her hand. Jean was sitting up in bed and he wrapped his arms around her. "I'm so sorry for this Jean. This is all my fault."

"Don't you dare blame yourself. What I want from you is to force them to stop. I know you can take care of us, now take care of whoever is behind this; and Larry, I mean take care of them, once and for all." She started to cry and Larry held her even tighter. It was then that he noticed the principal and little Larry. He shook the man's hand and hugged his son. "Thank you very much, Mr. Peters. I won't forget your kindness."

"I'll leave you with your family and whatever troubles you and your family have, I'll pray that they are resolved quickly." It was obvious Peters overheard some of what Jean had to say.

Two hours later, Susanne regained consciousness and asked for her mother. All four of the family hugged each other and thanked God that everyone was okay. Larry stepped out and called Minh.

Minh was still in his office when the call came in. "We tracked a Vietnamese National by the name of An Chien; he flew from Denver to Los Angeles where he was detained by our people and the FBI; I had to read them in on the situation or they wouldn't help. Chien claimed diplomatic immunity and demanded that he be allowed to board his flight to Hong Kong. The FBI called the State Department and was told to release him. Although we didn't have jurisdiction, we were allowed to fly with him to Washington. On the way, one of our guys told him that if he was ever seen outside his country, no one would see him again, or words to that effect. We'll see if he understood the message."

"Do you think he's the one?" Larry asked.

"As sure as we can be, but it was taken out of our hands. The agency will put him on our tracking list; if he shows up again, he'll wish he hadn't. I think he accomplished part of his mission; they'll get someone else to finish it."

Over the next three days, Larry gave his predicament serious thought; he and Jean discussed what he saw as his options. She listened and made some comments, but he knew this was something within his expertise and he'd make the decision.

Commander Tran could not believe that two of his best men had gone missing. There had been no response from them for ten days. It was as though they were disposed of like garbage. They sent another agent to ram the flyer's vehicle; instead they attempted to kill the wife and daughter. This was complete incompetence. Whoever was leading the delegation was either an idiot or could not understand the gravity of the situation. There was only one way to handle the situation. He asked for a meeting with the regional committee and presented his argument as well as a plan to eliminate the American.

When his plan was approved, he sent for Major Nguyen. "The Central Committee wants to know why this

American has eluded capture. He evaded us in country and managed to neutralize our agents in America. He must be having a big laugh at our expense. I want him here and I want him now. If you have any plans for moving up in rank, then you have to bring that renegade here. I'm sending you to American as part of our UN Delegation. You will implement a plan to kidnap Captain Stephens and bring him here so justice can be done."

"Sir, you realize my English is rusty and I'm not experienced in surveillance or kidnapping techniques."

"I don't want to hear any excuses. Get the job done. You've had several chances; there will be no more. You're dismissed."

When the Major explained to his wife that he was being sent to America on temporary duty, she asked if she could come along. When her husband told her that wasn't possible, she just shrugged and went into another room. He packed his things, said goodbye to his two sons, and was driven to the airport by a member of his staff. He was two hours early, but it was more comfortable to wait in the airport lounge than his own home. He wasn't happy about his assignment but he'd make the best of it. Nguyen had a couple of drinks, boarded his flight and thought about an American blonde. He had a smile on his face.

Nguyen was met by a staff member from the delegation and taken to their headquarters. The chief of the delegation handed him a file on Stephens. A meeting with the team that had been monitoring the American flyer was set for tomorrow at ten in the morning. Most of the information in the file was known to the major, except the skill Stephens had in martial arts. Nguyen was proficient in boxing and wrestling while at college in the states, but he knew that he'd be no match for the American in hand to hand tactics. Perhaps that was the mistake that Dong and

Link made. They had confidence in their skills and probably overlooked those of their adversary. Nguyen vowed not to underestimate Stephens.

At the morning briefing Nguyen could tell immediately why there was failure on this end. Most of the staff had little knowledge of the American culture and few spoke passable English. When he asked about the CIA's surveillance of the delegation, there was only a token response by the UN Delegation Head. He was promised support in terms of money, supplies and armament, but limited help in extraction. Nguyen realized that he'd have to put together a plan himself and, other than logistics support, nothing else would be forthcoming from this group.

The first thing he decided to do was to become familiar with the area where Stephens lived. He wasn't ready to make any overt move toward the American until he had a good feel for what he was dealing with. He took a week and outlined a preliminary plan to deal with Stephens, which included some information on what Linh and his associate planned. The following week, he flew to Denver, rented a car and drove to Steamboat Springs. He stayed in an up-scale motel and treated himself to a good night's rest. Early the next morning, he had breakfast at the only diner in town, picked up some maps at a local gasoline station and drove past the hospital where Jean Stephens worked and the street where the family lived.

The following morning Nguyen dressed in slacks, a sport's shirt, a leather jacket and, wearing a Denver Avalanche cap, visited the park's office. He spent some time looking at the various trail maps located on the walls in the spacious office and observing all the employees. It was nearly nine o'clock when he saw a man who resembled the American flyer leave the office and start one of park ranger's vehicles and drive off. He reached in his pocket and carefully looked at the flyer's ID card; he was sure it was Stephens. He waited an hour and carefully observed all of the rangers as they departed the building just to be sure none of them were the flyer. He didn't follow the American, but he did drive the route Larry would take to get to the area he managed. Rather than stay longer and create suspicion, he drove to Denver, got a room at a Holiday Inn, and spent the rest of the day carefully writing a report of what he saw. He flew back to New York the next morning.

He had a pretty good idea how to capture the American. Dong and Linh, the two assassins who disappeared, had a plan to follow Stephens to the area that Stephens managed and subdue him in a secluded place. But that was playing into Stephens hands. The flyer knew the terrain and could easily set a trap; his two countrymen were at a disadvantage. Nguyen could see that the best spot to intercept the American was along the route to the man's station. There would be some traffic, but two teams with two cars could do it. One would lay in wait and block Stephens' car as he drove to his area, while the other would follow him at a distance. When he was forced to stop they'd have him in a vise. Every plan had some drawbacks, but there was a good chance his would succeed.

Larry maintained his flying proficiency after he retired and occasionally rented an airplane to fly around the area. Jean and the two children would fly with him but they didn't seem to enjoy it as much as he did. He especially liked to do touch and go landings while checking out the small landing strips in the area, many of which were unmanned. Occasionally, he flew as far as Denver to attend Buddhist services, since there wasn't a temple in Steamboat Springs. He built a small meditation room off the kitchen in his home and made sure that he spent at least an hour every day reading some of Buddha's sayings. The abbot in the Denver Temple welcomed Larry, but he recognized that the weather would curtail the American's visits and therefore, couldn't be counted on to perform any of the weddings or funerals at the temple.

The decision was made. He had some vacation time accrued and submitted a request for ten days. When he was sure it would be approved, he asked Jean if her parents could stay with her while he was busy. "I'll feel more comfortable if someone is with the children all the time while you're working," Larry told Jean.

The parents flew into Denver a month later and rented a four wheel vehicle and drove to Steamboat Springs. The father was helpful, but Jean's mother didn't understand why Larry was leaving his family for over a week while Jean was working at the hospital, thereby leaving the children unattended for a few hours. Jean didn't know how much she could divulge to her parents. Finally, she told both parents about the accident and the two assassins that Larry neutralized. Her father seemed to grasp the situation but her mother heard what she wanted to and subsequently confronted Larry. "The FBI is better equipped to handle this than you. Don't you feel any responsibility to your wife and children?" Her mother asked him.

Finally Jean took her mother aside and told her point blank what Larry's capabilities were and that the decision for her husband to leave was a joint decision. "Mother, if do don't shut up, you can go back home; you're no help with this attitude."

"I'm sorry Jean, I'm just so worried."

Larry called Minh a week after her parents arrived in Steamboat Springs and told him to expect a visit in the next few days."

When he was sure that he'd receive help at the other end, Larry flew a rented airplane to the east coast. He landed at a small air field in New Jersey, between Philadelphia and Cape May. The services available were minimal but they did have aviation fuel and a telephone to call a taxi.

The taxi cab dropped him off at a hotel in the small town two miles from the air strip where he called Minh at his home outside DC. "You should see me in the next few hours at your motel. Reserve a room for Felix and me. You still want to go through with this, don't you?" Minh asked.

"Are you backing out?"

"No, but I hope you understand the implications. They'll know someone helped you and hint that we were involved. We'll cover our tracks; just don't you screw up."

While he was waiting, he went over his plan and checked his equipment. Jean helped with the medical supplies; he took care of the rest. The airplane was gassed soon after he landed at the small airfield and Larry performed a thorough preflight check in case he had to take off in a hurry. His flying skills were such that he'd have no problem taking off at night with limited runway lights.

He asked Minh to furnish a set of night goggles, a hand held telephone and transportation to and from the airport where he parked his airplane. When Minh arrived, Larry checked the equipment Minh brought and felt confident he could carry out his plan. Over the next three hours, the CIA men showed Larry pictures of the complex the Vietnamese were renting for their delegation as well as that of the surrounding area. Minh had checked out the area over a four day period and rented two rooms on the fifth floor of the Highland Hotel overlooking the Vietnamese complex, starting tomorrow.

Minh and some of his crew had tailed the latest addition to the Vietnamese Delegation for a few days to establish his daily pattern, concentrating on when he left and returned to his apartment. His name was Major Nhu Nguyen. When Larry heard his name, he knew what his role was and what he was here for. He remembered hearing Sergeant Quon tell his squad about his supervisor's orders to bring Captain Stephens to Hanoi. His superior was Major Nhu Nguyen and now he was here. Nguyen and his bodyguard normally returned to their lodging around four in the afternoon and stayed in their residence for the rest of the evening, unless they went out to dinner. Twice each week, he went with his bodyguard to Denny's a block away, once a week to a nearby MacDonald's, and another night to the Fish Grotto within a block of their complex.

"He seems to like American fast food. Whenever he goes back to those three restaurants or to some other place, he generally walks. He must think the streets of New York are safe," Felix told Larry.

"He isn't any different from us. When I used to go to Philadelphia, I'd walk to the Italian section of town and stuff myself with Cheese Steaks at least twice a day."

"Here's what we know about him. He's a Major in the Vietnamese Army and was a Battalion Commander stationed at Da Nang. He's thirty-two years old, married, with two young sons; his wife is in Hanoi. He arrived over three weeks ago. My guess is that you're a high priority for him and that's why he's over here; his uncle is Commander Tran of the Hanoi District. Chances are he'll return to Hanoi as soon as you're taken care of, though they may want to take you back to Hanoi. His bodyguard seems competent but they may have their guard down because they think we're soft and won't challenge them on our own territory, no matter what they do to provoke us," Minh said.

"Gentlemen, I'm very familiar with Major Nguyen, though I've never met him. He directed the two squads they sent to bring me back. Commander Tran is the real enemy. I caused him to lose face and he wants me in the worst way. If he succeeds, I fear what will happen to my benefactor in Vietnam. This is very personal to me, not only for the attempt on my family but because he is who he is."

"I'll need a vehicle to take me and the major back to my airplane."

"Felix will drive you and bring the car back; it has rental plates. If you pull this off cleanly, I'll stay at the hotel for a couple of days to take care of any fallout," Minh said.

"What do your superiors say about your freelancing like this?"

"They don't want to know anything and if we screw up, they won't know any of us. Realistically, I couldn't do this unless there was some tacit understanding with them and what could be accomplished. They like the idea of being in the passenger's seat," Minh replied.

Minh, Felix and Larry drove to their hotel the next afternoon, occupied two rooms, and set up a schedule of surveillance from four in the afternoon until ten at night. From seven in the morning to eleven at night, one of the three would monitor the Vietnamese Complex from the window perch in one of their rooms. Another would be near a pay phone one block away; the third would be stationed in the shadows across the street from the delegation's complex. The three would rotate every four hours.

They planned to make contact with Nguyen and his bodyguard as they were returning from dinner. Minh felt the two would be more relaxed after a good meal and not be as apprehensive. Larry and Minh would take out the two, while Felix would be ready with the car.

Major Nguyen had finalized his plans, selected the men he needed, and was planning to fly with his team to Denver at the end of the week. There were a few loose ends that had to be cleaned up but, for all practical purposes, he was ready.

Nothing happened the first two nights. On the third night, Nguyen and his bodyguard were picked up by a vehicle and taken out of the immediate area. On the fourth night the two came out of their complex at six PM and walked to Denny's. The bodyguard was vigilant and carefully screened the area as they approached the restaurant. When they reached Denny's, he went in first and, when he was comfortable that it was safe, he signaled Nguyen to come in. The two sat against the wall on one side of the thirty by thirty foot room that was nearly seventy percent occupied with hungry customers. Nguyen was relaxed as he ate a country-fried steak dinner, but the bodyguard didn't relax; he was vigilant.

Those going in and out of the restaurant were monitored by Larry, Minh and Felix. The three maintained contact through portable phones. The Vietnamese stayed inside Denny's for over forty-five minutes before exiting and making their way back to their apartment. Minh waited until the light turned red and then crossed the street and followed the two. When it looked like the two were finishing their dinner, Larry made his way to the Vietnamese Complex. Soon after the Vietnamese crossed the street with the bodyguard walking nearer the curb, Larry made his way toward them.

Larry started to stagger as he approached them and the bodyguard became visibly alert. As they were about to pass each other on the sidewalk, Larry staggered more noticeable and the bodyguard pushed his client behind him. Larry drove his knucklers into the bodyguard's solar plexus and, with his left hand, he chopped the man in the back of the head and the bodyguard fell to his knees. As he started to rise, Larry kicked him in the ribs and when the man fell on his stomach, Larry leaped up and came down on the man elbows. He could hear them crack and the bodyguard cried out in pain. Larry grabbed the chloroform rag he carried in his pocket and put it over the bodyguard's mouth until he succumbed.

Nguyen was stunned and started to back up while watching the fight between Larry and his bodyguard. He didn't see Minh come up behind him but he kicked out when Minh put a chloroform soaked cloth over his mouth. Although the target struggled, the chloroform gradually took effect and Nguyen relaxed and leaned against Minh. Larry put his hands under the bodyguard's arms and dragged him into a nearby alley; he was unconscious, but breathing normally. With Nguyen sedated, Larry took out the needle he carried in a box in his overcoat pocket and, after filling it from a vial, he injected the fluid into the arm of Major Nguyen. Minh and he held the man up until Felix arrived with the Black SUV. They put the unconscious man on the rear seat and Larry looked around before getting in the front seat; he couldn't see anyone who'd witness their actions. .They left Mink to take care of any unintended consequences.

It took them several hours to reach the airfield where the Cessna 210 was waiting. Larry had taken out the rear seats and welded a chain to the floor. He and Felix put Major Nguyen on the rear floor, fastened hand cuffs to his wrists behind him and attached them to the chain on the floor. Just to be sure, Larry gave him another shot. He did his preflight checks again and was ready for takeoff by six in the morning. Felix stayed until Larry was airborne. The plane could fly at two hundred twenty-five miles an hour with a fuel range of nine hundred miles. Although the ceiling for the plane was 27,000 feet, Larry would fly between nine and ten thousand feet most of the way; he planned to stop twice for fuel. Although he carried enough of the drug for three shots, Jean said two should keep the prisoner under for twelve hours. Larry hoped to be in Colorado before then.

Minh went back to the hotel where they'd been conducting surveillance on the Vietnamese Delegation. Thirty minutes later, two members of the delegation came out of their apartment complex and walked to Denny's Restaurant. Within ten minutes they returned and went into their living quarters. Soon six men came out of the building. They divided into two man teams; each going in a different direction, obviously looking for Nguyen and the bodyguard. Minh watched as they returned, spread out, returned and then looked in cars and alleyways before they found the bodyguard. He was unable to walk without help from his compatriots.

The hotel where Minh, Larry and Felix stayed had replaced all their windows with one-way glass in the last year. As Minh looked down at the sidewalk in front of the Vietnamese lodging complex, he could swear the six were looking up at him, though none made a move to come to his building. He assumed they were thinking, "This couldn't happen in America", but it was a common occurrence in their country; he was sure they were spooked.

Chapter 29

Larry rented the Cessna airplane for ten days and planned to complete his mission within that time frame. Most of the flight to Colorado was without incident, though he did have to divert around some thunderclouds over Kansas. Nguyen had been quiet during the flight, though occasionally, he'd say something in his own language; once it was about the abbot. It was nearly sundown when Larry landed and brought the airplane to a halt near his SUV.

There had been a light snow while he was gone, but his SUV started immediately and, although it was an effort, he put the Major on the rear seat with his hands cuffed behind him; Larry covered him with two blankets. Just to be sure, he gave his prisoner another injection and drove to the shack he built in the northern end of his area of responsibility. It was dark as he stopped on the dirt road off route 40, southeast of Steamboat Springs, and unfastened the chain blocking access to the trails he managed. He repositioned the chain after he drove through the barrier, then got back in the car and drove the remaining five miles. His prisoner was still unconscious when he arrived at the shack so he went into the little hut and made a cup of coffee. He sat down and went over his plan again; everything was set.

He semi-carried his prisoner into the building and placed him on a cot on one side of the one-room cabin. He put bracelets on his feet, took off the cuffs, put them back on with his hands in front of him and tied a chain from his hands and feet to a ring attached to the floorboards. This allowed his prisoner to turn somewhat but he wouldn't be able to escape. Larry had been up over twenty-four hours and his eyelids were heavy. He put on his parka and gloves and quickly fell asleep on the other cot at the opposite side of the hut; he felt entirely safe. He woke a couple of times during the night; his prisoner hadn't moved.

Six AM came early and Larry was fixing breakfast for two on the electric frying pan he'd bought for this situation. His prisoner was awake but hadn't made any move to get up. The tranquilizers were probably still having some effect. "I'm fixing scrambled eggs with sausage and potatoes. I'll have some coffee ready in a few minutes." Larry spoke in Vietnamese.

The major started to move but was constrained by the ankle bracelets and hand cuffs. "Who are you?' he asked.

"I'm Larry Stephens, the American you've been trying to kill."

"I don't know what you're talking about. I'm a member of the cultural section of the North Vietnamese Delegation. You must have me confused with someone else. I have diplomatic immunity. You are in serious trouble for kidnapping me."

Larry smiled. "I'm not the one who's tied up. You're wasting your time trying to tell me you don't know who I am, especially since you personally sent two teams to bring me back to Hanoi"

"Where are we?" Nguyen asked.

"We'll talk about that later. I'm going to take off your hand bracelets so you can eat. I must warn you that I'm capable of neutralizing you at any minute. It wouldn't be wise to try anything physical. Your men already found that out."

As soon as his hands were free, Nguyen sat up and tried to put his chain around Larry's neck. But Larry was ready and with a closed fist, he backhanded the Major and the man fell back on the cot. His lip was split and his nose was bleeding.

"I can see you're someone who won't listen to advice. If you try anything again; you won't like what I can do to you."

Nguyen sat up on the cot and Larry gave him a clean rag to wipe the blood from his face. "I don't know whether you're hungry, but I am. I'll put some breakfast on your cot and you can decide. My suggestion is to eat and keep up your strength. I want the fork back when you're finished eating."

After Nguyen ate his breakfast, Larry asked for the tray and fork, but the Vietnamese only returned the tray. Larry backhanded him again and his lip split further while his nose started to bleed again. "Let me have the fork."

The prisoner returned the fork and Larry told him to use the cloth he'd given him to clean the blood off his face. The Vietnamese stared at him with hatred in his eyes. "I'm going to ask you some questions and then I'm going to tell you what's going to happen over the next week," Larry said.

"You'll get nothing from me. You're just wasting your time. When I get a chance, I'm going to kill you."

"Are you serious? You sent two groups to bring me back. They couldn't accomplish the task, what do you think you can do?'

The Asian spit at him. You are a murderer. You killed many of our soldiers."

"Actually, I didn't kill anyone. I roughed up some of them, but that was all. Others killed your men."

Over the next hour Larry asked six or seven questions and got nothing in return. He waited an hour and asked the same questions over and over, but Nguyen showed nothing but distain for his captor; one time he laid back down on the cot and closed his eyes. Larry served him an early lunch and allowed him to relieve himself on a Porta Potty that was next to the cot.

Around four o'clock in the afternoon, Larry told the Major what was going to happen. "No matter what you do, you'll not break me. Eventually I'll win. You are a weak American. I saw your type in the Hanoi Hilton. I'm going to kill you with my bare hands." The man was snarling as he spit out the words.

Larry took off the Asian's handcuffs. "Put on this jacket and gloves. It's going to be cold tonight."

As soon as the jacket and gloves were on, Larry put the handcuffs back on with Nguyen's hands in front. He undid the leg bracelets to the floor but connected the chain to a metal ball. He lifted it up and handed it to Nguyen. 'Let's go, you first." Larry directed.

Once outside, Larry led the way down a narrow path to a clearing with a large tree in the center. Next to the tree was a chair, a large plastic bottle of water and another Porta Potty. A chain was hanging down from a thick branch. Larry attached the chain to Nguyen's handcuffs and disconnected the ball that he'd forced Nguyen to carry. "There's enough slack in this chain so you can sit down, go to the bathroom or sit on the ground. You'll be out here all night. There's an abundance of wild animals throughout the forest but the only ones you need fear are the wolves and bears. The wolves travel in packs but the bears are singular. I hope that I can return quickly enough to save you if a predator comes upon you."

"You won't let me die. You want something from me. I can take anything you can throw at me," the Vietnamese said.

"Don't fool yourself. If you won't talk, even if a predator comes after you, then you're no use to me. I can let you die and not shed a tear. I can tell you this. You're never going to see Vietnam ever again. The main question is, do you want to live. We'll find out in a few days."

"Your government won't let you kill me. As soon as the head of the delegation knows I've been kidnapped, he'll contact the State Department and you'll be found, if I don't kill you first."

Over the next two days, Larry brought Nguyen his meals, but the major just smirked. "There are no wild animals out here; you cowardly Americans killed them all. I've suffered through your blanket bombing, lived underground for three months at a time and dragged myself two miles with a broken leg. You cannot break me. I will be at your execution. My people are not dumb. They will come for me."

"Maybe the wolves and bears don't know you're here. I'll just leave some scraps of meat leading up the trail and see if that'll bring them. Larry responded. The Asian wasn't smirking anymore.

With listening devices set up all around the tree, Larry could monitor the Vietnamese from his shack. If there was imminent danger for the man, Larry could be there immediately.

Around two in the morning, he heard Nguyen scream. Larry got up, put on his parka and grabbed his rifle. As he approached his prisoner, he could hear screams. Rather than shoot to scare off any predator, he hurried to the clearing. Three coyotes were picking at the scraps Larry had placed on the path. Perhaps Nguyen had never seen this species. He probably thought they were wolves. Larry scared them off and came up to his prisoner who was at the end of his tether. His face was red and he kept looking in the direction where the animals had been. "Are you ready to talk and answer my questions?"

"I will never talk. I may have been scared but I'll let the predators eat me before I give you any information."

"If that's what you want, I won't come if I hear you scream next time."

Commander Tran learned about the abduction of his nephew and the assault on the bodyguard within twenty-four hours of the event. He demanded that their UN Delegation Chief file a protest and seek the immediate release of Major Nguyen. So far, the US State Department denied any knowledge of the situation but vowed to recommend that the FBI investigate. The CIA had no comment.

Chapter 30

Jean's injuries quickly healed and within a month, she was back performing at least one surgery a day. The other doctors who were picking up Jean's duties were glad to help their co-worker, but they were even happier when she came back full time. Susanne took a little longer to heal, but with her grandmother's encouragement, she was back to school after six weeks. Susanne was amazed at how many of her classmates said they missed her. The local police department had the house under surveillance for two weeks until Jean felt she and the children were not in immediate danger; it really was Larry they were after.

Larry had rigged up a telephone in the shack. He'd page Jean every day when he had a chance to talk and she'd call the number. Are you making any headway with whoever you have?" Jean asked

"It'll take a few days, but I'm sure he'll come around."

"What are you going to do with him when this is over?"

"That hasn't been decided yet. I assume the CIA will have something to say. They may want to turn him."

Minh watched the extra activity around the Vietnamese complex, but at no time did he see any local police presence. He did learn that the assistant chief of the delegation filed an official report with the US State Department and that an inquiry was passed on to his supervisor, who asked Minh if he had anything to do with the disappearance. Minh gave a plausible denial.

It was near dawn the following day when Larry heard his captive scream. He took his time getting his parka and gloves on before he grabbed his rifle. The screams were more intense this time and Larry hurried to the site; a wolf was pulling on the Asian's jacket. The man was backed up to the tree and was trying to hold off the wolf. Larry heard the terror in the scream, but he did nothing but watch. Nguyen saw Larry and pleaded with him to intercede but Larry waited. The wolf turned and looked at Larry, who stood there with his rifle ready; the wolf eventually walked off. "Do you want to talk?" he asked The Asian.

"Take off these chains and bring me inside where it's comfortable and I'll answer your questions."

"That's not going to happen. You're going to tell me everything while you're chained to the tree, then I'll bring you inside."

"Kiss my ass, I won't be here another night. You'll see." Nguyen shouted at Larry.

"I'm going to take my time in responding next time. You might think about that tonight. A predator may take a bite out of you before I can get here."

Larry repeated the delivery of three meals to his captive the next day and on each occasion asked Nguyen if he was ready to talk. His question was met with the same response, "Never".

After he delivered the evening meal, Larry tossed more food on the ground leading to where Tran was chained; some he placed near his chair.

"What are you doing?" Tran asked.

"I'm just trying to give you further incentive."

Around ten that evening, he could hear his prisoner scream. He waited and then he distinctly heard the words, "I'll talk."

Larry rushed to the site with his rifle. When he entered the clearing he saw three wolves on top of the Asian tearing at his clothing. Larry shot twice and the wolves ran off. Nguyen was hysterical and seemed to be fighting off the wolves even though they'd run off. Larry helped him up and told him to sit down. He gave him some water and waited until he was rational.

"Are you ready to talk?"

Nguyen didn't answer, so Larry repeated the question.

"I think you scared them off; I don't think they'll come back. I'll take my chances."

"That's fine by me. I think the next time you scream, I'll just stay in the shack and have a beer." Before he left his prisoner, Larry threw some more morsels on the ground and the major screamed obscenities at him.

He knew it was only a matter of time before Nguyen capitulated. The main concern would be how many lies he'd mingle with the truths. If he thought Larry would be easy, he was mistaken. Early in the evening, the screams started slowly, then intensified. Larry held back until Nguyen was begging for him to intercede.

Larry finally rushed to the clearing. Nguyen was on his back fending off the three wolves again; there seemed to be blood on his face. Larry yelled at the three wolves but they ignored him so he shot one and the other two ran off. The Major wasn't moving. Larry approached slowly and saw that his right sleeve had been torn off and his arm was bleeding through his shirt. He took off the cuffs, then his parka and examined the man's wounds. Nguyen's eyes followed him as he opened the medical kit Jean provided and attended to the bite marks and gashes on the Asian's arm. A lot of the fight had gone out of the Major because he didn't try to attack Larry when his cuffs were off. After putting some hydrogen peroxide on the wounds, Larry bandaged the affected area, put the parka and then the cuffs back on and helped the Asian to his feet. "Sit in the chair," Larry ordered.

"You'll not be able to survive another attack and I have no intention of bringing you back to the shack until you answer all my questions truthfully. Are you ready?" Nguyen nodded.

Larry went through a series of questions to establish a rhythm and see if the Vietnamese was going to cooperate. After he had established his name and what directorate he worked for, he asked his captive, who directed the attacks on Larry and his family. Nguyen was hesitant but named Commander Quon Tran and the Central Committee in Vietnam as the originator of his orders. When asked why they wanted him dead, Nguyen said that Larry's escape was an insult to the regime.

"How many American POWs are still in Vietnam?"

"Nine."

"Where are they now?"

"They're shifted every two months between six sites. I don't know where they are at this time but the six sites are…." Larry placed the tape recorder close to Nguyen's mouth and he listed the six sites.

"Give me the names of all those in your delegation and what their specialties are."

Again Nguyen listed each person, what they did and what experience they had.

"Who in my government assisted you with your mission against me?"

"I don't know what you're talking about."

"Of course you do. You wouldn't have had this much access and latitude of movement without some inside help. So who was it?"

"I don't know what you're talking about."

"You're going to stay out here until I have all the answers to my questions."

"You promised I could come in if I answered your questions and I did. There's no one helping me."

"I'll be in the shack. I can hear what's going on out here. How soon I respond is dependent on your cooperation. Now I'm going to verify the information you gave me. If any of it is wrong or incomplete, I'll assume everything is a lie and act accordingly."

"You son of a bitch. You promised." If Larry heard anything else, he ignored the outburst.

Back in the shack, he called Minh on the secured phone and gave him the information Nguyen furnished. He paged Jean and when she called back, he told her he had most of the information, but would need at least another day to get the rest. "I love you Larry, please come home soon," Jean said.

Twice that night he went to the clearing to chase off some wolves but Nguyen still wouldn't answer his questions about any American assistance he received to kill Larry and harm his family.

The next day was a duplicate of the previous one and Larry went back to the cabin at six in the evening. About ten that night, the captive was shrieking and begging Larry for help. Sensing that it was more than a couple of wolves, Larry raced to the clearing and saw a brown bear pawing at Nguyen who was near hysterical trying to fend off the animal. Larry fired a warning shot over the bear's head and the animal ran off. Larry knew this was the best time to get his information.

"I'm heading back to the hut unless you give me what I want."

"Charles Thompson and Maurice Jones from your State department have been assisting us in finding you and keeping the whereabouts of the POWs away from their superiors."

"Did they sabotage our attempt to rescue the POWs?"

"Yes."

"What was their motivation?"

"They're Russian moles. That's all I know. I've never met them. We exchange information by drops in Washington and New York. You're not going to leave me out here now, are you?"

"I'm not going to bring you into the cabin, but I have a place where I'll tie you up. It'll be close enough to the cabin; you should be safe. We'll be out of here tomorrow. What do you want to do? Your people will kill you for releasing this information."

"I'm requesting asylum at this time."

"I'll pass on your request. I have no official status with our government. That's up to them."

"Do you have family in Vietnam?" Larry asked Nguyen.

"I have a wife and two sons. I rarely see them and the marriage was arranged."

He moved Nguyen to a secondary site within twenty yards of the cabin. Larry felt comfortable that he'd be able to protect the Major tonight. Tomorrow they'd be gone.

Larry paged Jean, who called back immediately. "I have everything I want. I'll return my prize to Minh and then stay in Washington for a couple of days. There's still a couple of loose ends that must be tidied up for us to remain safe."

Minh agreed to meet him at the airfield in New Jersey the next evening and provide him transportation for a few days. "I want Nguyen kept under wraps until I finish one more thing. There're two individuals in our government who've been helping him. I'm going to talk to them." Larry said

"Who are they?" Minh asked.

"You've stuck your neck out for me so I'm going to keep this information from you. You'll not be involved. By the way, Nhu Nguyen, Vietnamese Army Major, wants asylum."

"Why am I not surprised? I'll see you tomorrow."

He sedated his prisoner with the last of the drugs Jean provided and placed him on the floor of his SUV. After he cleaned up the areas where he held his captive, including the shack so there'd be no trace of the major, he drove to the airplane. He approached the field cautiously and, when he was sure there was no one around, he lifted Nguyen up, carried him to the plane and placed him on the floor behind the pilot's seat. He chained him to steel plates imbedded in the floor.

After a thorough pre-flight check and cleaning off all the snow and ice that had accumulated over the past several days, he was on his way. He had about three quarters of a tank of gas to go the first leg. Since he was flying west to east, he'd have tail winds and the duration of the flight would be shorter. At the next refueling stop at a remote airfield, he filled up, did a quick walk around the plane and took off; the Asian was still sedated.

There were very few landing lights at the remote airfield in New Jersey as he set the plane down and braked until he came to a stop. He turned the plane around and started taxing toward two cars parked near the touchdown point and then stopped; he kept the engine running. He wasn't sure who was waiting for him so he decided to pass on a message. He revved up the engines a couple of times to let those waiting understand that he had some options. He waited five minutes and when there was no movement from the two vehicles, he called Minh on the portable phone. "I thought there'd be only one car to meet me. Who's here besides you and Felix?"

"It couldn't be just Felix and me. The Deputy Director of Operations had been read in on this and he insisted on coming. I couldn't keep this action only between us; I'm sorry. There are also two agents out of the Special Actions Division that will take custody of Nguyen. The director wants to talk to you in private after we take custody of the major."

"It isn't that I don't trust you Minh, I just don't trust anyone else. I'll wait right where I am with the engine running while the deputy director walks to my plane. I don't want anyone else to leave those vehicles or I'll take off and make my deal another day."

After a few minutes, Minh answered. "He doesn't like it but if it will make you happy, he's on his way. Just don't be a dork, listen to what the man has to say."

It took a few minutes for the Deputy Director to walk the distance. Before Larry would allow him into the airplane, he made the CIA official turn out all his pockets and take off his windbreaker. When he was sure there were no concealed weapons, he opened the cockpit door and helped Frank Jordan into the seat next to him. "You're a very cautious man, Mr. Stephens. Perhaps you should work for my Directorate."

"I did work for the agency for nearly a year and didn't like it. What's on your mind, Mr. Jordan?"

The CIA official looked behind his seat and saw the Vietnamese stretched out. "Is he okay?"

"He's in pretty good shape. He'll come around in a couple of hours."

"I understand you have the names of two State Department employees who are Russian Agents. I want those names."

"No way. This is personal with me. They not only conspired with a foreign government to have me killed, but they probably sabotaged the attempt Minh and I made into

Vietnam to rescue the POWs. And then there's my wife and daughter."

"You mean you want to kill them."

"I may give them the opportunity of committing suicide rather than be strangled."

"That's pretty selfish, and besides, it's dumb."

"What do you have in mind?"

"We certainly don't want them dead. We want to turn them. This is a potential gold mine and I can't have you jeopardizing this coup, even though you're the one that found this out. Be reasonable, man. I know you're a patriot. See this from your country's viewpoint. Here's what I'll do if you give me the names. I'll make sure that no one, and I mean no one, will ever come to your house or place of work and put you and your family in peril, ever again."

"That's ridiculous; you can't promise something you can't deliver."

"Well, I won't have someone living in your house but trust me, I will have you under surveillance and better yet, I'll have everyone attached to the Vietnamese Delegation or whoever comes into the country from North Vietnam on a short rope. What do you say?"

"Why didn't you do this in the past and we wouldn't be talking about it now."

"You're right, we screwed up, but we can make it right."

"What about the magazine reporter? He's not going to back off for you or anyone else."

"We'll trade with him by giving him something better to pursue."

"What about Curtiss?"

"He's no longer an issue."

"If I give you the names of the two moles, how will I know that they'll be out of circulation?"

"They have two choices. They can either be turned or interned if you know what I mean. There are no other options on the table for them. Nguyen and whoever he worked for and those two may not be the only ones coordinating on the hits on you and your family. If there are others involved, they'll talk. Why not come with us when we take them down. You can view the interrogation if you wish. You've earned the right."

"Their names are Charles Thompson and Maurice Jones of the State Department. Nguyen didn't know which directorate. He indicated both were Russian moles and had been assisting his delegation in finding me and impeding the POW rescue."

Jordan made a series of calls while he was sitting next to Larry. Within thirty minutes, he had their addresses, phones numbers and the name of the sections the two worked at within the State Department. The next calls he made were to stage a take-down of the two men. It was seven in the evening and they set the take-down time at midnight. Minh and Felix would take Nguyen and the two cars to Washington. Larry, Jordan and the two Special Actions men would fly in Larry's plane to DC and be met by Jordan's assistant. The effects of the sedatives that Larry gave Nguyen were still working, so he undid the locks to the cabin floor. Minh and Felix drove up to the airplane and unloaded Nguyen. The two CIA Agents boarded and all

four were airborne by seven thirty. They planned to land at
Dulles International; Jordan made the arrangements.

__Chapter 31__

Larry **touched** down and taxied to a remote section of Dulles Airport. There was a black SUV with a driver waiting for them. Jordan put his hand on Larry's shoulder and assured him they were going to take down the two moles. Larry still had his portable phone and, after Jordan departed the plane, he called Jean and asked if she could join him in DC for a couple of days.

Jean called back an hour later and said she'd fly in tomorrow with a landing time of six in the evening on American Airlines, Flight 5336. In the meantime, Jordan set up a stakeout at the home of the two state department employees living in Falls Church, Maryland. From the information, furnished to him by his assistants, both men were assigned to the Vietnam Desk. Thompson was thirty four years old, weighed one hundred ninety pounds and stood six feet tall. His file listed an undergraduate degree from USC in Business Administration and a Masters from Columbia in Political Science. Jones was from Arkansas, stood five foot ten and weighed one hundred eighty pounds. He went to college at Princeton and has been with the State Department for ten years; he was Thompson's supervisor.

CIA agents tracked the two men as they drove home in a standard Chevrolet Sedan around eight PM. The stakeout group monitored them until they retired around eleven. Jordan's people took the two into custody at midnight without firing a shot, without warrants and without any physical altercations. He directed they be brought to a building in a remote section of eastern Virginia.

A crew of six questioned them throughout the night. Larry wasn't permitted to be present during the interrogation but would be able to see the prisoners in two days, if he desired.

Jean arrived on time and Larry met her at the airport; she brought a couple more changes of clothes for him and they took a room at the Ritz-Carlton. They hadn't had a night to themselves for a long time; they would cherish every minute. They awoke at ten the next morning after finally falling asleep at five in the morning. Luckily, they'd ordered room service for that time and were able to eat outside on a small veranda, overlooking the capitol grounds. They planned to see the Supreme Court Building and the White House today.

At ten the following morning, they were picked up by a black sedan and driven to a remote CIA site in Virginia where the two state department detainees were being held. Mr. Jordan was there to greet them. "We had a lengthy interrogation that lasted twenty four hours. They finally admitted they were Russian moles and had been coordinating with the Vietnamese to refute the fact that there are POWs still remaining in their country. They admitted that they were helping the Vietnamese find you, but wouldn't admit that they were part of any assassination plan."

"Do you believe them?" Jean asked.

"To a degree, but we'll keep them here for at least two weeks to find out who their Russian contacts are."

'Can we see them? Larry asked.

"They're in an interrogation room that has a viewing area. Why don't we go down there and you can see who they are and what they're saying."

As they sat down on in the viewing area, they could hear the questioning by the CIA interrogator. "Have either of you met Captain Stephens or any of his family?" The response by both was no.

"Why did you finger Stephens for the Vietnamese?"

"We were asked to find out where he was living and who he worked for. We weren't asked to do anything else."

"You must have known that he was on a hit list."

Both responded that they did not.

"What do you think will happen if we give your names to Captain Stephens?"

"You can't do that. We expect that you'll carry out your bargain and give us protection," Jones responded.

"Just so you honor your bargain, Captain Stephens was the one who gave us your names and he's sitting behind that glass panel watching both of you. How does it feed to have a target on your back, so to speak?' Both turned and look in Jean and Larry's direction. .

At that moment Jean grabbed Larry's arm. "Can they see or hear us from that room?"

Jordan responded. "They can't hear or see us."

"I saw the taller of the two men at a coffee shop in downtown Steamboat Springs last month," Jean said.

"Are you serious?" Jordan asked.

"I was having lunch with another doctor when the man on the right and a woman came into the establishment and sat down at the same table. "At one point, he looked directly at me," Jean responded, pointing at Thompson.

"Would you be willing to look at a lineup to be sure you could pick this man out?" Jordan asked.

"Certainly, how soon can you set it up?'

"Give us an hour. Perhaps you and Larry could have some coffee or lunch while you're waiting. We have a nice cafeteria on the second floor. Just take the elevator up; you can't miss it," Jordan responded.

When they returned from the cafeteria, Jordan had set up a lineup of five men with similar builds and complexions. "Boy, I've never seen so many handsome men in a row. It's number four; maybe I could have the phone numbers of the others." Jean chuckled, as she hugged Larry.

"Are you certain?' Jordan asked again.

"Yes."

"Could you work with a sketch artist this afternoon and try to identify the woman he was with?"

Jean looked at Larry who nodded a yes.

"Those guys lied to us. There may be a bigger network involved than they want to divulge. Let's see how they hold up under more interrogation in the basement. I'm pissed that they thought they could get away with this. Mr. and Mrs. Stephens, thank you. When did you plan to head back home?"

"We were going to fly out early tomorrow morning. Why?"

"Our problem may be greater than we suspect. If you don't mind, I'm going to fly two agents to your city to follow up on the woman your wife saw. They'll be in contact with you; there will be some surveillance of your home and place of work, if you don't mind."

"We'd like to meet them so there're no surprises."

Jean worked with an artist for over an hour and when she was finished, Jean, Larry and Jordan met in the cafeteria. Jordan pulled out a folder and laid the sketch on the table in front of them. "That's her. Boy, did he do a good job," Jean said.

Jordan and Minh took them to dinner that evening and Jean and Larry danced for the first time in years. "I can't tell you how happy I am that you returned and we're together. There was a time when I wasn't sure you'd take me back."

"You have nothing to apologize for. I would have taken you back no matter what. I'm starting to have some dialog with the children, which pleases me a lot. I hope we can put this latest episode behind us, but I'm a little skeptical. There may be more people out there who mean to harm us. We have to be vigilant."

"It's been hard on the children, especially your son. After the accident, Larry Jr. has become very protective of his sister and doesn't interface with his friends. Hopefully, when we get back home, he'll relax into being a teenager. He feels as though he's the protector of the family right now. He'll come around."

Jordan filled them in on the identity of the woman that Jean saw with one of the State Department moles. "Her name is Naomi Walsh. She works as a linguist for a multinational company headquartered in Denver. We don't intend to pick her up just yet; she'll be under constant surveillance from this moment on. Hopefully, she'll lead us to the other members of her cell and we can pick them up too," Jordan said.

The most significant information Jordan relayed was the fact that the State Department sent a message through channels to the North Vietnamese Government. It states that Major Nhu Nguyen asked for asylum and that he identified Commander Tran as the individual who sent assassins to America to kill or kidnap an American citizen. "That ought to slow Tran down," Jordan said.

Jordan made one final pitch to Larry to come back to the agency. Jean laughed. "He's happy working for the Forestry Service. They don't shoot at him." Jean said.

They decided to stay another night in DC and take the Potomac Dinner Cruise. The next morning, they held hands as Jean read the preflight checklist and Larry checked off the items. Jordan and his driver showed up at the plane prior to takeoff and asked to have a moment with Larry alone.

The two men spoke for about two minutes, shook hands and Larry walked back to the plane. He and Jean embraced as he helped her into the cockpit and they took off.

"Are you going to tell me what Jordan had to say?" Jean asked.

Larry smiled. "They've opened up a line of communication with the North Vietnamese and are putting together a team to go to Vietnam. The President asked if I wanted to be part of the team."